HER HUSBAND'S WIFE

Book 2
Deadly Intent

*To Rick Lutz —
Hope you like my
interpretation of your
story.*

Robin W. Titchen

Robin W. Titchen

This book is a Self-Published First Edition from Paisley and Tumbleweed Publishing

HER HUSBAND'S WIFE

The author can be contacted at: www.robinwtitchen.com

ISBN-13: 978-1493528332
ISBN-10: 1493528335

DEDICATION

Dedicated to family, living and passed—from ancestors who took a chance to come to the new world and loved those who were socially unacceptable to love—to those more recent in my family tree who made difficult choices leading them in an unexpected direction in their own life. All these choices, the brave and not so brave, through the march of time, have had an impact on my own environment, reality, and life.

ACKNOWLEDGMENTS

I want to thank Rick Lutz for his contribution of an introduction to Vietnam. A huge thanks goes to my family, friends, and fans who have kept me motivated and encouraged to complete this work. Without you, I would have given up this quest to build on the lives of Mariah, Morgan, and Riley, the victims they sought to help and protect, and their crew of nemeses and accomplices.

KIDNAPPERS

He stood, concealed in the bushes as the nondescript, white pick-up truck—slightly lifted with steps on either side at the doors—turned down the narrow, dirt drive leading to the old, abandoned house. The truck came to a stop beside his own faded-red Chevy pick-up. Dust from the truck's passage drifted south, over the field in front of the house. The driver's door opened and a slender, shapely ankle above a three inch, high-healed, black pump appeared beneath the door and landed on the side step. The foot turned as the second foot, toe pointed to the ground, touched down on the dirt drive—the first foot following a half minute behind. The woman took a step back and slammed the door closed, adjusted her purse over her right shoulder, and turned. The well proportioned woman, with short blond hair swept from the sides of her face—a feathering of bangs across her forehead—turned and looked around. In the perfect oval of fine porcelain skin, her beautiful blue eyes peered out from heavily lined lids and long, thick, dark lashes. Her mouth, the perfect bow, and painted bright red, accentuated the flawlessness of her skin. She wore a black, long-sleeved sweater adorned by a three strand necklace of pearls, the longest tier brushing the swell of her breasts. Below the sweater, a matching pencil skirt stopped just above her knees.

"Quit acting like a fucking peeping tom and get the hell out here," she yelled, belying her beauty with the coarseness of her vocabulary.

He was angry with himself for being so easily deceived by her beauty. He imagined there was virtue where none existed, simply because she looked like an angel. He didn't know what happened in her past that broke her beyond repair, but he learned, too late, how heartless she had become since their childhood friendship.

Just plain mean and hateful! he thought.

Her goal in life seemed only to destroy everything good in the world. He wished he'd realized the depth of deception in her before he got involved—regretting, as he stepped from behind the bush and pretending to zip his pants, that he ever knew her.

"Sorry. I had to take a whiz. Are you ready for them?"

She turned at the sound of his voice and glared.

"Noooo." she said slowly, her voice rising at the end of the word as though correcting an errant child. "When I'm ready for them I will tell you. I told you that before."

"You never told me the job would take this long. My wife's really sick and I need the money now or they wont start the treatment."

"Yes dear," she sneered. "That's one reason I called you. Here's half the money." She reached into her purse—he flinched, expecting her to pull a gun and shoot him. She pulled out a wad of cash instead.

"This should be enough to get the treatment started."

She sauntered toward him, arm outstretch and waving the greenbacks.

"I have another job for you too. That means even more money for you." Her grin was forced and to him, looked sinister.

His stomach churned.

This is bad, I know it is, he told himself. "Now what?"

He took the money and stuffed the cash in his back pocket. She reached up and he flinched again. She gently brushed the hair from his forehead and caressed the side of his face.

"Why do you fear me? I told you I would pay for your help, didn't I? I'm only trying to help you take care of your sick wife. I never said I would hurt you."

She smacked her palm hard against the side of his face and pinched his cheek between the heel of her palm and all four fingers.

"And yet you fear me," she sneered.

She released his face with a push, throwing her hand into the air, and turned, walking toward her truck. He reached up and rubbed his throbbing cheek, knowing it would be bruised the following day.

"I'm hurt," she yelled turning back to face him. "Be here tomorrow with your van at four P.M. I'm bringing another one. You'll need to prepare tonight to have the place ready."

"What?" He swallowed hard. "The deal was only for one, and there's two already. I agreed to only one."

"I'm paying you extra. You'll need the money for your wife's treatment, after all." She paused and glared at him. "Or you can quit. Keep what I've paid you for your troubles."

He watched her as he thought about the offer. She would kill him before she would let him walk away. She told him that before, when she took the second girl. "How long is this going to continue?"

She advanced on him until she was a hands width away. "Until I'm done," she snarled, her upper lip curling like a rabid fox.

He backed up a step and whined, "But we need to wrap this up before we're caught."

"Yes. We. That is the operative word—WE! If I go down, you do too and where will your wife be then? Huh? Just shut the hell up and do what the fuck I tell you. Everything will work out fine."

His heart pounding in his chest, he looked at the ground in front of his feet and nodded his head.

"Okay. I'll be here." There was no animation in his voice. He had no choice. If he refused, she would kill him on the spot.

SUNDAY

Exhausted and hoping for a peaceful, nightmare-free sleep, Mariah went to bed at eight o'clock. Paisley, her rough coat Jack Russell Terrier, slept with her back against Mariah, all four legs spread out toward the other side of the bed. The little pup started yipping and her feet twitched as she dreamed of chasing her prey, and Mariah fell asleep with a smile and thoughts of a long run on the beach with her four legged friend.

I'm sitting in my camp chair, enjoying the warmth of the sun caressing my skin. A plastic cup of Merlot sits in the cup-holder of my chair as I listen to The Bent Arrows playing on the stage to my left. The afternoon is hot, but clouds float in and out of the sun's way, giving the people in attendance intermittent relief from the burning rays. The Willamette River flows in front of me with numerous fishing and sailing vessels anchored close to shore, and the people around me are kicked back, and relaxed—enjoying the wonderful weather at this annual Fourth of July Blues Festival in Portland Oregon.

Strains of 'Smoke in the Lavender Fields' are carried on the soft breeze over the noise of the crowd. The second band sets up on the stage to my right. The field before me is littered with spectators who are dancing to the music, sitting in their camp chairs, or lying on their blankets.

Numerous food and trinket vendors are set up along the walkway behind me catering to the throngs of people moving to and fro like ants at a picnic. The many food vendors fill the air with tantalizing aromas of grilled burgers, hotdogs, chicken, sausage links, pulled pork with roasted onions and peppers, funnel cake, cotton candy, and popcorn. I just finished a sausage on a stick and half a funnel cake so the thought of food is not uppermost in my mind. I'm content to sit and people watch as I listen to the music and sip my disposable cup of wine. Food is in abundance, wine and beer are flowing, and all the people seem to be having a good time.

"There's a fire in the mountains and smoke in the lavender fields. I ain't cryin' 'cause you're leavin', it's the smoke in my eyes. The smoke in the lavender fields …" the lead singer croons before the guitarist does a fabulous riff.

I look up to azure blue skies dotted with fluffy white clouds. A single small cloud begins to float across the sun, casting a shadow on the festival. Smiling, I lift my face to the summer breeze and the warmth of the rays and I close my eyes for a moment to take in all the sensations of touch, sound, and smell.

Opening my eyes, my gaze drifts down to the river where a large fishing trawler is coming around the bend to my left. Flying from the trawler's mast, is the largest United States flag I have ever seen. As the vessel comes more fully into view, the crowd becomes quiet and I, with everyone else, turns to follow its progress up the Willamette River. Even the band ceases its playing as all turn toward the river. The only sound is the squawking of seagulls and the slapping of waves on the riverbank and against the vessels anchored close to shore. The trawler rounds the next bend with only the flag visible over the horizon.

As the flag dips out of sight, the sea of people, with one deep breath taken in unison, watches for the trawler to come back into view. It does and in an instant, the flag breaks up and turns into *large balloons—red ones and white ones—that line the mast.*

"Ooooh," says the crowd as one voice.

The largest of the balloons is white and is the lowest on the mast, then a slightly smaller red one, next another, even smaller white one, until the smallest of them all, a red one, is at the very top. The tiny red balloon is floating over the top of the mast as though filled with helium.

A tall, red-haired man walks to the bow with a large whip in his hand. His blue eyes pierce through the distance and the crowd, like the lights of a lighthouse signaling to the passing vessels, and draws me to him as if by magic. His eyes are so bright and clear, I could see him looking straight at me with a kind smile. It seems as if I were standing only inches away. His shoulder length, red hair sports hues ranging from deep auburn to bright orange with thin streaks of yellow, giving the illusion of fire as the breeze lifts his hair and blows it around his head. His bare skin from the waist up is the weathered deep brown of a man who works tirelessly in the elements. His sculpted muscles are outlined under his sweat-glistened, tanned skin and tight fitting blue jeans.

He unfurls his whip and starts swinging it above his head like a lasso. With the slightest twitch of his wrist, he snaps the whip and pops the lowest balloon on the mast.

"Aaaah", and "Ooooh" everyone says as he repeats this over and over until only the top balloon remains and the trawler moves out of sight around the bend again. The only thing visible is the small red balloon floating above the mast.

The crowd waits with anticipation for the trawler to return so they can witness the rest of this unexpected performance. Everyone is mesmerized and wants more.

In a sluggish crawl, the trawler comes back into view—like watching a turtle cross a road, steady but slow. The crowd waits. A woman next to me says under her breath, "Did it break down?", and the kid to her right shouts, "Come on, man." Everyone is impatient for the show to continue.

The man with the head of fire and eyes of sapphires, still standing at the bow, swings the whip over his head, waiting to show the crowd his power over the last balloon. Everything becomes slow motion to me and each breath taken by the people around me appears like a pulse, as if the very earth is breathing with anticipation. The sound of the whip moving through the air is like the sound of helicopter blades; 'whoop, whoop, whoop'. The whip is twisting above his head like a snake getting ready to strike. With a twitch of his wrist the writhing snake jumps up to the top of the highest balloon and strikes.

At that instant, a large white sail unfurls and the trawler transforms into a sleek and beautiful sailboat—the weathered, red haired man is now attired in a tuxedo and top hat as he stands facing the crowd. He sweeps the hat from his head, stretches his arms out to each side and takes a bow. The crowd, delighted, cheers and yells while clapping their hands. Everyone is talking at once about the amazing transformation of a trawler to a sailboat.

The red-haired, blue-eyed man smiles and winks at me as the sound of the cheering dims in my ears and an enormous, black cloud moves across the sky and blocks out the light from the sun. Day turns to night in the blink of an eye and I know the terror to come. Only the lighthouse eyes of the red-haired man pierces the darkness, and even that looses the battle and fades away. I gasp in panic, waiting for the inevitable. I can't escape the terror to follow and I can't hold back my scream ...

Mariah cried out, and threw her arms up to shield herself from the intruder leaning over her. Her heart pounded as she peered into the darkness of the room, but the intruder was gone with the sound of a slamming door echoing in her ears.

She lay in her bed and cried while her heart crashed into the barriers of her chest as if trying to escape it's cage. The sound of her blood rushed through her ears and deafened her to any sound of an invader to her sanctuary and she forced herself to take deep slow breaths to try and calm her racing heart.

Paisley, hearing Mariah cry out in her sleep, licked the tears from her face. Mariah held on to her little companion and tried to see beyond the blackness of the night for any real threat, but like the previous incidences when awakened to this terror, there was nothing. She stared into the darkness of the room, trying to hear over the roar of her own blood flow and the tinnitus she acquired from the beating two years ago. She couldn't go back to sleep from fear of the intruder returning to her dreams.

As she lay in bed, she thought back to when the nightmares started. It wasn't until she got out of the hospital—not until they released her from the skilled nursing facility—not until Uncle John declared her strong enough and fit enough to take care of herself, and returned home to Texas. Not until she was back home on her own, alone with Paisley and sleeping in her own bed—that's when the nightmares started. That's when the haunting shadow first appeared.

****

From that beating she took two years ago at the hands of a man she considered a friend, she suffered broken and missing teeth, a fractured skull, a broken nose, a cracked jaw, broken ribs, broken fingers and toes, and a fractured femur, not to mention the many cuts, scrapes, abrasions, and deep tissue bruises. At the end, her abductor pulled out a galvanized tub and swung it around in front of Mariah, smashing her bare feet. He lifted each foot and dropped it into the tub before emptying five gallons of water into it. The pain from her broken thigh bone seared through her like a red hot knife when he moved her leg to drop her foot in the tub, and she screamed. Only through tiny slits of swollen flesh around her eyes, could Mariah see him standing in front of her, preparing to electrocute her. She braced for the final shock, but before he succeeded, she witnessed his head exploding, staining the wall behind him with dark-red blood, pink brain tissue, and bits of shining white bone. She passed out and didn't regain consciousness until she heard voices nearby.

"How's she doing?"

"Resting. She came out of the coma last night."

"Good. That's good news."

Mariah tried to recognize the voices.

"Why don't you go to the house and get some rest, John. I'll sit with her tonight. She'll be safe with me."

"Thanks, Morgan. I think I will. Call if there's any change."

Mariah tried to say something, but could only groan. She heard rustling and then someone gently took her hand.

"Everything's going to be okay now. You're in the hospital and we're here with you, Mariah."

She recognized her Uncle John's voice as he patted her hand. "You're not alone. One of us is with you at all times, so you rest now. You're safe now, baby. Thank God, you're safe, now."

Mariah, her eyes swollen closed, couldn't speak. She could barely nod her head before drifting off into a dreamless, drug induced sleep.

Mariah underwent emergency surgery when she first arrived at the hospital. Her femur was a clean break and needed only to be stabilized and casted. The pressure on her brain, due to swelling, was relieved and her jaw and nose were repaired. Later, when the doctors believed her strong enough to withstand it, she had reconstructive surgery on her face, and finally dental implants and caps to repair the damage to her teeth.

Four days after coming out of the coma, Mariah, finally coherent enough to hear how she came to be saved from certain death, listened as Riley wove the story for her.

"Since everyone thought me and Jeri were dead—killed in an auto accident in Europe, which was a ruse—I stashed Jeri in a tiny hamlet in the South of France and came back to the States, incognito. I conducted my own undercover investigation to make sure the threat to my family and friends had really been put down. I wasn't going to bring Jeri back home until I was convinced it was safe."

In the course of his investigation, Riley discovered some things about Mariah's friend, Jerry, that she needed to know about. Unfortunately, he was too late. As he approached her home, he spied the man tossing an unconscious and bound Mariah into the trunk of a car parked at the curb in front of her house. Riley followed as Jerry pulled away. They passed through town at a sedate speed and headed into the Sandia Mountains.

Riley had to abandon his vehicle and hike up to the cabin on foot. Using his rifle scope, he observed the madman preparing to electrocute Mariah. Unable to extract Mariah from the enemy in time, his only hope to save her life was to scope in on the killer and take him out, ending Mariah's ordeal.

After, "Thank you," all she could think to add was, "I could have saved us all some trouble if I had just grabbed my gun off the nightstand. I feel so stupid."

No one in the room blamed her. Morgan reminded her that betrayal from a trusted friend or loved one is hard to conceive at the time of occurrence. The mind shuts down in disbelief.

Once the wounds healed and she was well on the road to physical recovery, a thankful Mariah saw the skill of her plastic surgeon. Other than a few small scars, no one could guess at the pounding her face had taken or the damage it sustained. The emotional and psychological damage, Mariah was finding out, would take a lot more time and work to overcome.

The specter of the events in the cabin haunted her. Mariah, tired of being tired, knew from experience that peaceful sleep would again fail to come to her, so she got out of bed and went to the bathroom. She studied her reflection in the mirror as she placed a hand on each side of the sink and leaned forward. The image of her face, puffy from crying, with tears streaming down her cheeks stared back at her from the mirror. Her long strawberry-blond hair, in a disheveled mess, fell over her shoulders almost touching the rim of the sink, and draped her bare, rounded breasts.

"What are you crying about," she asked the image in the mirror. She shook her head and sighed before she answered herself in a ragged voice.

"I'm so tired." She squeezed her eyes shut and took a deep, shuddering breath. Tears chased each other down her face like droplets chasing each other down a rain streaked window. She hung her head low until the stretch in the back of her neck began to hurt, the tears dripping from her eyes and plopping into the sink. After a heavy sigh, she raised her head and looked back into the watery image of herself in the mirror.

"I'm scared," she whispered. "Oh God. What if this never ends?" Her eyes closed tight, and she shook her head again.

"And I'm ANGRY," she declared through gritted teeth. She pounded the counter with both fists at the same time—one resounding bang.

"Why didn't I see him for the sick bastard that he was? How could I have been so blind?"

Mariah wept. Paisley whimpered at her feet. At last, sniffling, she grabbed a tissue from the box on the counter and wiped her eyes and nose before throwing it in the waste basket. She took a deep breath and looked at Paisley.

"It's okay, girl." She reached down to scratch her little Jack Russell behind the ears and patted her on the head.

"I'm alright, baby."

Mariah turned on the shower before stepping in the tub and pulling the door closed. Stretching her arms out to the back wall, with her back to the hot spray, she thought of the many times she took that stance in the shower with Paul. He would stand behind her, washing her back before gliding his soapy hands around to cup her breasts, pulling her close against his hard wet body, and kissing the back of her neck.

With that memory, the tears started again and turned into loud, racking sobs. Mariah crumpled to her knees on the tub floor. She turned to a sitting position, pulled her knees to her chest, and wrapped her arms around her legs. The water beat down on her head as she laid her forehead on her knees and continued to sob. She remembered the passion she and Paul shared so many times in the shower before taking it to their bed. She whispered his name.

"Paul. … I miss you so much."

Drained by the emotional roller-coaster and exhausted from lack of sleep, Mariah turned off the water which had become so cold, her fingers and toes became numb. She opened the sliding door and stepped on the bath mat, grabbed a small white towel and wrapped her hair in it before she dried herself with a large, fluffy, yellow towel. She walked back to the bed leaving the yellow towel on the floor where she dropped it.

"Come on, Paisley. Let's try to get some shut eye."

After she patted the bed, Paisley jumped up to stretch out next to Mariah.

Still too wired to close her eyes, Mariah stared at the green light on the smoke alarm that hung right inside the bedroom door and she thought back to a time before the intruder … a time before the beating … a time when she was happy and felt safe … a time of love. She thought back to the day she met Paul.

****

Engrossed in her research at the university library, Mariah startled when a book dropped in front of her on the table where she sat studying. She looked up from her notes with a scowl at the clumsy and inconsiderate lout blundering around and disrupting the peace with his racket. The scowl was replaced by a slow hint of a smile when she saw bright blue eyes set in a handsome, masculine face topped with auburn red hair.

"I'm very sorry" Paul whispered.

Mariah had seen Paul around the campus on several occasions and felt a strong attraction, but she never had an opportunity to speak to him. Instead she asked her roommate, Jewel, about him. Jewel and Mariah shared a house off campus and Jewel had a government class with Paul. Although Paul wasn't her type, Jewel said he seemed a very nice guy— authentic, generous, and kind.

Mariah was happy he happened to drop books on the table where she sat studying.

"It's alright. You startled me, is all."

He pulled the chair out across from her and sat down.

"Hi. I'm Paul. I saw you here yesterday, but you left before I got a chance to speak to you. Mind if I sit here?"

"No, it's fine. I'm Mariah. It's nice to meet you, Paul."

She didn't see him the day before, but she was glad he noticed her and finally talked to her.

"I've seen you around and have been looking for an opportunity to talk to you."

"You have?" Mariah was surprised.

"Yeah." He shrugged his shoulders and grinned. "Imagine my surprise when I saw you here at this big table all by yourself. Are you going to be here long?"

Mariah blushed.

"I'm afraid so. I'm on a time crunch and need to finish this research today. I have a paper due Monday, so I have to get it done. How about you?"

"I expect to be here most of the day. My paper is due next week. I'm invited to a Halloween party tomorrow night, but I won't be able to go if I don't get this research done."

"Me too. Wouldn't it be funny if we are going to the same party?"

"We can make that happen. You want to go to my party with me and then we can go to yours?"

Laughing, Mariah said, "Where's your party?"

"My buddy …"

"Shhhh," the guy at the next table glared at them.

Paul lowered his voice to a whisper. "My buddy and his fiancé are throwing it at their new place on 85th Ave. … Mathias and Chastity."

"Matty and Chass," Mariah said a little too loud, earning a growl from the guy at the next table.

"Ah, you know them too," Paul whispered.

Nodding her head, she whispered back, "Yes. Chass is in my Adolescent Psychology class and we've teamed up together for several of the assigned projects. I'm going to their party too."

"Matt and I grew up together. So, I'll pick you up?"

"Sure, I'd like that, Paul. I better get back to work though if I'm going to get this done."

The guy at the next table muttered, "It's about damned time." Paul and Mariah smiled at each other before turning to their studies.

It remained hushed, in the library until one o'clock in the afternoon when the guy at the next table slammed his book closed and scraped his chair across the floor while he stood up. In unison, Paul and Mariah both looked at him and shushed him. He glared at them, whispered "fuck you", and gathered his books, leaving the study area. Paul and Mariah smiled at each other.

Another hour passed before Paul leaned back in his chair and yawned.

"I've got to take a break and get something to eat. Want to join me?"

Mariah looked up and stretched her neck and shoulders, arching her back and spreading her arms out.

"Sounds great. I was thinking the same thing, but I hate to put everything up just to come back and search for the reference books all over again."

"Leave them out. I'll tell Mel we'll be right back. No one

will bother them."

"Oh. I didn't think we could do that."

"We're not supposed to, but I spend a lot of time here and they know me. It'll be fine."

"Okay."

Mariah stood from her chair and Paul took her hand leading her to the counter. The warmth of his touch sent little shivers up her spine.

"Hi, Mel," he nodded toward Mariah. "This is Mariah. Mariah, this is Melissa."

"Hi, Melissa."

"Hi, call me Mel. Everyone does."

"Mel it is." Mariah smiled.

"We're going to grab a quick bite for lunch and be right back to finish studying. Mind if we leave our books out to save time? I promise we won't be long."

"Sure, no problem. Would you bring me back a coffee?"

"Be happy to. Same as usual?"

"Yeah, and a Danish if there are any left. Just a sec while I get some money for you." Mel reached under the counter for her purse, but Paul stopped her.

"Don't worry about it, my treat. We'll be back soon." Paul took Mariah's hand and headed to the stairs leading to the café and student lounge below.

"That was very sweet of you," Mariah told him as they started down the stairs.

"Not really. Mel's a friend, but it also ensures that no one will mess with our books, so it's not such a selfless gesture."

"Oh, so you're calculating, hmmm?"

From what Jewel told her, she knew his offer to pay for Mel's coffee wasn't just a ploy to grant him special privileges.

"Yep, I'm very calculating," he said with a mischievous grin and a wink. "I'm a physics major. We do lots of calculating." With a robust laugh he put his arm around her shoulders and led her down the rest of the stairs.

Mariah liked his sense of humor and joking nature. The way he dismissed his thoughtfulness and generosity with a joke impressed her even more.

At six o'clock, she closed her last book and placed it on top of the stack beside her. She slid a piece of paper across the table to Paul and whispered, "I need to go and get this paper written. Here's my phone number and address. What time do you want to pick me up tomorrow?"

"Are you wearing a costume?"

"Yes, I'll surprise you." She smiled.

"Okay. I'll call you before I come by."

"Sounds great. I'll talk to you later." Mariah gathered up her books and left.

The next day, mid afternoon, the phone rang as Mariah finished printing out her paper.

"Hello?"

"Hi Mariah. This is Paul. I'll have my paper done in a couple hours. How about if I pick you up at six for the party tonight?"

"I'll be ready. Are you going to tell me what you're going as?"

"Nope, I'll surprise you too."

"Well," she joked, "I hope you're not coming as Prince Charming, because that would be weird since I'll be Cinderella."

They both laughed.

"I'm no prince charming. I guess I'll be a thief so I can steal a kiss *and* your heart. I'll see you in a couple hours." Before she could respond, he disconnected the call.

When Mariah opened her door to Paul's knock, she took one look at him and laughed.

"What are you, a shadow?"

"I told you I was coming as a thief."

"I thought you were kidding."

"Nope. And you're not dressed like Cinderella, either."

"So … all black … are you supposed to be a cat burglar?"

"You're dressed as the cop. What do you think?"

Mariah started to answer when Paul waived his hand for her to stop.

"Here. Let me put the rest of my costume on." He took a black strip of cloth from his back pocket and put it over his eyes, positioning the eye holes so he could see, and tied the ends at the back of his head. He pulled a black knit beanie over his red hair and spread his arms out to his sides. "Now, what do you think?"

"Definitely a bandit. Be careful or I might have to arrest you before the night is over."

"Oh, be forewarned. I intend to steal something very special tonight. I guess you'll have to arrest me." With a chuckled he puckered his lips, closed his eyes, and leaned forward.

Mariah, laughing, put a hand on his shoulder to hold him off.

"Don't think I won't arrest you, mister," Mariah joked back. "I'm the one with the handcuffs, after all." For emphasis, she pulled the authentic, police issue handcuffs from the leather case at the back of her Sam Browne duty belt and held them up. "And, I'm the only one with the key."

With a soft laugh and a glint in his eyes Paul came back with, "You can handcuff me anytime you want to, Mariah Jeffries."

Mariah blushed, mumbling, "Um, I have no comment." She grabbed her authentic police jacket—a gift from her Uncle Richard when he got a new one, and asked, "Are you ready to go?"

Paul laughed, "I'm sorry. I didn't mean to make you uncomfortable." With a flourish, he opened the front door and extended his arm with a little bow. "Your chariot awaits. Uh ... or should I say patrol unit?!"

Mariah grabbed her keys, put them in her jacket pocket and stepped out the door in front of Paul with a little twitter of a laugh.

"You're funny. Are you going to ride in the back seat like my perp?"

"Maybe when we leave the party." Paul pulled the door closed. "You want it locked?"

"It should be locked already."

He tested the knob to make sure and took Mariah's hand as he walked her to his Dodge pick-up parked at the curb. As she climbed into the cab he asked, "Is that an authentic Sam Browne you're wearing?"

"Yes. It was my uncle Richard's. He gave me all the gear I'm wearing—the Sam Browne belt and leather cases, handcuffs, and baton—when he was promoted to detective. I've got the Sam Browne synched up as much as I can, but still it's a little loose on me, so I'm especially thankful for the keepers that came with it."

Paul gave a gentle pull on the belt and Mariah fell into him.

Paul caught her and helped her reseat herself.

"Ooops." Paul giggled and Mariah blushed.

A little embarrassed, Mariah continued, "Look. I added the mace case and the can of mace myself."

"Nice. Toy gun, huh?" Paul didn't need to touch it to know it was plastic.

"Yeah, but the cuffs and baton are real."

"Well, feel free to use the cuffs on me, but please don't hit me with your baton." He gave her a mischievous little grin.

"Not as long as you behave yourself, Paul Carlton."

Paul winked as he closed the door and went around to the driver's side.

On the way to the party, Mariah learned that Paul was a year and three months older than her. He grew up in Roswell, New Mexico, graduated High School from the Military Institute and is now in his junior year at the University of New Mexico, studying physics. On the drive home after the party, Paul learned all about Mariah's aspirations to become a forensic psychologist, her father's career as a firefighter, her mother who worked for years as a paralegal, and her Uncles—John, Dan, and Richard.

Paul did get that kiss before the night ended, and he

didn't have to steal it. As Mariah expected, he was the perfect gentleman. When they got back to her place, they could hear through the door a scream from the horror movie Jewel was watching on the television. Mariah put her hand on Paul's shoulder, leaned up, and kissed him.

"Thanks for the evening. I had fun."

"Me too."

He took her in his arms and gave her a kiss complete with butterflies in her stomach and tingles throughout her body.

When he broke from the kiss, he asked in a husky voice, "Can I see you tomorrow?"

Mariah, catching her breath and holding his arm so she didn't topple over, nodded her head. "I would like that."

Paul and Mariah saw each other every day after that party. Paul claimed he recognized her as his soul mate the moment he first laid eyes on her but it took him a while to get up the nerve to approach her. Mariah, already drawn to him, fell under his spell and couldn't help but look forward to the times they would spend together.

The sound of Mariah's alarm brought her out of her reverie of Paul and she groaned. She rolled over to turn off the alarm before reaching behind her, and patting Paisley.

"Come on, girl. Let's get up and start another day."

MONDAY

"God. I thought class would never end," she muttered under her breath as she walked out the back door to the parking lot, her arms loaded with books.

I'm never gonna make basketball practice in time if I don't run, she thought before uttering, "Ugh! I can't believe I left my gym bag at home this morning." She stopped at the curb to the parking lot, pulling her foot back as a pick-up pulled up and stopped in front of her, blocking her path.

"Hi Savannah," the woman behind the steering wheel said through the open window.

"Oh hi. I haven't seen you in a while. We thought you got married or something. Where have you been?"

"Nope. I've been working on a big project. I heard about Tina and Chelsea. Does anyone know what happened yet?"

"No. At least, I haven't heard—just that they're missing. It's terrible." Savanna, remembering her own plight added, "Hey, I'm in a big hurry. I forgot my gym bag at home and I have basketball practice in twenty minutes, so I've got to run."

"I'm sorry. Hop in and I'll give you a ride. You can tell me how the rest of the team is doing."

"Oh, great. Thanks." Savannah smiled and walked around to the passenger side as the driver put the truck in park and leaned across the seats to push the door open for her.

Savannah dumped her armload of books on the floorboard at her feet and stepped up to settle into the seat.

"I saw your game last week. What a fight. Too bad you girls lost."

"I can't believe the ref's last call. We would have won if not for that penalty." Savannah arranged her feet around her books on the floor. "So what are you doing here? Finish your big project and get bored?"

"No, not finished and certainly not bored. Can you reach the plastic bag at your feet? The crinkling sound is making me crazy." The woman pointed at the floor in front of Savannah's feet before putting the truck in gear. "Just thought I would pop by while I was in the neighborhood and check on you girls and how your games are going. We had a lot of fun at the games and the road trips, didn't we?"

"Yeah. You disappeared so suddenly, everyone wondered what happened." Savannah leaned forward before buckling her seatbelt and reached for the bag stuck under the edge of the mat far to the front of her feet.

"Why didn't you say goodbye or let ... uh, I can't reach it." She grunted as she stretched further.

"Why didn't you tell someone you were going away? Everyone was worried about you."

The woman glanced around carefully before pulling away from the curb. Savannah was still bent over trying to get the plastic bag as the driver pulled out of the parking lot and turned east to head into the less traveled residential area. Savannah got a finger hooked around the offensive bag and started to tug.

"The bag is hooked under the mat," she said tugging. "I can't ... Here." She sighed as she pushed a couple of her books on top of the rustling plastic grocery bag.

"I put some of my books on the bag."

Before Savannah sat all the way up, the driver said, "No, no, keep pulling. The bag has to come free. I can't stand the sound." The driver turned on an empty street with open fields to either side of the road, her right hand on Savannah's back.

As Savannah bent to pull at the bag again, the woman pulled over to the side of the road and pushed Savannah over further.

"Here, let me help." With her left hand, she reached into a pocket and took out a rag, leaned over, and slapped the rag over Savannah's nose and mouth. After a brief struggle, Savannah went limp.

****

Mariah returned phone calls and made inquiries for a new case, but by three-thirty in the afternoon her exhaustion set in and she was having trouble focusing on anything. She closed her laptop, grabbed her purse, and crossed the hall from her office to Morgan's, her partner and best friend, and knocked on the threshold of his open door. Morgan looked up from his computer and smiled.

After Mariah's recovery, she and Morgan went into a partnership with their friend, Damion Riley, to purchase and run *The Watchers: Investigation and Reporting* located in Portland Oregon. Damion, before retiring from the FBI, rescued Mariah from the mad man who abducted and beat her. Morgan and Mariah had formerly been partners on the Albuquerque New Mexico Police Department, and before that, Morgan and Riley served in the military together.

Damion (who goes by Riley) and his wife Jeri, sold their home in Idaho Falls, Idaho and relocated to Portland so Riley could become a private investigator. Jeri wanted to be closer to her sister and brother-in-law, Janice and Clive (an Oregon State Trooper) Henderson. Janice and Clive were happy to have the Riley's move closer after Jeri's harrowing abduction by the mob during the same investigation in which Mariah was almost killed. Riley and Jeri rented a condo in downtown Portland on the west side of the Willamette River.

Morgan retired from the Albuquerque Police Department and moved with his wife Molly, their son, Maximus (who goes by Max), and their daughter Mia to the Portland area. Molly researched the schools before moving and she and Morgan chose to move to Hillsboro, Oregon—just outside of Portland—for the schools. They found a beautiful home not far from the high school and an easy commute to the city.

Mariah sold the vacant lot where her home once sat before being blown up by the mob in an attempt to kill her. She sold her psychology practice plus the office building to a psychologist from Las Cruces New Mexico who wanted to relocate to Albuquerque. After losing everything in the explosion, she decided to wait a while before buying again and found a little cottage to rent only two blocks from Janice and Clive's home in southwest Portland.

Mariah loved the energy of Portland and her new career as a private investigator. Working with the two most important men in her life—second only to her three uncles who lived in Texas—filled her with happiness. The only other thing she wanted in life was a good nights sleep.

"Hey, congratulations on the win, Jeffries. That was quite a case." Morgan said, bringing her focus back to the present.

"Thanks. I sometimes wish the craziness of some people and the things they do surprised me more."

"I understand, but someone has to be the guardians to help and protect the unsuspecting. Someone has to see the ugliness in the world and strike back at it."

"I know. I'm taking off early and heading home if you don't need me for anything else today."

"Nope. You earned yourself some time off. Why don't you take a few extra days?" Morgan, aware of her nightmares, worried about her.

"Nah, I can't. I still need to write up the report on the case and send out the bill for payment. Besides, what would I do without work to come to?" She smiled and shrugged a shoulder. "I'll be back in the morning."

"Okay, if that's what you want, but call me if you change your mind."

"I will Morgan, but don't hold your breath." Mariah smiled and turned to leave, throwing over her shoulder, "Talk to you later."

"Alright. See you tomorrow you workaholic." He watched her walk down the hall until she was beyond his line of sight before returning his attention to the report in front of him.

****

"I'm happy you had the good sense to bring your utility van this time," she said with a sneer.

"Yes ma'am." He looked at the ground, hating this woman more and more with every passing day.

"Well? What are you waiting for. Get the girl and put her in your van. You know what to do!"

He eased past the woman, walked to her pick-up truck, and opened the passenger door. He grabbed Savannah by the shoulders and rolled her out of the floorboard of the truck. He pulled at her shoulders letting her feet fall to the ground, and shuffled backward` until he got to the back of his white utility van with red lettering that read HOFFMAN MAINTENANCE SERVICE. He lowered the girl to the ground in front of his feet and reached over her to open the back doors. Savannah, feigning unconsciousness, kicked up with all her might and kicked him in the groin while he was leaning over her and vulnerable. He cried out and fell to his knees, holding himself. She scooted back and scrambled to her feet. She started to run but the woman, only a step away, stretched out her leg and tripped her. The woman jumped on Savannah and punched her in the face. The girl screamed and fought back, grabbing the woman's hair with her left hand and punching with her right. Savannah, screaming, tried to roll over on top of the woman, but the woman kept her balance and slugged the girl in the face two more times shouting, "Shut up, you little bitch."

The man got back to his feet and ran over to the two fighting females. He grabbed Savannah's hands and pulled them away from the woman. The woman slugged the girl one last time and leaned back, sitting on the girls thighs.

"Hold her down, you fool. I'll get some more chloroform."

The woman stood and brushed dirt from her slacks and sweater, both black, while her reluctant partner turned the screaming girl to her stomach and secured her wrists with a nylon cable tie. The woman hobbled to her truck, one three-inch black heel on her left foot, her right foot bare. She came back with a rag and a small brown bottle.

Savannah struggled to rise, but only managed to roll back to her back.

"Why are you doing this to me," she yelled.

"Because your parents paid us to. They're tired of your constant complaining and they don't want to put up with you any more."

"That's a lie. You're a lying bitch. Let me go!" The girl screamed and grunted with effort, kicking her feet to keep the man and woman away from her. The man finally captured her ankles and held them, but the effort didn't stop the girl from bucking and hollering.

The woman leaned down at the girls head and said, "Shhhh!"

The girl stopped her screaming to catch a breath and whimpered, "*Pleeeese* ..."

In a syrupy soft voice, the woman said, "I'll let you go when you learn your place in life." She grabbed the girl's hair and turned her head so she could place the soaked rag over the girls nose and mouth. "Breath my pet. I think you will be the favorite. You'll bring in a lot of money until you're finally broken. Breath in deeply, now."

****

The sand shifts beneath my feet as Paisley and I run along the beach. The water rushes in from the ocean, trying to ensnare our feet, but I keep us out of reach of the waves. The sound of crashing waves on the beach is peaceful and I give silent thanks for this beautiful, sunny day. Sweat runs from between my shoulder blades down to the small of my back and tickles me, but the cool breeze blowing in my face dries the sweat before running into my eyes. My hair, divided into two braids are draped over my shoulders, the ends tapping on my chest above each breast while I run.

Paisley stops and begins to dig in the sand. She stops digging and sniffs around the shallow hole before digging again to the left of the first spot. She leans back on her hind legs, then pounces at something to the left of the second spot. Her tail is a blur, wagging back and forth and she whines as she starts digging yet again. I smile leaving Paisley to her entertainment and take a few steps closer to the waves, digging my bare toes into the cold, wet sand. Looking back in the direction we came from, the silhouette of a man stands in the distance. A wave rushes over my feet, up to my ankles and I look back to check on Paisley. She is laying in the sand, watching me. I glance back down the beach, but the figure is gone. I turn and call to Paisley, "Come on, girl," and start running up the beach. Paisley follows, overtaking me and runs ahead. She turns up the beach, away from the waves and starts circling around, her nose to the sand. I come upon a large heart dug into the sand with writing inside.

"Help is coming!"

'What an odd thing to write inside a heart,' I think. Looking around, there's only Paisley and me. Only our footprints in the sand are visible behind us, and those are being washed away by the incoming tide. There are no footprints ahead of us.

Paisley starts digging in the sand again. She is deep in a hole by the time I cross the beach to her, and I have to peer over the edge to find her. The incoming tide would soon fill in the hole so I call to her, "Paisley, get out of there." Panting and bright eyed, she turns to me and wags her tail.

"Come on, let's go home."

She jumps to me, but the hole has grown to a pit and is too deep. She hits the side and slides back to the bottom. The first wave to reach the pit, pools in the bottom around Paisley. I drop to the sand and lean over the edge to grab her, but every time she gets close, more waves pour in and push her further away. The pit is filling with water and growing wider and deeper. Paisley is paddling to the edge where I'm reaching for her. She whines. A whirlpool appears in the center of the very large, dark pit and starts to pull Paisley in. I try to stand so I can jump in and save her, but seaweed has entangled my legs. I panic and start yelling at her to swim to me. She tries, but the pull of the whirlpool is too strong and she can't break free.

"PAISLEY!" I scream as she is sucked under.

As the waves retreat back to the ocean, the seaweed pulls me across the beach to drag me to my death in the depths of the sea. I struggle against the waves rolling me to my back, and fight against the seaweed wrapping around my waist and legs. I gasp for breath when my face breaks the surface of the water, before I'm pulled under again. As waves wash over my face, a red haired, blue eyed man stands over me and says, "Help is coming, Mariah. Don't despair."

A large shadow moves across the sun, the image of the man waivers in the sluicing of water, and disappears. Darkness descends. I groan, unable to escape the waves or the seaweed, the grief of losing Paisley, or the nightmare stalking me. I try not to be afraid and surrender to the ocean as an overwhelming sense of defeat weights me down beneath the waves. I think of what Uncle John taught me—to love life. As long as I have life, I have something worth fighting for, and to never give up. He taught me that life is more than a functioning, breathing body. Life is thought and purpose and action. He told me that his father, my grandfather, taught him and his brothers, my father included, that to live was to resist oppression and meaningless dogma—to reach beyond fear and to fight for the right to be free thinking and to act on your own moral code of goodness and compassion. I am not ready to give up and die. I reach with my head for the surface as a wave recedes, gasp for breath of precious air, and scream.

Mariah woke to Paisley's whining and licking her face. She clutched Paisley and checked the clock. *Only two hours*, she thought. *Only two hours of sleep.* She sighed and rolled over with Paisley in her arms. "I love you, Paisley girl. I'll keep you safe," she whispered as she closed her eyes and drifted off into a dreamless sleep.

ROBIN W. TITCHEN

TUESDAY A.M.

Mariah, dressed for the crisp fall morning, set aside her ever present exhaustion to take Paisley out for her morning run. As a child, her grandfather and uncles, all in law enforcement, taught her to be unpredictable in her daily routines, so after trying multiple routes for their run, Mariah settled on four that gave her the best evasive and defensive options. Two of the four took her and Paisley passed a very nice dog park. A couple of times each month, she threw in one of two additional paths for variety and to keep things mixed up, even though neither of the two directions were favorites.

Mariah's breath misted in the cold fall air as they jogged down the front walk and turned left on the sidewalk. In the beam of the street lights, beads of frost glistened on the windows of the cars lining both sides of the street. In spite of all the hard work in the neighborhood to bag up the fallen leaves in their yards, the ground and sidewalks were littered anew with the colorful discards of the majestic trees. The crunch and rustle of leaves under her feet made a sweet sound to Mariah and she smiled as she jogged with Paisley beside her. She remembered how she always loved this time of year back home in Texas and later in Albuquerque New Mexico. But in Oregon, she realized, the beauty was more than she ever imagined.

Three quarters of a mile down the road, Mariah took another left, and then a right at the next corner. After another quarter of a mile she crossed the street to the dog park, entered the first gate with Paisley, unhooked her leash, and opened the second gate for them to enter the park itself.

Mariah always thought the dog park she and Paisley went to in Albuquerque was great until she found this one. A mixture of deciduous and evergreen trees and bushes lined the outside of the fence, giving the illusion of a rural setting. Looking around, Mariah thought of how magnificent the fall colors had been the last couple of weeks. Inside the fence were three towering oak trees to the right of the entrance. Under the trees were four picnic tables with benches, and water buckets of various sizes scattered around the ground for the dogs to drink from. To the left of the entrance was a doggie water park with a cement slab, five foot by five foot, and a drain in the center for washing the dogs after rolling in the mud and the muck. Behind the slab and against the fence stood a vertical pipe with a water faucet attached sporting a hose with a spray nozzle at the end. On either side of the slab lay blue plastic kiddy pools for the dogs to play in during warmer weather.

In front of the two park areas ran a paved, quarter mile, oval track with a large grassy area in the center. Around the outside of the track were brightly painted, metal benches for visitors to sit and converse while watching their dogs run and play. On the far side of the track were two smaller, fenced in parks for those dogs learning to socialize or the more aggressive dogs to run and play without risking injury to others. This park was well maintained, often supervised, and always a pleasant place to visit.

As the sky began to streak with hues of blue, purple, and pink, Mariah advanced on the track and began her workout, alternating between sprinting, jogging, and walking. Paisley started following her nose, first sniffing around the water buckets and picnic tables before chasing all the good scents along the track and in the field.

Mariah thought back to the slow and painful process of

recovery after the beating two years ago. She reveled with every step she took—thankful she was able to again do her usual strenuous exercises of running and martial arts that she practiced most of her life. She finished her two mile run and bent over, hands on her knees to catch her breath before walking to the middle of the field to start her Tai Chi Chuan exercises. Paisley chased and jumped at the birds swooping down to feed on the early morning bugs.

The squeak of the gate opening brought Mariah out of her meditation. She checked around the field until she spotted Paisley before she glanced toward the gate.

"Hi Bobby," she called and raised her hand in greeting. Bobby waived back and turned to close the gate after his white, standard sized poodle entered.

Mariah took her phone from her jacket pocket to check the time. "Paisley, come on girl. Time to go," she yelled, spotting the little terrier across the field. Paisley turned her back to Mariah and started chasing another bird, her tongue hanging out the side of her mouth. Mariah couldn't help but laugh before muttering, "standard operating procedure, huh girl?"

She walked toward Bobby and the gate, keeping an eye on Paisley. The small, fourteen pound dog stopped mid chase and watched Mariah. She turned her back to Mariah again and ran up the field, jumped at a passing bird one last time before running to catch up with Mariah.

"Good to see you and Bonnie Girl again. Were you on vacation?" Being one of the first people Mariah met after moving to Portland, she and Bobby became friends, often sitting at the park and chatting about local current events while the two dogs chased and played with each other.

"No , I've been sick," Bobby said. "This is the first time I've gotten out in a while."

"I'm sorry," Mariah said and leaned over to scratch behind the poodle's ears, earning a nudge on the thigh. "Hi there, Bonnie Girl."

As she bent to hook the leash on Paisley's harness she said, "If I had known you were so sick, I would have checked in on you. I'm glad you're doing better now."

"I'm happy to be better. You and Paisley are looking good. Already heading home?"

"Yes, we've been here an hour, and I've got work to do. Take care of yourself, Bobby. Maybe we can catch up later in the week."

"That would be nice. I hope to come out here at least once a day now that I'm back on my feet."

Mariah waived goodbye and left through the gates with Paisley in tow.

Back at home, Mariah removed Paisley's leash, harness, and collar, before sitting on a bench by the front door, and removing her shoes. Paisley jumped and howled at the shadows cast on the wall each time Mariah bent over. She hung her coat in the hall closet and padded into the kitchen where she grabbed a handful of raw almonds from the fridge and popped a k-cup in her Keurig. While waiting for her beverage to brew, she snacked on the nuts. When her steaming, fresh coffee was ready and waiting in her favorite, over-sized mug, she carried it to the master bathroom, Paisley following beside her.

Showered and shivering, Mariah wrapped her hair in a towel and dried off. She stepped around the corner to her walk in closet, removed clean undergarments from drawers, and a pair of Levi's from a hanger. Half dressed, she searched through hangers of shirts but couldn't find anything she wanted to wear. She bent to another drawer, pulled out a tan camisole, and from the next drawer down, grabbed a rust colored cable-knit sweater, pulling each on over her head.

In the kitchen, Mariah rinsed out her coffee mug and put it in the drain rack, gave Paisley a treat, and left for the office.

******

The Watchers: Investigation and Reporting was housed on the north side of the sixteenth floor of a twenty story office building in downtown Portland. Mariah pulled into the parking garage, under the office building and parked in prime parking—nearest the elevators. Morgan's assigned parking was next to hers, and Riley's to the other side of Morgan's. The assigned parking was included in the office lease.

She took the elevator up to the sixteenth floor where the light from the windows at each end of the hall reflected off the polished floor of the wide hallway. The original owner of The Watchers was the son of the original owner of the high-rise, giving the P.I. company some cushy digs. When the owner of the building passed away, the building, with the exception of the suite of offices housing The Watchers, transferred through a trust into the hands of a board of directors who also managed a number of other office buildings in Portland. The one stipulation in the contract was that the P.I. Company retain their current location at the same, original rent, for as long as they were in existence, regardless of ownership. Having such prestigious office space lent a certain air of success to the business and drew in wealthy and important clientele.

Mariah turned right after stepping off the elevator and walked passed the offices of a civil law practice specializing in corporate law. They handled lawsuits against corporations— whistle blowers, and class action suits. The law partnership was made up of five attorneys and their staff. They took up the center portion of the sixteenth floor. The offices at the far end of the floor housed a big CPA company and The Watchers were at the opposite end of the floor.

Mariah unlocked the door to their suite of offices, turned on the lights, flipped the sign to open, and closed the door behind her. She walked down the carpeted hall to the break room to fix a cup of coffee. She stood at the window, looking down over the city around her while she enjoyed the aroma of the dark roast brewing. She could feel the building sway slightly which tended to catch her off guard and give her a rush. The view out the break room and conference room windows took Mariah's breath away, rain or shine. They overlooked the Willamette River and part of the northwest side of downtown Portland. On clear days she could see Mt. Saint Helens and Mt. Adams, and sometimes even Mt. Rainier.

Mariah most loved looking down on the tall buildings near their offices, and the gardens laid out on the rooftops. The flowers and potted trees grew bigger than she ever expected possible and she enjoyed looking down on the bits of serene nature in the midst of all the hustle and bustle of city life.

She carried her coffee to the front office and checked for messages, finding none. She placed the full, steaming cup on the desk before she walked down the hall to her office, retrieved a file, and returned to the front. She sat and opened the folder, staring at the paper in front of her without seeing anything on the page. Her thoughts, as they often did, drifted off to her recurring nightmare. She tried to remember if the shadow possessed any facial features. All she remembered was a human shaped, dark blob advancing on her or leaning over her before she woke in terror.

Lost in her musings when the door opened, Mariah gasped and jumped up taking a defensive stance, her heart pounding in her chest. Morgan stood just inside the door, holding the knob with his right hand, "What's the matter Jeffries? Everything alright?"

Sinking back into the chair, she exclaimed, "Oh! Morgan! You scared me."

Morgan turned and closed the door, "Obviously, but why?" He turned back to Mariah. "I just walked into the office like I always do. What's going on?"

"I know!" she said with a little too much venom. She shook her head and took a few calming breaths. "I wasn't expecting it."

"Mariah, I walk into the office almost every day around this time. What is wrong?" Concern laced his voice.

"I KNOW, MORGAN!" she shouted, her head spinning from the adrenaline rush and her mounting frustration.

Morgan pulled the chair out in front of the desk and sat facing her. He leaned forward, arms resting on the edge of the desk.

Tears pooled in her eyes and threatened to spill over.

"I'm worried about you, Jeffries. You need help. I'm here for you," he said, spreading his hands out. "What do you need? What's going on? Let me help you."

She shook her head. "Nothing!" She shrugged her shoulders and shook her head. "I'm exhausted, Morgan. I'm still having bad dreams ... really bad dreams." She looked up at him, tears breaching the boundary of their rims and spilling to her cheeks.

"That's not surprising considering what you went through back in Idaho and Albuquerque. I was hoping the move would help. Give yourself some time, Mariah. You were back at work as soon as you were able to navigate. You didn't give yourself much time to deal with everything you went through. Are you still in counseling?"

"Yes, but it hasn't helped a bit. I feel like I'm throwing good money after bad. Morgan, I went back to work as soon as I could because ... well, I had to. Working gives me something to focus on and think about besides the nightmares. Not working would have been a lot worse for me."

"I know. Do you want to talk to me about any of it?"

She took a deep breath and slowly blew it out through pursed lips.

"No." She shook her head. "You're too much like family, Morgan. Plus, you're a business partner now. Maybe I need to find a new psychologist—get a different perspective. You know?"

"Sure, maybe that will help. I can research them and help you find a good one who deals with post-traumatic stress disorder."

"Thanks but I'll start the research myself." With a weak smile, Mariah continued, "You have enough to do."

"I don't mind helping, Mariah. I care about you. You're the little sister I always wanted."

"I know. I care about y'all too. I'll let you know if I need help. I promise."

Morgan got up from the chair and started down the hall before turning back, "You promise you'll let me know if there's anything Molly and I can do for you?"

Mariah nodded.

"And don't go karate chopping any of our clients who walk in the door. It's bad for business." He smiled and winked before walking down the hall to his office. Mariah wiped the tears from her eyes with her fingertips. The front door opened again and she dropped her hands to her lap and wiped her damp fingers on her jeans as Riley walked in, turning his back to her as he closed the door.

"Morning Jeff … Ah, what's wrong?" he asked when he turned back and saw her crying. "Are you alright?"

"Ignore me, Riley. I'm exhausted."

"Still having those bad dreams?"

"Yeah. Counseling doesn't seem to be helping. I'm about at my wit's end."

Riley walked over to the front of the desk, planted his hands, palms down, on top of the desk, leaned toward her and asked, "Do you trust me, Mariah?"

"With my life, Riley. You know I do," she whispered in a choked voice while wiping tears from her eyes again.

"Call Jeri and tell her what's going on. Please. Her sister might know of someone who could help you. Just hear her out before you write it off as crazy talk."

She looked at Riley, puzzled. "What do you mean?"

"Do it. Please? Talk to Jeri and she'll explain what I'm talking about. If you're interested, you can contact Janice."

She nodded her head, "Okay Riley. I trust you—of course I do. As soon as I finish up my report on this case, I'll go visit Jeri."

"Great. I'll call her and tell her you're coming by." Riley straightened. "Talk to you later. I have to go talk to a client in the clink—managed to get himself arrested last night and wants me to find evidence for his attorney to get him off." He watched Mariah a moment before nodding his head and walking down the hall to his office to retrieve a file. On his way out, he said, "I'll be back in a couple of hours," before the door closed, chasing his back.

"Finally!" Mariah sighed, relieved to think there might be help on the horizon. She typed up the final report on the divorce case she finished the previous Friday, and made out the billing statement.

Mariah was hired by the petitioner's counsel to investigate the husband on suspicion of philandering, and found enough evidence, and witnesses, to win the case. Not only did she find proof of one long distance, internet affair, she found proof of multiple affairs, one resulting in the birth of a child.

When checking several online date sites, Mariah found nothing obvious connecting the husband to an account, so she consulted with Norela Morales who was a huge help in the Albuquerque case.

Not only is Norela an expert in surveillance and personal protection, but as it turned out, she is also a genius at computer hacking. Mariah's Uncle Richard, another computer genius, and Norela got into a deep discussion on hacking at Morgan's retirement party before the move to Portland and taking over *The Watchers*.

Thanks to Norela's help, they found the husband on three different free dating sites and one which charged a monthly fee. He used a different alias on each site, but the pictures on all of the sites were of him. The paid site showed the heaviest activity, and Norela tracked down his financial transactions regarding his fees. He used a pre-paid credit card so the wife couldn't track them. Norela extracted emails from all the sites and Mariah did a lot of pavement pounding to find the women and interview them.

Mariah learned from the first woman she interviewed that their affair was informed and consensual. The woman was aware the man was married. She was too, and therefore she refused to answer questions or testify in court stating it would destroy her already tenuous marriage. The petitioner's counsel could have called her as a hostile witness, but they had enough willing 'victims' to cinch the case, so they chose not to assist her in wrecking her own marriage.

Two of the others were shocked and very angry when they learned he was married, and each testified that he presented himself as single and available. They each went out on several dates with the man. A fourth lived in Atlanta, Georgia, and told the story of him flying out to spend a romantic weekend with her. She provided dates and times, plus car rental and hotel information, and told Mariah he asked her to come to Portland for a visit only two weeks earlier. A fifth woman who lived in Plainfield New Jersey, became pregnant by him on one of his visits, and when she told him of the child, he disappeared, blocking any contact with her. Needless to say, the divorce hearing was quite the show—something you would expect to see on a late night television drama.

Mariah put the completed report in the case folder and slid a folded copy of the report in an envelope to mail to their client. Walking to the file room, she filed the case folder alphabetically by their client's last name, closed the file drawer and went to Morgan's office. She knocked on the threshold of his open door to get his attention. Morgan looked up from a report he was reading and raised his eyebrows, "What's up?"

The phone rang as she started to answer, and Morgan raised his hand to stop her while he answered the phone, "Watchers, this is Morgan."

The person on the other end of the phone seemed to have a lot to say. Every time Morgan opened his mouth to reply, he was interrupted by the caller and couldn't get a word in edgewise. After several attempts, he leaned back in his chair, waived his hand in the air, and winked at Mariah.

Mariah smiled.

"I see," he said at last. "Let me get your name and phone number and one of us will call you back to schedule an appointment … yes, but … I understand. Unfortunately, I'm headed out the door to an important meeting and our secretary has the day off. ... Sir, ... can I ... one of us will call you back in a couple hours. I promise, either I will or one of my partners, will call you before the day is out. ... Yes. Of course we can see you." Morgan nodded his head while he scribbled information. "Thank you, Mr. Silkeney. We'll see you when you get into town this afternoon." He hung up the phone and looked at Mariah. "You alright?"

"Well, I wanted to talk to you and Riley about the business. We need some staff—at the very least a secretary slash receptionist. We've grown a lot, and with us having to take turns sitting at the office or closing up during regular hours to conduct our investigations, it's costing us money by cutting into the cases we can take."

"I agree. This guy," he lifted the note he wrote, "is desperate to talk to us. He wants us all here this afternoon ... a matter of life and death, he said. He's driving up from Medford and will be here in a few hours. Think you'll be here?"

"I've got some personal business to tend to, but I shouldn't be more than a couple hours."

"Great. Riley should be back. I'll call him on my cell and give him a heads up. Go ahead and pencil in a meeting on the board to discuss staffing. Let's shoot for nine tomorrow morning."

"Sounds good, what meeting are you headed to?"

"Mia's Math teacher. Mia was accused of cheating on her last test because she didn't show her work." He shrugged his shoulders, "She does calculations like I do—not the way it's taught, but it works."

"Oh! Sorry to hear it's causing her problems in school."

Morgan stood and grabbed his keys and cell phone off the desk.

"Will you be back in time for Mr. Silkeney's meeting?" Mariah followed him down the hall.

Morgan turned in at the break room. "I should be, but go ahead and start without me if I'm not."

"Okay." Mariah penciled in a nine a.m. partner's meeting

on the calendar for the next day. "Give Mia a hug for me."

"Will do. I'll see you later." He walked out the door. Pulling it closed behind him.

Mariah grabbed her purse with her baby Glock cradled inside before she changed the sign to 'closed', locked the door and headed out.

When she exited the elevator on the first floor, she pulled her cell phone out of her back pocket and called Jeri while she rode down the escalator to the sidewalk below.

"Hi Jeri. Riley suggested I come and talk to you about some bad dreams I'm having. Do you have a few minutes? ... I'm leaving the office now and I'm walking, so I'll be there in about fifteen minutes, would you like me to stop and pick anything up for you on my way—a coffee or Bento Bowl? ... Alright. See ya soon."

****

"Hi Mariah." Jeri wrapped her arms around Mariah's neck and hugged her tight. "I'm so sorry you're still having those awful dreams. My abduction can't compare to what you experienced, and yet I was haunted something awful. Come in and let's talk. I'll tell you all about what I did with my sister's help."

Mariah took a deep breath, savoring the rich scent of cinnamon, ginger, and nutmeg from the cookies cooling on the counter and baking in the oven.

"Would you like some iced tea? I just made some fresh."

"Thanks, Jeri. That would be great." Mariah walked to the kitchen table, pulled out a chair and sat, hooking her purse on the back of the chair, while Jeri poured a glass of iced tea for each of them and brought them to the table. She handed a glass to Mariah and sat across the table, taking a sip of her tea before setting the glass down.

"Riley called and said you're still having bad dreams. You

look exhausted."

"Gee, thanks." Mariah chuckled. "I am exhausted. I …" The timer went off and Jeri got up from the table.

"Just a sec while I pull the last batch of cookies out. Want one?" She walked to the kitchen and grabbed a mitt to pull out the baking sheet. "They're best when they're fresh out of the oven," she called as she bent to her task.

"No. Thank you."

Jeri transferred the cookies from the pan to a wire rack, turned off the oven, and came back to the table. "They're Riley's favorite—I can't keep them in the house." She chuckled and shook her head. "I don't know how he stays so trim."

Mariah smiled at her. "Yes you do. He goes to the gym seven days a week."

Jeri sat back in her chair across from Mariah and nodded with a silly grin plastered on her face. "True, plus he works out at home." She took another sip of tea. "Do you want to hear my story?"

Mariah nodded.

"Every time I closed my eyes, I would start to relive the abduction all over again—the two men kicking in the back door, grabbing and gagging me before tying me up and throwing a hood over my head. They carried me out of the house and tossed me in the trunk of their car like a sack of potatoes. I hit my head and it hurt like crazy. I feel guilty even saying that after what you endured. I can't begin to imagine what it was like for you after the injuries you sustained."

Her eyes glazed over as she watched her abduction unfold in her mind. "I was terrified—their threats of using me to lure you, Morgan, and Riley in so they could kill each of you …" She was almost whispering—a far off look in her eyes. She shook her head and her eyes refocused as she looked at Mariah. "… and their descriptions of how they were going to do it." Her jaw clenched. "Riley held me in his arms every night and whispered to me that I was safe." Her eyes glistened with tears. "He held me night after night whispering, 'I'm here. I'll protect you. Nothing and no one will hurt you. I am your wall of defense.' Over and over he repeated those words, as if his will alone would keep the nightmares away. I hated what it was doing to him." Jeri wiped at her eyes before going on.

"I wanted so much to be able to go to sleep. I wanted his presence and his words to be enough, but nothing stopped the nightmares. I trust Riley, you know? I do! He would die trying to protect me. So many nights I couldn't get past the nightmares. By the time we moved to Portland, exhaustion ruled our days and started impacting mine and Riley's health. I was getting worried he might have a heart attack. His blood pressure was rising and he was having heart palpitations. Neither of us was getting any sleep. It was horrible. I didn't know how to stop the madness invading our peaceful life, and that Mariah, was the worst."

Jeri took a deep breath to quell her rising anger. She sipped her tea and swallowed before continuing. "Janice realized something terrible was going on. One day she came over for coffee and to visit. She didn't beat around the bush and came right out with what was on her mind. She used to suffer from severe depression and after all the tests, the doctors couldn't give her a cause for it. They only offered medications to manage the depression. She didn't like the way the meds made her feel or the side effects and it concerned her that no one seemed interested in *why* she was depressed.

"A friend of hers introduced her to a counselor who does past life regressions."

"Past life regressions? That's real?"

"Yes. Janice told me she'd exhausted all her other options through traditional medicine and decided to try this counselor. The therapist regressed her a number of times and she began to understand why she suffered from depression. It's a compelling story."

"Do you really believe in that," Mariah asked with a hint of skepticism.

"Well, I didn't, but I saw such a dramatic change in Janice

46

that I figured there must be something to it. When I couldn't stop the dreams, Janice convinced me to try regression. Mariah, if I didn't believe before, I do now. I can't explain how real it was to me. Would you like to hear more?"

Nodding her head, Mariah said, "Yes. I've reached the point where I'll try anything."

"I'll call Janice and ask if she can meet with you. I want you to hear about her experiences too, but she needs to tell you, herself. Let me try to get her on the phone. Just a second."

Jeri got up from the table and walked into the living room and picked up her cordless phone, pushed a number and waited before saying, "Hi Jan, this is Jeri. Give me a call at home when you get a chance. Everything is fine, just need to talk. Love you."

She disconnected the call and turned back to the kitchen doorway. "I'll see when she is available to sit with you and then give you a call. Will that be okay?"

"Yes, of course. It sounds interesting and if you think this therapist would help me, I'm game. I can't go on like this much longer, Jeri. I'm exhausted. I'm getting little sleep and you know how bad that is, especially in my profession. I need to be able to think clearly for some of the work we do."

"Riley's been telling me how tired you are and that you're not sleeping well. Considering what you've been through, we all understand. He and Morgan are worried about you. We all are. I've been after him to have you call me, and I'm glad he finally did."

"Me too. But Jeri, you can call me any time too. You don't have to contact me through Riley."

Sitting back down across from Mariah and setting the cordless phone on the table in front of her Jeri said, "I know. I also know from experience how personal these things can be and I didn't want to intrude if I didn't need to. Riley didn't either. Anyway, let me tell you about my regressions.

"We knew where my nightmares came from. It wasn't a question of past life issues … at least I didn't think so."

"What do you mean?"

"Well, the first thing we addressed was the whole situation with Riley going missing, my abduction and rescue by you and Morgan, the trip out of the country, and the cryptic message from Jim. We went through all that and then she asked me if I wanted to be regressed to see if there were any events in my past lives contributing to my nightmares. I was a little afraid at first, but curious too, and remembered what a life altering difference regression made for Janice.

"The first life I went to was way back in Ancient India. I was a young bride and my husband went off to war and was killed. I was blamed for his death and ridiculed in the streets before they stoned me to death."

Mariah grimaced. "Why were you blamed?"

"Something about bad karma back then. If I'd been a good wife, he would have lived, or something like that."

"Interesting."

"I wondered why that would be significant in my recent sleeplessness and learned that widows were often tortured and humiliated. Men of ancient India were discouraged from marrying a widow because widows were considered a disgrace to their family and carried bad karma. During the time in Idaho, when Riley first got involved in your abduction until the whole case was resolved, I had been so afraid for Riley's life. It made sense to me after the first regression. Of course I don't want Riley hurt and I don't want to lose him, but on a subconscious level I also feared going through the torture and humiliation of being a widow. That's where the dreams were coming from. As irrational as it is in today's world, my soul still feared that horror of being widowed in ancient India—still harbored the memory of it and wasn't able to reconcile the past with the present. I had to acknowledge those events and accept that they weren't relevant in my current life so my soul would be at peace with the past events.

"In the second life that called me, I was an old black woman living on a plantation in the south. I lived a long and hard life, slaving in the fields for the plantation owners until I died of pneumonia, old and all alone in a little shack. I saw the progression of that life, from myself as a little girl being sold away from my mother and family to work in the kitchen of a plantation, then being sent out into the fields, falling in love and jumping the broom to marry my man just to have him sold to another plantation owner after our second baby was born.

"I saw my first born son sold as a teenager and ripped from my arms and later, my second born son beaten to death by the overseer after he escaped and was caught and brought back. It was a sad, lonely life.

"Realizing how losing my mate in my past lives had devastating effects, helped me put my fears of losing Riley at rest and to be at peace. I'm aware that I'm likely to survive Riley. I've always known that and have always been terrified of being widowed. As terrible as that loss will be to me, this is a different life and I'm not going to let the time I have right now with him be destroyed by fear. I'll cross the bridge of widowhood if and when I have to."

With skepticism Mariah asked, "And you believe all that was real?"

"I do. I can't explain it, but it was so real. I didn't know anything about ancient India but after that session, I did some research and widows really were reviled back then."

The phone rang and Jeri picked up the cordless phone, checked to see who the caller was, and answered. "Hi Jan. ... Yeah, Mariah's here. She's having terrible nightmares from all the New Mexico stuff and I've been telling her about my sessions with Roselee. She's interested in hearing your story and I think she would like to start a session herself ... fifteen minutes?" Jeri looked at Mariah with raised eyebrows in silent question.

"Fine with me," Mariah responded, nodding her head.

"We'll be here. Love ya!"

Jeri pushed a button and set the phone back on the table. "She has a fascinating story. You'll be convinced to give Roselee a try."

"I already am. Are those the only two past lives you

visited?"

"Oh no. There were others, but those were the only two that called to me about my nightmares."

"Did you have any good past lives. Ones that don't lend themselves to nightmares?"

Jeri laughed. "Of course. One was of me as a child at Christmas, another of me as a young man at an anvil working as an apprentice to a black smith. Those two were brief glimpses because they didn't call to me. As Roselee put it, they didn't relate to the causative experiences I was looking for."

The two women chatted about Jeri's past life regressions until the front door to the living room opened and Janice stepped inside having used her own key.

"Helloooo," Janice sang out, closing the door behind her.

"In the kitchen," Jeri called out as both Jeri and Mariah stood from the table.

Walking into the kitchen, Janice hugged Jeri first and then came around the table and hugged Mariah.

"I'm so glad to see you again," Mariah said. "Jeri has been telling me about her experiences with Roselee, and I'm sure hoping this will be the answer to my prayers. Nothing else, not even traditional counseling, seems to be helping me,"

"Oh. It will," Janice replied with certainty. "Regression made all the difference in the world to me, and to Jeri, too."

Jeri brought to the table a glass of iced tea for Janice in one hand, and a pitcher of iced tea to refill their glasses in the other. She placed them on the table and retrieved a plate of fresh baked gingersnap cookies from the kitchen counter.

"Let's have a seat." She sat in her chair across from Mariah, and Janice pulled out the chair next to Mariah. Janice took a cookie from the plate.

"Oh yum! My favorite." Janice took a bite of the cookie and uttered a soft groan. "I wish they turned out as well for me as they do for you."

Jeri smiled at her. "You hate to bake and you know it."

"Okay, it's true. That's why I like to come over here." Janice swallowed the last bite. "Getting to the subject at hand, here's a little background information, Mariah. Twelve years ago, I developed a severe case of depression. No one could figure out why. I hadn't experienced any terrible trauma. We had a normal and happy childhood, and there were no dark hidden secrets in my life. My marriage was solid and happy. All the labs and tests came back good. The doctors didn't find any medical, psychological, physiological, or neurological explanations for the depression. They couldn't figure out why I was experiencing the depression and all they wanted to do was to put me on medications. I was near suicidal, and I felt hopeless.

"I hated the way the meds made me feel and I wanted the doctors to investigate further to find out why I was so depressed. I was told there weren't any other tests that could help them make a determination. I guess they did all they knew how to do, and throwing drugs at it was the only option left.

"That's neither here nor there now, however," she said with a flip of her hand. "When I complained to a friend, she introduced me to a counselor who does past life regressions. Out of ideas on what else to do, there didn't seem to be any other options, so I decided to give this gal a try. I'm sure glad I did.

"Roselee is wonderful. She is so genuine, caring, and compassionate and after two sessions of counseling, she told me that she believed there were things in a past life hanging on and causing my depression. In spite of my Christian upbringing, I always believed in reincarnation, so this intrigued me.

"The first regression took me to a life in which I was the wife of a stock broker at the time of the great crash. My husband killed himself when he learned that not only did we lose everything, but all his clients did too. He left a note for me—he mailed it before he shot himself in his office—telling me about some of his powerful clients who would torture him to death for losing their money.

"I was left destitute and afraid for mine and my children's

lives. We were kicked out of our home, and I didn't have any food for them, or the money to get to my family. I doubt my family could help, anyway. Everyone lost everything during that time. I couldn't cope with all the loss and fear so I wandered out into the woods in a blizzard, laid down in an open field and watched as the snow blew around me, and buried me. I froze to death, leaving behind my two young daughters to fend for themselves or be trusted to the care of strangers. After that regression, I was mortified that I wasn't strong enough to live for my children."

"What happened to your children? Did you see what happened to them?"

"No. The regression ended at my death. Roselee and I discussed that life though, and I began to understand my motivating drive - fear. Getting a handle on my weakness helped me with my current depression. After going over that life experience with Roselee for several sessions, I told her I wanted to regress again because I had this nagging sense there was something else—something more horrible still holding me back from a full recovery. As afraid as I was of learning I did worse things in past lives, the need to know what from my past was destroying my present, was even stronger.

"This time, I regressed to a Cheyenne Indian brave who's family was wiped out in the Sand Creek Massacre in 1864. I, along with other warriors from my tribe, were off hunting buffalo at the time of the raid. One of the young warriors, left behind as part of the small contingency to protect our women, our young, and our elders in the village, escaped the blood bath and found the hunting party. I was one of the first to return to the scene of the ambush and found my infant son, scalped and my squaw—my wife—along with my parents, grandparents, aunts, nieces, young nephews, and my friends families, all murdered and mutilated. I was devastated and I wanted revenge.

"I joined what they called The Dog Soldiers, a special group of tribal members who attacked and fought the military. I felt justified in ambushing and killing the soldiers, but every attack, every killing only brought more remorse. I wasn't raised to be a cold blooded murderer, that wasn't who I was or who I wanted to be, but it was too late. A marauding murderer was who I had become, justified or not. My life from the Sand Creek Massacre forward was angry, violent, and deadly until I was killed in a raid.

"I don't remember ever hearing about this massacre in any history class or anything, but since my regression, I researched it. I didn't know much about the Indian Wars at all until then. I learned that a militia of the Colorado Territory attacked a peaceful village of Cheyenne and Arapahos. They killed about a hundred and fifty Indians in that attack—the women, the young and infirm. They raped the women before killing them and mutilated many of the bodies.

"After seeing that life and counseling with Roselee about it, the last vestiges of depression lifted. Just like that." Janice snapped her fingers. "The anger? The sense of hopelessness, and guilt—at not being able to protect my loved ones as well as the later attacks I was a part of—was resolved and I was able to let go of the karma that had me locked in a cycle of destruction. In this life it manifested in this overpowering and unexplainable depression.

"It saved my life to be able to regress and resolve those very old tragedies. I'm a new person, Mariah—a much better person. My life is peaceful now, and I want you to find peace too.

"And, believe it or not, my wife from my life as a Cheyenne brave is my husband, today. Clive," she exclaimed and giggled like a schoolgirl. "We've been bonded to each other through these life cycles. I suspect, even though he refuses to be regressed, one of the reasons he got into law enforcement and is so dedicated to protecting the innocent and helpless is because of that experience at Sand Creek."

"Wow!" Mariah was a little in awe. "What a story."

"Would you like me to contact Roselee and schedule an appointment for you?"

Mariah nodded her head. "Yes. Something is haunting me.

I think it's Jerry, but maybe it's not. Maybe it's … I don't know. Could be something from a past life, I guess. I never thought about reincarnation much before. My Uncle John mentioned past lives before, but we never discussed it. I just never thought about reincarnation.

"If I don't figure this out soon though, I'm afraid whatever is haunting me, is going to kill me with exhaustion if nothing else. I don't know where else to turn for help. Traditional counseling is not helping me."

Mariah sighed and rubbed the back of her neck.

"I'm so tired. I'm just so tired." Mariah rubbed her face with both hands and then ran her fingers through her hair to the back of her head. She cradled her face in the crook of her arms, her elbows braced on the table. In a muffled voice she pleaded, "I've got to resolve this so I can get some sleep and have a real life again."

Janice got up from the table, left the room, and returned a moment later with a box of tissue she retrieved from the bathroom.

"Here, Mariah. Wipe your eyes. Everything is going to get better from here. I'm calling Roselee right now." She plopped the box of tissue on the table in front of Mariah and retrieved her cell phone from the purse she sat on the floor next to her chair. She scrolled through her phone list and pushed a button to dial Roselee. She paced back and forth at the end of the table while she waited for an answer and when the answering machine picked up, she sat in her chair.

After the recorded message, Janice said, "Hi Roselee, this is Janice Henderson. I have a dear friend who is in need of a counselor with your unique style. Please give me a call back to schedule an appointment for her." Janice recited her number and disconnected the call.

Once she hung up, she looked at Mariah. "I'm sorry I couldn't get right through to her. Her office staff is part time and the calls sometimes go right to voicemail, but she is good about calling back. Do you want me to schedule you for her next available appointment or give her your number so you can work something out?"

Sniffling and wiping her eyes, Mariah said, "Go ahead and schedule the next available appointment. I'll be able to work my schedule around since there aren't any upcoming court appearances. Will one of you go with me?"

"Of course!" Jeri said at the same time Janice replied, "You betcha!"

ROBIN W. TITCHEN

TUESDAY P.M.

Arriving at the office, Mariah found the door unlocked. She stepped inside and hollered, "Anyone here?" as she turned to close the door behind her.

Riley popped his head out of his office. "Hi Jeffries. I got here about thirty minutes ago and the doors were locked. Where's Morgan?"

"Mia's having problems at school." She walked down the hall to Riley's office and leaned against the door jam. "I went and talked to Jeri and she called Janice who came over. Thanks for suggesting I talk to them."

"You're welcome. I've been keeping an eye on you and I could see your dreams were getting worse. Jeri and I have been there. So, what do you think?" Riley closed a filing cabinet drawer and walked behind his desk. As he took a seat in his swivel chair, Mariah stepped into his office and sat in the chair across from his desk.

"Well, if regression helps me past these hauntings, I'll be happy. I'll reserve judgment until I meet this Roselee." Mariah glanced at the wall behind Riley and asked, "Do you believe, Riley?"

"I do, Mariah. I've always believed in the paranormal. I could tell you some stories of angel visitations and warnings that kept me alive. I keep this stuff to myself in order to maintain my credibility. A lot of people think it's crazy talk, but when you experience it yourself, you know better."

"I know what you mean. My family … we display umm … certain talents, if you will, that other people think is kind of smoke and mirrors—like Uncle John who is an intuitive. Me too for that matter. Uncle Richard is an empath like my dad was, and Uncle Dan is a dream clairvoyant. Their mother could see ghosts and talk to spirits. I never felt I could talk about it much with other people. I wish I could see and talk to spirits like my grandmother did. I miss my dad and would love to talk to him."

"He's with you, Mariah. Just know he loves you and he's with you."

Mariah sighed. "So tell me one of your stories, please."

"Sure. I was on a stakeout in the desert one night—not far from the farm where you escaped the night your nightmare started. This was back in 2008 and the crime rate had surged—increased burglaries, strong armed robberies, assaults, and murder. We had information of a criminal organization working out of this farm and it was my watch.

"The night was bitter cold and the visibility was poor—a pitch black night, overcast with moisture laden clouds and a heavy fog rolling in.

"I noticed the activity at the farmhouse picking up, and traffic to the place increasing. I needed to get closer and find out what was going on. I started moving in toward the farmhouse, belly crawling until I got behind a ridge where I got up and ran behind the cover to gain a little ground.

"I'm not sure what happened. I'm surefooted, and very good at watching for traps, but as dark as the night was …," Riley shrugged, "I missed something. I tripped and hit my head on a rock. It dazed me and I rolled over on my back and could hear people hollering and a dirt bike or ATV start up. It was apparent I set off an alarm or something. I tried to get up to run, but pain shot through my lower leg and I got dizzy from the head wound and fell back down.

"All of a sudden these two … for lack of a better word …

ANGELS appeared before me. They were tall, about eight or nine foot tall and one of them asked, 'Are we too late?'

"'No, not yet' said the other. 'But he'll be dead if we don't get him out of here. Confuse the pursuers,' the second one said before he knelt beside me.

"'You're in a dangerous place and we need to move you,' he told me as he touched my head wound.

"'There's no time, save yourselves,' I moaned, and he smiled at me.

"He said, 'You don't understand. We are here to save you. We are not in danger, but you are. I'll help you walk.'

"I nodded my head. I could hear all these guys yelling and ATV's running, but every time the sound came close, confused yelling increased and the noise would move away.

"The second angel helped me off the ground. My left ankle was injured … broken or something by the way it felt, so the angel helped me back away and cross the desert to a small cave inside a rock formation. We didn't seem to take more than five or six steps after he helped me up before we stopped, and he told me we were safely away. The angel reached down and cupped my ankle in both his hands, and a warm tingle flowed through my whole leg. The first angel showed up and told me, 'stay here until the snow storm ends.'

"'What snow storm,' I asked. Riley chortled.

"He continued with, 'You will be safe here. When you come out …'"

"'Come out? Come out of where?'

"'Damion, when you come out of this cave,' and he point down to a small rock formation before continuing, 'hike due East and you will find your vehicle to drive home. Do not come out of this cave until the snow stops and the sun is up. You will be safe and warm here.'

"I reached up and felt blood on the side of my head. The second angel put his hand on the wound and again, the warm tingle flowed through me. I nodded to the two angels and crawled into the cave which was barely big enough for me to curl up on my side.

"The first angel continued, 'While you wait for the storm to pass, the healing process will complete. Remember, this farm is the place you are looking for, Damion. It is filled with dark spirits and you must clean it out or wickedness will take root in your town and destroy your community. Tell your superiors there are trip wires and warning systems set up because they are hiding major crime activity. With the necessary search warrants you will find evidence of many crimes. Your search warrants will be for drugs, firearms, stolen property from the home invasions and burglaries, and ledgers showing pay offs.'

"The second angel cut in. 'Believe in prayer, Damion. It has saved you many times in your life, and prayer is what saved you this night.'

"As both angels shimmered and started to disappear, the first angel said, 'Sleep.' A bush grew up before my eyes in front of the little cave, concealing the opening, and snow began to fall while my eyelids grew heavy and closed."

"Oh, Riley! You're kidding, right? That sounds like something out of a fairy tale or, or ... the Bible or something."

"Now you understand why I don't talk about some of this stuff."

"Are you sure you weren't having hallucinations from your head injury?"

"Mariah, first of all, I triggered a warning and they were coming for me, but they couldn't find me or my tracks. There is no rational explanation for that. Second, I never heard of little caves out there before or since this incident. And ... what about that bush growing up within seconds to shelter the cave opening? I suppose some people could explain away some of it by arguing I was hallucinating but that doesn't explain how they failed to find me, or the rest of it."

"The rest of it?"

"I immediately fell asleep and slept for two and a half days, until the storm broke and the sun came out. I never sleep more than five or six hours a night." Riley shook his head.

"You're thinking it was the head injury, but it wasn't. It was pure restful sleep. The angel put me to sleep. For two and a half days I had nothing to eat or drink, but I wasn't weak or famished or thirsty or even frozen to death. I crawled out of that cave and hiked due east through knee deep snow for two miles and found the FBI checking out my truck and staging a man hunt. Two miles, Mariah."

"What did you tell your superiors about that night? How did you get the search warrants?"

"On blind faith, I lied. I told them the storm hit after I saw and heard enough to get the search warrants. That I got lost in the storm and found this rock cave—which as it turns out was almost three and a half miles from the farm where the angels found me—and I crawled in for shelter to wait out the storm. They carried me over three miles into the desert to a tiny little rock cave that probably didn't even exist before that night."

"And? …"

"We ran the search warrants and found everything the angels told me we would. After we made our arrests and cataloged all the evidence, I went to my doctor who x-rayed my ankle and it showed a recently healed medial malleolus fracture."

"What about your head?"

"No mark or scar on my head, no sign of head trauma except my hair was matted with dried blood, and Jeri washed blood from my clothes after I got home." Riley raised his eyebrows as he looked at Mariah.

"You had hair?"

Riley scowled at her.

She raised her hands and laughed. "Sorry. … I believe you, Riley. I don't think you're making any of this up. I've never heard of anything like this before, that's all."

"That's why I don't talk about these encounters."

"These? There are others? Like what?"

"Yes—a couple when I was in the military, a couple more from the FBI—don't enter that intersection, look up, or turn to the left. Stuff like that. Stuff that probably saved my life. Most of the time it's more of a uh … supernatural sense to do something that I wouldn't have naturally done."

Mariah frowned at him.

"Like stopping and looking both ways before entering an intersection with a green light. Just as I slowed down, a drunk blew the red light and would have plowed right into my drivers side door."

Mariah nodded. "Have you been regressed, Riley?"

"No, and I don't need to be. I know I've lived before. I believe, but I don't think I need to be regressed and view my past lives in order to be happy. Maybe someday something will happen and I'll want to, but for now, I don't."

"I never told anyone, Riley, but ... after they released me to go home from the skilled nursing facility—I was off all the pain drugs, all the meds actually—I woke up in the middle of the night with this horrible sense of dread ... like someone was coming for me. That's when the nightmares started, I think. In a panic, I was going to get out of bed and run but as I threw the blanket off, a sudden sense of calm came over me. I turned on the light next to my bed and I saw angels. There were two on the left side of my bed, one at the foot of my bed, one on the right side of my bed, and one leaning against the wall by the door. They were big like you described—about eight foot tall. They were shimmery, or ... or transparent. I'm not sure how to describe them..."

"Gossamer."

"Yeah, gossamer. I saw these gossamer beings standing around me and an overwhelming sense of peace filled me. I knew I was safe that night. They never said anything, they just surrounded me and guarded me against ... "

The slamming open of the front door and a buzzer sounding startle Mariah and Riley.

A man yelled, "Is anyone here?"

Riley jumped up first, darting around the corner of his desk and reached the door to his office before Mariah got to her feet. Both of them rush to the front office.

Riley slowed to a stop and said, "Hi. How can we help you?" to the back of a man who was gently closing the front door. The man turned with a sheepish grin. Tall, with short, dark hair graying at the temples, the man said, "Sorry about the bang. The door swung opened easier than I anticipated."

His full, well groomed, salt and pepper eyebrows framed soft brown eyes, and the long dark lashes behind silver wire rimmed frames were almost feminine in his masculine features. When he smiled, the soft laugh lines around his eyes and mouth suggested he was a happy man who laughed easily. Deep dimples broke the smooth plain of his cheeks on his clean shaven face. His voice was deep, but eluded to kindness and understanding. His posture and the Armani suit made him look distinguished and well put together—like a man accustom to dressing well and getting what he wanted.

"No problem. It happens all the time," Mariah said looking around Riley. "I'm Mariah Jeffries and this is Damion Riley." Mariah stepped around Riley and extended her hand. "How can we help you?"

"Hi Mariah. Damion," he said shaking first Mariah's hand and then Riley's.

"Call me Riley. Everyone does." Riley stood, feet apart, with hands on his hips and a scowl on his face. "How can we help you?"

The man wore a light blue dress shirt, crisp with starch, under his dark grey suit. A pink and blue tie, and grey loafers completed his ensemble. In his left hand he carried a dark brown leather briefcase, and an overcoat draped across his forearm.

"I called earlier, while on my drive here from Medford, and talked to Morgan. He told me to come on in when I got to town, but I didn't expect to be here before three. I thought I would still be on the road, but I arrived sooner than I anticipated and came in to see if I could catch someone. Traffic was …"

"Mr. Silkeney?" Mariah asked. Riley relaxed.

"really light. Yes, I'm Martin Silkeney."

"Hi Martin. We're glad you came in. Let's go back to the conference room and you can tell us about your case."

"Is Morgan here too?" Martin followed Mariah down the

hall with Riley bringing up the rear. "I've done my research and I need the help of your whole team. You're the best in the State and I believe your prior experiences will be a big help in this case. Young women in the Rogue Valley are in serious trouble. It's a matter of life and death."

Mariah cocked an eyebrow and glanced at Riley as they entered the conference room.

"Morgan is out at the moment. If he isn't back before we finish hearing your story, we'll be sure to fill him in. We all work together here, wherever the need is." Riley interjected waiving Martin to a chair. "Have a seat."

"Can I get you something to drink?" Mariah asked.

"No. Thank you."

****

Riley and Mariah took seats across the table from Martin and each grabbed a legal pad and pen from the stack in the center of the conference table.

"Please spell your last name for me," Riley said as he sat poised to jot it down at the top of the page.

"Silkeney," Martin said. "S-I-L-K-E-N-E-Y."

Riley wrote **Silkeney, Martin**, at the top of the page in block letters, and asked, "Do you mind if we record this meeting? I recommend it so we can refer back and make sure we don't miss or overlook any important information."

"Of course not. Do what you think is necessary."

"Thank you." Riley set up and started the recorder. "You said some young women are in serious trouble in the Rogue Valley. What young women, and how much trouble? Why don't you start at the beginning and fill us in, please."

Martin Silkeney took a deep breath and paused a moment, gathering his thoughts before beginning.

"At first we didn't realize it was all related, but in researching things, I believe it started two weeks ago when

Tina Webb went missing. She's a fourteen year old girl who plays basketball and softball on both school and independent teams. She's been raised in what appears to be a happy and loving home. The family are members of the Nazarene Church in Medford and attend at least once a week. In fact her mother is in the choir and teaches Sunday School for the pre-school kids. There are no clues as to what happened to her. She went to school, attended all of her classes and no one has seen or heard from her since she walked out of the last classroom. I am acquainted with both of her parents and I would be surprised if they had anything to do with her disappearance, but anything is possible."

"So what else is going on that you believe is related to this disappearance?" Riley asked.

"Two more young girls have gone missing since then."

"Two more? How young?" Mariah asked, her brow furrowed.

"Mid-teens. Fifteen and sixteen. I have three daughters around that age range, and I want to make sure something is done before any more girls go missing."

"So, your girls are safe?" Riley asked.

"Yes, I sent them to their uncle for safety's sake."

"Where's that?"

"Carlsbad, California. I was concerned for their safety. Two of the girls who disappeared are close friends to my girls. It's hitting too close to home for my comfort."

"Why do you believe they're all connected?"

"First of all, I don't believe in …"

A loud buzzer sounded and Mariah stood, "Excuse me, someone came in the front door. I'll be right back."

As Mariah started down the hall to see who walked in, Riley asked Mr. Silkeney if he minded taking a short break.

In the front office, Morgan stood over the desk writing something on a note pad.

"Hey Morgan. We've got …"

"Did you call that guy back for me?" he asked distracted as he continued writing.

"What? Yes, I was telling you he's in the conference room. He wants to explain his case to all of us. It sounds serious. Can you come and sit in on the meeting? We just got started."

"Oh, sure. Sorry," he said ripping the paper from the pad and stuffing it into his jacket pocket. "Let me go to the bathroom real quick and I'll be right in."

Back in the conference room, Riley introduced Morgan and brought him up to speed before saying, "Please continue Mr. Silkeney."

Mr. Silkeney mumbled under his breath while looking at his hands in his lap.

"Yes, umm … where was I?" He looked up and smiled. "Oh yes, as I was saying, I don't believe in coincidences. For three girls to go missing in only two weeks, there has to be a connection. Plus, I've been doing some of my own investigations and research. The police aren't talking and they won't for investigative purposes, but I happen to know for a fact that all three of these young girls are connected to each other. As I told you, two of them are good friends with my daughters, and I've talked to the parents of all three girls."

"Mr. ah …" Morgan leaned over to peer at the name at the top of Riley's notepad. "… Silkeney, is it?"

"Yes. Silkeney, but call me Martin. Please."

"Sure. Martin, what is your background? Or more specifically, what kind of background do you have in investigations and research?"

"I was a Las Angeles detective for eight years. During that time I trained at Quantico and went to school on the side until I got into law school. I now have my own private practice in Medford. I either work closely with my investigator or do my own investigations depending on the case."

"Thank you. It's good for us to understand what your background is. Please continue."

"The police are working on the case as are the FBI, but in two weeks, they haven't come up with much and young girls keep going missing. I would like to hire your firm to do your own investigation to see if you can uncover anything the police and FBI are missing. I've researched each of your backgrounds and I believe if there is anything the cops left uncovered, you guys are our best bet to uncover it. Along with your fees and expenses, I will extend to you the use of all the resources of my firm and its personnel if you need it."

"How do you know the police and FBI don't have anything?" Riley shifted in his chair and crossed his legs. "They don't advertise their findings until they've closed the case and sometimes, not even then."

Martin sighed. "Back in L.A., I have a buddy on the force. He knows people working the case and he disclosed information to me." Martin raised his hands in front of his chest, palms out, fingers splayed, and waggled them. "It was innocent. He's worried about my girls and it just came out. That's all. The point is, I know."

"I read about a girl named Chelsea Dunn who recently went missing from Ashland Oregon." Mariah looked from Martin to Riley. "I think they said she is sixteen years old. I wonder if it's related."

"That's right, she was the second girl to go missing. The third one is Savannah Massey. She's fifteen and went missing yesterday."

Pushing a legal pad in font of Martin and sliding a pen over to him Riley said, "Please list each girl and everything you know about each one, their activities, and their families.

"No need. I have it all written down right here," Martin responded, picking up his brief case, placing it on the table and opening it. He pulled out a thick manila envelope and slid it across the table to Riley. Here's a complete dossier on each of the girls and their families. You'll want to do a background check on me also, so I included all the information on myself and my family that you'll need, to save you time. If you need anything else, just ask. I have nothing to hide."

"Thank you, Martin. Let us go over this information and do a little research of our own. We'll let you know if there's anything more we can offer on the case. Where can we reach you?"

Martin took out a business card and scribbled down the phone number to his hotel room. "How soon do you think you'll have an answer for me?" He slid the card over to Morgan.

"We'll try to make a decision before the end of day tomorrow. This case will take us to the other end of the State, so we'll have to figure out how to manage that with our current case load."

"I understand. Here's my business card with my cell phone number." He handed a card to Riley and Mariah. "I look forward to doing business with you."

Standing, Riley said, "We'll be in touch. If we take the case, we'll have a contract drawn up for you to sign."

"Cost is not an issue. My grandfather left me very wealthy. I just want the kidnappings to stop and the culprits caught."

The others stood and shook hands with Martin before Morgan escorted him to the front door. As the two exited the conference room, Mariah's cell phone started ringing. Looking at the caller I.D. she swiped the screen and put the phone to her ear.

"Hi Janice—perfect timing." She walked down the hall to her office. "Uh huh … tomorrow morning? … Sure, nine o'clock is perfect." She sat at her desk and picked up a pen, flipped to a clean page on her notepad and prepared to write. "Okay. Go ahead." Mariah jotted down the address and phone number. "Do you want to meet me there or should I come to your house? … I'll pick you up about eight. … Okay, see ya then."

****

"A new case?" asked Morgan as he walked in and sat in the chair across from Mariah's desk placing his right ankle on his left knee.

"No. That was Janice."

"Jeri's sister? Is everything alright," Riley asked, stopping at her door.

"Yeah. Janice got me an appointment for tomorrow morning with the counselor she and Jeri went to."

"Oh, that's great." Riley bobbed his head as he continued down the hallway. "I hope she helps you as much as she helped Jeri and Janice."

"Me too," Mariah yelled at his retreating back.

"Glad you found a new psychologist," Morgan said as the office door closed behind Riley.

"Actually, she's a counselor who also does past life regression."

"Past life regression? That sounds interesting."

"Janice and Jeri both swear by it. I figure at this point, why shouldn't I try it?!

"Right." Morgan nodded his head. "I hope this new therapy works for you. Let me know how it goes, will you?"

"Of course I will."

He uncrossed his legs and leaned forward, preparing to stand.

"Um, Morgan. Before you go … "

Morgan leaned back in his chair.

Mariah frowned. "Do you believe in reincarnation?"

Morgan took a deep breath while looking at her. The air in the room became thick with hesitation as he weighed his answer.

"Yes!" He nodded his head, more to himself than to Mariah. Confident she could handle the truth, he continued, "I do."

"Can you tell me why?"

Morgan stared at her for a moment before looking off to the right, seeing something in his past. He took another deep breath and with slow control, exhaled.

"I don't talk about it much," he said quietly, as he shifted his gaze to the floor in front of his feet. "When I was being held by the El Salvadoran FMLN, before Riley and his Special

Forces team rescued us ..." he glanced up at Mariah. "I told you we'd been beaten and starved, right?"

She nodded her head. Morgan shifted forward in his chair, forearms on his knees, hands clasped, and averted his eyes to the corner of the room.

"Several of the men from my unit died during that capture." Morgan took in another deep breath and blew it out, slow and measured, as his eyes strayed back to the floor. In a quiet voice, almost as though he were talking to himself, he said, "I died too." He peered up into her eyes. "Three times, I died."

Tears welled up in his eyes and he swallowed hard. He shook his head before continuing, "The first time, I rose above myself and watched as they beat my lifeless body. An angel— that's the only reference I can think of, although he didn't appear as the kind of angel I grew up hearing about in Sunday School, but an angel none-the-less appeared beside my ... entity—up above the scene. I asked this being, 'Why?'"

Morgan paused, tears filling his eyes as he bowed his head, eyes turned to the floor at his feet again. Mariah witnessed a lone tear slip past his cheek and drip to the floor before he swiped the rest away.

"What did he look like, Morgan?" Mariah needed to hear his answer, but was hesitant to interrupt his story.

"He was big, and a bright light shown around him. I say him, but I couldn't tell a gender." Morgan shrugged. "It was a bright being, in the shape of a human without real features." Morgan raised his head, eyes riveted on Mariah's and asked with a frown, "Sounds crazy, huh?"

"I don't think so. I imagine you're trying to say you couldn't distinguish any particular features like hair, eye color, bone structure, and gender?"

"That's right." Morgan sat back in the chair.

Mariah looked past Morgan at the bookcase behind him. "What did he tell you?"

Morgan wiped at his eyes again and coughed. He closed his eyes, leaned forward, placed his elbows back on his knees, and ran his fingers through his hair before sitting up straight and looking at her again.

"He said I chose it." Morgan shook his head. "He told me, before I reincarnated I chose my path—being a soldier, being captured. When I asked why anyone would choose to be captured and tortured, he said it was for my spiritual growth. I needed to experience the hate and cruelty of war because in a past life, I didn't value my life, or anyone else's—I was cruel and deceptive, dealing out misery, just for the sake of power and wealth.

"He told me, 'You can come back with me, to the other side or you can go back to your life on earth. If you choose to return to your life on earth, it will be difficult. You will be beaten and tortured some more, but I and others like me are here with you and will help you. Rescue is coming.' That's what he said. I've never forgotten his words."

Morgan shook his head. "I asked him 'Why would I want to go back to that?' and he explained, 'Because it is preparing you to do more, to make the earth a better place. There are people you love, and will love, whose life paths depend on you being there to rescue and protect them. If you choose to cross over with me, their life path will go in a different direction. They will still face their obstacles, and without you, it might be harder or take longer. It's your choice and your choice will not be held against you by anyone.'"

Able only to whisper, Mariah asked, "So you went back to the torture?"

Morgan nodded. "They quit beating me by then and when I went back into my body, it was like an electric shock. I gasped and they drug me back to my cell and threw me on the floor. Three days later with only a daily piece of moldy bread and a drink of dirty water from time to time, the beatings began again. The first day wasn't too bad. The second day, I died again and Anthony, my guardian angel, was there with me. I asked him how much longer and he told me I would be rescued soon. I asked him about the rest of my unit and he said, 'some of them will survive with you, but many of them have crossed over. It was their choice and their life paths were complete for this life.'

"I wanted to quit, but I thought of Molly. We met only a few months earlier and I was already in love with her. The thought of her suffering because I was too cowardly to go on was more than I could bare. I went back into my body and was thrown into my cell. I was so weak and in so much pain that the slightest move stole my breath away—part of that was from broken ribs and maybe a ruptured disc in my back. Even breathing was excruciating. I was past being hungry and they gave us only enough water to keep us alive. I wasn't beaten any more after that. The last time I died, was in my sleep."

Morgan's breath caught as he squeezed his eyes closed. He reached up and pinched the bridge of his nose. "Actually, I'm not sure I died that time, but Anthony came to me—in my sleep, maybe." Morgan opened his eyes and leaned back in his chair. "I don't know," he said shaking his head. "Maybe I wasn't asleep. Maybe I was so far gone, that it seemed like a dream. I can't be sure, but I know he came to me one more time." Morgan opened his eyes and pierced Mariah with his intent gaze. "He touched me and I felt this incredible warmth … soothing warmth, flood through my body. He lifted my head and shoulders into his lap and I felt my broken ribs move back into place , my shattered ankles and my knees start to heal, and my left arm bone move back together and mend, my muscles grew a little stronger, and the pain was lessened. Something in my spine popped—not painful but I felt a pop. It was a good kind of pop. Then, Anthony gave me something to eat and drink. 'Morgan,' he said, 'it is time for you to be strong. Your rescuers approach and you will need to run. The surviving members of your unit are being administered to as I am doing with you. Rest now. You will be awakened soon.'"

Morgan looked at the floor in front of his feet again and cleared his throat. "You saw some of the scars when you rescued me from Compton's thug. Remember?"

"I do. I knew you'd been tortured, Morgan. Somehow, what you described is so much worse than I imagined."

Mariah wiped tears from her own eyes. "I'm one of those people he spoke of, aren't I?"

Morgan nodded his head. He wiped his eyes again and coughed before giving her a small, crooked smile. "You and many more. You were there to help me with some of the others. When we took down the mob we saved countless lives. I can't help but wonder how many lives were saved from taking down Compton."

"You saved my life a time or two, and Jeri's too."

Morgan nodded. "I went back for another tour of duty after I recovered. I was able to save the lives of some of the men under me—they got to go home to their families."

"And don't forget, Officer Tisdel in that bar fight. Remember? He'd be dead if not for you."

Morgan smiled. "Yeah. I broke that guy's wrist before he could pull the trigger. Teddy Tisdel went on to save all those lives in that bus crash. They would all have died if I hadn't been there to save Tisdel's life. How many more, Mariah? How many more lives would have been lost if I had given up? Think of the lives you've saved."

The small office grew quiet as Morgan and Mariah's thoughts filled the room with unspoken words.

"Morgan, do you suppose that I chose being kidnapped, beaten and almost killed, too? I didn't have an angel appear to me. I sure could have used one."

"You had an angel with you. You still do, Mariah. How do you think Riley was able to find you in time? There are no accidents. We always have free choice, but if we don't fulfill our life path—learn the lessons we set out to learn—we come back to experience the same challenges until we do learn those things and grow from them. Your life path isn't finished yet, that's all."

Mariah nodded her head as she wiped away tears with the back of her hand.

"I don't talk about it, Mariah. Most people wouldn't understand and it's not something I will defend. They don't need to know about that part of my … life and … death. Riley knows. He's seen angels too. Not like me, he never died, but he's seen them surrounding him. He understands."

"I won't say anything to anyone, Morgan. Thank you for telling me, though. Somehow, knowing your story is comforting to me."

Morgan nodded his head, took a breath and wiped his eyes again. He coughed to cleared his throat as he stood and started for the door.

Mariah asked, "So what are we going to do about Mr. Silkeney's case?"

Morgan turned back in the doorway and faced her. "Riley's going over the notes that Martin left and I'm going to do background checks on Martin and all the parents of the missing girls. Can you do the media research on the case and see if there's anything else you can come up with—any gaps or inconsistencies? Once that's done, we'll take the case." A steely glare encroached Morgan's visage. Jaw clenched, he continued, "I didn't survive those beatings to let some monster kidnap children and hurt them."

Mariah nodded. "Sure. I'm on it."

Morgan's sudden rage cooled. "When's your appointment?"

"Tomorrow morning at nine o'clock."

"Isn't that when you scheduled the Partner's Meeting?"

"Oh crap!" Mariah threw up her hands. "I forgot." She rubbed her forehead.

"No problem. Let's meet tomorrow after lunch, then. Will that work for you?"

"Sure. Thanks, Morgan. How did your meeting go with Mia's teacher?"

He sighed. "She wasn't happy, but she was reasonable. She said she'll devise a new test for Mia and administer it one on one. She's seen this once before, so she'll work with us if we will work with her."

"Well, at least she's being reasonable. I've heard of some teachers who can't or won't work with the students and either fail them or insist the student do the work the way it's taught.

It's funny. They tout thinking outside the box, but they don't teach it much, do they?"

"No. Not much. Not most teachers, but in their defense, they have rules and regulations they have to follow or risk losing their jobs. I'm sure it's not easy for most of them."

"I hadn't thought of that."

"Well, I'm gonna get to work on the backgrounds. Good luck with the new counselor. Let me know how it goes, will ya?"

"Thanks again, Morgan. I will," Mariah said as he walked out of her office and turned to go to his own. Mariah opened her laptop and started typing.

WEDNESDAY

Mariah, unsure of what to expect, was a little surprised by the modern and comfortable front office she and Janice stepped into.

From the glass fronted door into a large, airy reception room, Mariah took note of the surroundings. A six foot tall Fichus tree stood to the left of the door with a play area for young children to the left of that, filling the corner. Against the wall on the right side of the room, were two upholstered chairs in a gray and pink tweed fabric. An end table with a tall porcelain table lamp—off white with a brass base, filled the space between the chairs. The lamp had gold trim and pastel flowers in pink, blue, and yellow accentuated by pale green leaves all of which appeared hand painted. The shade was a soft pink throwing a rosy hue against the pale blue wall, and blended with the pink in the upholstery. Across the room, against the left wall, was a matching arrangement—two chairs, table in the middle with identical lamp and shade. On the wall, above each grouping were large abstract paintings in bold, primary colors with a splash of pastels. To Mariah, they almost looked like Rorschach images. She thought it was quite humorous and grinned. Across from the front door, was a long, hallway with a couple doors to each side, and two more at the end of the hall. To the right of the hallway, in a small enclosed office area, sat the receptionist behind a counter with a sliding glass partition facing the front door. The floors were covered with a light tan Berber carpet. The silence was eliminated by soft, gentle, and relaxing music.

As Mariah approached the front counter, the receptionist glanced up from her computer screen and with a warm smile, slid the glass partition open and asked, "Hello. May I help you?"

"Mariah Jeffries. I have a nine o'clock appointment."

"Mariah, yes ..." She looked at her screen and picked up a clipboard with papers attached. She handed the clipboard to Mariah.

"Please fill out this paperwork. There are three pages, front and back. The first page is for your demographics and insurance information. The rest are a series of questions. Answer all the questions as completely as you can, and sign and date them here, and here where I highlighted in yellow. Before you start, may I get a copy of your insurance card and a picture I.D. please?"

"Yes. Of course." Mariah reached into her purse for her billfold. "Here you go." She handed over her insurance card and driver's license.

Dora, according to her name tag, took both documents, walked over to the copy machine against the right wall behind her, imaged each document, front and back, returned to the front counter and gave them back to Mariah.

Mariah took the paperwork attached to the clipboard, and sat in one of the two chairs closest to Dora's desk. Janice was seated across the room, flipping through a magazine she scavenged from the rack on the wall next to her. She had a second magazine in her lap. After completing the paperwork and returning it to Dora, Mariah took a seat next to Janice and whispered, "Well. Sure hope this works."

Janice lowered her *People* magazine and smiled at Mariah. "It will."

Mariah picked up the copy of *Good Housekeeping* from

Janice's lap and opened the cover. She was too nervous to concentrate on the words, so she flipped pages and looked at the pictures. Dora left her cubicle with a folder and walked down the hall before returning to her desk empty handed. After a brief wait, an attractive, older woman entered the reception room from the hall and asked, "Mariah Jeffries?"

Mariah stood, dropping the magazine back on her chair and replied, "Yes?"

"Hi. I'm Roselee."

Roselee, almost six foot tall with a slender build, had thick, brown, curly hair and dark brown eyes. She had a soft, friendly smile that made the corners of her eyes crinkle. She was dressed in a long, full skirt and scooped neck, cotton blouse. The outfit was accessorized with a dark brown leather belt and brown leather boots with a one inch block heel and rounded toe box.

As Mariah took Roselee's hand she said, "Thank you for getting me in so quickly."

"As it turned out, we had a cancellation. I find that things have a way of working out." She smiled and gestured with her right hand for Mariah to walk with her. "Let's go back to my office where we can talk. Would you like something to drink?" She guided Mariah down the hallway. "There's coffee, several different kinds of soda, and bottled water, whatever you would like."

"How about a little coffee with a whiskey chaser," Mariah said with a nervous laugh.

Roselee chuckled. "A little nervous?

"Yes. Some water would be fine, please." Mariah felt foolish for being so nervous considering she was a practicing psychologist for so many years, but she felt like a fish out of water as the client.

"Sure. There's nothing to be nervous about. You'll see."

"Thank you."

"Paula, would you please bring us each a bottle of water?" Roselee asked an attractive, overweight woman with bleach blond hair, who sat at a desk in an alcove off the hallway.

As they approached the end of the hall, Roselee ushered Mariah into her office by extending her arm to the room on the right. "This way." The other room at the end of the hallway was a small kitchen/break room. "Please, have a seat."

They entered a room furnished with a deep maroon, overstuffed couch against one wall, facing two matching overstuffed chairs with a glass topped, wrought iron table between them. Matching tables stood at either end of the couch. Covering the polished, hardwood floor between couch and chairs was a large area rug made of the same tan, Berber carpeting as that in the reception room. Scattered around the room on top of shelves, and table tops were lit candles and various potted plants—ivy and jade in particular. On the table between the two chairs was a beautiful, potted Bamboo plant.

The walls in this room were also painted the same pale blue as the reception room. The lighting was muted with track lights pointing up to the top of the wall where it met the ceiling, and in the corner to the left of the couch was another potted Fichus tree. The sound of a gurgling brook was the gentle background noise, making the space warm and peaceful.

"Thank you," Mariah said and walked around the chairs to sit on the end of the couch.

Roselee took one of the chairs facing the couch as Paula came in with two bottles of water. She handed one to Mariah and the other to Roselee.

"Will there be anything else?" she asked Roselee.

"No. Thank you, Paula. Please close the door on your way out."

As Paula left the office, closing the door behind her, Roselee spoke.

"I can see you've been under a great deal of stress. Your aura tells me this, but so does your appearance. Your skin is dull, your hair is limp, and you are clearly exhausted."

"I am exhausted. I've been having trouble sleeping for quite some time now."

"Before you go into that, please give me a little background about yourself."

Mariah told her about her happy childhood under the loving guidance of her father, the heroic fireman, her mother the paralegal, her father's two law enforcement brothers and his older brother who guided Mariah in the arts of hand to hand combat and meditation. She explained how her father was killed rescuing a woman from a burning building and how she learned the truth about the fire, and his death, only two years ago. Mariah recounted to Roselee how she followed her high school love to college just to be dumped by him—her brief marriage to the love of her life and his tragic death as a test pilot for the United States Navy, and her various careers and activities through the years. She told the counselor of the deterioration of her mother's health with Alzheimer's and the loss and sorrow she was feeling over that.

"It sounds like you've suffered some major losses in your life, including that of your husband."

Mariah nodded. "I understand that everyone suffers loss at some point in their life. I always considered myself blessed, though."

"And it all came apart," Roselee stated.

"Yes. It all came apart."

"Tell me what happened."

Mariah told Roselee about the abduction two years ago. She gave a brief summation of the ensuing investigation, the bombing of her home, being on the run from local law enforcement and the FBI, the betrayal from a trusted friend, being beaten and almost electrocuted, and her rescue from the cabin in the woods by Riley.

"That is a lot of trauma."

"Apparently more than I can cope with."

"You're not telling me everything, though."

"I've been having terrible nightmares ever since."

"No wonder. Tell me about them, will you?"

Mariah went on to detail her dreams, most of which were pleasant until the shadow shows up trying to suffocate her.

"What stands out from each dream that seems to be a common thread through them all?"

"Paul, my late husband, is in most of them—either trying to get to me, or just in the distance watching, and the shadow ends the dream by trying to kill me."

"Who or what do you think the shadow represents?"

"I want to say it's Jerry, but I'm not sure. It makes sense to me, that it would be him. I just don't know. My girlfriends, Jeri and Janice, told me that past life regression might help me figure out who or what is haunting me. I've been in counseling ever since I got out of the hospital two years—well going on three years now, but it's not helping. I don't know what else to do. I've never been the helpless type. I've chased down murderers, and brought down the mob—twice. I'm a crack shot with just about any type of firearm, and for years I taught hand to hand and Martial Arts, yet I'm jumpy and fearful now. I don't want to be this person for the rest of my life. I want to be strong and confident again. Do you think you can help me?"

"Well, we can try past life regression. I can't guarantee it will help, but from my experience, I believe it will." Roselee glanced at her watch and said, "I have another appointment scheduled in five minutes. How about tomorrow?"

"I can make tomorrow work. What time?"

Roselee stood. "Let's go up front and check with Dora to see what's available." Mariah stood and followed Roselee down the hall.

A ten o'clock appointment was scheduled for Mariah the following morning. She paid for her visit, and received her appointment card and receipt before leaving with Janice.

Janice got in the car behind the steering wheel and watched Mariah settle in and buckle up. "So, how'd it go?"

"It was okay. I did most of the talking—filling her in on my background. We're going to do a regression tomorrow morning at ten. Do you want to be there?"

"I would love to sit in, if you're comfortable with it."

"I would appreciate it. I'm a little nervous—mostly about what I might discover."

"It sounds scarier than it is. Don't let yourself lose any

sleep over it."

Mariah looked over at Janice. "Is that a joke?"

Janice pulled out into traffic. "What? … Oh, sorry. No pun intended." Janice laughed. "Want me to pick you up in the morning?"

"We're having a meeting at the office this afternoon about a new case. I plan on being at the office in the morning to follow up on a few things, so I'll pick you up. If anything changes, I'll call you."

"I'll be ready. Are you excited?"

"Nervous more than anything."

****

Back at the office that afternoon, Morgan, Riley, and Mariah were sitting around the conference table discussing the Silkeney case.

"Here are copies of all the news reports on the missing girls. There's not a lot—the police and FBI aren't releasing very much information—primarily just their names, family names, schools they attended, when they were last seen, and their social activities." Mariah handed a set of copies each to Morgan and Riley. "The biggest common denominator is that they are all in this AAU Basketball group of girls. Tina Webb, the youngest of the girls is a kind of prodigy at basketball. She and Savannah go to the same school. Chelsea Dunn lives in Ashland and goes to school there, but is on the same AAU Basketball team as Tina and Savannah.

Morgan handed out a set of reports on each of the girls. "Here's what I got on the girls, their families, and their closest friends and their families."

Riley handed out a set of copies of the reports that Martin Silkeney gave them. "There's going to be a lot of overlap between all these reports. We should each go through them and make comparisons on our own. We can come together later to compare notes. At least one of us needs to go to Medford and start snooping around. Mariah, I think you would be the best candidate, since we'll need to talk to a lot of their girlfriends. Do you think you're up to that?"

Mariah took a deep breath. "I can't leave before tomorrow afternoon. I have an appointment with the counselor tomorrow at ten."

"If you feel you need to stay and continue your counseling, I'll go," Morgan added.

"We're doing a regression tomorrow and I want to get it over with. I guess it will depend on how that goes."

"Okay. I'll go ahead and be packed and ready in case you decide you need to stay here."

"Thanks, Morgan. I'll plan on being ready to go after the appointment. I'll give you a call as soon as I'm finished with it. So, what are we going to do about hiring some staff around here? We at least need a receptionist to keep the place open and answer the phones."

"I can contact a couple placement agencies and start doing interviews. Do you two want to sit in on the interviews or should I handle it?" Riley asked.

Morgan nodded. "Why don't you narrow down the choices and when you have … say … two or three good candidates, we can do a group interview and make a decision," Morgan suggested.

Mariah shrugged. "Depends on how this case goes. We need someone now, so if you can hire someone while I'm down South, do it. Don't wait on me to weigh in on the decision."

"Alright, then. I'll call the agencies today and get the ball started."

THURSDAY

Early the next morning, to ease her nervousness, Mariah took Paisley for a long run. The quiet, empty streets at four-thirty in the morning, made Mariah happy and she smiled as she turned north to circle the neighborhood and head to one of the local parks with a paved walking/jogging path. Having her baby Glock tucked in a shoulder holster under her insulated winter jacket, in case of trouble, gave Mariah a sense of empowerment and safety. With a knitted beanie pulled down low to cover her ears, and tight fitting leather gloves to fight off the frigid air, she was set to go. She didn't expect any trouble, but after her abduction, she wasn't about to take any chances, so she always had one of her new guns with her.

After five miles, Mariah headed back home at a jog with Paisley running along beside her. Paisley already had a chance to do her sniff/pee/poop business earlier in the run, so Mariah kept up the pace on the return trip.

After showering, Mariah filled Paisley's food bowl, and washed her water bowl before giving her fresh water. She fixed herself a cup of coffee before going back to the bathroom to dry her hair, put on some make-up, and dress for the day.

She sat down and started going through all the reports from the previous day. At eight-thirty, she left Paisley at the house, and headed over to Janice's place.

"Oh, Mariah. I'm almost ready. It's been a crazy morning so give me a sec, okay?"

Janice stepped away from the open door to let Mariah enter.

"No problem, Janice," Mariah replied to Janice's retreating back. Mariah closed the door and started to follow Janice who was shooing her yellow lab, Prince, and the new golden retriever pup, Ireland, that she rescued from a puppy mill, back to the doggy play room.

As Janice disappeared around the corner, Charlene, Janice and Clive's oldest daughter, came into the living room carrying her one year old, Shalette.

"Hi, Charlene. I didn't expect to see you this morning."

"Hi Mariah." Charlene started to tear up.

Mariah reached for Shalette. "There's our sweet baby. How are you, beautiful?" Shalette leaned into Mariah's arms. "What's the matter Charlene?" Mariah bounced the little girl in her arms and smiled at her as Shalette put her little hand over Mariah's mouth.

"Nathan and I split up." Charlene started sobbing and Mariah put an arm around her shoulder.

"I'm so sorry."

Seeing her mother crying, Shalette started to wail. Charlene took the child back into her arms, wiping her own eyes, and cooing, "I'm sorry. Hush baby. Mommy's fine. Shhhhh." She bounced the baby in her arms in an effort to calm her.

"What happened? Do you want to talk about it?"

"Okay, ready," Janice shouted before entering the room and seeing Mariah and Charlene.

"No, I don't want to keep you from your appointment."

"We have a few minutes if you want to talk about it."

"Oh, we had a terrible fight last night so I packed up the baby and came over here to mom and dad's. It's all my fault, I don't know why I got so mad. He called three times last night and asked me to come home, but I wouldn't. I'm too stubborn for my own good. Now I can't get hold of him and

I'm afraid he'll never take me back."

"What was the fight about?"

"He wanted to go out to Denny's Pub with a friend of his after work and watch a ballgame last night. I'd been home all day with the baby and all I wanted for the evening was his company, but he wanted to go out with his buddy instead. I went off on him and ruined everything."

"Oh, I see."

"Honey, he's not going to divorce you over that," Janice said. "You'll see. You can stay here a few days if you need to, but you'll work it out. He loves you and Shalette too much to not work this out. Are you sure he's not working today?"

"I don't think he was scheduled to work today. Besides, he always texts me or calls me back within an hour when he misses my call. It's been hours." Charlene started to tear up again and Shalette, taking the queue from her mother, started whimpering also. Charlene reined in her emotions and start to rock the baby again.

"More than likely, he had a bad night too," Mariah speculated. "It's obvious he wanted you to come back home last night so he probably just needed some time and figures you do too. You should try to rest, and give him time to call you back. If he doesn't call by the time we get back, we'll sit down and figure out a way to reach him."

"That would be good. Thank you. I'll talk to you after your appointment." Charlene, sniffling, hugged her baby.

Arriving at Roselee's office, Mariah checked in with Dora. Within two minutes, Roselee came down the hall and greeted her.

"Hi Mariah. Are you ready to start?"

"Yes, I think so. Do you mind if Janice sits in on my session?"

"Hi Janice."

"Hi Roselee."

"That's up to you, Mariah. You'll receive a recording of the whole session as part of my service, but if you still want Janice to sit in, she can." Looking at Janice she continued, "You remember the rules? You can't say anything."

"Yes, I know." Janice smiled. "That won't be a problem."

"Okay. Follow me back to the office, then."

They walked down the hall, Roselee in the lead with Mariah in the middle and Janice following behind. Mariah took one end of the couch and Janice sat in one of the chairs across from her. Roselee closed the door, turned on some soothing, instrumental music very low, and walked to the couch, sitting next to Mariah.

"Sit all the way back in the couch, feet flat on the floor. When I touch your third eye, or forehead, you will see your spirit's trail through time. You will follow that trail back to a life that calls to you. Don't ask how you will know where to stop, you just will. Trust me.

"If I touch you on the left shoulder, you will step back and be an observer of that life. You will experience no fear or pain, but you will see everything and be able to report it.

"If I touch you on the left elbow, you will move forward in time to a later place in that life or a later life.

"If I touch you on the left wrist, you will move backward in time to an earlier place in that life or an earlier life. Let your spirit's trail guide you.

"If I touch you on the back of the hand, you will awaken, refreshed, and remembering everything."

"So this is more like hypnosis?"

"Yes and no. It's more like intense meditation. It takes you to your repressed memories … your soul's repressed memories."

"Okay."

"The entire session will be recorded. Are there any questions?"

"What if I can't do this? Regress, I mean? What if I don't have any past lives? Is that even possible?"

"Regression is easy. Some people are resistant to the whole idea and therefore are not successful, but I think you'll be able to. If you're not, then we'll work on your problem another way. As far as past lives, I think you will be surprised at how many lives you will encounter."

"Today?" Mariah was surprised.

With a soft and gentle chuckle, Roselee said, "No. You're not likely to view more than one or two lives today. It just depends. Most people take several sessions before they find full resolution.

"Okay." Mariah took in a deep breath and blew it out. "How do I started?"

"Relax. Close your eyes and take a few deep, cleansing breaths."

Mariah followed her instructions.

"Good. Let yourself drift … relaxed … in a warm pool of water." She waits for Mariah's breathing to become steady and slow. "The water dissolves and you are now floating in nothingness. There is only you. There is peace in this nothingness. Do you feel it?"

Mariah nodded her head. "Yes. So peaceful," she whispered.

"Look around for your spirit's trail." Roselee touched Mariah's third eye. "Everyone's is different. Do you see something?"

Frowning, Mariah said, "No." She turned her head and a smile lit her face. "… oh, yes. There it is."

"Follow it."

Mariah's face contorted into a grimace.

"What do you see? Tell me."

Mariah leaned forward, rounding her back. The muscles in her body tensed and clenched. Her face is the picture of agonizing pain and she screams.

"AAAHHHHH!" "Stoooooop … STOP!" She threw her head back, sweat and tears mingling together ran into her hair. Mascara ran down her cheeks as she panted and groaned. Her muscles relaxed and she sank back into the couch and sobbed. "Please, … no … more. Stop."

Janice watched, wide eyed. She guessed she was watching Mariah's torture back in New Mexico.

Roselee touched Mariah on the left wrist, and Mariah moved back to an earlier time.

"What do you see now?"

"Looking down, the hem of my full skirt is swishing and brushing the tops of my dusty boots while I'm walking down a wagon trail toward a wooded area." Mariah's voice took on the quality of a budding young woman with a French accent. "I'm smiling. I'm happy. In my right hand I'm carrying a strap holding a couple of books, and in my left hand, a tin pail."

"What's your name?" Roselee asked her and glanced over at Janice. Janice's eyes were big with surprise.

Mariah stared at Roselee a moment before answering.

"Caroline."

"Where are you going, Caroline?"

"I don't like school and I decided I'm not going to school today. Why should I?"

"Why don't you want to go to school, Caroline?"

"All I want is to be a wife and a mother. Joseph's wife," she said in a sing-song voice. "I don't need to learn history and math and all that stuff. I can read. I love to read and when I get married I'll read to my babies."

"How old are you, Caroline?"

"I'm almost fourteen and a half—old enough to know what I want for the rest of my life."

"So Caroline, if you're not going to school today, what are you going to do?"

Mariah, as Caroline, smiled.

"Caroline? What are you going to do today?"

"I'm going to go on a picnic. I'm going to a special little grassy glade that I found in the forest and I'm going to read my books, and eat my lunch when I'm hungry. And then I'll walk home."

"So nobody knows where you're going? If something happens, no one will know where to search for you?"

"What could happen? I'll be fine ... I'll be home before it's dark. Nothing will happen."

"What year is it, Caroline?"

Mariah's brow wrinkled.

"Why, it's 1819."

"Where do you live?"

"Darling's Lake, Nova Scotia."

Mariah sat up straight and raised her right arm straight up over her head. She starts waiving her hand and her face brightens into a wide smile.

"Who are you waiving to?"

Mariah sighed and said, "It's Joseph. We're going to have a picnic together."

"Who is Joseph?"

Mariah's eyes opened wide in surprise at the question.

"An Indian boy." Her eyes turned to the ground, thumbs hooked in front of her as she twisted her torso first left and then right. "My parents don't like me seeing him but I love him so much, and he loves me too." Her head raised and a smile spread across her face again as she stared off at nothing, seeing in her mind, the Indian boy. "We're going to be married some day. He told me we would."

"So you're skipping school to spend time with your secret boyfriend in a secret hiding place in the woods near Darling's Lake Nova Scotia?"

Mariah, as Caroline, looked at Roselee. "Well ... yes but don't make it sound so bad." Her gaze dropped to the ground in front of her feet. "Well, it is bad—Mother and Father would be terribly upset with me if they knew, but I love him. You don't understand."

"I'm not judging you, Caroline. I'm just trying to understand." Roselee touched Mariah on the left shoulder so she could observe what happens without fear or reliving any pain or emotions. "Tell me what you see."

In her own voice, Mariah states, "Joseph is walking toward Caroline from the forest. He's smiling. He's five … ten-ish, black hair past his shoulders, flowing free. He's wearing buckskins—a leather shirt, breechcloth, and leggings. Moccasins cover his feet and calves up to his knees. He's carrying a bow slung over his left shoulder and a quiver of arrows on his back. He's Paul … he is my late husband's spirit. I can see him.

"Caroline hollers 'Joseph!' and runs into the boy's arms. He catches her and spins her around, both of them laughing, before he sets her on her feet.

"They kiss with passion while holding each other tight and then Joseph puts his arm around her waist and they start walking into the forest."

Roselee touched Mariah on the back of her left hand, awakening her from the regression. Mariah took a deep breath.

"Wow! That was amazing. It's like I was reliving that life. I could feel her emotions … the love. So real! Is that how it was for you, Janice?"

Janice and Roselee looked at each other before Janice said, "Well … not exactly."

Mariah's brow furrowed in puzzlement. "What do you mean?"

"Most people don't step right into the life like you did, Mariah." Roselee said. It's unusual that I'm able to converse with your past entity, Caroline, through you. That was interesting for me. How do you feel?"

"So, you're not saying it was a bad thing, are you? Everything is okay, right?"

"Yes, of course. I've heard of sessions like this one, but I've never had a client go so deep into their past life that they temporarily became it. That's all."

"I want to do another regression to find out what happened to Caroline. I can't believe for a minute that Joseph was the one hurting her."

"So it was Caroline's lifetime that screamed at the first session?"

"Yes!"

"I wasn't sure if it was her, or another life."

"It was her. I don't understand how this life, at least the part we … I … saw has anything to do with my hauntings. The first part, where Caroline was screaming in pain might, but not the second part."

"I think delving further into that life is a good idea. We stopped there for a reason. I have another appointment in a few minutes, but we could schedule another session for next week. Before we do that, tell me what you can about the lifetime you first dropped into, when you were screaming."

"It was Caroline. While she was screaming in pain, a woman is saying, "It's your own fault, Caroline. You were warned. Now you have to bear the fruit of your bad choices. Caroline didn't respond to the admonishment. She just closed her eyes and tried to catch her breath before the pain started back up."

"So, it was the same lifetime. That's what I was wondering. Before we schedule your next appointment, let me ask you … do you meditate?"

"Yes, every day… well, I used to. I still try, but I have difficulty clearing my mind most days."

"But you used to meditation with regular success, right? You know how and have experienced it?"

Mariah nodded.

"I thought so. You went into regression easier than most of my clients. Keep meditating. It will come back to you. When it does, you'll start to glean some understanding about this experience and how it relates to your troubles. We can discuss them in our next session. Regular meditation, even the attempt without success, will help to get your aura back in order."

"I'm going out of town for a while on business. I'm not sure how long it will take, but I hate missing a session."

"Where are you going?"

"Down to Medford on a case. It's complex, so I expect to be there a week or two, at least."

"Oh, that's good! My mentor lives down there, in Medford. She knows about regression and helping people interpret the lessons from those lives. Everything I learned, I learned from her. I could contact her and ask if she can see you sometime in the next week."

Mariah gave herself a minute to think about it. She had to find the reason for the sleep disturbances, but wondered what awaits her in Medford regarding the case.

"Okay," she said after a moment. "Let's find out if she has any time available. I'll work around it, at least for one visit."

"Great. Give me a minute and I'll meet you in the lobby with more information."

"Thank you." Mariah and Janice stood.

Roselee held the office door open for the two women, and closed it as they walked down the hall to the front.

Before getting to the reception room, Janice asked, "What did you think?"

"It was interesting. It was so real, not like a dream ... amazing."

"Do you think you'll be okay with this lady in Medford she was talking about?"

"Oh yeah. I don't see why not. I'll at least try her out once. I can't take much more of these nightmares. Maybe tonight I'll dream about the love between Caroline and Joseph instead of my dream stalker." Mariah tittered a little laugh as they stopped at the front desk so she could pay.

After paying for the visit, Janice and Mariah sat together in the empty reception room.

"That was remarkable for me to witness. When you first went into regression, your face took on a little bit different appearance. And, your voice was different. You had an accent. I know my voice didn't change because I have the recording, and neither did Jeri's. I wonder if my appearance changed when I was regressed?"

"What do you mean?"

"Well," Janice said, turning in her chair to face Mariah, "When you were first regressed, it sounded like you were actually in your past life body, re-experiencing the event. That didn't happen to me or Jeri. Then Roselee touched you on the shoulder and told you to step back and be an observer. Before that, when you seemed to be in the other life, you almost looked like a teenaged girl with a little bit different countenance. It's hard for me to explain."

"Hmmm. That's interesting. I need to ask Roselee about it—or maybe the other gal."

Roselee entered the reception room and handed Mariah a piece of paper. "Here you go. Velia can see you tomorrow at eleven-thirty in the morning. Here's her phone number and address. If you can't make the appointment, be sure and call her. I also printed off directions to her place from downtown Medford."

"Velia? Okay, thanks. I appreciate this."

"Call me if there's anything I can do for you when you return to Portland. Take care, Mariah. I hope you'll let me know how things go for you."

"Thank you, Roselee. I will."

"Bye," said Janice, as they left the office.

****

Mariah and Janice entered Janice's front door and found Charlene and Nathan in the living room embracing each other.

"Well, well," Janice said. "Good to see you Nathan. Did you two work things out?"

Charlene turned to them with a broad smile and slid her left arm around Nathan's waist.

"Yes. Shalette and I are going home. Thanks, Mom."

Janice hugged Charlene first and then Nathan. "I'm glad to hear it, not that I didn't enjoy having you and the baby here, but you belong at your home with your husband. Where's Shalette?"

As Mariah hugged Charlene, Nathan said, "She's down for her nap."

"I'm glad y'all worked it out." Mariah hugged Nathan. "I'm taking off. Thanks for going with me, Janice."

"You're welcome. Keep me posted, will you?"

"You got it." Mariah and Janice hugged as they said their good-byes. "Let Jeri know how it went for me. I'm not sure I'll talk to her any time soon. See y'all later." She waved goodbye to everyone in the room and went out the front door to her car.

Mariah drove straight home, loaded her suitcase into the trunk of her car, collected Paisley and her paraphernalia, and left for the office. Riley and Morgan were waiting at the office for her.

"How'd it go?" Morgan, sitting at the front desk asked when Mariah and Paisley came in the door.

"Well, it was very interesting."

Paisley ran over to Morgan and jumped into his lap. Morgan reached to the shelf behind him and pulled out a treat for her. She sniffed his fist with great interest, while Morgan lifted her from his lap and placed her on the floor.

"Watch this," Morgan said as he sat up.

Paisley sat in front of Morgan and watched him as he pointed his finger at her, pistol style, and said, "BANG!"

Paisley flopped over on her side, eyes closed with her tongue hanging out the side of her mouth.

Mariah laughed and clapped her hands but Paisley didn't move except to peak one eye open.

When Morgan said, "Okay," Paisley jumped up and Morgan threw her the treat.

Riley walked into the room and leaned against the wall. Paisley jumped back into Morgan's lap, and Mariah gave them a brief run down of the regression experience.

"Do you want to stay here and continue your counseling? You could help Riley with the interviews."

Mariah made a face. "No. She made an appointment for me with her mentor who happens to be in Medford. Besides, I trust Riley with the interviews. Paisley and I are headed south. What are you going to be doing?"

"I wasn't sure if you'd be able to go, so I made arrangements to go to Medford myself."

"You don't have to. Why don't you stay here with your family. If I need help, I'll call. There's no sense in spending the time and money for two of us to be down there until we know it's necessary. Has Mr. Silkeney checked in?"

"Yes," Riley replied. "I told him one of us would check in with him in Medford this evening." He reached into his pocket and pulled out a handwritten note. "Here's his contact information and the hotel room he rented for us. He'll be waiting for your call."

"Okay. I need my laptop. I left it in my office."

"Here you go." Morgan said putting Paisley on the floor as he stood and picked up the laptop case from beside the desk. He handed the case to Mariah. "There are some new notes in there too. I expected you would move mountains to make this trip so I made sure things were ready. Keep us informed and call if you need anything."

"Will do." Mariah hugged Morgan and Riley. "I'll call one of you tonight. Who should I report to?"

"Me," Riley said at the same time Morgan answered, "You can keep me posted."

"Never mind. I'll keep you both up to date with email." Mariah laughed.

"Just call one of us—or both of us if you need to," Morgan said.

Mariah waved and led Paisley out the door.

"I will."

As Mariah hit I-5 and headed south to Medford at twelve-fifteen, Paisley sat on the perch that Morgan built for her. It was a flat wooden platform was braced in the back floorboard and extended from the back seat, between the two front seats, and over the console stopping at the gear shift. It had a hinge at the back to allow access to the console beneath, and it gave Paisley a safe place to sit and watch traffic without inconveniencing space or access. Paisley loved to sit and watch out the front and side windows when riding. She used to try to lie down on the perch but with only the non-skid covering over the wood, it was too hard for her, so Mariah bought a queen size feather pillow, covered it in a black flannel material with colorful peace signs all over and laid it over the perch for Paisley's riding comfort. Now she can sit, stand and lie down right next to Mariah whether they're taking a short trip in town or a longer trip across the state.

Mariah, a superb driver—never having had a traffic citation, much less a wreck—also tended to be a bit of an aggressive driver. She hated being held up by slower traffic in front of her, instead focusing more on the final destination than on the trip itself. She recognized this as a fault of hers and tried to relax and enjoy the journey, but she couldn't seem to help it. Her natural inclination was to get there yesterday. As a result, she yelled at the other drivers and told them off while driving down the road—not that any of them could hear her. Unless they read lips, they probably thought she was rocking out to bad music, but she was laying down the law to the other drivers. She wasn't sure if that was a stress reliever or a bad habit, but she had reached a point in her life where she wanted to change that, so her mantra for this year had become *Stay Calm and Speak Gently*. Unfortunately for Mariah, between her exhaustion and the drive out of Portland Oregon in noon-time traffic, staying calm and speaking gently was quite a challenge.

The traffic was outrageous—not only crowded, but the drivers were impatient and combative. Mariah got stuck behind an eighteen-wheeler doing fifty miles an hour in the outside lane on the outskirts of Portland. The Honda Civic just in front of the eighteen wheeler's cab in the inside lane, blocked any traffic wanting to go around the semi. No one could pass the big truck because of the idiot driver in the Civic. Mariah's patience wore thin as she waited for a break in the traffic. Each time the trucker slowed down to let the white utility van behind the Civic pass, the Civic would slow down to block them, and each time the trucker would speed up to try to pass the Civic, the Civic would speed up. The speed limit had increased two miles back to sixty-five miles per hour and Mariah couldn't be more frustrated.

"Come on, you idiot. Either drive or get off the road!" Mariah shouted, pounding the steering wheel and looking over her left shoulder. She flipped on the left turn signal and slipped in behind the white utility van, and in front of a black Ford F-150.

"Come on, damn it! Move for crying out loud!"

No one was giving an inch and the Civic was staying just close enough to the front of the trucker so no one could go around.

"Shit!" Mariah hit the steering wheel. "Paisley, this is going to be one long ass drive if this keeps up." Sitting on her perch right beside Mariah, Paisley stared straight ahead like a good shotgun passenger should.

The F-150 that was behind Mariah slowed down and slid behind the eighteen-wheeler and a State Trooper pulled behind Mariah with his lights flashing. Mariah tapped the brakes and slowed down to slide in behind the F-150, and as the trooper pulled up beside her, she glanced over. It was Clive Henderson.

"Woohoo!" Mariah shouted as she smiled. "The cavalry to the rescue."

The utility van slowed and slid in behind Mariah and Clive pulled up behind the Civic driver. Clive sounded his siren and the driver hit his brakes to let everyone pass him in order to pull in behind the utility van. Clive followed the Civic to the side of the highway.

"HA!" Mariah shouted pumping her fist in the air. "Serves you right for driving like an asshole! I hope he writes you a big fat ticket, dumb ass," she shouted as she pulled around the eighteen-wheeler and hit the gas bringing her speed up to seventy. With all the yelling, Paisley jumped into the passenger seat, faced Mariah and stared at her as though she was a raving lunatic. Mariah realized she was acting like one.

Mariah took a deep breath, relaxed her grip on the steering wheel and told Paisley, "I'm sorry, girl. I know I'm supposed to stay calm and speak gently." Mariah shook her head. "That wasn't speaking gently, was it?" Paisley jumped back on the perch and laid her head on Mariah's shoulder and sniffed her neck before turning to look forward and keep an eye on the road. Once they got past Salem, the traffic thinned out and the drive became quite enjoyable.

The prior owner of Mariah's car installed a custom stereo system with a six CD changer. Mariah was thankful for that and enjoyed a mixture of some of her favorite tunes on the drive down interstate five to Medford. She was pretty eclectic in her taste in music, and since she'd been trying to stay calmer, she had a mixture of classical, country, pop, and only one classic rock album loaded in the player. It made for some excellent driving music.

Just passed Salem, Paisley laid down on her perch, rested her head on her front paws, and closed her eyes. Passing through Eugene, she sat up to keep an eye on all the increased traffic around them. When they got through the city, she jumped down into the passenger seat, made a couple circles before she curled up, and went back to sleep.

Mariah enjoyed the drive and the scenic beauty along I-5. There were so many places she wanted to pull over and take in the scenery but the traffic was too heavy, or there were no pull off places plus, her need to get to Medford and meet with Mr. Silkeney superseded any delay.

****

Mr. Silkeney reserved a two-bedroom Suite at the Medford Suites of the Rogue Valley, on Center Drive, with an open ended check out date for the agency's use while they worked on the case.

After checking in, and carrying her and Paisley's gear into the suite, Mariah took Paisley for a quick walk to stretch their legs and to give Paisley a potty break.

Back in the suite, Mariah did a little exploring to check out her accommodations. Each of the two bedrooms had a queen size bed, a dresser, and a small desk or writing table. The sofa in the living room pulled out into a sleeper as well. The kitchen was equipped with a refrigerator, stovetop, microwave, and dishwasher—the cabinets sported cooking and dinning equipment as well as cleaning supplies. There was a phone and a nineteen inch, flat screen TV in each bedroom and another one of each in the living room. The living room TV, being the largest of the three, was twenty-seven inches. According to the placard placed by the phone in the living room, the suite came with voicemail for the phones, cable service to include premium movie channels, CNN, ESPN, HBO, pay-per-view, and radio. In one of the bedroom closets, Mariah found an iron and ironing board.

Satisfied with the accommodations, she called Morgan's cell phone.

"Hi. Did you make it okay?" Morgan asked when he answered the phone.

"Yep. Got here safe and sound. The suite is nice—two bedrooms and a fully equipped kitchen. If you and Riley come down here, it will be comfortable enough for the three of us. The only inconvenience is the single bathroom, but we've managed that before. How are things up there?"

"Fine. Nothing new here. Molly says 'hi'. She's got dinner on the table, so call me tomorrow and let me know what's going on, okay?"

"Sure. You wanted me to call when I got here." Mariah smiled as she continued, "I'm sorry to take you away from dinner. Give my love to Molly and the kids, will ya?"

"Yeah, will do."

"Oh, and give Riley a call for me. He wanted me to check in with him as well, once I got here. I'm calling Martin as soon as I hang up with you."

"I'll let him know. Talk to you tomorrow."

Mariah laughed at Morgan's enthusiasm for his dinner. Molly must have fixed her famous brisket dinner with baked beans, mashed potatoes smothered in cream gravy, whole kernel corn, salad, and home made rolls—Morgan's favorite.

She gave Martin Silkeney a call. The phone rang three times before a voice on the other end said, "Martin Silkeney here. How may I help you?" in a professional, yet friendly tone. His voice, Mariah realized, is as smooth as melted butter.

"Hi, Mr. Silkeney. This is Mariah Jeffries."

"Mariah. I hope you made it in without incident?"

"I did. Thank you."

"How are the accommodations?"

"Perfect. If the guys come down, there's room for all of us in this suite. Thank you for securing them for us."

"Thank you for taking the job. I feel much better knowing you guys are on the case. Are you hungry?"

"Yes. I was going to go exploring to find a burger place. Do you have any recommendations?"

"I'm just leaving the office. I was hoping you'd arrive early enough so we could have dinner together. How about if I pick you up. I know of a fish and steak place not far from where you're staying."

"That sounds good. I'd like to talk to you about a game plan and where I might start tomorrow."

"I'll pick you up in ten minutes. Will that be all right?"

"Perfect. I'll freshen up and meet you in the lobby."

Mariah put some food and water down for Paisley before she went to the bathroom and washed her face, brushed her teeth, put on fresh make-up, and brushed her hair. She hugged Paisley and told her to be a good girl before putting her in her crate and brushing the dog hair off her blouse. As she walked out the door, she said, "I'll be back soon, Paisley. Love you, little girl." She closed the door and headed to the lobby.

As Mariah stepped out the front lobby doors, Martin pulled under the canopy at the front. He put his silver Audi, four-door sedan in park, got out and came around the front to open the passenger door for Mariah.

"Thank you," Mariah muttered, a little embarrassed seeing as how she's quite capable of opening her own car door. She'd always been a little uncomfortable with those sweet gestures of chivalry. She tucked her purse, cradling her baby Glock, between her feet in the floorboard and checked out the luxurious interior of his vehicle while he walked back around the front of the car. Beautiful decorative inlays adorned the dash and console, as well as the panels on the interior of the doors. A huge sunroof, and ambient LED interior lighting, as well as buttery soft leather seats were accoutrements fit for royalty or, at the very least, the very wealthy. A button in the door panel turned on the seat heater and she found the power controls on the right side of the seat, close to the floor.

"Nice ride," she said as Martin got back into the driver's seat.

"Thanks. I like it,"

Casey's Fish and Steak House was a quiet restaurant where they were able to talk without a lot of interruption. The food was good, the service excellent, the atmosphere pleasant and relaxing, and the news that Martin gave Mariah was terrible.

"Another girl went missing today."

"Oh my God. I hadn't heard."

"I heard it on the news while driving over here. They can't find a trace of her."

"Did they say who she is?"

"Duskie Banks—a seventeen year old girl—went to all her classes and disappeared when she walked out of the last class. Poof, into thin air, or so it seems. She's on the same AAU basketball team as the other three."

"Well, I guess that's where I'll be starting tomorrow. I'll go to the school and start talking to the other students. Where was … "

The waiter stopped by the table and asked, "May I get you a drink?"

"May I see the wine list?" Mariah asked.

"Yes. The wine list is right here." The young man handed her a bi-folded menu of specialty martinis, wines, and beers.

Mariah perused the list and said, "How about the Malbec?"

"A glass or a bottle?"

"A glass, please."

The young man nodded his head and glanced at Martin.

"I'll have a Margarita on the rocks with salt."

"Excellent. I'll be right back with your drinks."

Mariah looked at Martin. "As I was saying, Where did she go to school?"

"JFK Memorial High School. She's a Junior. Her last class was science, in room three of the science building, right by the back door. The back door opens out to a parking lot and across from that is the football practice field, baseball fields, and tennis courts."

The topic of conversation remained on the kidnappings during the entire dinner. Mariah pumped Martin for every bit of information she could think to ask for, including speculation as to who he considered a likely suspect in the kidnappings. He was at a loss for answers to that question.

"Thanks for dinner, Martin. It was better than anything I would have whipped up and much better than fast food. I enjoyed the company, just sorry another girl has been taken."

Martin pulled up under the canopy at the Suites. He turned the ignition off and opened the door. "You're welcome. I'm feeling a lot better about shipping my girls off to their uncle in San Diego." He stepped out and closed the door, jogged around the car, and opened Mariah's door for her. As she stepped out, he said, "I'll leave you to your investigation, but please keep me posted and don't hesitate to call if you need anything—day or night."

"I will. Good night."

"Good night, Mariah." He closed the door and walked back around the car as she turned to go into the Suites.

Back in her rooms, she harnessed Paisley and went for a short walk. The sky was clear and the stars were shining bright. There was a warm, almost tropic, breeze as they walked all the way around the large hotel complex and parking lot which included Medford Suites of the Rogue Valley and Bear Creek Suites of Medford. When they returned to the rooms, Mariah sent off an email to Riley and Morgan telling them about the accommodations and outlining her conversation with Martin.

Mariah showered, switched off the overhead lights, climbed into the queen-size bed, propped herself up with the pillows and turned on the television.

Paisley jumped up on the bed and demanded Mariah's attention, so they played and wrestled a little bit before Paisley curled up beside Mariah. With a wide yawn, her tongue curling upward, she laid her head down on Mariah's leg and closed her eyes.

With one hand resting on Paisley, Mariah operated the TV remote to flip through the channels with her other. Nothing of interest caught her attention, so she switched it off, turned off the bedside lamp, stretched out and thought about the case until she drifted off to sleep.

FRIDAY A.M.

Sitting in the camp chair and listening to the Blues band on the stage to my left, a voice calls out my name. "Mariah!" I look up and see a bronzed, blue eyed, red haired man walking toward me from the edge of the Willamette River, carrying a bouquet of red roses in his left hand and a bottle of wine with two empty glasses in his right. His hair, shoulder length and shaggy, shines like a radiant rainbow of red in the sunlight that had just broken through from behind a puff of cloud. He's calling my name and trying to tell me something, but I can't understand him over the sound of the music playing. He's dressed in a tuxedo but with each step he takes in my direction, his clothes fade, eventually becoming tattered rags. I stand from my chair. The roses wilt before my eyes, the petals dropping and leaving a bloody trail in his wake. He loses his right shoe with one step, and with the next he loses his left shoe. His skin becomes pale, then ashen, and finally dusty. With each subsequent step his legs crumble and disintegrate into dust—blown away by the breeze, starting with the feet, the calves, and then the knees. Each time a part of his body reaches the ground, it crumbles and drifts away on the wind. I try to turn away so he'll stop his advance, but I can't tear my eyes away from the decimation taking place before me. I try to cry out to him to stop, to warn him that he is killing himself, but I can't utter a sound.   He continues to advance and with each step, each pull of his arm, his ashes blow away a little at a time until the last of him fades away into nothingness—blue piercing eyes under a rainbow of fiery red hair were the last to go.   At the moment that he disappears, a disembodied voice says, "Poof, into thin air, or so it seems."

I search for the red-haired, blue eyed man, but I can't find him. When I sit back down, I'm in the cockpit of a fighter jet. On the control panel is a picture of me and Paul on our wedding day. I reach out and take it from the panel, flip it over and scrawled on the back are the words, '**I will forever love you.**' I close my eyes drinking in the warmth of his love and the sorrow of his death. I feel it all again as though the joy and the pain were brand new—the ecstasy and the agony all at once takes my breath away.   The precious memories of our love once shared and of our love lost through tragedy constricts my chest making it difficult to pull in a breath, but I don't want to let the memories go either. They're a part of me. As painful as they are, they're also precious and valued. I gasp for breath and reach to put the picture back on the panel but the panel is gone and I'm sitting on the ground, cross-legged, in front of a camp fire. The picture flies from my hand into the fire and I watch as the words **forever love'** are the last to go up in flames.

I lean back and all around me, are American Indians, dressed in buckskins and animal furs. Many of the women are preparing food, the men are sharpening and repairing knives, spears, and bows and arrows. A few of the men have long guns—some kind of rifle or musket. A group of children come running up from behind me, and course around me as if I were a rock in the middle of a river. They are shouting and laughing and as they continue running in front of me, the entire scene and all the sounds fade away into a heavy mist.   A shadow starts to emerge from out of the mist. Menace emanates from the shadow and terror wells up in my chest. I start to shrink back but I remember that I want to discover the identity of the threat. I must find out who is haunting me. With *my heart in my throat, as the shadow descends upon me, and is leaning over me, I try to discern features, but there are none. It's a big, dark, menacing mist. Panic wells up inside me and, screaming, I try to push the shadow away.*

Mariah woke to Paisley trying to get to her side as Mariah fought her off in the terror of her nightmare. She reached for and clutched Paisley who licked the tears from her face and whined.

Mariah wrapped her arms around Paisley and hugged her tight. She tried to tell the little dog that she was alright, but the words of assurance stuck in her throat and she started to choke and gag. She moved her left arm from around Paisley and wiped her eyes.

I wanted to find out who the shadow was. I tried so hard, but I couldn't. I tried to be brave, but I was terrified, was all Mariah could think.

Knowing she wouldn't be able to go back to sleep for a while, she turned on the bedside lamp and hit the 'on' button on the TV remote control. She flipped through the channels and found a rerun of *I Love Lucy*. Thinking that would be lighthearted enough to help her relax, she settled on it. Paisley settled back down, curling up at Mariah's side, groaned, and drifted off to sleep again. Sometime after two A.M. Mariah's eyes drew heavy and she slipped into restful slumber. She was awakened by the sound of her alarm at seven.

Mariah took Paisley for a long run first thing in the morning. They jogged out to the sidewalk on Center Drive and turned right toward a shopping center.

Across the street from the hotel was a hair cutting franchise and a little drive that separates it from a large parking lot, which ended in a huge nation wide retail store.

On the hotel's side of the street was a paint store and beauty salon in a strip mall with The Bear Creek Rink—ice-skating rink—in another building across the parking lot. A large specialty store for tools and supplies was across from the parking lot to the Rink. A sandwich shop, yogurt and ice-cream shop, bakery, pizzeria, and wireless service store were in another strip mall a little further down the street.

Mariah and Paisley crossed a four-way red light intersection that led into the shopping center which included a fast food restaurant at the corner. Across the parking lot was another large retail store that specialized in groceries and household supplies, and in front of that store was a gas station.

Around the corner from the grocery store, on the corner of Stewart and Barnett, sat a cafeteria style restaurant.

When they turned at the cafeteria and retraced their steps back to the suite, Mariah noticed on the other side of Stewart was a bank, a restaurant, a sporting goods store, another sandwich shop, an office supply store, and a discount grocery store. Across the parking lot from those businesses stood a fast food hamburger joint, a karate gym, and a liquor store. As they rounded the corner back to Center Drive, Casey's Fish and Steak house, where Martin had taken her to dinner the night before, appeared across the street from her. Another strip mall with more small shops sat back from Casey's and ran the length of the lot to the traffic light.

Mariah was pleased to find a grocery store and so many restaurants within close proximity to where she was staying.

Paisley enjoyed exploring the new area, often stopping and bracing herself with such determination to check out a new scent, that Mariah's momentum would jerk her arm and turning her around. Mariah made a mental note to find a dog park in Medford where she could take Paisley to run off leash in a safe environment once in a while.

Back in their suite, Mariah did her Tai Chi Schwan exercises and then showered.

She dug through her suitcase and took out a pair of wool blend socks that covered her calves to her knees, and pulled them on. Next, she donned her favorite pair of Rockies dark blue denim jeans, and a black, cotton, long sleeved, button-down shirt. She tucked the tails into her jeans, pulled on her western belt and her all-purpose hiking boots. She strapped on her shoulder holster, grabbed her lined windbreaker, gave Paisley a treat for going into her crate, latched the crate door, and headed out to meet her new past life regression therapist.

****

According to the address Roselee gave her, Velia's place was in Medford but the Garmin took her out Crater Lake Highway to White City, and then East down Highway OR-140 toward Klamath Falls. After two miles, Mariah, convinced she plugged the address in wrong, slowed and prepared to pull over to the side of the highway to double check her information, but before coming to a complete stop, the Garmin directed her to take the next right on East Antelope Road, back toward the Northeast side of Medford. This road took her to the back side of the mountain. Mariah continued on, taking the turn and the first curve to the left. She passed a busy golf course, and a half mile further, curved around to the right, past some farm and ranch country. A short drive down the road, the Garmin directed her to turn right on Dry Creek Road and up the side of the mountain, until she came to an electric security gate. Mariah pulled up to the speaker box in front of the gate, rolled down her window, pushed the button and waited. After a short wait, a disembodied voice asked, "Yes?"

"Hi. I'm Mariah Jeffries and I'm here for an appointment with Velia. I hope I'm at the right place." Without a verbal response, the electric gate started to open.

The drive, blacktopped and a scant two car width, had trees of all kinds on either side. The woods were thick with Madrone, Poplar, Cottonwood, Pine, Fir, and Spruce trees. The drive was wide enough for emergency equipment— ambulance and fire trucks—but due to the encroachment of trees and the switchback of the road, it would not be easy.

While coming around a shaded curve in the road, Mariah came upon a bit of comic relief by way of a family of raccoons.

The raccoons, a mother and four of her young, frightened by the approaching vehicle, ran in circles around a discarded McDonald's bag with French fries scattered in the middle of the road. She encountered the family on a steep incline and because of her reduced speed and cautious navigation, was able to stop before plowing into the group. Mariah watched the raccoons until they scurried off into the surrounding woods before proceeding up the mountain.

Her breath caught when she crested the top of the mountain and she saw the valley with Medford laid out below. The smoke rising from the chimneys in the city below, took on the shape of pine trees in the sky. She saw the image of white trees hanging still in the sky as a good omen—confirming to her that she would get to the bottom of the ghosts unleashed the day she was abducted and taken into the woods to be murdered. The image gave her peace.

Mariah approached the three story house from the southeast along the crest of the mountain. The asphalt of the road ended at a large brick fence with opened wrought iron gates. The open end of the gates rested in the dirt outside the compound on either side of the drive. At the fence, the concrete driveway began and led up to a four car, attached garage on the south side of the house. To the right of the drive, a parking pad with eight spaces marked out in white paint appeared. She pulled into the one nearest the gate, put the parking brake on, and turned off the ignition. Hers was the only car in sight.

Mariah looked up at an enormous white house with black trim—*more like a small luxury hotel than a house*, she thought. The wilderness grew right up to the estate where professional landscaping began inside the fence line. Mariah got out of her car, locking it out of habit, and walked across to the opposite edge of the driveway to look out over the valley. The clear blue skies, the grids of vineyards and pear orchards across the valley, and the twinkling of light reflecting off windows in buildings and off moving vehicles mesmerized Mariah with its beauty. A sidewalk ran across the cliff-side of the house to a covered, red-brick patio with a round fire pit in the center. The fire pit was made with the same red-brick as the rest of the patio. White wrought-iron patio furniture surrounded the fire pit. A small strip of fresh cut grass bordered by a low rock wall baring the edge of the cliff, ran outside of the sidewalk.

Mariah turned and walked back across the driveway to the sidewalk leading around to the other side of the house.

From the parking pad, Mariah passed through a short alley lined on both sides by well groomed, six-foot tall boxwoods, into the front yard of the estate.

This yard must be ablaze with color in the spring and summer, Mariah thought, *but even in this chilly fall, it's alluring.*

The yard was thirty-feet deep by sixty-feet long, and superbly manicured. A beautiful rhododendron garden stretching half the depth of the yard down the right side of the fence, greeted Mariah as she passed through the boxwood alley. Beyond the rhododendrons, a magnificent rose garden occupied the rest of the right edge of the yard, snaked around to the back corner and ended about twelve feet along the back fence. The entire rose garden was bordered with a concrete edge barring grass and weeds from creeping in on the roses. The center of the yard, monopolized by a large Japanese rock garden with an elaborate bronze sun dial in the center grabbed her attention. A large gazebo with built in benches all around the inside except for the opening which faced out toward the rock garden filled the back left corner of the yard. Wisteria, honeysuckle, and lavender, among other shrubs and bushes surrounded the sides and back of the gazebo giving it's occupants a sense of seclusion. The left side of the yard had what appeared to be Hosta, geranium and Manzanita plants. Mariah followed the sidewalk around from the boxwood alley toward the front door. Between the front of the house and the sidewalk more well manicured Hosta, lavender, and Manzanita filled the deep flower bed along with other plants she didn't recognize. The two story high, twenty-foot square roof, supported by two large pillars, covered the patio at the front door. To the inside of each pillar stood a large, three-foot tall, terracotta pot with some kind of ornamental tree planted in each. The double, red doors, surrounded by a black frame, and flanked by two narrow, stained-glass windows looked out of place.

Mariah rang the doorbell, but she didn't hear anything on the inside. She wondered if the doorbell was broken so she knocked and waited about a minute. After there was no response, she knocked again.

"Dadgum it!" a woman exclaimed as she swung the door open. "I'm not deaf, just slow. You must be Mariah. Come in." She shuffled backward holding on to the door knob. "Come on in." She took another step back and swung the door all the way open for Mariah to enter.

Mariah started to apologize for knocking but was interrupted by the woman who waived her right hand, "Don't apologize. The doorbell works, but Cheryl is off today and I don't get around as well as I used to. I was sitting in the library waiting for you to arrive."

She looked about seventy years-old while at the same time only forty. Her mixed features made it hard to distinguish age. Her hair, snow white with a thin streak of black, was brought together into one long, thick braid that reached to her waist. Her skin was olive and creased with either laugh lines or frown lines, Mariah couldn't be sure which, but they gave her face character. Her dark brown eyes peered out from a face with eyebrows so pale she almost appeared devoid of any at all. Her teeth, although yellowing, were straight and even. She was dressed in a sea-creature motif caftan and brown leather sandals.

After Mariah entered, the older woman pushed the door with such force, it closed with a resounding slam. "Follow me," she said and turned to shuffle down the hall. "I'm Velia, by the way. We'll go up to my therapy room." Velia walked with a limp and was bent over at the waist, her long braid falling over her left shoulder.

Mariah followed her down the hall wondering how the woman was going to climb stairs when Velia stopped them in front of a wood panel door. She pushed a button and the door slid open with a whisper to reveal the well-lit, interior of an elevator. They entered the elevator and the doors closed behind them, Velia pushed the button for the third floor. There was a slight jerk and the elevator started rising in a smooth ascent. "The maintenance guy comes out every six months to service this thing. My grandfather had the first one installed years ago for my grandmother. She passed away three years later. It was out of service for years after he passed away. That was two years after Grand. I had it upgraded five years ago after I was thrown from my horse and broke my back. I'm lucky I can walk at all. Windstorm, my horse, was spooked by a rattlesnake. Sure was glad she stomped the thing to death or I would have been bit and most likely died. When Windstorm couldn't rouse me, she ran off and brought help. Amazing horse. I cared for her like she was family until she got old and so sick, the humane thing was to put her down. Broke my heart to let her go. She was my angel."

"Yes, the loyalty of animals to their people is amazing. I have a little dog, a rough coat Jack Russell, who is my companion. I couldn't imagine my life without her." The elevator stopped and they exited turning right. Mariah walked beside Velia down the short hall to a set of heavy, wooden, carved doors. The carving—a single scene across both doors—was that of snow peaked mountains. The left door had the sun peaking over the ridge and an eagle in flight, while the right door had an eagle perched on a tree branch, the rays of the sun reaching it.

Velia pushed through the right door and Mariah followed into a room bright with natural daylight. The entire west wall of the room was glass and overlooked the valley below. Mariah caught her breath. The view was spectacular and it felt like she was walking on a cloud as she approached the window and peered out across the valley.

"Beautiful, isn't it?"

"Yes," Mariah whispered in awe as she stood and took in the scene. "The view is breathtaking. I would spend every minute of my day here if I could."

"This is where I spend most of my time—studying, meditating, and counseling."

Mariah pulled her gaze from the scene before her and turned, looking around the room. It was beautiful in it's simple decor. The glass windows, from floor to ceiling, extended across the face of the long west wall and shorter north wall. To the north end of the room, on Mariah's left as she stood with her back to the long window, was a seating area. The gleaming hardwood floor was covered with a brilliant Oriental rug in a dragon motif of reds, gold, blues, and greens. The overstuffed love seat was a pale, sea foam green, sitting on the north edge of the rug and facing the center of the room. There was a matching overstuffed chair on each side of the rug making a semi-circle of seating. In the center of the seating area was a round, glass-topped table with a beautiful crystal vase full of fresh-cut yellow, pink, and peach roses. Above the table was a chandelier that looked like it was made of real crystal.

In the center of the room, set close to the windows, was a white leather massage table. Across the room from the massage table, against the wall, was a wet bar. The south end of the room was dominated by a very large, rock face fire place. The mantel was a spectacularly carved piece of mahogany, about ten feet long. Two screaming eagles graced the front with their wings spread wide, the tips touching in the center, and turned up at each end. The wingspans, backs and top of the heads formed the mantle shelf. The bottom side of the shelf showed in detail the splayed wing and tail feathers. Their legs aimed out as if ready to land or grab prey, their talons wide open for grabbing. Each end of the mantel was supported by an equally large piece of mahogany, each support carved with woodland creatures—deer, bear, fox, birds, squirrels, raccoons, mice, spiders, and other animals as well as trees and bushes. They looked like totem poles but were shaped more like unrolled scrolls.

Mariah crossed to the fireplace slowly, mesmerized by the

intricacy and beauty of the carvings. She stopped in front of it and reached out to touch one of the support pillars of the massive mantle. She couldn't bring herself to touch it, her hand just hovered in front of it for fear her touch would spoil the peace and tranquility of the work.

"My great grandfather was a wood carver. People came to him from all over the United States and Canada to commission him for work. The pieces up here, including the doors we entered, were his greatest works and he wouldn't part with them."

"They're ..." Mariah shook her head. "I have no words to express how beautiful this is. It's exquisite. The whole room is breathtaking."

"I have to get off my feet. Let's have a seat and visit before we start." Mariah crossed the room to the sitting area that Velia had already reached. They sat and Velia said, "My great grandfather had a large place outside of Moses Lake in Washington. My grandfather, his son, was a very successful playwright before becoming a director in Hollywood. He bought the land that we now have up here. I inherited a large part of this mountain, bought by him so many years ago. He's the one who built this house and had a lot of parties up here—movie stars, directors, producers all came. This room was originally the ballroom. When he and Grand reached their mid seventies, my mom and dad moved in to help take care of them and the grounds. The place was left to me when my grandfather passed away. He left it to me to avoid all the taxes that would have had to be paid if my dad had inherited it. I don't understand how all that works, but back then, it was the thing to do, I guess. My dad was their only child and I was his only child, although I have an older half brother and sister—twins, on my mother's side."

"Well, this room is magnificent, but the whole house is so big for one person. I would be lost, I think."

"Oh. I don't live here alone. My parents live here still. They each have a personal nurse. Cheryl is my nurse-slash-assistant, and she lives here with her husband. Of course, my husband lives here and our kids and grandchildren come to visit often. Down the hill and off the main drive, there is housing for the grounds keepers and their families. I used to have stables down there, and of course we had housing for the stable hands, but I sold all of our horses, except Windstorm, years ago after my accident. The horses were my passion, but I couldn't ride them anymore."

"I'm sorry. That must have been difficult for you."

"It was sad, but it was a spiritual time of growth for me. In hind sight, I'm not the least bit sorry because I've grown and developed so much from that adversity. At the time, of course, I thought my life would never be fulfilling again.

Mariah nodded.

"Speaking of adversity, I understand that you have gone through quite a traumatic experience not too long ago. Why don't we get down to business before time slips away from us."

"Okay, but may I ask you a question first?"

"Of course!"

"There seems to be a common theme here of eagles. Did your great grandfather just like eagles or was there more to it?"

My great-grandfather's animal spirit guide was Eagle. It was very strong in him. Wild eagles would come to him in the woods and watch him. Once, a pack of eagles—flock of eagles? I don't know—they attacked a black bear and chased it off when the bear was chasing my great-grandfather. They saved his life. He honored Eagle in his woodcarvings. In every carving there was always an eagle. Sometimes very small, but he worked one in on every single carving he ever made."

"That's devotion, but I can understand why he would when they saved his life."

"Do you know what your animal spirit guide is, Mariah?"

"Fox, and more recently, dragonfly ... so I've been told."

"I'm not surprised. The fox is a good guide for someone in your profession, and the dragonfly asks you to be mindful of your deeper desires. If you follow dragonfly's guidance, it will bring you to transformation. Mine is hawk. Hawk is the messenger of the spirit world and gives me strength and guidance in my work … and my personal life." Velia grinned. "Any other questions?"

Mariah shook her head and smiled. "Nope, I'm ready to start."

Roselee went over the kidnapping and a transcript of the first regression with Mariah.

"Do you want to discuss any of this or go right into your next regression?"

"Since you have the information about my first regression, I would like to regress to before I, as Caroline, was being tortured. I'm puzzled by that segment, but I'm worried that it will be too hard for me to witness, especially in light of what I've been through."

"I understand. About going back to a certain point in time—that's no problem. You focus on the period you want to regress to and follow your spirit trail. And regarding witnessing it—if you remember, you can step back and observe without emotional attachment. The emotional trauma will not be the same as it was at the time of the event. Any other questions?"

Mariah took a deep breath and shook her head. "I'm ready."

"Good. Let's go over to the massage table." Velia stood and hobbled to the table. She pulled a wooden stool out from under the table. "Just lie on your back, hands at your sides, or on your stomach with one hand over the other."

Mariah sat on the edge of the table, swung her feet up to the foot of the table, and placed her head in the hole at the head of the table. She tried resting her arms along each side, hands flat on the table, but it didn't feel comfortable, so she put her hands on her abdomen—right hand over left. She closed her eyes and took a deep breath. Velia pulled the stool up close at the head of the table and sat.

"Comfortable?"

Mariah took another deep breath through her nose and slowly blew it out through her mouth. She nodded her head.

Velia leaned in very close and spoke softly into Mariah's left ear. "When I touch your third eye, you will see your spirit's trail through time. When I touch your left earlobe, you will look forward to another, more recent time from where you stopped, and when I touch your right earlobe, you will look backward in time. When I touch your left shoulder, you will step back and be an observer without emotional involvement. When I touch your right shoulder, you will awaken, refreshed, and remember everything. Any questions?"

Mariah shook her head.

"Open your eyes, turn your head and look out the window. Don't look down, just out to the side to the unobstructed view of the sky, and clear your mind of all thought. You are floating through the sky—relaxing, observing—keeping your mind clear. Relax your muscles starting with your toes. Feel them shed the tension, the relaxation moving up your legs ... your torso ... arms ... shoulders ... neck ... and now your face as you float through time and space. There is no pressure from outside forces ... no tension in the muscles of your body ... no stress in your mind. You are free now to go to the prior life of your choice."

Velia touch Mariah's third eye and immediately a trail of sparkling light appeared for Mariah to follow. Mariah followed the sparkling path as she floated through the void until she came upon a wagon trail.

"'I missed you Caroline. Where have you been? Joseph asks me.

'I missed you too. Mother was watching me. She said if they caught me with you again, they would send me away to live with my aunt. Joseph, what are we going to do?'

'We'll have to make sure they don't catch us together. I love you Caroline. I would marry you right now if we could but you're not old enough to go against your parents wishes. We have to be patient.' Joseph kisses me and I kiss him back, my fingers tangled in his long black hair.

"I'm following my spirit trail again."

Mariah's face contorted in pain.

"Aaaaaahhhhhhhh!" she cried out before clenching her jaw, and breathing hard. She continues to whimper and cry for the pain to stop. The pain is so excruciating, she imagines her body is being torn in two.

Velia touched her left shoulder and Mariah stepped from the past life to become an observer.

"A woman is sitting on the side of Caroline's bed, talking to her in a calm, quiet voice. She's holding her hand. Another lady walks from the end of the bed and wipes Caroline's brow with a damp rag.

"'It's your own fault, Caroline. You were warned. Now you have to bear the fruit of your bad choices.'

"Caroline doesn't respond to the admonishment. She closes her eyes and tries to catch her breath before it starts again. Caroline groans as the pain starts anew.

"Caroline has some kind of cotton looking nightgown on. It's all sweaty and hiked up to her waist. OH! I'M HAVING A BABY! But I'm just a young girl! The other lady in the room … she's my Aunt Beatrice. She tells me it's time to push. The one sitting next to me is my … Caroline's mother. The ladies are dressed in long dresses—the kind with petticoats, and they're wearing those long aprons—bib aprons, I think they're called. Aunt Bea is telling me to push and I'm pushing. Oh, look. It's a little boy. A beautiful little boy. They're putting him in my arms now."

"Oh, he is so beautiful—perfect in every way. Just look at his little fingers and toes, and a mass of jet black hair that sticks out everywhere, and … oh my, he has quite a good set of lungs.

"Caroline laughs.

"Mother is talking. She says, 'We will name him Daniel.'

"I respond with, 'Mother, NO! I want to name him. He's my baby.'

"'No. He's not, Caroline. He will be my son when we

go home. No one can know that you had a baby. Your life would be ruined. No one would marry you and take care of you and your baby. This is not a kind world for unwed mothers and half-breed children. You will be Daniel's big sister and your father and I will raise him as our son.'

"I'm hugging Daniel and crying. Mother sits beside me and hugs me. 'Why do you think we came to stay with Aunt Bea for so long? When we get home, we'll tell everyone that I was pregnant and had a very difficult pregnancy. You and Bea were taking care of me.'

"What if I refuse? Mother, I'm *his* mother."

"'You mustn't refuse, Caroline. You will see him every day. As his big sister you will be taking care of him much of the time—watching over him and teaching him.'

"Can we at least name him Joseph, after his father?"

"'NO!' Mother shouts and quickly stands. She turns to face me and says, 'We will not name him after that filthy savage—that we are going to keep a half-breed and raise him as our own is enough.'

"Aunt Bea walks up behind mother and touches her shoulder. Mother calms down.

"'I'm sorry, Caroline. We will name him Daniel. Period! Besides, people knew you were running around with that Indian boy. If we name the baby after him, they will know and your reputation will be destroyed. What kind of life do you suppose a half-breed boy will have? Huh?! None at all. He won't fit in with his father's people and he won't fit in with ours.'

"I'm crying ... I mean Caroline is crying and holding her baby. I'm so heartbroken ... I mean, we are—she is.

"'Do you understand what I'm telling you, Caroline? You have to promise that you will not ever tell anyone the truth or you will destroy not only your own future but this baby's too. You can't even tell Daniel. Never! Your father and I can provide for him a decent life, a good education, a future he'll never attain if he's known as a half-breed. Your precious Joseph's people will reject him and white people will too. You have to give him up to us for his own good and for yours too, and you have to agree that you'll never see Joseph again. There's no future for you with him and certainly no future for any children the two of you would have. Your children are our grandchildren and we want the very best for them—and for you, too.'

"She sits back down on the bed next to me and pleads, tears in her eyes.

"'Please, Caroline.' She takes my hand in hers. 'Please say that you understand and agree.'

"I'm holding Daniel and sobbing while Daniel is squalling. Finally I nod my head and Aunt Bea says, 'You need to calm down, it's affecting the baby.' She reaches for Daniel. 'He needs to get started nursing.' I nod my head again, still sobbing.

"'Mabel.' Aunt Bea calls out, and an older woman opens the door, enters the room and takes Daniel away.

"No. Where's she going with my baby?

"Mother says, 'Remember, Caroline. She's the wet-nurse we hired to come back with us, we will bind your breasts to dry you up before heading home. You need to get your girlish shape back so that no one will be the wiser.'

"I ... Caroline nods her head, the tears running down her face. I ... Caroline is so sad—beyond sad. I ... she rolls onto her side and sobs into the pillow with Mother and Aunt Bea patting me ... her, and trying to console her."

Velia touched Mariah's right shoulder and she came back to the present opening her eyes.

"Just stay still and keep your eyes closed while I massage your temples and we talk about it. That was quite detailed."

"Yes. They wanted to get married, but she was too young. She's so young, and from my last regression, he's not much older."

A tear seeped out of the corner of Mariah's eye as she watched a bird flit by the window. The tear ran into Velia's fingers as they massaged Mariah's temples.

"Why are you crying?"

"They were so in love, Velia. Joseph wanted to marry Caroline, but her parents denied them that, even when Caroline got pregnant. Her parents took her away until the baby was born and then stole her baby from her, not even allowing her to tell Joseph about his son. It's so sad. Why would someone steal our baby?"

"Caroline and Joseph's baby!"

"Velia, Joseph is ... was ..." Mariah sighed.

"What about Joseph? You recognized him from this life, didn't you? Who is Joseph in this life?"

"My late husband, Paul Carlton. I always believed we were soul mates, but now I know for certain. We've been together before. I have to regress back and find out if they were able to have a life together. Why is our life together always cut short? Why can't we have a happy life and live into old age together?"

Mariah started crying.

"You will go back to see what happened with Caroline and Joseph, along with little Daniel, but not today. Your time is up today. How about next week? In the mean time, I want you to remember that Caroline and Joseph was a past life and although knowing about that life, and any others you might have had, can be helpful in learning this life's lessons, you shouldn't get caught up in that life's events and outcomes. Those were for lessons you needed to learn then. Okay?"

Velia handed Mariah a tissue. Mariah nodded her head as she wiped her eyes and sat up. "I know you're right. I was just so surprised to see Paul's soul and how much in love we were then, just like we were in this life. I miss him so much every day."

"You're not supposed to stop missing him. You're supposed to learn how to move on with him in your heart instead of your arms."

Mariah, wide eyed, looked at Velia. "I never thought of it

that way but …" She nodded. "… of course, you're right. I know he is always with me, I just can't touch him."

"Maybe he is the one who is coming to you in your sleep."

"No—he tries to come to me, but something menacing stops him. The shadow stops him and tries to smother or pull me into death. I try to see who the shadow is but I'm so terrified, I wake up before I can see anything other than a big, dark grey, blob of a shadow. Paul wouldn't menace me. Whoever the shadow is, it's terrorizing me."

"Keep trying to recognize who is stalking you in your dreams. Do you want to wait a whole week, or do you think we should meet sooner?"

"Any chance I could come back tomorrow? I'm barely sleeping. If I'm doing alright, I'll call and reschedule for later, but for now, I believe sooner would be better than later for me."

"Yes. That will be fine. How about late afternoon, around three PM?"

"Thank you. I'll be here."

Velia noted the time in her appointment book and Mariah paid with her debit card. They went down in the elevator and Velia walked Mariah to the front door. "I hope you don't mind that I don't walk you to your car."

"Of course not. Thank you, Velia. I'll see you tomorrow.

FRIDAY P.M.

Once Mariah got back to town, she stopped at a pizza place for what she hoped would be a quick lunch. It wasn't, but the food was great. It was two-fifteen when she pulled into the parking lot of JFK Memorial High School, and found a visitor parking space. Students were milling around the campus giving Mariah the impression they were between classes. Inside the front doors, Mariah saw a big sign announcing, ALL VISITORS MUST REPORT TO THE OFFICE with a bright yellow arrow pointing to the right. Being a good girl, she turned right and entered the office which had a seating area for those waiting for an audience with the principal or a counselor. Across from the row of seats was a long counter separating the waiting area from five secretary's desks in the open area before the principal, assistant principal, and counselors offices. Mariah walked up to the counter with a little trepidation. She wondered what it was about going to the principal's office that, even now, makes her angry and resentful. She remembered her Junior year in High School when she was acting out and skipping school to drink and smoke with some friends until her Uncle John got hold of her and straightened her out. As much as she loved her mom and dad, she was going through a phase at the time—staying in trouble, and the only one who could reason with her was Uncle John. They always had a strong bond and still do.

John, her father's oldest brother, served in the Viet Nam war and moved to Okinawa when he got out of the army. He lived there for twenty years, training in the different martial arts. When Mariah was six years old, John moved back to Texas and began her martial arts training. He was a demanding task master but she loved the martial arts and took to it like a duckling takes to water. She has been an expert at hand to hand combat and taught martial arts at the YMCA for years.

Mariah watched a cute blonde student, about sixteen, talking to a boy in the same age group while she stood at the counter waiting for assistance. The girl was playing with her hair and batting her eyes in obvious, although inexperienced, flirt mode. Behind her, two other girls were pointing at their teeth, making faces behind the girl's back, and giggling. Throwing a glare over her shoulder at the two girls, the young blonde noticed Mariah at the counter and broke away from the group.

With a wide metal filled grin she asked, "May I help you?"

Mariah's attention was drawn to a piece of green leafy vegetable stuck in the girls braces and pointed her finger at her own mouth. "Um, you have, uh, in your teeth, … I mean braces …"

The girl put her hand to her mouth and turned beet red. "Oh. Excuse me," she said from behind her hand and looked down at the counter. "I was eating my lunch right before Tommy asked me about working the copy machine. I'm so embarrassed. No wonder he was staring at my mouth."

"I'm sorry. I guess those other two girls are not your friends or they would have told you." Mariah pulled out a mirror from her purse and handed it to the girl.

"Here, I'll stand in front of you so you can pick it out."

"Thank you."

The girl picked at her teeth reflected in the mirror. Mariah gazed over the girls shoulder, giving her some semblance of privacy, and kept her eyes on the boy, Tommy, as he said something to the two other girls, pushed them toward the back door, and then bent to the copy machine. He kept glancing at the young girl in front of Mariah. After just a moment, the girl returned the mirror to Mariah.

"Thank you. Those girls, Evie and Joanell, think they are so cool. They're always making fun of me because I have braces and I don't have the fancy clothes and shoes like they do."

"You like him, don't you?"

"Who? Oh, Tommy?" She blushed a bright pink and dipped her head.

"Yes. The boy you were talking to."

"I thought he liked me too, but I guess they all just wanted to make fun of me."

"Um. I think he likes you. He told Evie and Joanell to knock it off and get lost. He watched you walk all the way over here before turning to the copy machine, and he keeps glancing at you."

"Really?" Alexis started to smile again.

"It's true." Mariah nodded her head and smiled back. "He made them leave, practically shoving them out the back door, and he keeps looking over here at you."

"Thanks." She smoothed her hair back. "I'm Alexis. Can I help you with something?"

"Well, maybe. Do you know Duskie Banks? I understand she goes to school here and went missing yesterday."

"Oh!" Alexis' smile faded and she started to tear up. "She's my best friend. We've been neighbors our whole lives. We were born in the same hospital a day apart and our moms shared a hospital room. Why? Are you the police?"

"I've been hired to work on the case and would like to talk to people who know her and the other girls. Do you think your parents would mind if I came by your house sometime this evening and talk to all of you. It sounds like your whole family knows her and her family."

"Um. I'll ask. What's your phone number and I'll call you and let you know?"

Mariah gave her a business card. "I don't want to talk to

129

you without your parents present. Please, please, be very careful. All of the girls taken so far know each other, so that could make you a target too."

Alexis frowned. "I know. My dad is talking about sending me away to my grandma's to keep me safe, but I don't want to go. I'll talk to my parents and give you a call."

"Ask one of your parents to call me instead. That way, they won't worry about you talking to a stranger who, as far as they know, might hurt you." Mariah lowered her voice, "Don't give up on Tommy. I'm pretty sure he likes you too."

Alexis blushed as her eyes turned down to the counter top, a grin spreading across her face. "Thanks. Talk to you later."

"Okay, but before you go, I'd like to speak to the principal if I could."

"Oh!" Alexis paused. "Let me see if he's in. Wait here."

Alexis turned toward the back offices and took a step when Mariah called her back.

"Alexis?"

Alexis turned back to the counter. "Yes?"

"Here. Give him my card." Mariah handed her another card. "Keep the other one for yourself."

"I will. Wait here, I'll be right back." Alexis smiled before she turned from the counter and headed to the back office, tucking one of the business cards in her back pocket. After a few minutes, a tall, lanky, balding man with tufts of blond hair on each side of his head, approached the counter from one of the back offices. He was dressed in a dark brown suit, white shirt, and brown tie. He walked with a bit of a limp and his right hand curled into a tight fist.

"Mariah Jeffries?"

"Yes."

"I'm Robert Beaumond. How can I help you?"

Robert Beaumond had soft green eyes that peered out from behind gold rimmed glasses and reflected pain. His brow was creased. He had laugh lines around his mouth and eyes but he wasn't laughing, or even smiling this morning.

"I'm here to investigate the kidnappings. Would it be

possible to talk in private?"

"To what end? I can't disclose any information about the girls or their families without written consent from their parents or a subpoena from the courts."

"What about the staff here at the school?"

"What about them? The police and the FBI investigated all of us and we've all been cleared. Who brought your firm into this investigation anyway?"

"It's confidential. The police and FBI aren't getting anywhere and an interested party felt another group of investigators would be helpful."

"Well. I guess we're at a stalemate. Your information is confidential—my information is confidential. I have work to do. You have other people somewhere other than this school to harass, so I guess you should be leaving now."

"Mr. Beaumond, why the hostility? I'm only trying to help find these missing girls—alive and unharmed if possible, and the sooner the better. Why don't you want to help us in that endeavor?"

Mr. Beaumond stared at her a moment before blowing out a puff of air and lowering his head, shaking it. "Follow me."

I walked around the end of the counter and followed him into his office at the back of the room.

"Here, take a seat." He indicated an old, hard, wooden chair with wooden armrests positioned in front of his desk. He walked around the desk to his swivel chair, eased himself down into it, and leaned back and sighed.

"You seem to be in a lot of pain," Mariah commented.

"You think?" He tapped his finger on the armrest of his chair. "I have Rheumatoid Arthritis and all the stress of these girls going missing is exacerbating it."

"I'm so sorry. I guess that could make anybody hostile at a situation they have no control over."

"I suppose so. Look, these are all good girls. They're hard working, involved in athletics, dedicated, liked by the faculty and student body alike. Sure," he said, waiving his left hand in the air, "a kid here or there might not like them or is jealous of them, but who of any of us can say everyone likes us? It's just life. There isn't a single student who would harm these girls. Not really harm them or their families. Not like this, and certainly none of the faculty would."

"Do you think it's possible these girls have conspired to take off together, but they're doing it one at a time so they're less conspicuous?"

Mr. Beaumond's brow furrowed and his mouth puckered. "Nobody's broached that angle before—at least not to me. Hmmm."

He thought for a moment, shaking his head. "It doesn't make sense—not with these girls. There are a few others who might pull a stunt like that, but not these girls. I can't see it."

"May I check out the rooms where each of the girls were last seen?"

Mr. Beaumond stared at her. "I'll have to give that some thought. I'm not sure I'm comfortable with you poking around here. The police and the FBI checked out the whole building. What do you want to see the rooms for?"

Mariah sighed. "If I could examine where they were last seen…" She stared out the window a moment. "I need to observe where they were last seen, where they exited the classroom, the general number of people around the area at the time of their departure, the modes of transportation immediately available to them. That information would help me devise a hypothesis of how they disappeared."

"I see. Come on, I'll give you a brief tour."

"Thank you."

Mr. Beaumond eased himself from his chair and grabbed a cane. "Classes have let out for the day and I usually walk the halls while they clear out of the buildings."

They took a left out of the administration office and walked in silence for a few minutes.

"Would it be possible for me to meet with each of the girls teachers—at their convenience, of course?"

"Not without written consent. You bring in written consent from their parents and I'll make the arrangements and help you in any way I can."

"Fair enough."

A moment later they stopped in front of one of the classrooms. "No one has seen Savannah since she left this classroom. This is the last known place she was."

Mariah nodded at him and stepped past him, into the room. Mr. Beaumond remained at the door and watched as she walked around the room, touching desktops and bulletin boards. She sat in a chair, her back to the door, and closed her eyes. Focused on her breath, she began to see a young girl, the image of Savannah, laughing and telling a friend 'later' as she walked to the classroom door. She saw a sparkling path where the image of Savannah passed, much like her own spirit trail in her regressions, but wrote it off as residual memory on her part. She stood in a slow, fluid motion and followed the trail that lingered, to the door where it led around the corner to the right and faded in the distance. Mariah shook her head.

"What?"

With a frown, Mariah said, "I don't know. I had a sense of something, but I'm not sure what it meant."

"Huh," Mr. Beaumond huffed. "In my experience, that just means I have gas."

Mariah laughed and nodded her head. They turned and walked to the end of the hall, turned right and exited the building. They walked across a breezeway and entered another building. Several students spoke to their principal and seemed to like him. As they approached the end of the hall, he pointed and told Mariah that Tina's curriculum was advanced for her age. She was actually a student at the middle school, but attended high school classes in Science and Math during the afternoon. He pointed to the last room on the left.

"This is where she was last seen."

Mariah nodded her head.

"Thank you."

She stepped into the room and a woman stood from her desk at the front of the room.

"This is Mariah Jeffries. She's looking into the

disappearance of the missing girls and wanted to see the room where Tina was last seen."

"Oh. I see. I'm Pat Jenkow. Anything I can do to help you?"

"No. Thank you. I just needed to see her last known location." Noticing the back door, leading out of the classroom, Mariah asked, "Which door did Tina use when she left that day?"

"This one over here," Ms. Jenkow said indicating the back door. "It was the last class of the day and many of the students use the back door. It leads to the parking lot and the bus parking."

"Do you know how she usually got home after this class?"

"I think her mother usually picked her up, but I'm not sure. The police and FBI asked the same thing. Are you with them?"

Mariah ignored the question as she walked around the room, touching desks and books in the room.

Ms. Jenkow looked at Mr. Beaumond with a frown and shrugged. He shook his head and indicated for her to wait.

Mariah walked to the back door and placed her hands on the bar used to open it. She closed her eyes and focused on her breath, but got nothing this time. She dropped her hands, turned, and walked back to Mr. Beaumond.

"Thank you, Mr. Beaumond. I'll get those consents and be back Monday."

"You're welcome. I'll walk with you back to the office."

****

Once seated in her car, Mariah called Martin Silkeney's office and asked for an appointment. He told her he was free and she could come right over.

"Hi Mariah. Come on in."

134

Martin waived to one of those stackable, convention type chairs with the back and seat upholstered in a blue tweed material. He walked around his desk and sat in his leather-tufted, swivel chair, and leaned forward, forearms resting on his desk.

Mariah sat in the chair across the desk from Martin. "Thanks for seeing me. I need some help."

"What can I do for you?"

"I went to the high school and talked to the principal, Robert Beaumond. He either can't or won't give me any information without a written consent from each girls parents. I can't even talk to any of their teachers. Do you think the girls' parents would be willing to give their consent for me to gather information from the school on their girls?"

"Bob's only following the rules. He could get in a lot of trouble in today's atmosphere if he disclosed information on the girls. You want to talk to the parents too, don't you?"

"Yes, of course. You said you would set up the meetings. Have you had a chance to work on them?"

"I talked to Tina Webb's parents and they are willing to meet with you. Do you want to go to the home of each girl or meet them here?"

"I think it would be best to meet at each home—talk to the family, check out the girls rooms if the parents will allow me to. Being in their space will give me a feel for their state of mind ... help me connect with their personality. I need to know what their surroundings are like, how close the girls live to each other, what the family dynamics are like—stuff like that. I can't tell you how many times one itty bitty detail made a difference in bringing things together."

"I'll get right on it, then. Will tomorrow be soon enough?"

"I'd like to get started as soon as possible. I have an appointment tomorrow afternoon at three and I don't know how long it will take. I could do one or two in the early part of the day and the others the next morning. I'll need the authorizations Monday."

Martin was taking notes on a yellow legal pad.

"I'll have them ready for you. I'll draw up an authorization form for each girl's parents to sign, and ask the parents to come in and sign them in front of my notary early Monday. I'll write it so any representative from your firm will have permission. That way, when Morgan and Riley come down, they will have the same authorization if they need it."

"That will save a lot of time and confusion for everyone. Thanks."

"No problem. They'll be ready for you by noon. Anything else?"

"Yes. I would also like two extra copies of each signed and notarized consent form, in case anyone else will demand it before talking to me."

Martin jotted the request down on his pad and nodded. "Anything else?"

"No. That's it for now. Please email the schedule for meeting the parents along with their addresses and phone numbers, to me. I'd like those as soon as possible."

"How much time do you want between each visit?"

"Hmmm." Mariah, with eyes closed, thought for a moment. Quietly, as if talking to herself, she muttered, "I don't want to rush the families and press for a lot of information all at once ... just a chat ... give them time to open up to me."

She nodded her head and opened her eyes. "Give me two to two and a half hours with each family—that should be plenty of time. If I need more time with them, I'll ask for it. What I hope to do is sit down and chat with them, letting them talk at their own pace—more of a normal, informal conversation, rather than an interrogation. I want time to check out each girls bedroom, the yard, and the neighborhood. I doubt I will need two full hours, but I can use the extra time between meetings to complete my notes. I suspect some will go a lot faster than others."

"So you want to see two families tomorrow morning, and two on Sunday?"

"If that can be arranged. Tomorrow is going to be a full

day for me so no more than two of the families tomorrow."

"Would you like me to tag along? I can clear my schedule if you like."

"No, but thanks for the offer. The fewer outside influences, the better." She stood to leave. "Thanks for all your help."

"I want this to end, so anything I can do, I'll do. Don't hesitate to ask."

They shook hands and Martin walked Mariah out to her car. Mariah turned back to him from her open car door and asked, "Martin? Is there someplace you can think of in the surrounding area where someone could be holding the girls together—like an isolated farm, abandoned barn or warehouse, something like that?"

"There are a lot of places like that all over this valley. With these girls missing, everyone is watching for activity at abandoned places everywhere. I'm not saying it isn't possible, but it's going to be hard to track down. When are Morgan and Riley going to show up?"

"It all depends on what I come up with and whether or not I need them. I need a lead on something, otherwise we would all be spinning our wheels. They are working cases in Portland that need to be taken care of, but they'll come down if we need them. I promise you."

"Well, call if I can help with anything else. I want to bring my girls home."

"I'll call. Talk to you later, Martin ... and thanks, again."

"Bye."

He raised his hand to waive as Mariah closed the car door and started the engine. She watched in her rear-view mirror as Martin walked back into his office building.

Before pulling out of the parking lot and into traffic, she looked up the nearest outlet store. Finding what she was looking for, she headed to the store on Crater Lake Highway and bought a five pound bag of apples, a big bunch of bananas, a box of protein bars, a three pound bag of walnut halves, a three pound bag of pecan halves, a three-and-a-half pound canister of cashews, and a three pound bag of almonds. Finished there, she stopped at the pumps to fill her gas tank. Next she went to a superstore in the same shopping center and bought a box of gallon zippered plastic bags, a box of zippered sandwich bags, and a case of bottled water. Her next stop was a nearby sporting goods store where she purchased three boxes of 5.7x28 mm ammo for her FN Five-seveN, three boxes of .45 ACP ammo for her Glock G21, and four boxes of 9mm for her Baby Glock (the G26). She had a suspicion she was going to be doing some stake outs on this case and she wanted some portable nourishment and plenty of ammo on hand for quality target practice, as well as enough to keep on hand. The last stop was the local grocery store where she picked up some eggs, spinach, romaine lettuce, cucumber, tomato, onion, bread, deli turkey, deli ham, pepper jack cheese, mustard, and mayo. She took the groceries home and put the cold stuff in the fridge, before taking Paisley out for a walk. After the walk, she crated Paisley and headed out to the range.

This being late afternoon on a Friday, the range was pretty empty, which suited Mariah. It was too late in the day to do any shooting, dusk was at hand when she pulled up to the gates, paid her three dollars, and drove past all the alleys to check out her options. She wanted to pull up to the last alley, and get some target practice in, but she turned and drove back to the gates where a range master was waiting to lock up. On the drive back to the suite, Mariah thought about how much she loved shooting—focusing on her sights, the challenge of connecting the bullet to the target, and seeing the resulting impact made by the projectile she sent with the mere pull of a finger.

FRIDAY EVENING

Mariah opened the door to Paisley's crate as soon as she returned to the suite. Paisley stepped out, stretched and yawned before she jumped up on Mariah's legs, wanting to be picked up. She picked up the little dog, and talked to her a moment, Paisley paying rapt attention. After Mariah put her down, the little terrier ran off to look for one of her squeaky toys. She pranced back to Mariah with a toy duck made of colorful fabric. It had a squeaker in the nose and she raced all over the suite—in and out of every room—shaking her head, squeaking her toy, tossing it in the air, and catching it. Her gleefulness was delightful to Mariah and she couldn't stop herself from laughing. Paisley ran to Mariah and as Mariah bent to take the toy, Paisley ran out of reach just to come back and repeat the game. Mariah indulged Paisley a few minutes before she broke away, refreshed Paisley's water bowl, and filled her food bowl.

Mariah grabbed her laptop and set it up on the little table. She turned it on and while it powered up, she went to the kitchen to fix herself a ham sandwich. She ate standing at the kitchen counter and watched Paisley who stopped playing to watch her eat.

"No beg!" she admonished the little dog who backed away three steps and sat looking away from Mariah. Mariah smiled.

She finished her sandwich, took out a treat for Paisley and walked to the table, the little dog jumping at her side. Mariah gave the silent command for 'sit', and Paisley sat, received her treat, and ran off to the living room to devour her reward.

Mariah sat at the table and started a timeline of her activities on the case which, at this point, didn't amount to much. She checked her emails and had one from Morgan telling her to keep in touch and to call any time if she needed to. Riley's email was much the same.

****

Mariah sat back on the couch and picked up the TV remote, but she was restless. Something was gnawing at the back of her mind and she couldn't bring it forward. Instead of turning on the television, she phoned Morgan first and got voice mail, then tried Riley with no success before she got out the notes she had so far on the missing girls. She scrutinized every detail, committing them to memory.

The persistent, gnawing thought still clawed at the back of her mind. In frustration, she decided to try to relax in hopes the thought would be released from her subconscious. She turned on the television, and started flipping through channels. Before she knew it, she had zoned out, thinking about the girls instead of hearing the television while, at the same time, she mechanically changed channels. She imagined what they might have seen and done when they walked out of their last class, and she hoped against hope they were still alive and in the area. Something on the TV suddenly caught her attention. It was a rerun of Matlock. Some guy in a bar looked at Matlock and asked, "What missing girl?" She turned the television off and started pacing. Paisley paced with her—trotting along beside her, head turned up and watching Mariah. Mariah stopped in the middle of the room, put her hands on my hips and gazed down into the beautiful and intelligent caramel colored eyes of Paisley. "What is it, girl?"

Paisley sat and stared up at Mariah, giving a little whine.

"What am I missing? I'm getting things set up to talk to the parents and the teachers. I need to talk to the parents and find out who else the girls hung around with and get their support to talk to their friends, so that will follow." She squatted down and started scratching Paisley behind the ears.

"There's something I'm missing." Paisley snorted and laid down as Mariah's magic fingers started scratching down her spine. Mariah shook her head, stood, and started pacing again, Paisley jumping up to follow. After a few steps, Mariah sat down in the middle of the living room floor, crossed her legs and patted the floor beside her. "Come on, Paisley. Let's meditate."

Paisley circled around Mariah and sat down on Mariah's left. She hung her head and closed her eyes, taking in a deep breath and huffing it out.

Mariah sat up straight, placed a hand on each knee, palms up, touching each thumb to middle finger, closed her eyes and took three deep cleansing breathes. Paisley huffed a breath along with her.

Mariah sought her calm center, clearing her mind and blocking out any thought. She felt the calm take over her and she rested there. Without warning, the shadow, with a loud roar, barged into her calm and Mariah gasped, falling over backward. While scrambling to her feet, Paisley yelped and danced around to the side of Mariah, trying to get out of the way.

"DAMN IT!" Mariah exclaimed, stomping her foot. She closed the bathroom and both bedroom doors, grabbed her jacket and shoulder bag. She gave Paisley a treat, not even bothering to put her in the crate, and left.

It was early—only six-thirty p.m.—so the bars weren't hopping yet. Mariah found herself on Front street where there were a few bars and restaurants, one of which was El Jefe Grill and Bar. She hadn't had good Mexican food since moving from Albuquerque NM to Portland OR, so she decided to give it a try. She pulled into the parking lot at the side of the building and walked into the bar. There were a couple high round tables with stools to the left of the door. To the right was an area for a band to set up. The bar ran the length of the right wall after the band area, with round bar stools for seating. Between the bar stools and a row of high round tables with stools, was a meager walkway. A row of booths sat along the left wall beyond the bar and tables. Between the round tables inside the door and the booths across from the bar, was an open doorway to the restaurant side of the business. Mariah decided to sit at the bar in the hopes of chatting up some of the locals. The bartender took her drink order and when she brought the beer, she also brought a menu. After a brief perusal, Mariah ordered the beef and chicken enchilada plate.

An older gent, late sixties to early seventies, sat one stool over from Mariah, nursing his draft beer while watching the bartender, a pretty brunette with perky, half exposed breasts and sporting a little broken heart tattoo just above the neckline of her top on the left breast.

"You come here often?" Mariah asked him.

He glanced over and looked Mariah up and down. "Mind if I sit here?" He indicated the stool between them.

"Nope, not at all." Mariah smiled.

He scooted over, sliding his beer along the counter. "I come in here most days. I chat with my daughter when it's not busy. Know what I mean …" he tipped his head at the bartender, "… run off the assholes who try to hit on her. They don't mess with her much now, but when she first started here, it got real bad. I had to kick a few asses and bend a few ears to get my point across. Know what I mean?"

"Oh. I bet she appreciated that. She's your daughter?"

"Yeah, late life child. My pride and joy—her and the girls. Her man got himself kilt in a loggin' accident. She was left alone with two li'le ankle biters, so she went to some bartendin' classes, got her license, and took a job here. Know what I mean?"

Mariah nodded.

"Jason, the owner, is an old school friend a mine and put her to work here, but he warned her 'bout some a the grief an attractive bartender could be subject to. He's good about lookin' out fer his employees, but I figured I could help. Know what I mean? I come here more out a habit than need now. She's well respected by the regulars and nobody's gonna let anythin' happen to her now, but she had to earn her stripes, so to speak. Know what I mean?"

"Yes, sir. I sure do. She never remarried?"

"Nah. She dated some, but her husband was a great guy. He was crazy 'bout her and those li'l girls and she was head over heels over him. They were high school sweethearts. Know what I mean? Broke my heart when he got kilt, not to mention what it done to her. Know what I mean? I mean, if it weren't fer those girls a hers, she'd a kilt herself, too. Sure glad she didn't. Know what I mean?"

"Yep. I can imagine. How old are her girls?"

"Here you go." The bartender set the piping hot plate on the bar, and out of her apron pocket handed Mariah a fork and spoon wrapped in a paper napkin. She warned, "Be careful, the plate is very hot."

"Thanks."

"Would you like another beer?"

"Yeah, I'll have one more."

"Daddy, you want another" she asked the old gent.

"Sure, honey," he responded with a gentle grin and a nod of his head.

As she went off to get their drinks Mariah said, "Hi. My name's Mariah," and extended her hand to shake.

He took her hand and came back with, "Jeffrey."

Mariah leaned back suddenly and arched an eyebrow.

"How do you know my name?"

"You just told me. Know what I mean?"

"I told you my first name and you …"

"And I told you my first name. What's going on here?"

Mariah laughed. "I'm sorry. Your name is Jeffrey?!"

"That's what I said."

"My last name is Jeffries."

Jeffrey laughed along with Mariah. "Now I understand," he said, still chuckling.

The bartender brought them their beers and Jeffrey stopped her. "Katherine, this is Mariah. Mariah, my baby girl, Katherine."

"Hi Katherine," Mariah said extending her hand.

Katherine took the proffered hand and said, "Call me Kate. You new in town?"

"Just here on a little business. Your dad was telling me about your daughters. You must be worried about them with all those girls going missing."

As Kate wiped invisible spots from the bar in front of them, she said, "Nah, my girls are seven and ten and a half. I'm worried about those missing girls, sure, but I don't think my girls are at risk. At least … if anything happened to them, their uncles and grandfathers would be out for blood. That would be a bad scene," she said with a smile and a wink at her dad.

"You got that right. No one's gonna mess with my girls. Know what I mean? Hey Kate, get this. Mariah's last name is Jeffries." He shook his head chuckling and continued, "She thought I knew her last name when I told her my name. Isn't that funny?"

"Really? Yeah, that's pretty funny. I bet you were surprised, Mariah."

"Confused is more like it."

Jeffrey was still laughing when he turned back to Mariah. "You got any young-uns, Mariah?"

"No sir. Not sure I want any with this kind of madness going around. I can't imagine who would be taking these girls.

It's a terrible thing." Mariah shook her head. Looking at Kate she asked, "So you have a lot of family around here—brothers and all?"

"I have two older brothers. One lives in Eagle Point and the other is in Grants Pass, so they're pretty close if I need them. We don't see each other much, but if there were trouble, they would help. I have two younger brother-in-laws too. Same with them—we don't talk to each other much, but they'd be there if there were any trouble."

"That's good." Mariah nodded her head.

Kate left without a word to get a couples order who had come in and taken a booth behind Mariah. It was seven and the place was starting to pick up.

"Yep, these girls going missing," Jeffrey said, "sure is a terrible thing. Has a lot a people stirred up in town. Know what I mean? I mean, hell! If it was Kate who'd gone missin' I'd be out beatin' the bushes with a shotgun. Know what I mean? I mean, some-un would die fer sure! Know what I mean?"

"Yeah. If I had any children, I'd want heads to roll if someone hurt one of them."

"That's how it is when yer a parent. Give yer life's blood for 'em, you would."

"What's the scuttlebutt about the kidnappings? Have you heard anything?"

"No. It's like they're disappearin' into thin air. It's got a lotta folks scared. Know what I mean? I mean, some jackass is goin' 'round tellin' people it's aliens suckin' 'em up to their space ship to have sex with 'em so they can start to populate the earth with clones. Dumbest damn thing I ever heard of." He shook his head and took a big swig of his beer. "Damn fool jackass is tryin' to distract folks from the truth. Hell, he's probably the one takin' the girls and just deflectin' the focus off his self. Know what I mean?"

"Well, I would imagine the police checked him out. Don't you think?"

"I s'pose so." He drained his glass of beer before pounding

it down on the bar so hard Mariah thought it would shatter.

They both turned their heads to watch a couple of young guys come in the front door carrying some band equipment.

"Oh, is there going to be live music tonight?" Mariah asked.

"Looks like it. They usually have live music Friday and Saturday."

Kate walked back up to them and reached for her dad's empty glass.

"Kate, honey. What's up with the band tonight?"

"Ah, it's a new group trying to get established. Jason is going to be here and if he likes them, he'll book them again for next month. Stick around, Mariah. Might be entertaining."

"I'd love to but I've got an early meeting tomorrow. Guess I'll pay my tab and get out of here."

"Sure, I'll be right back with your ticket."

"Here's my card," Mariah said handing over her credit card. "Put it on here, please."

"Sure thing." Kate took the card and headed to the restaurant side of the business.

"I enjoyed meeting you, Jeffrey. Thanks for keeping me company."

Jeffrey tipped his head. "Maybe I'll see ya in here again afore you leave town. Know what I mean? Come on out tomorrow night and I'll cut a rug on the dance floor with ya." His eyes closed and his grin widened as he raised his hands in front of his chest and shook his shoulders.

Mariah laughed. "Sounds like fun."

Kate returned with the card and a register receipt to sign. Mariah tipped twenty percent and signed the receipt before pocketing her copy and the credit card.

"Thank you, Kate. Look after those little girls and maybe I'll see you again. Good night."

Jeffrey and Kate murmured "good night," as Mariah walked away from them, crossed the small dance floor, and exited the door as a guy arrived with a bass drum. She held the door open for him to enter before walking to her car.

****

As she closed the car door, her phone rang. She check the screen to see who was calling, but didn't recognize the 'five-four-one' area code number. "This is Mariah Jeffries."

"Hi. This is Bruce Givens—Alexis' father. She gave me your card and said you wanted to talk to us about Duskie."

"Yes. Um, it's seven-fifty," Mariah said checking the time. "Is it too late to come by now?"

"No. Not at all. We're happy to help in any way we can. Besides that, Alexis is anxious for you to come by. You sure impressed her with your kindness."

"I'm leaving El Jefe Grill and Bar right now. Can you give me quick directions?"

"We're on Dakota Ave., across the street from Polk Elementary School. Go south on Front Street and turn right on 11th St. Continue down 11th until you come to Oakdale where you will turn left. At the Y, keep to your right and continue around the curve. Turn right on Dakota. We're across from the school building. It's a blue house with white trim. I'll turn the porch light on."

"I'll be in a black, Toyota Corolla. Give me a few minutes to get there—it shouldn't take long."

After the insurance settlement from her house in Albuquerque being blown up, along with her Mercedes Benz parked in the garage, Mariah paid off all her debt, and bought a 2001 Toyota Corolla in Black Sand Pearl with 38,375 miles on it for only $1500. It was in pristine condition, without a scratch or a dent anywhere on the body, nor a single mare on the interior—the light charcoal cloth seats were without stain, snag, or rip. All in all, for fifteen-hundred dollars, she purchased a gently broken in, 'new' car that had been fully loaded with all the available bells and whistles at the time of the original purchase. The original owner had been an eighty-five year old widow who passed away peacefully in her sleep ten years to the day after buying the car.

Arriving at the house, Mariah saw Alexis waiting on the front porch with an older man who Mariah assumed to be the girl's father. Mariah pulled a u-turn just passed the house and parked in front. She put the car in park and grabbed her shoulder bag in which she kept a notepad, and tape recorder. Mariah locked the car door before she closed it and waived to Alexis who stepped off the porch and walked down the sidewalk to greet her.

"Hi, Mariah. This is my dad, Bruce," she said as she opened the gate to the four foot tall chain-linked fence encompassing the front yard.

"Hi Alexis. Good to see you again." She turned to Mr. Givens, "How do you do, Mr. Givens. I'm happy to meet you."

"Fine. Nice to meet you too. Twila just opened a bottle of wine. Come on in and we'll pour you a glass"

"That sounds good, but I think I'll pass. Thank you, though." Mariah didn't want another alcoholic drink on top of the two beers she already consumed. "I would like a glass of water, if that's okay."

"I'll get it," Alexis said and ran ahead of them into the house.

The front yard was small. A large Oak tree stood in the left front corner, it's leaves scattered on the ground and in the road. The broken sidewalk led up to the center of the house where the wooden door was worn—the paint cracked and peeling. The aluminum frame for the screen door was still in place, but the door itself was gone. To either side of the door was a sliding window, the screens intact. As Mr. Givens stated earlier, the house was blue—more of a slate blue—with peeling white paint on the door and window frames.

Stepping inside the front door, the smell of garlic and onion with tomato wafted up to Mariah. To her left was a small dining room with a round, wooden table and four Windsor style chairs. The walls were a pale yellow, the linoleum, which followed around a breakfast bar into the adjoining kitchen, was white with brown and green flecks in it. The table was clean with a small vase holding flowers that appeared real but were more likely silk. The kitchen had a pot sitting on the stove top and dirty dishes in the sink, but otherwise was as clean, neat, and orderly as the rest of the interior. The living room, to Mariah's right, was small but clear of clutter. The walls were painted a maroon with vertical white stripes. A dark blue upholstered couch sat under the front window. There was a matching chair against the far wall, and a torchiere floor lamp in the corner between the chair and the couch. Across from the couch, mounted on the wall, was a flat screen TV. Tan, plush carpeting covered the living room floor and stopped at the hardwood hallway floor leading from the front door between the dining room and kitchen, to the back end of the house. Down the hall stood an open door to the right just past the living room, another door, closed, to the left just past the kitchen, and a set of folding doors halfway down the hall. At the end of the hall stood another closed door.

"Please, have a seat," Mr. Givens said. "This is my wife, Twila."

"How do you do." Mariah extended her hand to the woman who stood from the couch.

"It's nice to meet you." Twila reached for Mariah's hand. "I hope we can help you find the girls. We're so worried." Her grip was limp and moist from the sweating wine glass containing a chilled white wine. "Alexis says you're a private investigator hired to look for the missing girls. That must be an exciting job."

"Not always." Mariah smiled. "Most of the time it's routine—track down tidbits of facts and information and put them together so they make sense."

"Please, sit down," Twila told Mariah indicating the chair as she sat back down on the couch and took a drink of her wine. Mr. Givens sat next to her.

"Here's your water." Alexis handed Mariah a glass of water

and sat next to her father at the end of the couch.

"Thank you." Mariah sat in the chair and turned slightly so she could see all three of them. "Before we start, would you mind if I record our conversation? It's helpful when I make notes so I don't miss any small details that might make a difference."

"No. Not at all," Mr. Givens said.

Mariah took the old fashioned cassette tape recorder out of her bag, checked the tape inside, turned it on and said, "It's eight oh five pm Friday evening at 912 Dakota Avenue in Medford Oregon. I'm talking with Mr. Bruce Givens, his wife Twila, and their daughter Alexis." Mariah then placed it on the floor in front of her feet. "Alexis tells me you know the Banks family well."

"That's right," Mrs. Givens responded. "Kayla and I were friends since High School. When she married Tim and moved in just a couple doors down, we were excited to be neighbors. We moved into this house about six months before I got pregnant with Alexis, so we've been here for eighteen, almost nineteen years now. Tim and Cassiday, Duskie's birth mother, lived down the street when Bruce and I bought this place. We became close friends with them. Then we got pregnant with the girls about the same time. The girls have always been close, but when they were about a year old, Cassiday was in a bad car accident and hurt her back real bad. She was never the same after that—lots of pain and emotional problems. We didn't know it at the time, but apparently she had become addicted to the pain drugs. One day she told me she wasn't feeling well and asked if Duskie could spend the night with Alexis since Tim was working late at the plant. Of course, I said yes. When Tim got home the next morning, he found Cassiday dead, with a needle sticking out of her arm. The police said it was heroin. Tim, poor thing, was devastated. He loved her so much. He's a really nice guy."

Mrs. Givens wiped a tear off her cheek and took a sip of her wine. "It took a while, but eventually he met Kayla at work. She moved back to the valley after her divorce and went to work at the plant as a forklift driver. They dated a while and when they fell in love, everyone could see it. They have been devoted to each other and to Duskie ever since. I don't know how he's going to survive losing Duskie now. She's such a bright and happy child." Twila's chin trembled with the effort of holding back her tears.

"How sad."

Twila and Bruce nodded. Alexis wiped the tears from her cheek.

"How old were the girls when Cassiday died?"

Twila wiped at her eyes. "Seven. No, eight. They had just started second grade."

"How did Duskie handle the death of her mother?"

"It was terrible. Tim was so grieved that he had a hard time seeing his daughter's pain, much less doing anything to help her. Duskie spent a lot of time with us. Gradually over the course of a year, Tim got a grip on himself and became more aware of Duskie and her sense of loss. For a while it was like she had lost her mother and her father. With a lot of encouragement from friends and family, he started going to a grief counselor and he took Duskie too. I think that saved her from becoming one of those really broken kids that never gets their life together. You know?"

"Yes. Grief can be very devastating sometimes. So, you think Duskie turned out pretty well adjusted?"

"Yes. I do. We enjoy having her around. She loves Kayla and was happy when Tim married her and gave her a mother. We talk about her memories of her mom, Cassiday, and she asks me questions about what her mom was like before she was hurt so bad. She wants to know about her mom, naturally, but she also sees Kayla as her mom. She's a very happy and well adjusted girl." Twila started tearing up and said in a choked voice, "She's like family to us and we're so worried. Please find her. Please."

As Twila started sobbing, Bruce put his arm around her and held her close, his own eyes sparkling with unshed tears.

Mariah waited a moment to let them gain their composure

before saying, "Thanks for all the background information. I'm going to do everything I can to find her and the other girls. Have you talked to Tim or Kayla since Duskie went missing?"

"Yes." Twila pulled a tissue from her sleeve and wiped her eyes and nose. "I went over there after work as soon as I heard about it yesterday, and again today to see if they needed anything."

"How did they seem tonight?"

"Beaten down. Tim just sits and stares at the TV. Kayla is trying to be strong for Tim, but she's hurting too."

"What do you do for a living?"

"I'm a receptionist for Dr. Pauls. She's an optometrist and has her own practice. It's small, but she's great—especially with kids."

"What do Duskie's parent do for a living, Mrs. Givens?"

"Please, call me Twila. Kayla is a phlebotomist at the hospital. She didn't like working at the plant and got hired and trained in the lab at the hospital. Tim is still working at the fiber board plant. They're both trying to keep soldiering on, but it's taking a toll on them.

"Mr. Givens, how about you. Have you talked to Tim or Kayla lately?"

"No one calls me Mr. Givens. I'm Bruce."

"Bruce." Mariah smiled.

"I'm a truck driver and was on the road this week. I just got home this morning, so I went with Twila when she got home from work. I'm not sure I would be in any better shape than Tim, if Alexis went missing. I told Alexis I was going to take her out of school and let her ride with me when I go back on the road tomorrow, but I don't think the company will allow it for liability reasons. I'm worried about her and can't even imagine what Tim is going though."

"Me neither. Alexis, what can you tell me about Duskie? Who did she hang around with?"

"She hung around with me mostly, and the basketball team, of course."

"Was there anything weird going on that you know of?

Has anyone given her a hard time or threatened her? Anything you can think of?"

"Not really. I don't know anything else."

"Did she have a boyfriend or a boy she liked?"

"Well, she liked Austen Smith, but he started going with Kimmie Huber, a tenth grader and a cheerleader. I'm the only one she ever told that she likes him though, so I don't think that would have anything to do with her being missing."

"Yeah, probably not. Are you on the basketball team too?"

"No. I was two years ago, but I wasn't very good. I'm on the Volleyball team and I run cross country."

"You like to run?"

Alexis nodded.

"Me too. Do you know where there's a good place to run where I don't have to avoid traffic?"

"Oh, there's lots of places. Bear Creek Park has a paved trail I like. It's part of the Green Way. It actually runs from Ashland to Central Point and is pretty safe."

"That's a matter of opinion," Bruce interjected, and cocked an eyebrow as he looked at Alexis.

"The cops patrol it pretty regularly, Dad."

"They can't patrol the whole thing all at once. What about that young man that was practically decapitated last year?"

"Dad!"

"Anyone who travels the Green Way, should do so with a group—especially the more isolated areas, and especially if they're out there at night."

"Yes, sir," Alexis replied, rolling her eyes. To Mariah, she directed, "Maybe we can go running together some time."

Mariah nodded and smiled, "I would like that. Maybe we should find some place other than the Green Way, though—for your dad's peace of mind." Mariah smiled at Alexis.

"Sure. There are lots of places to run. The track at the high school is usually open."

"Sounds great."

Mariah turned to Twila and Bruce, "Would that be okay with you two?"

"Yes." Twila said as Bruce said, "Of course."

"I'll call you then," Mariah said to Alexis. "Maybe tomorrow evening if I have some free time. Would that work?"

"Sure," Alexis answered with a big grin.

"Okay. Well, thank you so much for seeing me." Mariah picked up the tape recorder, hit the stop button, stuffed it and her notepad back in her bag, and stood. "It was nice to meet you both."

Bruce stood and thanked her for working on the case. "I sure hope those girls are found soon, and that they're all okay."

"Me too. Please give me a call if you think of anything else or hear anything new that you think might help in the investigation. I'm going to do everything I can to get those girls back."

"Yes, thank you," Twila said as she rose from the couch. "And come back to visit sometime. We'd love to have you over for dinner this weekend, if you would like."

"That sounds lovely, but I'll probably be busy on the case."

"Well, call us if you find yourself free," Bruce said. "I'll walk you out to your car."

"Thank you." At the door, Mariah turned to the Givens family. "Good night."

"Good night, Mariah," Alexis said. "See you tomorrow."

"Night," said Twila as Mariah stepped out the front door, Bruce following behind.

"Will you be okay with Alexis running with me while I'm here?"

Bruce followed behind Mariah in silence until they got to the gate. He reached around and opened it for her before he answered.

"I think it will be fine as long as you keep her safe. I would prefer you do not run very far on the greenway. There have been some problems in the past, but the school tracks would be good. She really likes you and I think you could be a good influence on her."

Mariah smiled. "I'll keep that in mind. Thanks again

Bruce."

"I wish you luck. Good night, Mariah."

"Good night."

Paisley greeted Mariah when she entered the suite, and the two of them played a quick game of tug-o-war with Paisley's squeaky giraffe toy.

"How about a run, Paisley?" she asked, ruffling Paisley's fur at the neck and scratching behind her ears. Paisley's eyes brightened, her mouth opened in her doggie smile and she cocked her head to the side.

"Come on." Mariah laughed as she went to her room and donned her jogging clothes, harnessed Paisley and took her out to the car. They drove around looking for a school yard or track area to take a long walk and think.

Without consciously realizing what she was looking for, she found the backside of JFK Memorial High School fifteen minutes later, Paisley perched beside her the whole time. There was a large open field, a couple baseball fields, a track and football field, tennis courts, and the back door to the science building Duskie disappeared from the day before.

Mariah and Paisley got out of the car and started walking. It was a cool night. The stars shone bright in the night sky and the air smelled fresh and clean. There were a lot of locked gates, but Paisley and Mariah walked around the campus where they could.

The back door of the science room opened directly to the sidewalk—the drive for the parking lot beyond that. Mariah tried to imagine Duskie's last moments on campus and where she might have gone after leaving class. She envisioned Duskie walking across the parking lot to the field, and from there to the road beyond. She pictured in her mind a beat up Ford … no a plain sedan, waiting to pick the girl up outside the classroom.

Mariah doubted Duskie was forcefully taken from the parking lot behind the science building. Classes had just let out and there would have been a lot of other people around to witness it. She either walked away, where she was then nabbed off campus, or she willingly left with someone.

As Paisley and Mariah walked across the open field, back to the car, Mariah decided she needed to see what happens behind the Science building when school lets out.

Once they were back in their rooms, Mariah made detailed notes in a word document on her laptop of the day's activities and information gleaned. She saved the document and opened up her email account. After she sent off an email to Morgan and Riley, with her notes of the day attached, she opened a new email from Morgan. Morgan attached a detailed and thorough background check of Martin Silkeney which showed him to be above reproach. Mariah wasn't surprised. She also had a new email from Riley. He was still working on the complete background checks on the parents of the missing girls and will send them as soon as they're finished. There was an email from her Uncle Richard keeping her updated on him, Uncle Dan, and Uncle John.

She received another email from Uncle John, who was checking up on her. He's the only one of the Uncles that Mariah talked to about the nightmares. She was aware of his worry over the recurrent nightmares and how much they interfered with her inner peace and centeredness.

She composed an email to Uncle Richard, telling him where she was and what she was up to—that she will let him know if she ever needed their help again. She expected him to share the email with Uncles Dan and John.

She composed a second email to Uncle John and let him know about the past life regression. She looked forward to hearing what he thought of that and was hopeful she would be able to tell him that it helped.

By the time she finished, Paisley was burrowed under her blanket on the bed, sound asleep. Mariah stripped her clothes off, leaving them in a pile with the previous day's clothes, showered, and slipped between the sheets exhausted, her hair still wrapped in a towel. She was sound asleep in minutes.

SATURDAY A.M.

As I enter the Givens' front door, a bronze-skinned, blue-eyed, red-haired man walks toward me from the far end of the hallway. The scene expands, dissolving the room around me into an open wooded area. He is carrying a baby, chubby little arms and legs waiving in the air. He calls my name and asks 'Why?' I try to walk toward him, but my feet are heavy and weighted down as if they are in lead boots. They will not move. The red-haired man is dressed in buckskins and as he takes a step in my direction, the baby falls from his arms and disappears. He stops and looks all around, clenches his fists, glares at me, and asks 'Why?'.

'Why what?' I ask him, but there's no reply. I shrug my shoulders and shake my head. He advances another step before eight children swarm him, five little boys and three little girls ranging in age from two to twelve. He's laughing and playing with the children and then he pauses to count them. When he's done, his brow furrows, he is puzzled and holds his hands out to his sides, palms up and asks, 'Why?' A tear rolls down his face and he turns into an old man as the children age to adults. Spouses appear and then children materialize in their parents arms or clutching their parents legs. He smiles at them and with a soft caress or pat, touches each one. Finished, he frowns and turns to me again, a tear

running down his weathered and wrinkled face. He glances off to the side. I follow his gaze to a grown Daniel with a beautiful wife and several children approaching the red-haired man. As Daniel gets close, he shoves the now aged man dressed in buckskins, pushing him down, and spits on him before walking past, his wife and children laughing. The old man lies on the ground and cries. In disbelief he again asks, 'Why?'

I stand in the doorway, looking out on the wooded scene, and I cry. 'I don't know. I don't know,' I scream as I watch the old man turn to dust and drift away in a swirl of wind. 'Please come back. Please! ... Come back...' But all I hear is the echo of his question, 'Why?' I weep as I repeat 'I don't know. Please, I don't know. Come back.' I fall to the floor and cover my face with my hands and try to stop the flow of tears. The hairs at the back of my neck begin to bristle and I raise my head to peek through my fingers as a shadow rushes at me. 'No! No!' I cry out throwing my arms up in protection. I gasp and yell 'Nooooo!'

Mariah awoke with a scream stuck in her throat and a whining Paisley licking the tears from her face.

After the usual morning ritual, Mariah started to crate Paisley but decided to leave the door open since she behaved so well the night before. She gave Paisley a treat, made sure she had food and water, and headed out to her first appointment.

Martin had emailed Mariah's appointments to meet with each of the girls' family. She had thirty minutes to drive to the home of Duskie Banks, the most recent girl to go missing.

Passing Alexis' house, she pulled up on the street in front of Duskie's home, exited her car and locked it. The narrow, concrete, sidewalk was lined on each side with recessed, red-brick. It went straight from the curb to the two concrete steps and front porch. In front of the steps, the sidewalk branched off to the left around rhododendron and snowball bushes, to a six foot tall wooden gate in the fence enclosing the back yard.

The exterior of the house was a light grey, faded almost to white, with a darker blue-grey trim around the door and windows. The windows were the old wood-sash, four-pane per frame style with screens over them. The front door had a white metal framed security/screen door, the kind where the top half is glass and the lower half is a sliding glass panel that can be lifted to let fresh air in through the intact screen.

Mariah pushed the small, round, lighted doorbell and heard a single 'ding' on the other side of the door. She waited a minute and raised her hand to knock when the wooden door opened and a tall slender women with wavy brown hair asked, "Yes?"

"Hi. I'm Mariah Jeffries, the investigator that …"

"Oh. Yes, please come in. We've been expecting you," she said as she unlocked the screen door and pushed it open for Mariah to enter.

"Thank you. I'm sorry to disturb you during this difficult time, but it would be helpful if I can talk to you and Duskie's father."

"Martin told us about you. We're very thankful you took the case. Tim's been on the computer this morning researching your team. We're impressed with your group and hopeful you can find our girl. I'm Kayla, by the way."

"We're going to do everything we can," Mariah said as she followed Kayla into a long, narrow living room with hardwood floors. Just inside the front door, to the left, hung a large mirror over a small table. On top of the table stood a vase with silk flowers, a statue of a sitting black, tuxedo cat, and a framed family picture of a man, the woman who opened the door, and a teenaged girl who resembled the pictures of Duskie that the news had been airing on TV. The front window to the right had beautiful white lace curtains hanging over a white gauzy material for privacy and in front of that stood an antique roll-top desk with an antique swivel chair in front of it.

A brick fireplace, painted white, with an oblong square of marble inlaid in the floor in front, occupied the center of the right wall. To the right of the inlaid marble slab was a stand with fireplace tools, and to the left of the slab, a wicker basket full of scented, waxed pinecones. The faint scent of evergreen and jasmine permeated the house. Across from the fireplace a door stood open to a bedroom. As Mariah passed by the open door, she saw a black cat sprawled in the middle of the made bed. The cat raised its head and watched her walk by. Beyond the doorway on the left side of the room was a black leather couch. Across from the couch, a small flat-screen TV hung on the wall. Just passed the couch, a stairway leading to the second floor and more bedrooms began it's ascent. At the end of the living room, in the center of the wall, was a seven foot square opening into the dining room.

As she entered the dining room behind Kayla, a man sitting at the table, his back to the wall on the right, raised his eyes from the laptop computer in front of him.

"Tim, Mariah's here," the woman said.

Tim closed the lid to his laptop, stood, and proffered his hand to shake.

Taking his hand Mariah said, "Hi Tim. I'm so sorry for what you and Kayla are going through."

"Thank you. Please have a seat. Would you like something to drink? Kayla can get you a coke or coffee? Water if you prefer?"

"A cup of coffee would be nice if it's not too much trouble."

"No problem. I just made a fresh pot. Tim, do you want a refill?" Kayla asked.

"Uh," he raised his mug and drank the last of the contents. "Sure," He answered and handed her the mug.

Mariah sat across the table from Tim as Kayla went through another wide doorway into the kitchen with Tim's mug.

"I've been reading up on you. I'm surprised you're even walking after what you've been through. That must have been terrifying," Tim said looking Mariah in the eyes.

"It was, and it's going to have an impact on the rest of my life, but work helps a lot. I find it cathartic to put other's problems before my own, focusing on their problem and how to help them solve it. That keeps my mind off my own nightmare experience."

He nodded his head. "Yeah. I can imagine. I'll have to keep that in mind."

Tim looked off at the family picture hanging on the wall in a wood and brass frame. Mariah glanced into the kitchen and saw Kayla splash a dash of Jack Daniels into Tim's cup of coffee. She turned her eyes back to Tim as Kayla came back in with a tray holding three mugs of coffee, a small bowl of sugar, a box of sugar substitute, and a carton of flavored creamer. She placed the tray on the table between Tim and Mariah, careful not to spill the coffee, and handed each of them a full mug.

"I wasn't sure how you like your coffee. If you need something else, please let me know," she told Mariah.

"Black is fine. Thank you." Mariah set the cup down on the table. "Do you mind if I record our conversation? It helps when I'm typing up my notes."

"Nope. Do whatever will bring my girl back," Tim said.

Mariah pulled the recorder out of her purse, put it in the center of the tray, and turned it on.

"It's nine-forty-two Saturday morning at 919 Dakota Ave. I'm talking with Tim and Kayla Banks regarding their daughter, Duskie Banks.

"I talked with Alexis and her parents last night and they told me a little bit about Duskie's birth mother. Tim could we start from your childhood and move into when and where you met Cassiday?"

"Me? What's all that ancient history got to do with Duskie being missing?"

"Yes, you. Sometimes 'ancient' history pops up in the present. I'm covering ground the cops and FBI may have overlooked. At this point there is no information too trivial. Everything needs to be considered, and only when proven to be insignificant to the case, can we disregard it. I'll be looking into the background of all the parents. For all we know, this could be someone from your distant past that's been harboring a grudge for decades. We have to consider that."

Tim and Kayla shared a glance and then he took in a deep breath and let it out forcefully, his shoulders sagging. "You're the expert. What do you want to know?"

"Where did you grow up? Do you have siblings? If so, where do they live? Are you close? Any falling out? This neighborhood—what was it like when you first moved in here? How has it changed? What neighbors came and went, what were your impressions of them? Did any of them have a beef with you or your family. Stuff like that—day to day things over the years and what stands out. Our subconscious mind is more powerful than we often give it credit for."

"I grew up here—in this house. My dad worked at the mill and my mom was a housewife. She was real active in church and helping in our classes with the different parties and field trips. I have a younger sister who lives in Eugene. She's married to an accountant and they have two boys and a girl. We keep in touch, but we don't see each other very often. My dad was killed in an explosion at the mill two weeks before his retirement and my mom died a year later. After my dad died, she went downhill. Ask me, she died of a broken heart, plain and simple. I'd gone to college and studied engineering but never graduated. Cassiday and I got married the summer before my senior year. My dad warned me to wait until I graduated, but I was crazy in love. What can I say? We planned to stay in married student housing so I could finish my degree, but before the first semester was over, she got pregnant. There was no way we could afford a baby without me going to work full time, so I left school, moved back here from U of O, and went to work at the mill. Six months later, she lost that baby. We were both devastated. It was a boy …"

Tim stared off for a moment before shaking his head and saying, "A year later, she got pregnant again, this time it took and we had Duskie." He paused, eyes going vacant as he delved into memories. "She was so beautiful. I couldn't take my eyes off her, and yes—she had me wrapped around her little finger from the moment I laid eyes on her." Returning to the present, his eyes focused on Mariah and he smiled a sad little smile. "It's amazing how that happens."

Mariah smiled thinking of her past life and giving birth to Daniel. She nodded at Tim.

"Oh. When Cassiday was pregnant the first time and we moved back here, my folks sold me this house and they bought a newer house in East Medford. They gave me a great deal and without that, we couldn't have afforded to own back then. So, when Duskie was born, we lived here. She's lived here her whole life—the same house I grew up in." Tim started to tear up. "I'm sorry," he said putting his head in his hands and raking his fingers through his hair. "I'm so scared for her."

Kayla rushed from her chair back to the kitchen. Mariah watched her as she stood at the sink, her back to the dining room. Her head was bent forward, face resting in her left hand, her right arm clutched around the front of her stomach, and her shoulders heaving in silent sobs.

"I know," Mariah said, "but I'm living proof, you can survive some bad stuff."

Tim nodded.

With soft tenderness, she went on. "Tell me what Duskie is like. Is she timid, tough, smart, savvy, a fighter or compliant?"

"Oh. She's tough." Tim smiled and swiped at the tears on his face. "She amazes me—a lot smarter and tougher than me and her mom. That's for sure. She's amazing in so many ways."

"Thinking back over the years. Has there ever been anyone in the neighborhood you were leery of? Or anyone she was associated with in any way that gave you pause or concern?"

"No. Not really. Not that I can think of right now. And believe me, I've been wracking my brain trying to think of someone who would do this."

Kayla returned to the dining room after getting her emotions under control, and Mariah asked about her background. Kayla filled her in with where she grow up, facts about her childhood, her parents, her siblings, her friends to current.

"Can either of you think of anyone from your past, even your teen years, who might have nursed a grudge against you?"

Tim and Kayla looked at each other before shaking their heads no and looking at Mariah.

"If either of you think of someone from your past who might have reason to hurt you through your child, please call me right away."

"We will." Kayla said as Tim nodded his head.

"May I check out Duskie's bedroom?"

"Sure. The police and FBI already searched it and took some of her personal stuff away." Kayla said.

"Did she keep a diary or journal?"

"Yes, and that's one of the things the cops took. I feel guilty saying this, but I would read her journal once a week just to make sure she was okay. I know it's an infringement on her privacy, but with kids today ... I just wanted to make sure she was safe. You know?"

"I understand. I'm not here to judge you. Did you notice anything of concern in her journal?"

"No. Just teenage girl stuff—some girl made a face at her or some guy smiled at her. You know? The usual teenage angst. She was really well adjusted in my opinion."

"Did she feel threatened by anyone or did she mention anyone threatening her in any way?"

Kayla shook her head, "No. Nothing like that."

"Okay. What about online activity? Maybe she met someone in an online chat room?"

"The FBI are looking into that too. They took her tablet and her cell phone."

"Thanks."

"Well, follow me." Tim said. "I'll take you up to her room."

Mariah followed Tim back into the living room and turned right to go up the stairs. The stairs were dark, steep, and narrow. Tim flipped a switch to turn on a bare 60 watt bulb at the top of the dark brown carpeted stairs. The steps were so shallow, they almost had to step sideways on them. At the top landing, there was a door to the right and another to the left. Tim turned right into a small bedroom, the door standing open.

He switched on the light and Mariah stood and took in the room. Across from the doorway was a small wooden sash window, raised about an inch, letting in a sweet fall scent and the occasional sound of a car driving by on the street below. To the right of the doorway was a laundry hamper, clothes draped over the edge and filling the bottom of the hamper. Next to that was a wrought iron chest with three wicker drawers. Beyond that, on the wall to the right, was an alcove with a bar for hanging clothes, then a twin bed with a Seattle Seahawks bedspread and a night table with a lamp and clock radio in the corner on the other side of the bed. Across from the bed was another smaller alcove with shelves filled with knickknacks, books, a jewelry box and pictures. On the wall beside that alcove was a large corkboard filled with pictures of friends, cards, notes, dried up flowers, a homecoming corsage, and some movie tickets.

Mariah stood in the doorway taking it all in, lost in thought when Tim cleared his throat and said, "Well, I'll leave you to it. I just ask that you leave it like you found it. It may be the last thing …" He choked, then wiped his eyes and said in a strangled voice, "… the last thing we have left of her."

Mariah turned to him and put her hand on his arm. "I will Tim. I'll be very respectful of her belongings. Don't give up on us or on her. You said she's strong and smart. Let's hang on to that. Okay?"

He nodded his head and started back down the stairs, wiping his eyes and sniffling. Mariah turned back to the room and took it all in again, noting every little detail she could see before moving into the room. At last, she crossed to the bed and gingerly sat at the head of the bed, slid her shoes off and swung her feet up onto the bed and laid down, her hands behind her head. She remained there, concentrating on her breathe, trying to get a feel for the girl who lived there, delving into the remnant of the girls aura and energy. Mariah could sense happiness and confidence. There was no fear or timidity flowing in this room.

Good! Mariah thought. *That will serve her well.* After several minutes, she leaned up on her elbows and looked around the room from that vantage point. She studied the cork board and all the items pinned to it. There didn't seem to be a lot of order to it. She sat up, swung her feet to the floor, put her shoes back on, stood, and straightened the bed before turning to Duskie's hanging clothes. She had jeans, some tops, several skirts, three pair of slacks, two dresses, and three different sets of basketball uniforms. One hanger held scarves and belts. On the floor were a couple pair of tennis shoes, a pair of boots and six pair of flip flops—four rubber and two leather—all neatly lined up. On the shelf above the hanging clothes was a box with some board games—Monopoly, Backgammon, Clue, and Jenga—underneath stuffed Raggedy Anne and Andy dolls, and a stuffed Easter Bunny. To the right of that was a box of CD's of some unusual music for a teenaged girl—Pink Floyd's *Dark Side of the Moon* and *The Wall*; *The Essential Barbara Streisand*, *The Best of Cher*, and *The Beatles 1*. In that box, Mariah found an unopened pack of Big Red gum, a bag of Peanut M & Ms, and a bag of bite sized Snickers. Next to the box of CD's were two pair of high heels, one black with white polka-dots and little black bows on the back, the other pair was emerald green with glitter.

Mariah got on her hands and knees and looked under the bed, but it was clean with nothing stored underneath. She examined everything on the shelves in the smaller alcove, finding a photo album full of pictures of her biological mother and father's wedding—her mother's pregnancy pictures, pictures of her as an infant and growing up, pictures of her mother who was beautiful and looked a lot like Duskie. After that were pictures of the wrecked car her mother was injured in, pictures of her mother in the hospital recuperating and pictures of Duskie bruised and scratched up, ending with pictures of her mother's headstone. Mariah checked the drawers in the night table next to the bed, and the drawers of the wicker chest. She checked out everything on the cork board last, lifting some pieces to see what was underneath. There did seem to be some order to the cork board—general school activities posted on the left, basketball memorabilia filled the center, and friends and family stuff occupied the right side.

Unless Kayla had cleaned, Duskie was a neat and organized young lady. The only affliction she had with hording or saving a bunch of memorabilia was the secreted candy, which in Mariah's estimation was nothing to be concerned with, and the corkboard memories.

Mariah walked to the door and turned, looking back into the room again, checking to see if she missed anything. She closed her eyes, took in a deep breath and whispered, "Give me a clue Duskie."

Mariah opened her eyes and saw an image of Duskie posting a picture on the corkboard. She walked back to the collage and looked again. There were a number of pictures of Duskie and her friends. One picture of four friends sitting at a table. Mariah looked on the back for an inscription. It was dated the previous July and said *Tiffany, Tyler, Josh, and Miranda.* Another was a selfie of Duskie and a boy standing in front of a wooded area. The inscription read, *Me and Devon.* Near the bottom of the board, under three pictures, she found a picture of all the missing girls and their teammates, in their uniforms and standing with two women. There were several more, most of them were group pictures, but Mariah couldn't put together a clue from any of them. She walked back to the bedroom door and flipped off the light, crossed the landing, and peeked into the other room. She felt along the wall for the switch and flipped it up when she found it. There was a desk under the window, an old, tube style TV, with an Xbox along one wall and two bean bag chairs facing it. Mariah entered the room to check it out further. In the far corner, there was a small but full bathroom—toilet, pedestal sink, and a large shower. Next to the bathroom was a small kitchenette with a single sink in the middle of a four foot long cabinet. A microwave oven sat on the left side of the counter-top, and the opposite side of the counter held a toaster. Beneath the microwave was a mini-fridge, and the drawer under the toaster held plastic utensils, one dull steak knife, a dull paring knife, and an assortment of bag clips, spoons, and forks. The single door under the sink concealed the usual cleaning supplies, dish soap, comet, toilet bowl cleaner, rubber gloves, dusting rags and dusting spray. The cabinet above the sink held paper plates and bowls, an assortment of cups and mugs, a box of microwave popcorn, an open bag of chips, a bag of chocolate chip cookies, some chocolate truffles, half a loaf of bread that was starting to mold, a jar of peanut butter, a box of crackers, a box of tea bags, a jar of sugar and a tin of ground cinnamon. Mariah closed the cabinet door and bent to open the refrigerator, where she found six cans of soda, a half empty quart of milk, a tub of margarine, three apples, an orange, two individual pudding cups, and a bag of shriveled grapes.

After searching through the room and finding nothing of note, Mariah turned the light off and went back downstairs.

When she came down the stairs, Tim and Kayla were still in the dining room, sitting at the table. Tim was on the computer and Kayla was staring at the wall behind him.

"Kayla," Mariah asked, "did you clean Duskie's room, or is it always that neat?"

"No." she said, shaking her head. "We haven't wanted it disturbed, so ... except to make sure the police didn't make a mess, I've only stood in the door and thought about her." Kayla started to cry, covered her face with her hands and then put her left hand at the base of her throat and fanned her face with her right hand trying to get her emotions under control.

"It's so hard with her gone. We miss her and we're so, so worried."

Tim slammed the lid of the laptop down and hung his head before saying in a strained voice, "Is there anything else you need?"

"No. I can only imagine how scary this is right now for you and all the other parents. If you think of anything, no matter how trivial it might seem, would you give me a call? Here's my card with my cell phone number on it."

"Sure." Tim said without looking up. Kayla nodded her head and reached for the card. "Please find her. Please?"

"I'll do everything I can."

Kayla started to get up from the table but Mariah stopped her, saying she would let herself out. Mariah went to the door and closed it with a gentle click.

Walking to her car, Mariah heard someone call her name. She looked up and saw Alexis standing in front of her house.

"Oh, hi Alexis. How are you?" Mariah called as she walked down the strip of grass to the girl's house.

"Fine. Are you busy?" Alexis asked as Mariah walked up to her.

"I have a couple more appointments today. How are you?"

"I'm fine. I was wondering if you wanted to go running with me? You said you might be able to today."

"I would love to, but I have these meetings I have to do first. When I finish, I'll pick up Paisley ..."

"Who's Paisley?"

"My dog. You'll love her. I can pick you up after I get her if your parents are fine with that. Do you know a fenced in park so Paisley can run off leash?"

"We could go to the dog park up on Barnett. It has a dirt track we can run on."

"That sounds great. I was hoping to find a dog park around here. My last meeting is at three and could last a couple hours. I'll call for your parent's permission when I'm finished and let you know when I'll be by."

"Okay," Alexis said, all smiles, braces shining in the sunlight.

"Talk to you soon." Mariah said as she turned and walked to her car.

****

Mariah's next appointment was with the parents of Tina Webb, the first girl taken, and the youngest. Mariah plugged the address into her Garmin and started her car. She drove East until she came to Oakdale where she made a right, crossed Stewart Avenue, and entered a newer neighborhood. She continued until she came to 595 Shadow Wood Drive.

Mariah parked on the Oakdale side of the house, locked her car and walked around to the front of the house to the short, steep driveway. Angling off the driveway, a curved sidewalk led to the front door. In the center of the small, sloped front yard grew a Japanese Oak Tree, the leaves mostly brittle and fallen.

Mariah rang the doorbell and could hear a very clear ding-dong resonate inside the home, then the clomp of footsteps before the door opened. Peering out at her stood a four foot tall, ghoul with black smudged make-up around the eyes and fake blood dripping from pointed, plastic incisors.

"Oh! No!" she exclaimed, feigning terror and holding her arms up in front of her face.

The child growled, "Argh!" and raised his arms toward Mariah, hands opened wide, fingers spread apart and flexed. Mariah growled back and he giggled.

"Hi. I'm a vampire."

"I can see that. Are your parents home?"

"Trevor, I told you not to answer the door," a teenaged girl said as she reached the door. She turned Trevor down the hall, "go wash that mess off your face and get ready for lunch."

"Awe, Mom."

The child turned left at a doorway halfway down the hall, and disappeared from sight.

"Hi. Mariah?"

"Yes."

"I'm Tawnie, Tina's mother. Please come in. We've been

expecting you."

"Oh," Mariah said in surprise. "You look so young I thought you were Tina's older sister." Tawnie was approximately five foot two inches tall. She had shoulder length, straight, dark-blonde hair, and freckles on her clear, fair skin. Her eyes were an almost Loden green—a bright, glittering contrast to her hair color. Her teeth were perfectly straight, and a brilliant white, and she had a figure that most women would die for. She wore stretch yoga pants and a form fitting, long-sleeved stretch knit yoga shirt which are unforgiving if you have an ounce of unwanted fat on your body—and Tawnie clearly did not. She looked all of sixteen years old—certainly not old enough to be the mother of a fourteen year old girl.

She smiled sweetly. "Thanks. I hear that all the time. Come on in, Gayle will join us in a moment."

Mariah stepped into a short hall with an opening to her left leading to another parallel hallway where Trevor disappeared earlier. Walking passed the opening, she spied Trevor standing on a stool at the bathroom sink directly across the hall from her, water running, and making faces at himself in the mirror.

"Trevor! Wash! Now! Don't make me come in there and wash your face for you," Tawnie admonished her son as she passed. She stepped around the side of the couch and motioned for Mariah to sit. "Would you like something to drink?"

"No. Thank you. I'm sorry if I'm interrupting your lunch plans."

"You're not. We were expecting you."

From what Mariah saw so far, a brown and grey swirled, slate-tile covered the floor throughout the house. The living room they entered was odd shaped, and a large cream colored area rug, six foot by eight foot, covered the floor in the middle of the room. The light tan sectional couch, matching chaise lounger, and end tables arranged around the edges of the rug were worn, but clean. Mariah sat on the end of the couch, and noticed a brick fireplace built into the corner to her right.

Across the room, the wall opened up to the dining room, a breakfast bar separating it from the kitchen around the corner. Tawnie sat on the edge of the chaise lounger, across from Mariah.

"Do you mind if I record our conversation?" Mariah pulled the recorder out of her purse.

"No. Not if it helps."

Mariah set the recorder on the floor at her feet.

"Hi," a man said behind her. She turned and saw a short, squat, slightly overweight, bald man with gold wire rimmed glasses on a round face. She stood and extended her hand.

"Hi. I'm Mariah Jeffries."

He shook her hand while saying, "I'm Gayle Webb. I hope I haven't kept you waiting. I just got in from work and wanted to change my clothes—get a little more comfortable."

"Not at all. I just got here. Tawnie …" interrupting herself, she turned to Tawnie. "Do you mind if I call you by your first name?"

"Not at all. Of course you can call me Tawnie."

Mariah returned her gaze back to Gayle and continued, "Tawnie doesn't mind if I record our conversation. Do you? It helps me when I type up my notes."

"No. I don't mind. I'm going to grab a beer. You want one?"

"No. Thank you."

Gayle looked at Tawnie. "Hon? You want something?"

"No Gayle. Please come and sit down." When he walked into the kitchen, Tawnie rolled her eyes. "He's been like this since Tina went missing. He can't sit still, bouncing from one thing to another—he goes to work every day—avoids talking about her or her disappearance. You probably won't get much out of him."

Mariah nodded. "We'll do the best we can. Avoidance is his way of handling the stress. We all manage it in different ways."

Gayle came back into the room and took a seat next to Tawnie. He placed his left hand on her knee and took a big

172

swig from his can of Bud Light. "How can we help you find our girl?"

Mariah went over much of the same with the Webbs as she did with Duskie's parents and then asked if she could examine Tina's room. Tawnie took her to the little hallway off the entryway where they turned right and went straight down the hall to the bedroom at the end.

"Thank you. I'm looking for any clues to her personality and where she was emotionally."

"No problem. Go ahead." Tawnie leaned up against the door jam, crossed her arms over her chest, her right foot in front of her left ankle, toe supported on the floor. It was clear Tawnie intended to stay and supervise.

Mariah walked into the middle of the room and turned around slowly, taking in everything she could. It, too, was neat and clean—a place for everything and everything in its place. Unlike Duskie's room, this room had been recently dusted and vacuumed. Mariah smelled lemon scented dusting spray and the vacuum cleaner tracks were still visible in the carpet.

"Tawnie, did you pick up and clean the room since your daughter's disappearance or is she always this neat and clean?"

Standing erect she asked, "Why? The police didn't say I couldn't clean or touch anything? Did I do something wrong?"

"Of course not—it would just be helpful for me to understand how neat and orderly Tina kept things, or if she's messy. If she's messy, what kind of messy is she?"

"Oh. The day after she went missing I came in here and started looking at her things, missing her, and thinking about her. I had to do something to keep from going crazy, so I started cleaning." Tawnie's voice rose as her agitation grew.

"I cleaned everything and went through everything, looking for a clue to where she might be. I didn't want to believe she'd been kidnapped. I thought the police must be right, maybe she ran away or something. The police thought she was a runaway—at first, before the next girl went missing, they thought she just ran away. But now ..." Her composure shattered and she cried out, "Oh my God."

Gayle showed up behind Tawnie. "What's going on here?"

"I cleaned," Tawnie wailed as she turned into Gayle's arms. He wrapped his arms around her, and held her head to his chest as he glared at Mariah.

"It's okay. You didn't hurt anything by cleaning. Don't worry about it." Mariah glanced at Gayle before she turned her attention to the room, giving Tawnie time to compose herself.

"I'm sorry," Tawnie said, sniffling and pushing out of Gayle's embrace. "I'm so lost without her and I'm sick with worry."

Gayle dropped his arms and Tawnie patted him on the chest. "I'm fine, Gayle." She wiped her eyes with her fingertips.

He nodded at her. "I'm going out to the garage, call me if you need me."

When Mariah turned back to the doorway, Tawnie was standing alone. "Is there any particular reason you thought she ran away? Did y'all argue or something?

"No. The police thought she was another runaway, so I got to wondering. If she was, there must be a reason. Kids don't run away from home without a reason. Tina's not mistreated. She's a good girl and she knows she is loved and we would do anything to keep her safe, so why? It didn't make sense, but I didn't want to think someone kidnapped her, either."

"I'll do everything I can to bring her and the rest of them back." Mariah looked back into the room.

"She's dead, you know."

"What?" Mariah spun back around to Tawnie, taken by surprise with the matter-of-fact statement. "What do you mean?"

"She's been gone for weeks. She must be dead. They're not asking for ransoms or anything. Some serial killer is grabbing our … grabbing our girls and … and doing … Oh, God. Who knows what before killing them." Tawnie was sobbing.

Mariah gave the woman a few minutes. When Tawnie had settled down, Mariah took a deep breath before replying. "That is a possibility, Tawnie. I won't lie to you. However, we don't have any evidence yet to indicate any of the girls are dead. Try to think positive thoughts—and wait until there's evidence before you start thinking the worst has happened. Put positive energy out there that she's coming home."

Tawnie nodded her head, tears running down her face.

"Are you going to find my sister?" Trevor asked, peaking his make-up smeared face around Tawnie.

"I'm going to try. You have to be a good boy and take care of your mom. She needs your help around the house now more than ever before. Can you be strong and help her?"

"Yes. I miss my sister, even if she likes to boss me around."

"Do you have any idea where she might have gone, Trevor?"

"Nu uh." he said, shaking his head no. Tawnie and Trevor led Mariah down the hall and back to the living room.

Gayle stood at the dining room table, going through the mail when Tawnie and Mariah walked back into the living room. "Did you find anything?"

"No. I didn't expect to find anything. I'm sure the police and FBI took anything that might give a lead. I wanted to get a feel for her personality. How organized was she?"

Gayle turned from the table toward Mariah, shook his head, a slow, easy smile spreading across his face. "She was a mess—funny, smart, messy ... but organized. She was always on the go. ... I miss her."

"I'm sure you do. Can either of you think of anyone who would want to hurt her?"

"No. Not really." Gayle sighed and turned his back to Mariah.

Mariah's glance turned to Tawnie. "You? Anything? Even the slightest suspicion of someone could warrant a closer look."

"Honest. We don't have a clue. I wish I knew, but I

don't."

"Thank you. If you think of anything, please give me a call. Day or night. It doesn't matter."

Gayle looked down at the table, reached for an envelope, but then tapped his fingertips on the table top. "We will."

He raised his eyes to Mariah, smiled and walked to the living room. "Thanks for everything you're doing. We'll call if anything else comes up."

Mariah shook hands with Gayle and then Tawnie. "Thank you for your time," she said and headed for the front door.

"She liked to run in the old forest. Daddy didn't like her going there, but she liked it. Maybe she went in secret and fell … and, and … hurt herself. Did you check the old forest?" Trevor asked, his bottom lip trembling and tears pooling in his eyes.

Mariah turned back to the room. "The old forest? Where's that?"

He shrugged his shoulders and said, "I dun know. I heard her telling someone on the phone one day."

"Who was she talking to?"

"Just one a her friends."

"How long ago was that?"

He raised his shoulders again, head tilted, and closed his eyes. "Ummm, don't remember. A while ago." He started to cry. "I should have told daddy. She's gone and it's my fault."

Tawnie bent down and turned Trevor to face her. "No, son. None of this is your fault." She pulled him into her arms and they both cried in the tight embrace.

Mariah turned to Gayle. "Did you tell the police about this?"

Gayle shook his head no. "I didn't know she still went out there. I told her a good six months ago she couldn't go to The Old Forest anymore. I felt it was too secluded."

"Where's the Old Forest?"

"The formal name is Forest Park, some people refer to it as the 11-hundred acre Park or The Old Forest Park. Take Highway 238 West out of downtown Jacksonville for about a

176

mile and turn right on Reservoir Road. At the kiosk, you'll find trail maps."

"Thanks, I'll look into it and contact you if I find anything."

"We should put together a search party. I'll go too," he said, excitement lacing his voice.

"Honestly, Gayle. If it were only her missing, I would consider it a likely possibility, but not with four girls missing and all at different times. It would be too much of a coincidence. Don't you see?"

His enthusiasm dissipated as quickly as it arose. For a moment he hoped and believed there was something he could do to bring his little girl home.

"I'm sorry. How was she getting all the way out to the park?"

Gayle walked to the couch and sat, braced his elbows on his knees, and dropped his head in his hands. He took a deep breath in. With the exhalation he said, "Well, her boyfriend. Tucker would come pick her up and they would go out there to run. I didn't like it and I told her she couldn't go anymore. If she wanted to see this boy, he would have to come spend time with her here, at the house, so we could get to know him. Last I heard, he stopped seeing her months ago."

"Do you have Tucker's address and phone number? I'd like to talk to him."

"No. I never even got to meet the kid. She met him at a basketball tournament. Supposedly, he lives in Jacksonville and is sixteen years old. She was too young to have a boyfriend anyway, and I told her that. She didn't like it, but she was only fourteen."

"Tawnie, did you ever meet him?"

"I think so. I meet so many random kids at those tournaments. I don't remember for sure. I might recognize him if someone introduced me to him again, but I couldn't describe him or even put his name to a picture of him."

"Alright. That's something else I'll check out. Thank you. And Trevor, thank you for speaking up. You were very brave and the information might help bring your sister home. I'll let y'all know if I turn up anything."

Mariah left the Webb's home and headed for Velia's. On the drive, she munched on an apple and sipped water from the stainless steel bottle she kept in the car.

SATURDAY P.M.

"What do you think?" Mariah asked Velia.

"I believe you're strong enough. You're ready to face whatever it is that's been haunting you. But, it's not about what I think. What do you think?"

"The case is accelerating, and I'm tired, Velia. I want this over and I'm determined to bring it to a rapid conclusion. I think I can do that with your help. So, if you believe I'm ready, and since I believe I'm determined enough … let's do it."

"Okay. You'll go back to where you left off with Caroline's life and continue to the end of her life or the end of the significance of her lifetime."

Mariah, sitting on the white, leather massage table nodded.

"Let's get started then. Lie back."

Mariah stretched out on the table and closed her eyes.

"Take a deep breath and let yourself relax."

"I'm going to tell Daniel that I'm his mother and take him to see Joseph, his real father. I'm eighteen now and you can't stop me," I tell Mother.

"Oh, yes I can! Legally, he is our son. If you ever tell him that you gave birth to him, your father and I will

cut you off. You'll never see him ... or us again. I will not allow you to ruin our boy's life!"

"Mother!" I shriek.

"No! You heard me," she yells back. An almost three year old Daniel waddles to the foot of the stairs and shouts up at us.

"Mama!" He raises his hands to us.

Mother turns and starts down the stairs. "Coming Daniel." He frowns at her, then spies me trying to hold back my tears. His little face puckers and he begins to cry, calling out, "Ca-rine."

"I love him, and he loves me. Can't you see that?" Running half way down the stairs to catch up to Mother, I hiss in her ear, "Why shouldn't he know I'm his mother and not his big sister?"

Without pausing, Mother continues down the stairs and picks up Daniel. She turns and glares at me. "Let me put him down for his nap. Then we'll talk."

I go back upstairs to my room and pace, waiting for Mother to call me.

When mother comes to my door, she asks me to follow her downstairs where we can talk without waking Daniel.

Downstairs in the parlor, I ask her again, "Why Mother. Why shouldn't he know I'm his mother and not his sister?"

"Because you'll have to tell him about his father, the savage, and the world will find out he is a half-breed. His life ... his future, will be ruined. Is that what you want for him?"

"No, but ..."

"But nothing. Do you think those savages will take Daniel in and love him like we do? No! They will ostracize him, just as they do the Kincaid kid. He's nothing more than a beggar on the street. Is that what you want for Daniel?"

"No."

I was deeply hurt when they had taken Daniel from me after his birth, but I knew they were trying to protect us both.

The poor Kincaid boy, only ten years old, has had a rough life. The boy's mother was only a few years older than me when she got pregnant, but everyone in town knew about her pregnancy and who the boy's father was. She never left the house except to go to church with her family after the birth. When she did go to church, she was ignored, scorned, and snickered about behind her back.

I tried to be friendly and speak to her a few times but I was always chastised by mother. "Shouldn't associate with her, she's an unwed mother. And worse, she is known to have been dallying with the savages," my mother would say. "Let that be a lesson to you, Caroline."

Becky Kincaid took her own life a year after her child was born. Because of that, I was grateful for my parents protecting my reputation and going to the trouble of concealing my pregnancy and Daniel's lineage. Things are different now, and I'm older.

The Kincaid boy—no one knows his name because his mother's family calls him 'boy', is badly treated and not allowed to go to school because the town's people don't want their children exposed to a half-breed. His mother's family, people from town, curse the child and berate him daily in public and, no doubt, in private too. His grandfather has been seen hitting the boy and one time, kicking him so hard it knocked him to the ground because he didn't move fast enough when they were leaving the general store.

"Joseph told me the boy's father would have taken him in to love and raise with the help of his extended family, but the Kincaids wouldn't allow it. Now his father, a man who was once one of Joseph's closest friends, is a drunkard. The girl he loved and who had given birth to their child bent to her parent's will and gave up her child to them. The Kincaids won't have anything to do with the boy's father or allow him to raise his child. That little boy is kept away from a man who would love him and raise him, teaching the boy skills and traditions. Instead he is mistreated by a family who hates and resents him. They blame him for their daughter's death."

"Caroline, we are not mistreating Daniel. We love him and as far as he, and everyone else knows, we are his parents. Why do you want to take that away from him and put him in harms way? You're just being selfish. Think about what's best for Daniel."

"That won't happen to us. I'm older now and Joseph assured me that Daniel will be much loved and accepted by his people, if not my own. My reputation in the community doesn't matter to me anymore because I'm going to marry Joseph anyway."

"No."

"Yes, Mother. I'll be shunned for that alone, but it doesn't matter. I just want my baby with me. We can love him and care for him."

"If you want to throw away your life, then that's your choice, but I will not allow you to destroy his. Daniel is already loved and cared for, and he has the best of everything."

"Joseph's family will adore Daniel and love him too. Life will be different for him from what the Kincaid boy endures. I hope for Daniel to have the best of both worlds. Not just what you and Father can give him."

"Your father and I knew you were seeing him again—that, Joseph!" she said with utter disdain. "I had to stop your father from kicking you out of the house just the other day. He is losing patience with you, Caroline. If you continue to spend time with Joseph, you will be treated no better than Becky Kincaid. People talk and they are starting to talk about you. Becky had a home and family she cared enough about to stay away from her savage lover. We've tried to help you understand the severity of your choices. If you don't stop, you won't have a family or a home. As hard as we've tried to prevent it, there are consequences for your choices that you could suffer, but Daniel will not suffer with you." She started sobbing. "Please, stop this nonsense Caroline, before it gets out of hand."

"I am done with this," I declare with calm resolve. "There is no way I am going to spend another winter away from Joseph and I am not going to give up my son either. I will never be a problem for you or Father again. I am going to marry Joseph. We will raise our son together." I push past her to the stairs.

"Come back here," she yells.

"Daniel!" As soon as I get his name out of my mouth, mother grabs my arm, spins me around, and slaps me hard across the face. Stunned at first, my anger soon rises.

A groggy Daniel calls me.

"Ca-rine," he cries, and I push mother away and dart up the stairs. Mother grabs at me as she rushes up from behind. She hooks my ankle as I reach the landing and trips me. While I'm trying to stand, she pushes me down and rushes ahead of me to block my path to Daniel's bedroom. Daniel is still crying out for me.

"Get out," my mother hisses at me. "Leave and don't come back," she shouts over her shoulder as she goes into Daniels room and scoops him up into her arms. I follow her into his room and reach for him, but she slaps my hands away and yells, "Leave him alone! Go to your Indian and his filthy people. Leave us alone."

"Come to me, Daniel," I say to him holding my arms out. He reaches for me, but mother turns his head away and Daniel struggles with her and yells, "Ca-rine".

"Get out, Caroline. Just leave this room." She lays Daniel on the bed and turns to me, pushing me toward the doorway. "If you're going to stay here, you must follow the rules. If you can't, we can send you to Aunt Bee's. There is an excellent school there and a nice social life for young people. You could find a nice man to marry and start your own family, but you cannot take Daniel. If that choice doesn't appeal to you, then leave. Know however, if you leave, you will leave without Daniel."

Tears sting my eyes as I gaze past her to Daniel who is sitting up on the bed, crying and watching us.

"Ca-rine" he cries plaintively, still reaching for me. Mother pushes me back to the landing where I turn from her and run down the stairs, grab a wool shawl from the hook, and continue out the front door into the yard, mother chasing me.

"Come inside, Caroline. It's freezing out here," she yells to me across the yard. "You can think about it inside. A storm is coming."

Tears flood my eyes as I yell to her, "I'll be back for my son." I turn and run away from my childhood home and down the road toward mine and Joseph's meeting tree.

"Caroline, come back. You'll freeze. CA-RO-LINE ..." Her voice is carried away on the rising wind as I continue to run down the trail.

Joseph once told me our meeting tree is about a two mile walk from my house and another three miles from the tree to his village. I've never been there before, but I need Joseph's help. He will come back with me to get our son.

It is cold for mid September, I think as I slow to a walk. In a rage, I didn't think of my footwear—I am still in my slippers, and the wool shawl only covers my shoulders against the blustering wind.

The wind is blowing harder now, and approaching 'our' tree, sleet starts to fall. *If I don't make it to the village soon, I will freeze to death.* I gather the shawl around me, bend my head into the wet wind and run.

The stinging sleet and bits of snow swirling around me, blind me beyond a foot in front of my feet.

I've heard of early storms like this but they are uncommon here in Nova Scotia. My throat is getting raw from gasping in the frigid air and because of the limited visibility, I stumble and fall. I am so cold now, my feet and hands frozen and numb. I want to just lay here and let the snow cover me, but I think of Joseph and how desperately I want to be in his arms and spend my life with him. Remembering something Joseph told me—about a time he was caught in a blizzard—I look for an evergreen bush. I spy one on the side of the trail and crawl to it where I find a large tuft of dried grass protected from the bush. I begin to pull it up and stuff it into my slippers. I search further and find an evergreen tree with more dried grass and stuff the sleeves of my dress. I pull the shawl up over my head, crossing the ends over my chest and pull my hands up into the grass filled sleeves of my dress to protect them from the harsh cold. I clasp my arms across my chest holding the shawl on and tucking my covered hands into my armpits before continue on, my face and lips going numb from the cold wind.

The sleet turns to heavy, wet snowflakes by the time I stumble into the edge of the village and fall against the door of the first wigwam I come to, collapsing as I knock.

I wake up covered in furs on the floor by a warm fire and can't remember, at first, where I am or how I got there. When I do, I bolt upright, the furs falling from my bare skin. I am shocked to find I am completely naked and glance around the small wigwam. A hunched old woman is sitting on the floor near the far corner and bending over something, her back to me.

"You were frozen half to death out there. I brought you in and removed all your wet, frozen clothing so you would warm back up before your skin started to die," she tells me as she stands with the grace of a ballerina, and turns around to face me.

She takes a wooden bowl and scoops out a liquid from the kettle hanging over the fire. "Here. Drink this. Be careful, it is very hot, but it will help you feel better."

"Thank you." I take a tentative sip of the pungent smelling liquid and my face puckers as my nose and sinuses tingle. "Ewe, what is this?"

"Medicine made from herbs and melted snow. Drink it all. You need the liquid, and the herbs will help you heal from the cold. You were not dressed very warm. Where did you learn to use the dry grass? Most whites don't know to do that."

I drink the rest of the liquid down as quickly as possible. After the first couple of sips, the pungent flavor doesn't pucker my face anymore. I lean over and put the gourd back on the rock she had taken it from.

"No, I wasn't expecting the storm to hit like that and I was trying to get to Joseph. He's the one who told me about the dry grass. He wants me to go on the migration west with him."

"So you're the girl he loves. You're Caroline?"

"Yes. Is there any way for me to reach him today?"

"No. Not tonight."

"Night?"

"Yes. The storm is raging and blocking any light from the moon. Maybe tomorrow it will be safe for you to go outside, but for now, you must stay here with me."

"I have to get to Joseph."

"What's the rush? The People will not leave for weeks."

The old woman sits down next to me on the furs and takes my hands, turning them over and looking at them. She starts poking my fingertips with a sharp piece of stiff straw.

"Do you feel this?" she asks with each poke while I try to jerk my hand away.

"Yes," I tell her each time.

"Let me see your feet," she demands as she deftly pushes the furs away from me. In surprise and modesty, I yelp and try to pull the furs back to cover my nakedness but she quickly, yet gently, grabs my left ankle and pulls it into her lap, spreading my legs wide and exposing everything. I reach down to cover my most private parts, but she doesn't seem to notice or care.

She checks out my foot by poking my toes and different parts of the foot with her straw poker. With each poke she asks me the same question and I respond by answering "yes". I try to pull my foot away with each poke, but she holds fast.

After enduring several more pokes, I cry out in frustration. "What are you doing?"

"I'm checking to make sure your blood is flowing back into your feet and the skin isn't dying." She grabs my right ankle and repeats the process.

"Am I ... am I alright?"

"Do you hurt anywhere? Any stinging or burning—maybe some tingling?"

"No. I feel quite fine. I'm not going to die, am I?"

"You'll be fine." She stands from the furs in one easy, smooth motion, and hands me a buckskin robe she takes from a hook on the wall behind me.

"Thank you." I cover myself with the robe. "When can I go to Joseph?"

"Ah." She grunts as she goes back to the basket she was weaving and sits facing me.

I watch her in the dancing firelight. She looks ancient, but she moves as fluidly as an athlete. Her hair is a solid drape of pure silver strands. Her face and her hands are a rich, dark brown, etched with wrinkles. Her dark brown eyes dart from her basket and then to me as her fingers fly, weaving the strands in and out.

"I am the healer for my people, and I live on the outskirts of the village. Joseph lives with his family at the other end of the village. It is too dangerous for you to go outside right now. You wouldn't be able to find your way in the blowing snow, and would freeze to death."

"But I must reach Joseph. When can I leave?"

I realize I'm whining and behaving like an ungrateful child. I should be satisfied I'm safe and warm—near Joseph and safe from the raging storm.

"Joseph isn't going anywhere. You will see him when the storm passes. Maybe tomorrow."

I don't respond and she bends to her weaving. After a few moments, she raises her eyes to me. "You have been with child. Where is Joseph's babe?"

I am standing and putting the robe on with my back to her when she asks that. Heat rises in my body as I blush all over. I try to answer her.

"I uh, um ... I um. Baby?"

"Young child. Yes. Did you drop the child in the storm? If you did, it is dead now," she tells me—her tone, matter-of-fact.

"No! Oh, my. No. Daniel wasn't with me." I turn toward her.

"But you have had a child. Did it die at birth?"

"No." I start to cry. "No. My baby didn't die. He is with my parents."

The old woman gets up and comes to me. She takes me into her arms. "Tell me everything."

With my head on her boney shoulder, I shake my head no and tell her in a choked voice, "I can't. I can't tell anyone."

"You must tell me. I keep many secrets when it is necessary, but you must let me help you. Something happened and that is why you came here in the storm. I am right. Yes?"

"Yes."

"Sit. Drink more juice. We will talk."

I drink the herb juice she hands me. After swallowing the last of it, I shudder from the pungency. The old woman takes the gourd from me and refills it.

"Again."

My shoulders sag and I look at the offering with disdain, but I can't refuse it after she saved my life. I take the gourd and empty it. By now I can detect a sweetness to it that I didn't taste before. She sits with impeccable grace next to me on the furs, and pats my knee.

"My name, in your language, is Orneda. You can call me Orneda. I am the healer to my people. I help with the birthing of babies. I heal the sick or make the dying more comfortable before they pass over. I give spiritual guidance to my people when the counsel asks, and I keep many secrets. Joseph's mother is my sister and I love Joseph as I love my own sons. You can trust me not to tell anything that is not good for him or for my people. When you tell me your story, I will advise you as to what is best for you and for Joseph and the child."

I gaze into her gentle brown eyes, the depths of which are like pools of liquid mud—hinting at warmth and comfort. Closing my eyes, I take a slow, deep breath before I start to talk.

"I got pregnant. His name is Daniel and Joseph is his father. When my parents found out I was spending time with Joseph, they forbade it. I couldn't stop seeing him. We couldn't stop seeing each other. I know we're young—well, I'm younger than Joseph, but we love each other. So we saw each other in secret, meeting each other whenever we could. Eventually we became ... intimate. It was the day after my fourteenth birthday. Oh, I was scared to death the first time, but Joseph was wonderful. He was so gentle with me. We hadn't been intimate very often when my monthly curse stopped coming and I was sick in the mornings. That's when mother started questioning me and determined that I was with child. They took me away to my Aunt Beatrice's house in

Plymouth Massachusetts to give birth so no one would know I got pregnant out of wedlock. That is a terrible disgrace with my people. My mother would not allow me to name him Joseph, like I wanted to. My mother said we were going to tell everyone she was the one who gave birth to him and because it was a difficult pregnancy, I went with her to my Aunt Bee's house to help. She and Father were going to name him and raise him as their own child. She said I could help raise him, but only as his big sister and he is never to know I am really his mother or that his father is a ..." I pause, not wanting to use the term my mother used. "an ... Indian."

Taking another deep breath, I look at her. "She said if anyone knew he was a half-breed, he would be abandoned by my people and by Joseph's people—he wouldn't fit in anywhere and his life would be ruined."

"Does Joseph know he has a child?"

"I didn't tell him. I was afraid to tell anyone for fear what my mother predicted would come true. I was afraid of being ridiculed and ostracized by my own people. I was afraid of other men thinking I was cheap and ... and ... thinking they could have their way with me, so I didn't tell anyone. I tried to stay away from Joseph because my parents insisted, and I was afraid of what they would do if I went against their wishes again. They threatened to kick me out into the street and I had no where to go and I wouldn't be allowed near my baby either." Tears well up in my eyes and I blink furiously to try to dispel them.

"After Joseph got back from the western migration, we were together again and he knew. I was afraid Joseph would be furious with me for being such a coward so I didn't tell him, but he guessed."

"Yes. There are changes to a woman's body after giving birth. It wouldn't have been hard for him to realize once you were intimate again."

"He was so angry. Oh, not at me—but at my parents. What they did was wrong, he said. He wants his son and he asked me to bring Daniel and come to the village so we could do the migration west together and not come back. When I told my mother I was going to tell Daniel I am his mother, she was furious and told me I couldn't—that I can't take my son, and if I saw Joseph again, my father would kick me out of the house.

"I can't go back there except to get Daniel. Once Joseph and I have Daniel with us, I'll never go back there, but I'll never see my parents again either."

Accepting the terrible loss of family, I can no longer contain the pain and wail in grief. Orneda wraps her arms around me and holds me while I sob to exhaustion. When the sobbing subsides, she lets go of me and I sink to the furs and curl up in the fetal position. Orneda pulls the furs up around me

"Sleep, Child." My eyes are already closed but I hear her stand and move around by the fire as I drift off to sleep.

A gentle shake of my shoulder wakes me. Orneda is squatted down next to me holding the gourd out for me to drink from.

"Drink this."

I take the gourd and sip from it.

"You were not sleeping well. This will help you to rest. We will talk more in the morning. Sleep now." She takes the gourd from me when I drain it, and sets it down next to the fire.

I roll over and close my eyes, drifting off to peaceful sleep.

Orneda is sitting across the room, cross legged, weaving her basket when I wake. "Did you sleep well?"

"Yes. Good morning." I push my limp, stringy hair out of my face. "Is the storm over?"

"Yes. It's cold, but the sun is shining."

"Oh, wonderful." Standing I search the small room for my slippers. "Now I can go to Joseph."

"No. We must talk first. I have been meditating on the situation." She puts the basket down beside her and stands. She crosses to a pot on the fire and spoons maize mixed with berries into a wooden bowl and hands it to me. "Eat first. We will talk when you're finished."

Sitting back down at her basket, she works in silence while I eat. The hot cereal is delicious and I realize how hungry I am. I finish eating and start to put the wooden bowl down when my stomach lets out a loud rumble. Orneda looks up and smiles. "There is more if you want it."

I scoop out another helping. "Would you like some?".

"No. I ate while you were sleeping."

We sit in quiet contemplation until I finish eating.

"Where do I wash this out?"

"Leave it by the fire and I will take care of it when you go to Joseph."

Finally! I think. "He will go with me to my parents home and we will get Daniel. You will love him, Orneda. He's such a sweet baby and looks so much like Joseph."

"First we must talk. I have been meditating and I decided you should leave Daniel with your parents."

"No. I ..."

"My people are not afforded the benefits of the white people. Daniel has people who will love him and care for him. He is well established in their world. You don't worry for his safety, do you?"

"No, but ..."

"He doesn't know your mother isn't his mother. Other people don't know that either, so he can grow up with opportunities he would never have if you bring him here. It is the best thing for him. It will be hard for you if you stay with my people and it would be hard for Joseph.

But real love is doing what is best for the other person and not what we selfishly want for ourselves."

Tears stream down my face as I stand looking at her. "But he's my baby. A good mother wouldn't leave without her baby, and I can't live without Joseph. I love them both."

"A good mother will do what is best for her child, even if that means giving the child up so he will have a better future."

"Joseph will never go for this. He wants his son."

"I will talk to Joseph. We will keep this between the three of us to protect Daniel."

Sinking to the furs, I weep in defeat.

Leaving the basket on the floor, Orneda stands and walks to me.

"The men of our family pass ancient talents to their female children. Daniel will carry that heritage to any female offspring he fathers. His sons will pass that heritage to their daughters and so on." She pats me on the back. "He may never know of his true heritage on Joseph's side, but he will still pass on the special traits a Medicine Woman carries."

"What does that mean?"

"Even though those offspring will not be taught how to use those talents ... one day in the far future a Medicine Woman will be born. She will receive training without knowing about her inherent talents. As long as she is taught to face her fears, she will come to learn of her talents and become a powerful leader."

"You see this for Daniel's offspring?"

"Yes."

"What about other children Joseph and I have?"

Orneda smiles. "They will be raised knowing of their heritage ... and their talents."

I lay my head down, weary from the emotional revelations shared and given. "Thank you, Orneda."

Orneda goes back to her basket weaving. I lose track of time, but I am brought out of my numbed grief by a knock at the door.

"Come in," Orneda calls out.

The door opens and I hear the person stomping their feet to rid the snow from their shoes and brushing the snow from their coat.

"I'm here to check on you, Auntie." Joseph's voice startles me out of my reverie. I look up as he steps inside and closes the door, and I gasp at the sight of him. Surprise spreads across his countenance when he sees me. He rushes to me, kneels and embraces me.

"Caroline. What are you doing here? Where is Daniel?"

"I can't ..."

"Why are you crying?"

"Daniel," is all I can say.

"We have a lot to talk about," Orneda says getting up and walking over to us.

"What happened to Daniel?" Joseph asks, fear tingeing his voice.

"We have to leave him with my parents."

"What? No!" Joseph stands and turns to Orneda.

"It is best," she tells him.

Everything is fading from my view and I am floating in nothingness.

I am walking arm in arm with Joseph in the meadow. It is summertime and I am large with child. Joseph turns to me. "They think you are dead—that you froze to death in that blizzard. They didn't realize you made it to our village and stayed with us until we moved west."

"Everyone thinks I'm dead?"

"Yes. Your parents were coming out of church with Daniel. He is getting big."

"Did you speak to him?"

"I started to cross the street to them, but your parents glared at me. I realized it would not be wise. Daniel didn't pay any attention to me, but why would he?"

"I'm so sorry. I ruined things when I listened to my parents. I made such terrible choices."

"You were barely more than a child. There wasn't much choice to make."

"I wish you had an opportunity to know him and for him to know you."

Everything is fading from my view and I am floating in nothingness.

I am walking up to my parents house, wearing the traditional Mi'kmaq tunic and long skirt. My mother is hanging clothes on the line and I walk toward her.

"Mother?" I approach her.

Mother turns and her hands fly to her mouth in surprise.

"Caroline?"

"Yes."

"But you're dead."

"No, mother. I made it to Joseph's village. We're married now."

"You're pregnant."

"Yes. We are very happy."

Her eyes narrow and her countenance hardens. "You can't have Daniel."

"We agreed Daniel's future would be better if he remains your son, but I would like to see him ... as his sister."

Just then, Daniel comes around the side of the house. "Ma?"

"Come here, Daniel. There is someone here ..." Daniel walks to her side and his eyes widen when he recognizes me.

"Ca-rine!" he shouts and runs to me. "I miss you."

"I miss you too."

"Where you been?"

"With my husband, Joseph. I live with his people in their village."

"Oh. You mean Indians?"

"Yes. The Mi'kmaq people. They are my people now."

Everything is fading from my view and I am floating in nothingness.

I am sitting at a long table with many people around me, Joseph is at my side and there is a babe suckling at my breast.

Across the room there are children laughing and playing while the adults at the table are talking.

"We must go now. Good night." Joseph tells the group as he stands from the table and helps me up. "Come children." Two little ones part from the group of children and run to us, shouting their goodbyes.

Everything is fading from my view and I am floating in nothingness.

I am approaching my parents home with a new wee one in my arms. I only visit after the birth of each new child so Mother can meet her newest grandchild. Daniel, now eleven years old, opens the door to me.

"Hello Caroline," he says.

"Hi Daniel." I reach to hug him but he pushes away from me and shouts, "No!" He runs to mother who is coming down the hall.

"Daniel, what's wrong?" I ask him.

"You. You left us and ran away. We thought you were dead. And you did it for those Indians. I hate you." I start toward him but mother tells me to stop.

"Leave him alone. You shouldn't come here anymore. He doesn't like the Indian children and we don't encourage him to.

Your father continues to refuse to see you and will not welcome you into our home. We don't want you to come here anymore. You are dead to us now."

"Mother. I'm not dead. I'm the same girl you raised. Why can't you forgive me?"

"We don't want your bad decisions to contaminate Daniel. He's a good boy and has a bright future."

"But, why now ... all of a sudden ... after all these years."

"There's been an incident with Daniel and some of the Indian children. We need it to stop, and that includes you staying away. I'm sorry, but I can't go against your father's wishes and Daniel's needs."

I look at her trying to think of something to say and realize nothing I say will change the situation. I turn around and walk away, tears flowing, but I hold my head up and my back straight as I leave, my new babe asleep in my arms.

Everything is fading from my view and I am floating in nothingness.

Joseph and I are walking down the street in town and Daniel, as a grown man—a wife on his arm and three children following behind, is walking toward us. My heart flutters with joy and I smile. I've kept tabs on him through the years, but never approached him or spoke to him.

"Good day," I tell him, tipping my head in his direction and beaming with pride. He glares at me and says, "Don't talk to me you filthy squaw." Joseph grabs his arm and says, "Don't," but Daniel pushes Joseph to the ground and spits on him. He turns to me. "My sister is dead. She died in a snow storm when I was a little boy.

You might look like her, but you will never be my sister. Don't you ever talk to me or my family again." He shoves his way past me, almost knocking me to the ground.

"Daniel," I sob as he storms away from me, his wife looking over her shoulder and giving me a smug smile.

Joseph stands and takes me into his arms, trying to sooth my broken heart as I try to sooth his. We walk back to our home arm in arm, our heads down not wanting anyone to witness our grief.

Back at home I tell Joseph, "This is all my fault. If I'd been more brave all those years ago, Daniel would be with us. He would be confident in our love for him. It seems like every decision I made since letting my parents take Daniel only made our lives worse."

"That's not true." Joseph puts his arms around me. "You weren't more than a child yourself when Daniel was born. You had little choice about him. If you didn't let fear rule so much of the rest of your life, you would see that. We've had a happy life, haven't we?"

Nodding, Joseph kisses the top of my head and holds me in his arms.

Everything is fading from my view and I am floating in nothingness.

I am standing in Joseph's arms under a tree. It is autumn and the leaves are falling. "Look at me, Caroline." I gaze into his soft brown eyes. The years show on his face and in his graying hair. "You can't continue to live your life in fear. Because you were afraid of your parents, you didn't tell me about Daniel until it was too late. He's been lost to us for a long time. But our son Joseph isn't. Face your fears and let Joseph go with your blessings. He's a man now and he needs to lead his own life. He will come back. You'll never lose him like you lost Daniel."

"But it won't be the same."

Joseph chuckles, "When has anything ever been the same. Life changes with every passing day. Nothing is the same today as it was yesterday, we just have to live with what life brings us."

"I can't lose another of my children. He's going so far away."

"He's going to make a life for himself. He's an excellent tracker and in great demand. He's always wanted to go west—ever since he was a little boy. We must let him go."

Everything is fading from my view and I am floating in nothingness.

I am sitting on the side of the bed and looking at a much older and very sick Joseph.

Joseph wheezes with each painful breath he pulls. "Don't be afraid. Our people will take care of you when I am gone," he manages to say.

"I can't live without you, Joseph. Please don't leave me to live the rest of my life alone."

"I will never leave you alone. Our love is a string that will keep us bound together throughout eternity. All you have to do is think of me and I will be with you," Joseph squeaks out in a weak, raspy voice. "Remember what Auntie Orneda taught you before she went to the Great Spirit—stop being so afraid or your fear will haunt you, even after the grave. Let go and face your fears—all of them. Until you do, they will always chase after you—fear will always haunt you if you don't ..."

Joseph starts to fade away and I heard again his last words, "Until you do, they will always chase after you—fear will always haunt you if you don't let go of it."

Everything is fading from my view and I am floating in nothingness.

"Just relax now." Velia massaged Mariah's temples while they both thought about the revelations.

"It seemed so real. I experienced everything through Caroline's eyes and emotions. Even if it wasn't ever real— even if it was all in my imagination, the message was very clear. '...*You have to let go and face your fears—all of them. Until you do, they will always chase after you—fear will always haunt you if you don't ...*' That's what he said and that's what's been happening to me. Fear has been stalking me ever since the abduction."

Velia continued to massage Mariah's temples and shoulders.

"They were so in love. WE ... we were so in love," Mariah mumbled.

"You were right the first time. They were different people in a different time."

Mariah rose up on her elbows and turned to face Velia. "But Caroline was me and Joseph was Paul. She was my husband's wife and he was very much my husband."

"Caroline was your past life. She was the wife of your past life husband."

Mariah pushed up to a sitting position and stretched to grab her ankles. She smiled. "It kind of goes around in circles, doesn't it?"

"In a manner of speaking, I suppose it does. But, you have to keep your perspective. That was the past. This is the present. Don't confuse the two." Velia eased herself off the stool and stretched her back with a slow, easy arch. "Let's go sit down. My assistant put out a delicious white wine on ice and a tray of fruit with cheese and crackers."

Mariah swung her feet over the side of the massage table, and hopped off. They walked together to the seating area, Velia taking her favorite chair and Mariah sitting across from her. Velia poured them each a glass of wine and leaned back in her chair.

"Do you consider yourself a mother?"

Mariah reached for a grape. "No. I don't have any

children."

"Then why do you consider yourself Joseph's wife?"

"I … we … because he's Paul. They're the same person."

"That's where you're wrong. They're the same soul. Every time we reincarnate, we are a different person. Your soul and Paul's soul were once united in life, in an older world, but neither of you were the same person when you met and married in this life."

"I don't understand."

"Our past lives influence us in our current lives because our souls grow, and learn, and evolve—the same way we grow, and learn, and evolve in our current life through each new experience. You're not the same person today that you were when you were five years old. The memories of the past lives stay with the soul, but the past *life* ceases to exist. Caroline and Joseph ceased to exist when they died, only the soul continued on. Caroline's soul was reborn in you. That doesn't mean that you were Caroline, it means that your soul carries the memories of Caroline's life."

"But isn't it true that the soul stays within certain groups of people … er—certain groups of souls. Those who have been close to you … them … in the past? Am I making any sense?"

Velia sighed. "Yes. You're correct. Look at it this way. The soul with Joseph's memories could have been born into your body. The soul with Caroline's mother or father or Daniel's experiences could have been born into your body. That wouldn't make you any of those people. You are you, not Caroline. Your soul carries the memories of a woman who lived a very long time ago and was in love with a man named Joseph. Caroline was not your husbands wife because she never lived the same time Paul lived. You are not Caroline's husband's wife because you never knew Joseph."

"I understand what you're saying. It's all so convoluted."

"Yes. It can seem that way."

"Does everyone connect as closely with their past life?"

"No. You're unique in the way you actually become your past life entity. I've heard of it before, and know of a woman who regressed like you. It's rare, though."

"Why do you think regression is different for us?"

"I'm not sure. Something to do with your other talents."

Mariah took a sip of her wine. "What other talents?"

Velia gave her a lopsided grin and tilted her head. "Your advanced intuition for starters."

"Okay, I'll give you that. But that's all I've got."

"Your talents are growing. You've displayed some ability as an empath and from what you told me today about your recent dreams, you're becoming a dream clairvoyant."

"Oh."

"When you first came to me, your aura was dark and out of whack, but it's starting to clear up. Reading aura's is one of my natural talents. You have talents you haven't even tapped into yet."

Mariah stared out the large windows to the clear blue sky before asking, "How do you know I have latent talents?"

"I see it in your aura."

"You see all those different "talents" in my aura?" She used her fingers to make quotation marks in the air. "What other talents do I have?"

"Well, your intuitive, empath, and clairvoyant talents we've discussed. I see a capacity within you for others, but I can't tell you what they are. You'll have to discover them on your own."

Mariah nodded and the two women sat for a while in silence, sipping their wine in quiet contemplation.

"Did you learn anything helpful in today's session, Mariah?"

"Yes."

"Do you want to talk about it?"

Mariah puckered her lips and furrowed her brow before answering. "Fear."

"Joseph was telling you fear is haunting you."

"Yes. I never considered myself fearful, and maybe I wasn't until after the attack. I've certainly been fearful ever since that happened. But Velia, how do I let go of fear? It's one thing to know you're afraid and that your fears are haunting you, but how do you let them go?"

"That's what you have to figure out. No one can tell you how to do that. If I could, I would."

Mariah nodded her head and drained the wine in her glass.

"Have some fruit and cheese before you leave."

"Thanks, Velia. How have you been?" Mariah leaned forward and fixed Velia a plate and handed it to her before she fixed her own.

"Oh, I'm fine—good days and bad, like always," Velia answered and accepted the small plate from Mariah. As they ate, they talked about the local vineyards and wineries.

"There's a good band playing at Del Rancho next Friday evening. Would you like to go with me and Grady, Mariah?"

"Grady is your husband?"

"Yes."

"That sounds like fun. Let me see how my investigation goes and I'll call you by Thursday afternoon to let you know."

"Fair enough."

Mariah popped the last grape from her plate into her mouth and stood.

"Well, I better be going."

"Do you want to schedule another appointment?"

"Let me call you. My case is heating up and I'm getting busier by the day."

"Just call me when you need to. I'll work you in."

SATURDAY EVENING

Mariah went back to the Suite to change into her running clothes and pick up Paisley. She grabbed two apples, a sandwich baggie full of mixed nuts, four bottles of water, and some treats for Paisley, all of which she tossed into a backpack. She harnessed Paisley, and called Alexis' home number.

With approval from Twila, Mariah headed over to the Givens' home. When Alexis got in the car, Mariah offered her an apple.

Alexis declined the apple.

"I just ate dinner."

While Mariah munched on some nuts, Alexis gave directions to the dog park. Mariah was surprised at how close the park was to the Suite where she and Paisley was staying.

They pulled into the back of the Dairy Queen on Barnett Road, and parked. Alexis led them across the street and down a long, sloping sidewalk—a concrete wall rising to their right. To their left was a swath of land covered with brush and trees all the way down the slope to the water's edge where the wide 'creek' appeared to run fast and deep. At the bottom of the sloping sidewalk, they had to turn left onto an iron bridge with recessed wooden slats to cross the thirty foot wide span.

It was dark and a soft rumbling growl came from Paisley until Mariah turned on the flashlight attached to Paisley's leash.

Mariah swept the light over the wide, sturdy bridge with guard rails along both sides. The light wasn't strong enough to penetrate past the end of the bridge. With some trepidation from Paisley, they started across the bridge to the Bear Creek Greenway on the other side.

The Bear Creek Dog Park, across the walkway from Bear Creek and the bridge they crossed, had indirect lighting from Barnett road on the south side. Mariah and Alexis walked a short way down the Greenway path and turned right to the entrance of the dog park. There weren't any security lights in this part of the park, which concerned Mariah.

"Are you sure the park is open this late?"

"Sure. I used to come with my friend Bethany all the time before Buster, her Lab, got hit by a car. There's enough light from the Barnett streetlights to keep from being totally in the dark once we are on the track. This part is dark though because of the trees. I forgot to bring a flashlight—I'm glad you brought one."

"Yeah, I keep one on Paisley's leash. I'm glad this dog park, like a lot of others, has the small enclosed area where the dogs can be unleash or leashed up before entering or leaving." Mariah unleashed Paisley before opening the gate to the main park.

As they approached the track area, Mariah was able to turn the flashlight off. Paisley had already wandered off, checking out the new scents. The two women stood at the edge of the track and did their stretches before starting to jog. They kept the pace down while they chatted.

"Tommy called and asked me out today."

"He did? When are you going out with him?"

"We're going to the movies tomorrow if my dad will let me. I haven't had a chance to ask him yet, but I don't think he's going to let me go—because of all this mess with my friends being abducted."

"To be honest, I would be concerned about you going out right now, too. Maybe you can invite Tommy over to your house for dinner and to hang out—let your parents get to know him."

"That sounds so old fashioned. I doubt he would want to."

"He might. If your dad says you can't go out until the disappearances are solved, you might want to explain it to him. If he really likes you, he will want to spend time with you, even if it's at your home with your parents around. Your parents seem cool and it would be good for them to get to know him and see that he will be trustworthy with you."

"Yeah. They are, but …"

Alexis tripped and almost went sprawling in front of Mariah before she caught herself and continued running a few more paces.

"Are you alright?"

"Yes. … No." She hobbled to a stop and bent over at the waist with her hands on her knees. Mariah stopped beside her and put her hand on the girl's back.

"I'm okay. I stepped on a rock and almost twisted my ankle." She raised her right foot as she straightened, and wiggled her foot around. "It's fine, though."

"Maybe we should stop. I don't want you to strain it any further if you did injure your ankle."

"No I'm fine."

"Let's walk then … a little ways, at least, and see how it does."

Alexis nodded.

"You set the pace Alexis, and I'll follow your lead."

They made a couple more laps around the track, Paisley repeatedly joining them and then running off to chase something only she could see or hear. Finally, around the last bend in the track, Paisley came running up from behind, slowed to a trot when she passed, and turned her head back to make sure they were following her.

Mariah whispered to Alexis, "Watch her. She's telling me she's ready to go." Paisley commenced to lead them toward the gate.

Alexis laughed.

"How's your ankle?" Mariah inquired.

"Fine … I think."

"Do you want to stop and do some Tai Chi exercises before we go?"

"What's that?"

"Tai Chi is a type of martial arts. Some people call it 'meditation in motion'. Do you meditate?"

"No. I've never done that either."

"Well, I'm a certified Tai Chi instructor. Do you want to learn a little bit of it?"

"Sure."

"Let's go to the middle of the field then." Mariah turned.

"No." Alexis caught Mariah's arm. "It's too dark to see where we're stepping and some people aren't very good at picking up after their dogs. The light's the best here, is this enough room?"

"It is. When you're good enough that the movements are natural, you can start to meditate while you do the exercises. Let me show you."

Mariah took her stance, closed her eyes, and took a deep cleansing breath. She ran through a series of moves with fluid grace, and when finished, she smiled.

"What do you think?"

"Cool."

Mariah walked Alexis through a simple routine of moves and stretches and they repeated it until Alexis had it down.

"Well, let's call it a night. Ready to go?"

"Yes. My ankle is starting to ache and I think it's swelling."

"Oh no. I'm sorry." Mariah put her hand on Alexis' shoulder. "Let's go to the car and I'll take a look at it. You can lean on me if you need to."

Mariah called Paisley as they headed to the gate. Moving out of the illumination of the street lights, Mariah turned on the little flashlight so they wouldn't walk into anything and hurt themselves. She found Paisley sitting patiently against the fence next to the gate. Mariah put the leash on Paisley, they exited the park, and started back toward the bridge. Before reaching the bridge, a homeless man stepped out of the shadows. "I been watching you two. What was that dance you were doing?"

Mariah stepped between Alexis and the man, giving her Paisley's leash. He was tall, about six foot. Mariah couldn't tell if he was fleshed out or skinny as a rail. He appeared to be wearing layers of clothing and had a backpack slung over his left shoulder.

"We were doing Tai Chi exercises. How are you?"

"It was pretty. Do you have a few coins you could spare? I'm real hungry, Ma'am."

"I'm sorry, but I don't have any money on me. I have an apple and some nuts in the car. Would you like to walk to the car with us and I'll give them to you?"

"Yes Ma'am. That would be real nice."

They crossed the bridge together, Mariah keeping herself between the man and Alexis, as they chatted. He introduced himself as Erick and he said he was a veteran down on his luck. Mariah told him there were places that helped veterans get back on their feet, but he said, "No Ma'am. I'm not taking any charity. I'll leave it out there for those boys and girls who didn't come back in one piece. I'll be fine."

"Well, think about it. Its getting colder out. I don't want you to freeze to death."

"Don't you worry about me, Ma'am." he said as they reached the car. "Our fine Government taught me how to take care of myself."

With the key fob, Mariah unlocked all the doors and told Alexis to get in with Paisley. Stuffing the keys in her front pocket, Mariah opened the driver's door and quickly hit the lock button on the door before grabbing her backpack and the change she kept in a cup holder. She stepped away from the door, pushing it closed, and extracted the snacks and a bottle of water from the backpack. Mariah felt a lot better with Alexis and Paisley in the car and all the doors locked.

"Thank you, Ma'am," Erick said as Mariah put the food and coins in his hand. "God Bless, and you two ladies stay safe. I hear there's been some mischief about toward young women."

"Are you talking about the kidnappings?"

Erick bowed his head and looked at the ground in front of him. "Yes, Ma'am."

"Have you heard anything about who might be responsible?"

"No Ma'am. I've asked around some, but no one seems to know anything. At least, they aren't talking if they do."

"Have you heard about the guy who is saying it's aliens?" Mariah asked with a little laugh.

Erick smiled. "That's old Tango. He's obsessed with alien theories. He's harmless and no one pays much attention to him."

"Tango?"

"Yes Ma'am. Tango Charlie is what he likes to be called. His name's Thomas Charles Tucker. He was a private in the army—got shot in the head and hasn't ever been right since, but he's a good guy. Everyone looks out for him and he looks out for everyone. He's broken up a couple fights and stopped some bullies from picking on people, so people like having him around."

Mariah nodded. "That's good. I figured the police had already talked to him."

"Yes Ma'am."

Mariah reached in her back pocket and pulled out one of her business cards, handing it to Erick. "I've been hired by a private individual to look into the disappearances of the missing girls. If you hear of anything Erick, would you give me a call?"

"Yes, Ma'am. If I hear of anything that might be useful, I'll give you a call."

"Thank you Erick. You stay safe, okay?"

"Yes Ma'am. Don't you go worrying about old Erick. I know how to take care of myself. Thanks for your kindness, ma'am."

With that, he turned and wandered off back toward the park, tossing the apple in the air and catching it like a baseball while whistling a little tune.

On the drive back to the house, Alexis told Mariah how scared she was when Erick stepped out of the dark.

"I thought I was gonna pee my pants," she said with a nervous laugh. "And then you invite him to *walk* with us. Couldn't you *smell* him? Oh my *God*, he stank!"

"Well, you would stink too, if you didn't have a place to bathe on a regular basis. He seemed nice enough." Mariah smiled over at Alexis. "Besides, part of that stink is Miss Paisley. She obviously found something to roll in which she loves to do."

"Yeah, she stinks for sure and so did Erick. But at first, you didn't know he wouldn't go crazy and try to hurt us."

"I know. That's why I put myself between you and him, and gave you Paisley's leash. If he had started anything, I could have taken him."

"Nu uh! He was a big man. I was scared half to death for you. What if he had a gun or a knife?"

"You remember those Tai Chi moves I was teaching you?"

"Yes."

"You keep practicing them. Practice them until the movements become second nature. Those are defensive moves to help you block blows and move easily out of the way of an attacker. I'm a master at several martial arts and I've successfully defended myself and others from attack with nothing more than my hands and feet. I'm also a marksman and keep a gun with me at all times."

"You had a gun on you while we were running?"

"Of course. As long as you're with me, Alexis, it's my responsibility to keep you, and myself safe."

They pulled up in front of her house and Mariah put the car in park.

"Thanks for asking me to run with you. I enjoyed the company."

"Thanks for taking me. I like hanging out with you, Mariah. Will you teach me some more Tai Chi?"

"Yes." Mariah grinned. "I'd be happy to. You have to practice the moves I taught you every day. I'm going to be pretty busy the next couple of days, but I'll call you when I have a break so we can go running again."

Alexis opened the door and got out of the car. Turning and leaning back into the open door, she said "I will. Thanks Mariah. Talk to you later."

"By Alexis. Keep an eye out and stay safe."

"I will." She patted Paisley on the head before she closed the door and ran to her front door letting herself in.

*****

Having bathed Paisley and herself, Mariah collapsed on her bed in exhaustion from the long, emotional day. Sleep evaded her. She couldn't stop thinking about Erick—his compassionate and intelligent dark brown eyes—his long, stringy, jet-black hair, so oily it reflected the moonlight like a mirror.

He looked and smelled homeless, but his eyes were too clear— and knowing! His posture too erect, his gaze direct, his manner friendly and … and … what? Mariah wondered. *…Protective! He was protecting us. As though he wanted to make sure we made it back to the car safe and sound.*

Something about Erick didn't fit the homeless persona he portrayed and Mariah couldn't bring the pieces together to make sense of them.

Something about Erick doesn't jive—not sinister, but what? … Mariah sensed Erick was more than he projected.

She threw the covers off, got out of bed and went to the living room. She sat on the couch with her laptop and started making notes from the days interviews, and her encounter with Erick. She typed until she couldn't think of anything else to write down. Finished, and before closing her laptop, Mariah stared off into empty space trying to remember if she recorded everything she intended to. She dozed off thinking about her notes and the days events when her head flopping forward jarred her back to consciousness. She closed the laptop and went back to bed, Paisley following close behind. The two of them were snuggled together and sound asleep moments later.

I'm in a dark fog bank or a cloud, and I can't see a thing around me. Paisley is barking in the distance and I try calling to her, but no sound comes out of my mouth. I start slapping the side of my thigh with my right hand so she can find me while I start shuffling toward the sound of her barking. I keep my left hand extended in front of me. The fog is thickest around my feet and legs and I can't see where I'm stepping. The fog thins around my hips, and at my waist the darkness starts taking over again. I stop and squat down to the break in the fog, but the darkness follows me down. I continue to slap my thigh, hoping that Paisley would come to me, but she doesn't.

I continue walking again and trip, almost falling. I reach out, but can't find what tripped me up, so I scoot over a step and continue toward Paisley's barking. I try again to call her, but I can't make a sound.

The darkness starts to fade as I move along and I can see a little further than the nose on my face. I stretch my left arm out in front of me and my hand disappears in the fog. Paisley's barking is persistent and I increase my pace, trying to reach her.

A figure emerges from the fog in front of me and I recognize Erick. His countenance is serious and sad. He reaches out toward me and says, "Don't go any further. You'll ruin it. Wait. Just wait!"

The fog starts getting thicker and he is disappearing into it.

"Erick, don't go. Where am I? What do you mean? Ruin what?"

He's gone, but out of the fog comes his voice. "Wait. Just wait!"

I can't wait. Paisley needs me, so I continue on through the thickening fog. I try to call Paisley again, but my voice fails me and I'm confused. Why could I call out to Erick, but not to Paisley?

I'm angry now and I start walking faster, not caring if I run into something. I must find Paisley.

I'm completely engulfed by the fog now. It's like a heavy gauze hanging over me, blinding me. The fog is icy cold, like a fall rain— a gentle mist, except I'm only getting cold and sluggish, not wet. Paisley's barking is fading away and I can't find her. I start to panic and run in wild, blind abandon. I trip and fall on the cold, hard packed dirt. In front of me is Tina's face, pale grey in death. Her empty eyes are staring out at me, her mouth gaping open in a silent scream. A trickle of blood is running from the corner of her mouth, across her teeth and dripping into the dirt beneath her.

"Tina, no." I whisper. I clench my fists and push myself up from the ground. "I'll find who did this to you. I promise!"

I stand in a foggy void of complete nothingness. I can't sense a thing in this place—the cold is gone, the wet is gone, there is no temperature to be aware of, no surfaces to touch, no sounds to listen to and nothing for my vision to detect. I have no idea which way to go, and no bearings to go by, so I stand still and go into the Wu Chi stance, calm my spirit and start my Tai Chi exercises. I am in a void, focused on my breathing and my movements. I keep moving, breathing, focusing. There is no sense of how much time has passed, but I'm getting tired when, finally, the fog clears.

I open my eyes to darkness at the fringes of ambient light that settles around me. Erick walks toward me, the echo of his heel strikes filling the void. Instead of dirty jeans and a down coat with a backpack hanging off one shoulder, he is in fatigues, a rifle hanging over his shoulder. Suddenly he ducks down on one knee, pulling his rifle around—ready to shoot. "Get down," he shouts and waives his left hand down toward the ground. I start to squat and look around to see what he is hiding from. As I turn my back to Erick a shadow flies toward me so fast I can't duck out of the way and I fall backward to the ground.

"Leave me alone!" I shout raising my hands to ward off the attack.

A shadowy form without features leans over me, slowly coming closer and closer. I gasp for breath but it feels like the shadow is sucking the air out of my lungs, and sitting on my chest. Big wet drops of rough moisture rise from the ground, across my cheeks and eyes, and into the suction of the shadow.

Mariah woke with a start, gasping for breath. Paisley who was leaning on Mariah's chest and licking her face to wake her, sat back and barked once when Mariah moved her head and took a gasping, ragged breath. Covered in sweat, her heart pounding, Mariah sat up and reached over to pat Paisley.

"We're okay girl. Just another nightmare." But she wondered, *did I have another nightmare, or was it an intuitive dream?* She didn't want to believe Tina was dead. She cried for the missing girls and for their families. An hour after waking, the anxiety spent, she got up and took a shower, wrapped her hair in a towel, changed the sweaty sheets on her bed and crawled back in, drifting into a restful sleep.

SUNDAY

Mariah slept in the next morning, forgetting she had a nine a.m. appointment with Chelsea Dunn's family in Ashland. She stretched and reached for her cell phone to check the time. As soon as she saw it was 7:30, she remembered the appointment and threw her covers off. Paisley rolled over on her back, stared at Mariah and yawned. Mariah smiled at her and stepped to the closet. She pulled on a pair of sweat pants, her favorite sports bra, a sweat shirt, wool socks, and her insulated hoodie. She pulled on her Nike's, donned her insulated windbreaker, harnessed up Paisley, and took her out for a quick run. At thirty-three degrees and a bit of a breeze, it wasn't too bad for a run. At least she didn't have to contend with the fog from her dream.

Back at the room, she showered, dressed in a clean pair of jeans and a sweater, some wool socks, and her waterproof hiking boots. She fixed herself a cup of coffee and a bowl of oatmeal. When she was finished eating, she put fresh water down for Paisley and filled her food bowl with kibbles. She gave Paisley a treat and headed out for Ashland, forgetting to put Paisley in her crate.

Chelsea Dunn's home, a two story, soft beige with white trim, single family dwelling with an attached two car garage sat about a mile up the side of the hill on the West side of Ashland. Mariah pulled up in front of the garage fifteen minutes after nine, and walked around to the front of the house. 'Ding-dong', she heard emanate from inside the house when she pushed the button beside the door.

A tall, slightly overweight, middle aged woman with short, black hair answered the door.

"Hi" I said. "I'm Mariah Jeffries."

"You're late. I was beginning to think you were going to stand me up. Come on in," she said and stepped back to allow Mariah passage.

"I'm sorry I'm late. This visit with you and your husband is very important to me, I assure you."

"No husband. He left us three years ago. It's just been me and Chelsea since her brother went off to college two years ago. Want some coffee?"

"Yes, please, if it's not too much trouble."

"I wouldn't have offered if it was. Take a seat at the table while I pour you a cup."

Mariah understood some personalities are abrupt and cantankerous by nature, but she wasn't sure if Mrs. Dunn fit into this category or that of a woman reacting to the unprecedented stress in her life. Mariah watched as Mrs. Dunn poured the coffee and walked around the open island separating the kitchen from the dining room. She plopped a full cup down in front of Mariah, the coffee sloshing over the sides.

"I don't have any sweetener in the house. Don't believe in the stuff. No milk or creamer either. That stuff is poison too, so it's black or nothing around here."

"No problem. I appreciate the coffee." Mariah took a sip. "Up until about a year ago, I routinely drank plain Folger's instant coffee. This is an improvement."

"So, Martin said you wanted to talk to me about my only daughter's disappearance. What do you want from me?"

No pussy-footing around with this woman—and she was not going to cut Mariah any slack for being fifteen minutes late either.

"Well, I'm interviewing the families of the missing girls, trying to get a clue as to who is taking them and why."

"Don't you think if we knew, we'd be out getting them back ourselves? Why don't you read all the police reports. They spent hours talking to all of us and, no doubt, logged countless more hours investigating."

"I have no doubt about that. But, Mr. Silkeney believes they might have missed something that could put us on a whole new path to finding them. It would be helpful to get some insights from you, but if you would rather not talk to me, I'll work with the information I've already obtained."

"No. It's not that I don't want to help." Her shoulders slumped and her gaze dropped to the table. Her tone softened when she said, "Of course I'm willing to help. I want my daughter back."

The steel returned to her voice as she continued, "I don't see what bringing in a whip of a private investigator is going to do when the FBI can't find a trace of her."

Mrs. Dunn's eyes sparkled with unshed tears. "Damn it!" she proclaimed, slamming the flat of her hand on the table and making the coffee cups jump. "I hate crying in front of people."

She got up from the table and went down the hall and closed a door. Mariah waited for her to compose herself. About three minutes later, she came back to the table, a tissue wadded up in her right hand and her eyes red-rimmed.

"I apologize. This has been the worst time of my life. I've never felt so helpless or hopeless in my life, not even when her father left us for another woman."

"I know it's hard to keep answering the same questions, but it could help. If it would be easier for you, we could have a conversation about her instead of a formal question and answer type of interview. I'd love to hear about her from her mother's perspective—what she's like at home when no one is around—what is she like with family, and her friends. What did y'all do together? What did she do to make you laugh? What did she do to frustrate you? What was she like as a child, going into her teens … just days and weeks before she went missing? How did she learn to drive, what foods does she like. Everyday life kind of things."

She nodded her head. "I would love to talk about her. No one seems to want to listen, it makes them uncomfortable for some reason." She aimed a weak smile at Mariah and said, "Thank you."

"Do you mind if I record our conversation? It would help when I type up my notes."

"No. I don't mind. Let's go into the living room where we can be more comfortable."

After they got settled in the living room, Mrs. Dunn started talking. "Dunn's father and I married twenty years ago."

"Dunn?"

"Chelsea. When she was a baby, we called her Little Dunn and later, we shortened her nickname to Dunn. Her friends call her Chelsea, but her dad, brothers, and I call her Dunn. She looked so much like her father when she was a baby that his parents started it. Anyway, I had just gotten my Doctorate in Philosophy and he worked in corporate law. Bob, most people call him Robert, is fourteen years older than me and divorced when we met. His ex-wife met a man on leave from the Marines and she ran off with him. They live in Germany and she never came back for her boys or anything. She and Bob had three boys. At the time Bob and I married, they were ten, eight, and six. I desperately wanted a child of my own, not that I didn't adore the boys. But … Bob had a vasectomy after Curtis was born, and we didn't think it would be possible for us to have a child together. We explored our options—adoption, artificial insemination … stuff like that and we learned that sometimes a vasectomy can be reversed. Bob decided to try that first and if it didn't work, then we could look into other options. He had the surgery and a year and a half later, I got pregnant. By then, I had given up hope the surgery would work, but it did.

"She was the most beautiful baby girl I ever did see— perfect in every way. I know everyone says that about their baby, but everyone told me that about her. Are you too young to remember the Gerber Baby?" Mrs. Dunn waived her hand in the air before continuing. "Never mind. She looked like that baby in the Gerber Baby Food advertisements from the sixties and seventies."

Mrs. Dunn took a sip of her coffee. "She was smart, too. She walked at eight months and had an insatiable appetite for learning. She was so full of questions that sometimes it exasperated me. She was sounding out words and teaching herself to read at five years of age. She amazed me in so many little ways … and big ways too.

"I've never in my life known a child with as much compassion as she has. As soon as she was strong enough, she would open doors and hold them open for people at the stores. She would smile and talk to everyone and helped with anything she could. In school, she always protected the kids that were being bullied, and comforted the crying, hurt, or frightened child."

Mrs. Dunn stared off into space for a moment. Mariah knew she needed to talk and reminisce, so she didn't try to ask anything and gave her time to ramble. After a few moments, Mrs. Dunn turned her eyes on Mariah again. "She's played basketball since she was big enough to dribble the ball. By the time she was in Middle School, she was good. She *is* good. There are five colleges looking at her, and her grades are good. She's got a three point eight right now. Since she started Middle School, she's fluctuated from a three point five to a four point oh, and between a three point eight and a four point oh since entering High School.

"And, oh! She's so excited about college. She is so looking forward to that. Most of her life she talked about being a veterinarian, but then she found out that a vet has to put down sick or injured animals. She didn't want to do that, so she decided she wants to go into, what she calls 'people medicine'. She's not sure what kind exactly. Last we talked she was thinking about Pediatrics or maybe Geriatrics. She loves older people and relates well with them, but she loves babies too.

"She loves to read. She'll read anything you put in front of her. She was reading the reader's digest in pre-school. Can you believe that?"

Mariah shook her head.

"She likes crime television when she slows down long enough to watch something, and for movies, she likes romantic comedies and sci-fi.

"The thing we both like best is sitting in here, with a cup of coffee or hot cocoa, and catching up. We would try to set aside time for each other at least once a week, usually on a Tuesday or Thursday. I have late classes on Monday, Wednesday, and Friday and she has basketball practice those evenings. Her games are typically Tuesday or Thursday nights or on the weekend, so we just worked around our schedules. No matter what, we always found at least one evening a week to spend together.

"Sometimes, especially in the winter, we would buy a one-thousand to two thousand piece jigsaw puzzle and work it together. See that picture over there of the Eiffel Tower? That's one of the puzzles we worked together."

Mariah glanced toward the picture that Mrs. Dunn pointed to. She got up from the chair and crossed to the framed picture.

"Wow. I didn't realize it was a puzzle. It's beautiful."

"And that one over there behind you, of the rose garden is another one."

Mariah turned to scrutinize the rose garden picture.

"Beautiful."

"The Eiffel Tower was my favorite and the Rose Garden was Dunn's. We've worked a lot of puzzles together, but those are the only two we framed.

"Sometimes we'll go to the coast and rent a room overlooking the ocean on the weekend and walk the beach, fly kites, and go hiking. When she comes home, I'm taking her to the coast for as long as she can stand it." Her bottom lip trembled and tears pooled in her eyes.

"I'm sure she will love that. Hopefully soon," Mariah said and smiled at her. "So you're a teacher?"

"Yes. I worked at Rogue Community College for years, and then Southern Oregon University offered me a position. I love it. That's when we moved to Ashland from Medford. Dunn was upset at first, but once she learned she could continue on the AAU team she got over it. She's made some wonderful friends here in Ashland too."

"What does her father do?"

"He's a corporate attorney for Harry and David. I'll never forgive him for running off and leaving us. He's no better than his ex-wife except he maintained a relationship with his children—all except Curtis, the youngest boy. Curtis was furious with his father and refused to have anything to do with him."

"Curtis is the one who went off to college two years ago?
"Yes."

"I wonder why Martin didn't tell me that you and Robert are divorced?"

"We're not. I said he ran off with another woman, I didn't say I granted him a divorce."

"Oh." Mariah said. "Wow, three years? Why are you hanging on? Isn't that kind of like cutting off your nose to spite your face."

Mrs. Dunn took offense at that.

"Well, aren't you little miss know-it-all?! I hate to admit it, but I refused to grant him a divorce out of pure revenge if you really must know—not that it's any of your business."

"I'm sorry. You're right, of course. It is none of my business unless it somehow plays into your daughter's disappearance." As Mariah took a breath to go on, Mrs. Dunn opened her mouth to protest but Mariah jumped back in soon enough to ward off her words.

"I'm not saying it does, but sometimes the smallest, most seemingly innocent things could turn the tides on an investigation. What has her relationship with her father been like most recently?"

"She adores her father. He was always the playful parent. He would back me up on discipline, but he would never enforce the rules, and he always took credit for the fun outings. When she or the boys would act out, it was always up to me to discipline and come down heavy on them, then he would loosen the discipline telling them I was being too harsh."

"But when he left, she stayed with you?"

"Yes. I think she wanted to go with him, but he told her it would be better if she stayed with me and come to visit him on weekends and holidays. Really! He just didn't want anyone interrupting his sex play and love fest with the little slut he ran off with." The last sentence she stated with strong vehemence.

Mariah was not about to encourage her bitter diatribe about her ex-husband, so she said, "Could you give me his address and phone number? I would like to talk to him too."

"Not about me, I hope. I don't need anyone running to him with tales about me and I told the kids that too. They are not to mention me to him. If he started talking about me or asking questions, they are to shut him down."

"No. No. I won't talk to him about you. I won't even tell him that we talked. I only want to get his insights on Chelsea."

"He lives in East Medford, up on the hill. I'll have to text you his address and phone number. I don't have it memorized." Mrs. Dunn fished her cell phone from her back pocket. "What's your number?"

Mariah gave her cell phone number and soon after heard the ding, announcing a text had been received. She checked and saw Mr. Dunn's information.

"Thanks. I'll get in touch with him later today. In the meantime, would you mind if I looked around in her room?"

"Oh, good grief!" Mrs. Dunn stood. "First the cops, then the FBI, and now you. I don't know why all you people think you'll be the ones to find that one little, special something that will solve the case. Really. Don't you think if the police and the FBI couldn't find any clues, then you won't either? You're not even a cop. I'm sure they've had more training than you, so what makes you think you're so superior?" The heat of her frustration resonated in her voice and colored her face a bright pink.

"First of all, Mrs. Dunn," Mariah said with complete calm and patience. "I'm a former police officer myself. I started out as a patrol officer and advanced to Detective. The Department sent me to Quantico, the FBI training center, which included training in this kind of investigative work. Secondly, I'm also a licensed forensic psychologist, so viewing her surroundings will help me develop a working image of her personality and where she was emotionally at the time she went missing. I know this is all intrusive for you and that you want to preserve her room. I will respect that. I promise you, I will not disrespect her belongings, your home, or your memory of her. To be honest, viewing her room and her things may not help, but if there's even the smallest chance it would make a difference, wouldn't you want me to see it?"

Mrs. Dunn stood there, her mouth open and her eyes red rimmed as she tried not to cry. Her mouth moved as though she were trying to say something but she only made mewing sounds before nodding her head yes. She started toward the hall and waived her hand to indicate Mariah should follow.

Dunn's mother stopped at the hallway and pointed up the stairs. She said in a choked voice, "Turn right, it's the last door on the left. I can't go to her room. I can't even stand to look in there, knowing she may never come home. Her room is probably a mess. Just close the door when you're finished. I'll wait here."

"Thank you."

Mariah walked passed Mrs. Dunn and started up the stairs. She glanced back at the distraught mother as she turned right at the top of the stars, and continued to watch her while she walked along the balustrade to Dunn's room. Mrs. Dunn stood in the same place, tears streaming down her face, her hands clasped together and held under her chin. Self consciously, Mariah turned her gaze from Mrs. Dunn when she reached Chelsea Dunn's bedroom door. She turned the knob and glanced back over her shoulder toward Mrs. Dunn who opened her hands and covered her mouth, a silent sob shuddering her body.

Mariah entered the room and closed the door behind her. Immediately to her right as she walked into the room, she saw a stencil in Script on the wall that read *Love Like You've Never Been Hurt* with flowers around it. To her left, a full length mirror attached to the wall, reflected her image. Stuck behind the top right corner were notes, possibly study notes or notes from friends, she couldn't tell. Mariah took the notes down and opened them, one at a time. She took pictures of each note with her phone camera.

Above the mirror, another stencil surrounded by roses read, *Family*. Next to the mirror was a nineteen inch, flat-screen television attached to the wall above a chest of drawers. On top of the chest of drawers stood a DVD player at the center back. Surrounding the DVD player was make-up and jewelry. On the wall above the television was another stencil of a bouquet of roses. In the corner next to the chest of drawers stood a make-up table sitting catty-corner with a chair in front and a mirror on top. In the center of the wall opposite the door, a window covered with wooden blinds dominated. A black, imitation wrought-iron, curtain rod sat above the window, holding two bathing suits on one end, and a duffle bag on the other. Above the window another stencil read *Dance Like Nobody is Watching*. To the right of the window, a white shelf attached to the wall held framed pictures of Chelsea and her mom, Chelsea and her dad, and Chelsea and three older boys … her brothers. The black wrought-iron, double-bed headboard stood against the next wall. Above that was another stencil that read *We grow great by our dreams.* In the corner to the left of the headboard, a short, square table held a large stuffed panda bear and an alarm clock. On the floor of the other side of the bed was an even larger stuffed panda bear. The next wall beside the bed included white, partially opened, folding closet doors. On the wall to the left of the closet hung a white board with different uplifting sayings, song quotes, and a heart drawn in the center, colored in pink. Friends and family names were written all around the heart—some written in cursive, some in block letters, some printed, all in different colors. There didn't seem to be any particular pattern. Mariah snapped a picture of the white-board.

On the floor were three different piles of clothes, several pair of shoes, two pair of boots, and a hair dryer. It was clear to Mariah the room hadn't been picked up or cleaned since the last time Chelsea had walked out.

Mariah checked in each drawer, felt under the mattress, and examined the space under the small table next to the bed. She found nothing of interest to the investigation. The closet floor was covered with clothes, basketballs, duffle bags, hair ties, books, papers, notes from friends, dress shoes, gym shoes, socks, sweatshirts, jackets and board games. There were more board games and stuffed animals on the shelf above the hanging clothes.

In the back corner of the closet floor, under a duffle bag and a jacket Mariah found a small wooden box. In the box, under a bunch of love notes and letters from a boy named Lucas, she found a diary. She didn't have time to read but she did take the time to snap a picture of each page and paper. She hoped some of the pictures would render helpful information down the road.

When she came out of the room thirty minutes later, Mrs. Dunn was standing in the same spot, her hands covering her face as she sobbed silently. Mariah closed the door and walked back down the stairs, taking the woman into her arms. Mrs. Dunn laid her head on Mariah's shoulder.

"I'm so sorry you're going through this. No parent should have to suffer this nightmare. I'm going to do everything I can to find your daughter and the others. I promise. And I'm going to find out who is behind this if it takes the rest of my life. They will pay, no matter what. I promise you."

Mrs. Dunn nodded her head on Mariah's shoulder and then pushed her away, wiping her eyes.

"Thank you. I believe you will, too. Please don't fail us, Mariah. I'm begging you."

"I won't. Will you be okay for now? I've got to leave."

"Yes. I'm fine. Just keep me posted, please."

"I will.

"You know your way out. Please leave now."

Without saying any more for fear she would start to cry, Mariah walked to the front door, and looked back at Dunn's mother. She stood with her rigid back to Mariah as she slowly slumped to the floor, her shoulders shuddering. Mariah opened the door and exited, closing it quietly behind her.

By the time she left the Dunn residence, it was time to visit Savannah Massey's family.

****

Mariah turned right into the drive for Savannah's house—a bi-level, sitting on a hill surrounded by vineyards, when she remembered that she hadn't called Morgan or Riley in the last couple days. She made a mental note to call one of them as soon as she finished interviewing the Massey family. After that, she intended to take a nap before going through Chelsea's diary.

At the end of the short, gravel drive, she had to turn right again and saw a long, two-car-wide drive sloping down to the right of the front yard, ending at the two-car garage. The garage sat flush with the front of the house, but on the lower level. Before reaching the slope to the garage, and to the left of the driveway, Mariah turned into a circle drive in front of the fenced front yard. A concrete sidewalk led from the gate to the wooden ramp and front porch on the second level of the house. Mariah parked in front of the gate and walked the long sidewalk to the front door. To the right of the front door, a locked, chain link gate barred passage to steep concrete steps leading to the driveway below. She pushed the doorbell and heard a big dog bark, plus what sounded like a horse running to the door. She braced herself.

"Chester, down!" a woman said on the other side of the door before the sound of the deadbolt turning, and the door swinging open. In front of Mariah stood a five-foot, eight-inch tall woman, wearing skin tight leggings and a long sleeved, skin tight top. Her make-up was perfectly applied and her hair beautifully arranged. She was a very striking and confident woman in spite of the fat rolls that were prominently displayed by her tight clothing. Her belly hung over her lap to the top of her thighs and when she turned to hold Chester back, the rolls of fat pushing past her racer back bra gave the appearance of having large breasts where her shoulder blades should be. She was wheezing so hard that, at first, Mariah thought she was whistling.

"Hi." She pushed Chester back from the door. "Mariah?"

"Yes."

"Please, come in. I'm Mona, Savannah's mother. Don't mind old Chester here. He loves everyone and so does Raina, our other German Shepherd."

"Thank you," Mariah said as she stepped into the narrow hall.

"Come with me. Sorry we couldn't see you over the weekend. Wade and the kids are in the dining room. Would you like a cup of coffee?"

"Oh yes, coffee would be wonderful. I haven't had anything yet this morning." As she followed Mona, Chester walked behind Mariah, sniffing her backside and poking his nose between her legs.

They turned right at the end of the hallway into another short hallway. To their right, a stairway led down to the lower level, and to their left they turned into yet another short hallway which housed a freezer, a water dispenser with a five gallon bottle of water sitting on top, and the dog's food and water bowls. Chester continued following behind, sniffing Mariah from feet to derrière. Mariah had to reached back and pushed his head aside several times as she continued to follow Mona.

The final hallway opened up into a large, untidy mess of a kitchen. The sink was full of dirty dishes, the stove top covered with pots and pans, and the counter tops were covered with all kinds of packaged foods and empty food containers. The cabinet door under the sink stood open with trash overflowing into the floor.

Mariah followed Mona as she turned right in the kitchen and crossed in front of the refrigerator, passed the breakfast bar covered with napkins, pizza boxes, and a half full box of donuts, into the dining area where the Massey family was sitting at the dining room table, sans Savannah.

Another dog came up behind Mariah, sniffed her legs and derrière.

"Raina! Stop that and go lay down. Both of you. Shoo!" Mona pushed the two dogs back through the kitchen and into a living room.

"I apologize for the mess. It's been hard to keep up with everything around here lately, and having our car stolen last night didn't help matters."

"Your car was stolen last night?" Mariah asked.

"Yes. We heard a car start up out front about three this morning which is unusual since there's nothing but vineyards out here around us. Please, have a seat." Mona pointed to a chair and walked to a cabinet for a coffee mug. "Wade got up and saw my car peel out down the driveway and take off down the road toward Jacksonville. The cops were here until five and we're a little exhausted," she continued before she introduced Mariah to the rest of the family.

"Oh, this is Wade, Savannah's father."

"Hi Wade. I'm Mariah. Nice to meet you."

"Hi," he said.

"And this is Alesha and Alonna, Savannah's twin sisters," Mona continued.

"Hi." Mariah eyed the two girls sitting at the table.

"Are you going to find Savannah?" Alesha asked.

"I'm going to try."

"And this is Wade Aaron. We call him Aaron— Savannah's baby brother," Mona added.

"I'm not a baby. I'm this many," Wade Aaron said holding up his left hand with all five fingers splayed.

"How many is that, Aaron?" Alonna asked him as Alesha said, "He's five. We're nine."

Aaron gave a huge toothy grin and nodded his head dramatically.

"Hi there, Aaron." Mariah winked at him.

"Girls, I need you to start cleaning up the kitchen. You can listen to us talk while you work, but it has to get done now."

Both girls groaned. "Yes, ma'am." They stood from the table and went around the bar to the kitchen.

"How can we help you, Mariah?" Wade asked.

"Right now I'm gathering information, trying to look at things from a different point of view than the police and FBI. I'm hoping to find clues that will give us all some better direction. Everyone seems to have hit a brick wall. Do you mind if I record our conversation?"

Wade shook his head no and waved his right hand as if to say, lets get on with it.

As with the families of the other girls, Mariah went over much of the same questions with the Massey's.

Savannah was fifteen years old and an avid basketball player. At one time during the year, she played on three different teams—her school basketball team, her AAU basketball team, and the YMCA teen girls basketball team. She also helped coach the five and six year old boys basketball team at the YMCA where Aaron plays. She had average to good grades, loved school, loved basketball, and adored her siblings. She had a boyfriend, Spencer, who was a science nerd and attended every one of her games as long as they didn't interfere with his school work and activities.

Spencer, sixteen years old, and two grades ahead of Savannah as he skipped second grade, participated in the Science club in school, and had organized several trips for his club to different places in the prior three years. The most notable trip was to Cape Canaveral for a tour. Spencer was not a suspect in any of the disappearances. He wrecked his motorcycle on his way to school the day before the first disappearance, and spent some time in the hospital with two broken ribs and a broken leg. He was in physical therapy the day Savannah went missing.

After spending an hour and a half talking to the family, Wade showed Mariah to Savannah's bedroom downstairs.

The downstairs area was an actual two bedroom, one bath apartment. Savannah had the bigger of the two bedrooms while the twins had the other one, the small bathroom was between the two rooms. There was a small sitting room with a door leading to a tiny, fenced in yard, and a kitchen with a door leading to the two car garage.

"Do you mind if I spend some time down here alone?" Mariah glanced at Wade with a questioning look. "I sometimes get a feel for a person—their personality, and emotional state—when I'm in their living space."

Wade's eyes bored into hers, but after a moment he answered, "I suppose so. We'll be upstairs."

Mariah walked through the whole apartment with the exception of the twins room. She peeked in their room, but didn't enter. There was a chalk board on the wall where a refrigerator would normally stand and it appeared the twins were the ones who used it the most. In the cabinets, Mariah found some microwave popcorn, cookies, a bag of jawbreakers, some packets of sour gummy candies, and peanut butter crackers. A few clean glasses were on the counter next to the sink. On the other side of the sink sat a microwave oven.

In the sitting room, a broken down old couch and recliner, with the foot rest up, faced a thirty-two inch flat screen TV with an Xbox on the floor in front. An old scratched up, maple coffee table sat in front of the couch.

The apartment as a whole was neat and orderly. Savannah's room could have easily passed as a boys room with posters of NBA basketball players on the wall, and a framed basketball jersey signed by Shaquille O'Neal over her headboard. The only thing that indicated it was a girls bedroom were the dresses in the closet, the vanity desk with make-up and nail polish sitting on top, and curlers, curling irons, and a blow dryer on the floor. A hamper stood next to the closet with a pile of clothes in it.

Mariah went through the dirty clothes, checking the pockets, and found seventy-three cents in the front pocket of a pair of jeans. In the back pocket there was a note from Tina Webb. Mariah put the change back in the pocket and opened the note.

I saw Spencer giving a note to Kathy after 3rd period. Probably nothing, but I'll keep an eye on him. Tina

Mariah folded the note and put it back in the jeans pocket. Before going back upstairs, Mariah stood in the doorway and looked into the open room. She closed her eyes and took a deep breath, releasing it with practiced ease. She waited. Her meditation took her to a flickering fire. In front of the fire, she saw Savannah sitting with knees pulled up to her chest, hands tied behind her back to a stake in the ground, and a gag in her mouth.

"Oh, dear God," she whispered, the connection broken.

Finished searching, Mariah went back upstairs. The kitchen had been cleaned and the trash taken out. Wade Massey stood at the fireplace in the living room, his left arm braced on the mantle and his forehead resting on his arm as he stared into the fire. As soon as he heard Mariah enter the hall from the stairwell, he straightened and turned.

"Well? What did you find?"

"Thank you for allowing me to spend some time in her room. That's a nice little set up for a teenaged girl. Did you ever have any trouble with her sneaking out at night?"

Alesha and Alonna came in the back door, talking and laughing at each other with both dogs, Chester and Raina in tow before Wade could answer. As soon as they saw Mariah talking to their father—their mother sitting on the couch—they quieted and stood in the doorway of the kitchen, both dogs pushing past them and coming to Mariah to sniff and check her out again.

"No," Wade said, closing his eyes and shaking his head. "Savannah is a good girl, and she had the twins down there with her. They would have told us if she had left. Isn't that right, girls?"

The two girls looked at each other and then at their dad. "You mean if she snuck out?"

"Yes. If Savannah had left without permission, you would have come and told me or your mother, right?"

Alesha gave a vigorous nod.

"Yes." She nudged Alonna with her elbow. "Of course, we would."

Alonna stood wide eyed, staring at her father and said "Uh huh."

A door slammed and then Aaron called out in a whining voice, "Mom! Alesha and Alonna ran off and left me outside."

Mona sighed and Chester ran off to the sound of Aaron's voice.

"Does anyone have anything else you think might be of help?" Mariah eyed the girls, sensing they were holding something back.

No one responded. Wade turned back to the fire.

Aaron pushed his way passed the twins saying, "Get out of my way," and went to his mother, Chester following close behind.

"Mom, they won't play with me," he intoned, dragging 'me' out in a pitiful whine.

Mona put her arms around him and pulled him up into her lap and started crying. "Just be still, little man. You can go to the shop with me in a little while."

Mariah asked no one in particular, "Did Savannah ever go to the Old Forest out of Jacksonville?"

"Yes, there were a couple of times that the AAU basketball team would go out there to jog the trails. They always had chaperones. I went with them about six months ago. Why?" Wade replied.

"I heard of one of the girls sneaking out to meet a boyfriend there."

"Oh no. That's terrible." Mona said.

"Now Mona. It's not really a dangerous place. It's just a bit isolated. I don't know of any real crimes that have happened out there."

"But it's so big. Anything can happen. What is it, a hundred miles of trails or something?"

"No. It's about eleven hundred acres and I think it has about fifteen miles of trails. It's really nice and a lot of people go out there to walk, hike, or ride bikes. Some of the trails are very easy and level, some moderate, and some more difficult. People take their kids or their dogs. I wouldn't want Savannah to go out there by herself, but simply because if there was trouble, she might not have anyone around to help or call for help. But I don't think it's a dangerous place. Besides, the girls were abducted from school from what everyone can gather. I don't think the park has anything to do with it."

"Okay. That's excellent information. Anything else?"

"No. I don't know anything anymore," Wade said in resignation. Mona and Aaron just held each other and rocked, while the twins stood in the kitchen doorway and watched Mariah.

"Well, thank you for your time. I'll show myself out."

"We'll walk you out," the twins said in unison.

The girls were silent as they walked down the long sidewalk to the front gate and Mariah's car. As Mariah opened the gate to leave, Alonna said, "She did sneak out a couple times, but we can't tell Daddy right now. He'll kill us for not telling him when it happened."

"She did? Do you know where she went or who she met?"

"Nu uh." Alesha shook her had no. "She told us she couldn't sleep and she was going out for a jog. She even invited us to go with her one time."

"How often did she sneak out?"

Alonna shrugged her shoulders, "I dunno. Once or twice a week, I guess."

"Do you think she ever met someone?"

They both shrugged their shoulders. Mariah gave the girls her card.

Call me if you think of anything else. It might be exactly what we need to find your sister."

"We will," the girls chimed.

Mariah's phone started ringing.

"Thanks girls."

She went back to the suite and changed into her running clothes, collected Paisley and took her to the dog park for some exercise. She was in desperate need of some stress relief and running always helped with that. She turned Paisley loose inside the park and started jogging the track. Paisley would run with Mariah for a little while until something interesting caught her attention, then she would be off chasing other dogs, or birds, or even bugs flying in the area. When she got tired, she caught up to Mariah and led her to the gate to go home.

****

Back at the suite, Mariah showered and dressed before checking her phone. She missed a call from Riley and two from Morgan, and a text message from Morgan asking how things were going. Mariah made a mental note to call at least one of them back today, but first she called Mr. Dunn from the contact information Mrs. Dunn sent her.

"Hi, Mr. Dunn, this is Mariah Jeffries. My firm has been hired by Martin Silkeney to find the missing girls, including your daughter. I …"

"What's Martin's stake in this?" he asked, cutting Mariah off.

"I beg your pardon?" The animosity in his voice surprised her.

"Why … did … Martin … hire … you?" He accentuated each word. "What's his stake in this?"

"He's concerned and wants whoever is responsible to be caught so the young girls in the area are safe again. He said some of the missing girls are friends with his daughters and he's terribly worried about the safety of his daughters as well as all the other girls in that age range."

"Meddling old coot!"

"I'm sorry you feel that way, but …"

"He's always been that way and I don't like the man. What are you supposed to do that the FBI cant'?"

"Look, I can go over my credentials and those of my partners if you would meet with me. All we're trying to do is find the girls and stop any further abductions. We work WITH the police AND the FBI and not against them. Do you have some time available to talk to me?"

"Sure," he said, his tone sarcastic. "I don't have anything else going on. My employers don't expect any production from me, so I can spend all the time in the world chatting with you." His sarcasm dripped like molasses—slow and thick.

Mariah took a steadying, calming breath before answering.

"I won't take much of your time. When would be a good time for you?"

"Meet me at my office now. I'll be expecting you at the Harry and David Corporate offices on Highway Ninety-Nine. How long before you're here?"

"I'm just around the corner and can be there in five minutes. Thank you."

"Please don't keep me waiting too long. I'll have to wait downstairs by the door to let you in. It's my day off, but I'm here because I *DO* have a lot of work to do."

By the time Mariah had reached Mr. Dunn's office, his ire had cooled and he greeted her with professionalism. He walked with a cane, leaning heavily on it as they traversed the lobby to the elevators. His office was across the hall from the elevator on the second floor. Standing behind his desk he said, "I would offer you something to drink, but I'm the only one here."

"That's fine. I'm not thirsty."

Robert Dunn, a man of moderate height—about five-ten, and very gaunt, wore a designer suit that hung on his frame like the skin of a dried up withered apple. He was bald, had prominent cheekbones and dark circles under his eyes. His skin shone with a sickly pallor, and his hands had a slight tremor. He sat with a sigh and waived to a chair for Mariah to sit.

Mariah pulled out her recorder and asked him questions about Chelsea. He verified much of what Mrs. Dunn told her, and a great deal of pride filled his voice as he spoke of his only daughter.

"Mr. Dunn, I understand that you and Mrs. Dunn have separated. How did Chelsea respond to that and how has it changed her behaviors or attitudes, if at all?"

"She was heart broken, of course. She loves both her parents and feared she would lose one of us. Valene and I assured her that would not be the case."

"Did you and Valene give her a choice as to which parent she would live with?"

"No. I wanted her to go live with her mother." He looked down at his hands, clasped together on his desk and trembling.

"I love Valene. I'll always love her and I knew that my leaving her would be devastating. If Chelsea had chosen me over her mom, it would have destroyed Valene so I encouraged her to stay with her mom."

"Is it true you left her for another woman?"

"No. Absolutely not."

"Well, if you love Mrs. Dunn so much and there wasn't someone else, why did you leave her?"

He raised his eyes to meet Mariah's. "Can you keep what I tell you confidential?"

"Honestly, it depends on what you tell me."

He shook his head and looked down at his hands. "Please don't tell Valene what I'm about to tell you."

Mariah nodded.

"I'm sick." he said, looking back at Mariah. "I'm very sick, and I didn't want Valene or Chelsea to witness my deterioration. I would rather they hate me than to see me for the pitiful wreckage of a man that I have become. I've been diagnosed with ALS and after researching it, I walked out, got my own place and hired a live-in nurse to help me. Of course, Valene thinks the woman is my lover. She also thinks she is depriving me of a divorce; however, I never asked for, or filed for one, nor will I. Everything I have, if there's anything left, will go to her upon my death."

"Does Chelsea know?"

"No. My two older boys know and they promised me they will not tell the girls or Curtis until after I'm dead. That's the last bit of dignity I have left before I go."

"I'm very sorry. Most people would want the support of their loved ones during a time like this."

Mr. Dunn tried to swallow and then coughed with as much vigor as he could muster. Catching his breath, he answered.

"Valene would have given everything up to help me. She's worked so hard to get where she is and she's going to need a good job when I'm gone. I'm going through all my assets pretty fast now, and if I don't die soon, there won't be anything left to leave for Valene and Chelsea's support. I couldn't let her throw everything away to watch me die. I don't have much longer. I was in remission for a while, but the symptoms are back and more aggressive than before. I need a wheelchair now, but I'm putting it off to the last possible moment. Once I go into a wheelchair, I will resign from my job and stay home and wait for death."

"I want to thank you for your time and your candor. I'll keep your secret as well."

"Find my daughter for me before I die. Will you?"

"That's my plan. Just don't die too soon."

MONDAY

Paisley is stretched out on the couch beside me, chasing something in her sleep and yipping softly while I'm working on my notes. I hear someone clear their throat and look up to see Paul sitting in the chair across from me.

"You're here" I say in a calm, quiet tone—not the least bit startled at his presence.

"I'm always with you, Mariah. You just can't always see me."

"But I'm only dreaming. You left me to fend for myself years ago."

"I didn't choose to My Darling Red," Paul's nickname for me all those years ago because of my hair color. Sometimes he would call me just 'Red'.

"Who's haunting me? Is it Jerry?"

"I can't tell you that, Red. Just remember that you are a fearless, strong, and independent woman. You are loved by many. Remember that."

A sob catches in my throat.

"I miss you so much. Why have we never been able to have a long and happy life together?"

"We have."

"*When? Why did I have to lose you this time?*"

"*I can't tell you what your life lessons are. You have to discover them yourself.*"

"*I don't want to do this by myself anymore. It's too hard, Paul.*"

"*You're not by yourself. You have Paisley, the uncles, and Morgan and Riley, their wives, and Jewel and Norela—and now, Jeffrey and Kate.*"

"*But they're not you.*"

"*No. They're not me, My Darling Red.*"

I stand from the couch and approach Paul who is now standing. He is wearing his favorite Dale Earnhardt lounging pants, his beautifully tanned skin from the waist up bare and rock solid. He takes me into his arms and with a soft growl I sigh, comforted in his embrace. We stand in place, holding each other for a long while, and I don't want it to stop.

I look up into Paul's blue eyes and he leans his mouth down to mine. We kiss—his hand slides up my back, his fingers tangling in my hair and pulling my head back as he slides his mouth down along my jaw line, whispering across my throat leaving shivers of delight. His mouth travels across my collar bone, before dipping down to my breast with little butterfly kisses and taking my nipple into his mouth. I gasp at the delightful pain that sets off a firestorm in my body. I hold him close and we sink to the floor which turns into a feather soft bed. I am transported back in time as we devour each other in our love and lust, just as we had done so many times before. Every inch of his body is explored and appreciated by me, while he sets every inch of my body on fire with his lovemaking. He brings me to the edge of ecstasy several times before finally allowing the competing sensations to explode within me. Exhausted at last, I roll on my side, sheltered in the protection of his arm curled around me, and I lay my head on his chest, but there is no heartbeat, no hardness of his muscles, and no warmth.

Mariah bolted up and looked around, feeling deceived and cheated that he wasn't really there with her. It was only a dream—a beautiful, tantalizing, enchanting dream—but only a dream. With a sad and heavy heart, she reclined on her side, tears dripping on her pillow, as she experienced the loss of Paul all over again and she drifted off to sleep. Paul did not come back to her. The dreams were broken and disjointed. Some silly little trivia, some made no sense at all. Then …

I am running across rooftops, leaping from building to building and looking back as a shadowy figure tries to catch me.

"Leave me alone," I shout, but the words are caught by the wind and carried away. I stumble and fall, coughing, my breath ragged. "Leave me alone. Please," I plead as the shadow makes a slow approach. Flat on my back, I scoot trying to move away. I couldn't stand and run, so the shadow moves in closer. "What do you want?" I ask trying to pick out features, but there are no features to make out and no answers to my question. The shadow stands there next to me for a moment—hovering over me. I wait. I remind myself that it's fear itself that I'm afraid of, so I resolve to stand up to it. I sit up and lean forward, pulling my feet back and getting on my knees. The shadow opens it's maw, but doesn't approach me. I raise to a kneel and plant my right foot on the ground. The shadow backs up a pace. I push off the ground and stand, facing my terror. "Get away from me," I shout. The shadow leans in, opens it maw and for the first time, I see inside. I observe Caroline's trepidation in telling Joseph about Daniel, and the loss of their first born child. I view my kidnapping, escape, Morgan's and Jeri's rescues, the explosion of my home, the Feds labeling us murderers and drug dealers, and the hysteria within myself caused by all of those events. I witness Jerry beating my bloody and broken body.

"No! This is not happening again. Jerry's dead and he can't hurt me any more." There is a loud crack and a hole appears in the shadow's head, above the large maw. Black ooze pours out. I hear someone behind me and I look back to find Erick standing in his

fatigues, his rifle in hand and aimed at the shadow. He nods his head at me and I turn back to the shadow expecting it to be gone or laid out on the ground, dead, but it's not. The shadow is standing there, smiling at me. It opens it's maw wide and a loud screeching siren sounds.

Mariah jerked awake, her heart pounding—the sound of emergency sirens passed on the street outside. She remembered standing up to her tormenter and smiled, realizing the enormity of what she accomplished. Paisley, who jumped when Mariah did, crawled over to check on her. Mariah put her arm around the little dog.

"We're alright, Paisley. Everything is going to be alright."

Mariah laid back down with Paisley curled up next to her. She wondered as she closed her eyes what Erick was doing in her dream—*the man is an enigma,* she thought. She reached over to the night stand and checked the time on her cell phone.

Five-thirty. Oh God! She was so tired—weighed down with exhaustion to the point she couldn't move. She must have drifted off to sleep because the next moment of consciousness, she was awakened by her seven thirty alarm going off.

She turned the alarm off before rolling over and patting Paisley. The little dog stretched out and groaned. Mariah drifted off to sleep again.

The sound of tires screeching woke her with a start and she check the time. An hour had passed and she had to get up and get moving.

Showered and dressed, she took Paisley out for a quick walk. In spite of the late morning start, the early morning sunshine hadn't yet penetrated the cold. Mariah and Paisley were glad to get back to the Suite.

Upon returning, she put fresh food and water down for Paisley, checked the iPod to make sure the battery was full, and plugged it into the speaker, set the music on random, and turned the volume up so Paisley wouldn't be distracted by the outside noises.

"Be good, little girl. I'll be back," she told the little dog and closed the door behind her.

Mariah sat in her car and called Martin to see if he had the signed and notarized authorizations from the girls' families. He advised his notary was out sick and the forms would not be ready until the next day.

Mariah decided she would take advantage of the free time and go out to the Medford range for target practice. It was a beautiful day with sunshine and few clouds, the temperature finally starting to rise.

She pulled up to the pay-box and made her donation for use of the range, then drove past the lanes toward the last one. There were a few men sighting in their hunting rifles in the first few lanes of the range, but she found blissful solitude pulling up at the last lane.

The Do-Alls she liked to use for practice are unpredictable when hit, flying and bouncing all around, and she enjoyed the challenge of locating them, readjusting her aim with each shot in rapid fire. After shooting, Mariah took her time cleaning each gun before packing up and heading back to the suite, Paisley, and lunch.

As she turned the key in the ignition, her phone rang. She sat with the engine running while she answered the phone.

"Hello?"

"Mariah?"

"Uncle John! How are you?"

"I'm good. How about yourself?"

"I'm good. Great really."

"I'm so happy to hear that. So you're doing past life regression therapy. What do you think of that?"

"It's been amazing, and it really seems to be helping."

"Wonderful … just wonderful. Do you feel like telling me a little bit about your experience with it?"

Mariah sat in her car, at the far end of the range, talking with her Uncle, mentor, and friend for over an hour about her progress through past life regression. They talked about her past life as Caroline and how real it seemed to her—about Joseph and Paul, and many other aspects of the treatment. John told her of his own past life regressions when he was a young man fresh out of the horrors of the Viet Nam conflict.

After the phone call, Mariah was feeling emotional—missing her uncles, remembering Paul, and thinking about the girls and their families, especially the Dunn family. She was emotionally drained, and hungry for nourishment and friendly conversation. She put her car in reverse, turned the car and ambled back down the row of shooting lanes. She decided to go to El Jefe Grill and Bar for a plate of enchilada's and a cold beer or two. Hopefully Jeffrey would be there for friendly conversation.

When she walked into the bar, Jeffrey waived to her from his stool in the corner at the bar, the stool beside him empty. Mariah walked up to him and patted him on the back.

"Good afternoon, Jeffrey. How are you?"

He smiled. "Well, hi Mariah. I'm just fine. Know what I mean? How ya been?"

"I'm kind of sad today. Mind if I sit next to you?"

"No. Not at all. Happy for the company, know what I mean?"

"I do." She pulled out the stool beside Jeffrey and sat. "How's the family?"

"Good. My girls are great. Know what I mean? How goes your work here?"

"Slow. Too damned slow for my liking. That's for sure."

"Well, let me buy you a drink and we'll talk about something different. How's that?" He waved for Kate to come over.

"Hi Kate."

Mariah raised a hand in greeting as Kate approached the end of the bar.

"Hi Mariah. I'm glad you came back. I guess the food wasn't too bad then?"

"No. It was delicious. I'll have the same thing tonight, Chicken Enchiladas and a Fat Tire, please."

"I'm buyin', Kate, so put it on my tab, please," Jeffrey said.

"Sure thing, Dad. You ready for a refill?"

"Yeppers. Fill 'er up, my beautiful daughter." With an expansive smile, he winked and nodded his head.

Kate chortled and walked off to put Mariah's order in and fill their drink order.

"Thank you Jeffery. You didn't need to buy my meal."

"Happy to do it. Maybe you can buy mine next time."

"I'd love to." Mariah smiled at him.

Kate came back with a basket of chips and salsa, putting them on the bar between Mariah and Jeffrey before getting their draft beers.

As Kate walked off, Mariah said, "I'll tell you Jeffrey. It's so hard talking to the parents of these missing girls. They're so broken, it just rips my heart out. I've got to find them. I don't think I'll be able to live with myself if they're not found soon."

"Oh. So that's your business? You a cop?"

"Guess I didn't mention that last time." Mariah aimed a weak smile at him. "Yes ... no." She shook her head.

"Um, yes, that's my business here and no, I'm not a cop anymore. I'm a private investigator. If you don't mind, don't tell anyone, please. Sometimes, I can extract more candid information from people if they're not aware of why I'm talking to them."

"Sure, no problem. I mean ... I can see your point. Besides, who would I tell? Know what I mean?"

"Jeffrey, do you mind if I ask you a very personal question?"

With a little tilted smile and a wink, Jeffrey answered, "I'm flattered, know what I mean? But you're just too young for me, Mariah. There was a time, I could have kept up with you, but not now, Honey. Know what I mean?"

Mariah's eyes widened in confusion and then surprise. Jeffrey laughed and patted her on the back. The confused expression on Mariah's face prompted him to go on. "I'm just kiddin' sweetheart. Know what I mean? You can ask me anythin', just don't be surprised if I don't answer. Know what I mean?" He started laughing again and Mariah joined in.

"You should a seen the look on your face. Know what I mean?"

"Well … now that I think about it … " They both laughed a little more. "That was funny, Jeffrey."

Jeffrey sobered and asked, "What's on your mind, kiddo?"

"Oh, never mind. Maybe I just needed a good laugh." She giggled again.

"No. No. You were being serious, so what did you want to ask? Looked like you had something important on your mind. Know what I mean?"

Mariah shook her head. "I had a horrible day yesterday and it's still with me. I was going to ask you what the worst day of your life was like … to take my mind off my day."

"Ah, I understand. I surely do. Know what I mean?" He contemplated a moment. "You don't want to hear about the worst, but I'll tell you a story about a really scary time in my life, if you want."

"Sure. I'd appreciate that."

"I enlisted in the US Army right before the Viet Nam Conflict started, know what I mean? My first night "in country" (he used his fingers in the air to make the quotation marks), I was laying in my bunk at the Strategic Communications Command Center, located in the heart of Saigon. I was a Specialist five then. Approximately oh-one-hundred hours I woke to the sound of gun fire and people scrambling around outside my room. Know what I mean?" he asked pointedly, his right eyebrow arched as he looked at Mariah.

She nodded her head.

"When I opened the door, I saw an MP running down the hall. 'What's happening?' I questioned him in my most courageous voice."

Jeffrey chuckled, shaking his head. "'Gooks all over the place outside' he answered.

"'What do I do?' I inquired in my now quivering voice."

He smiled at Mariah and laughed. "I was just a damned kid. What did I know? Know what I mean?"

"Yeah, it sounds scary."

"'Crawl under your bunk and stay there,' he shouted as he ran down the hall with bullets flying all over the place, people yelling out orders, explosions going off ... know what I mean? Hell ... and I was ordered under my bunk, helpless without a weapon. What a fabulous welcome to Viet Nam. Know what I mean?"

"You didn't even have a gun?"

"Hell no. I was in the command center. Know what I mean? I wasn't fully processed in. Crazy, huh?! Anyway, I assumed the fetal position under my bunk and listened to the battle going on outside my door. I was scared shitless. That's fer sure! Know what I mean? It seemed to go on fer *hours*."

He pounded his fist down on the bar.

"In actuality, it probably only lasted fifteen or twenty minutes. I didn't sleep at all that night. Know what I mean?"

"Wow, sounds terrifying."

"It was. The next morning, outside the compound were several piles of dead insurgents. In shock, and not sure I was believin' what I was seein', I suddenly experienced this intense gratitude that I wasn't one of them bodies in the piles. Know what I mean? What in God's name did I get myself into I wondered.

"That afternoon, I was processed and issued a side arm, a 45 caliber, and told not to hesitate using it if I thought I was in danger. I mean ... Oh, I felt so much better! ONE magazine of ammo! Crazy, huh? Know what I mean? One *stinkin'* magazine."

"Crazy." Mariah said, shaking her head.

"The next two nights were not as bad. Explosions were about a mile away with no gunfire at the compound. I felt relatively safe, but scared and worried, none the less. Know what I mean?"

"Yeah. How could you feel safe at all?"

Jeffrey shrugged his shoulders and went on. "Sweat soaked my freshly pressed fatigues as I left the relative security of the compound of Da Nang Airbase in the late afternoon of my fourth day in country. It was so humid you were never dry. Take a shower? No need to dry off 'cuz you're drippin sweat before you even put your clothes on. Know what I mean?"

Kate brought Mariah's plate and topped off the bowl of salsa.

"Dad charming you with one of his stories?"

"My intro to Viet Nam, Kate—great story, right?.

"It's interesting—crazy, but interesting," Mariah said.

Kate leaned on the bar as Mariah started eating, and Jeffrey continued.

"I was the FNG … know what that means?" he asked Mariah, leaning forward, his eyes opened wide.

Mariah shrugged and said, "I'm not sure … fucking new guy?"

"Yep. I was the fuckin' new guy. Pardon my French li'l lady, but that's how it was. Know what I mean? Anyway, the children outside the gates spotted me right away. They gathered round me and yelled, 'You got gum?, You want boom boom?' And 'Give me money, GI,' was shouted out by young boys and girls while they were grabbin' my arm, pullin' at me ever which way—hands on my back, all wanting me to give my attention to their requests. Know what I mean?"

Mariah nodded.

"I hurried along to meet my ride to my new duty station located across the bridge. I felt an unfamiliar tug on my left hand and looked down only to find that one of my new friends had my watch half off my arm. There was a tug at the back of my pants as another tried to dislodge my wallet. Know what I mean?

"Almost immediately I was surrounded by Vietnamese Police who were shoving and beating the kids away from me and yelling at them 'Di Di' and other unintelligible words at the top of their lungs. Know what I mean?"

Mariah nodded that she was still with him as she took another bite of enchilada.

"The kids left me alone after that and I was able to walk about another fifty feet to my waitin' ride. I mean, I get to my ride and these two soldiers were laughin' and pointin' at me as they lounged in their jeep. Know what I mean? The two guys who were going to give me a ride to my new home for the next year or so, were laughing and mocking me. I didn't mind, so much though. I was glad to see 'em. Know what I mean?

"'Welcome to Viet Nam', they said when I got along side a them. 'You gotta watch those kids … they'll rob you blind!' I was amazed. I had never seen children act this way and here I was in the middle of it. Know what I mean?"

"Yeah. I've seen movies of Viet Nam where they showed the kids that way. Were they just hungry or what?"

"I think so, but who's to say. Know what I mean? Now I'm in Da Nang, been attacked by an unruly crowd of children, meeting my first new friends from my duty station who were laughing at me and once again … weaponless. I mean, I found nothing to smile about right then. Right?

Kate walked down the bar to take an order while Jeffery continued.

"The trip to my duty station was about an hour on rough roads, thru narrow streets with people staring at me. Some waving, although my driver said they were flipping me off— some smiling and some angry looks. Know what I mean?"

He watched as Mariah took a sip of beer before nodding at him to go on.

"We drive a while down the road and stop at the entrance to the bridge that connected Da Nang to the location of my station.

"'Why are we stopping?' I asked because I didn't like the idea of being a sitting target. Know what I mean?

"'There are floating mines in the river', they said. 'We gotta wait 'til they get 'em all.' Just then a few shots rang out followed by explosions from under the bridge. I was cringing in the back seat, my duffel bag serving as my protection. I about shit my pants." He laughed.

Mariah almost choked on her fork full of Spanish rice when he said that. Jeffrey patted her on the back before continuing.

"Know what I mean?"

Mariah nodded and took a swig of beer.

"I'm sure the bridge was no more than 100 yards long, but it seemed like it took half an hour to drive across it. Funny how time slows down when you're scared half to death. Driving with no lights, except for the spaced, bare light bulbs along the side of the bridge, we finally got to the other side. Know what I mean?

"As I glanced at my drivers after we got to the other side, I detected a sigh of relief from both of them. That made me feel a little better. Know what I mean?

"Well, while we drove down a dirt road, surrounded by houses made of cardboard, corrugated metal and wood, my driver had his rifle in hand, locked and loaded, and pointing toward the houses. 'We know they're out there, but we don't know exactly where,' I was told. I thought, 'Oh great. Now I'm a moving target. Know what I mean?"

Mariah finished her meal and Kate came over and took her plate away.

"I don't think I'd ever been so fearful in my whole life. Nothin' good has happened since I landed in Saigon. Know what I mean? I mean, I knew I was destined to die any minute.

"My duty station was a rather large compound with fields of antennas pointing up into the sky. In a cloud a dust, we pulled up to the Orderly Room. Know what I mean?

"'You're here. We're gonna go grab a beer.' the driver said to me.

'Thanks' was about all I could mutter. I was so nervous I couldn't even find the front door to the office."

Jeffrey chuckled. "Know what I mean?"

Mariah nodded.

"When I got inside, the First Sergeant stood in his skivvies with a foul grimace on his face. Can you picture it?"

Mariah was surprised he didn't say 'know what I mean.' It threw her off for a second, delaying her response. "Oh. Yeah. What was he mad about?"

"Seems my arrival had interfered in his happy hour or somethin'. Great way to start off, I thought to myself. This had been a shitty week, and now my First Sergeant is pissed at me before I even get to meet him. Know what I mean?

"Picture this. A young kid, in a foreign land, having already survived an attack, not knowing anybody and so nervous he was about ready to piss his pants and suddenly ..." he paused for effect, eyes growing large.

Mariah waited.

"A hard slap on my back," he slapped his hand down on the bar, "and a 'where the hell have you been' yelled in my ear. I cringed, what did I do wrong already, I wondered. Know what I mean? Slowly I turned to the back slapper to give my story and who should be standing behind me but one of my best friends from High School. Chuck!!! I was as happy as a kid fishin' at the river on a Sunday mornin'. Know what I mean?" Jeffrey laughed and Mariah laughed with him.

"All I could do was hug him and tell him how glad I was that he was there—relief flowed through me instantly."

Jeffrey laughed out loud and clapped the bar again before leaning back on his stool and almost falling off. Mariah reached out and grabbed his arm, as he grabbed the edge of the bar with his other hand and continued his story without missing a beat.

"That's when I learned when the night is the darkest, someone will come into your life to help you out. Might be a stranger, might be an old friend, might be family. Doesn't matter 'cause you don't have to face the dark all alone. Know what I mean?"

"Yeah. I think I do, Jeffrey. Thanks. I needed to hear that."

"Well, that's not all. Chuck helped me process in, showed me the ropes and told me of the do's and don'ts around the place. Know what I mean? He had already been at the post for ten months and was gettin' ready to go home. Our time was limited but we made the best of it. Know what I mean? He even got me a side arm. I felt much better after that. Right?"

He shook his head and said, pensively, "Chuck went home shortly afterwards and I lasted out my year with many a story to tell my children."

"And we've heard them all," Kate said with a twinkle in her eyes as she walked back to their corner of the bar. "Every last one of them—at least five times each."

"What an exciting story," Mariah said. "And to think you made it back home alive."

"Yup. A year of fear and unknowing, but I survived. Know what I mean? When I got home, I tried to contact Chuck to no avail. Years went by and his memory gradually faded. Know what I mean? One day I was searching the internet—great thing, by the way—for anythin' about my duty station and found a registry of people in the same unit I was in. I found Chuck's name, and his address and phone number, too. Know what I mean? He lived about twenty miles from me! I couldn't believe it. Know what a surprise that was?

"Wow, all this time and he lived only twenty miles away?"

"Yup. We've visited often these past years. Although we were not the best of friends before Viet Nam—for the past 20 years we've been very close and supportive. Know what I mean?"

"Wow, Jeffrey. Glad you finally got back in touch with Chuck," Mariah said. "Thanks for sharing with me. I enjoyed hearing your story, but I better go home and take Paisley out."

"My pleasure. I enjoyed the company. Know what I mean?"

"Me too. And thanks for the dinner. As always," Mariah said turning to Kate, "it was delicious."

"You're welcome," Jeffrey said at the same time Kate said, "Glad you enjoyed it. Come back any time."

"I will and probably soon. Y'all take care."

After their goodbyes she made it to her car and headed back to the suite and to Paisley.

****

As soon as Mariah walked into the suite, Paisley jumped on her legs and danced all around her in happiness. Mariah bent and picked her up, hugging her as tight as her four legged roommate would allow before she set Paisley on the chair and put her harness on to take her for a walk.

It was a beautiful evening. The air smelled crisp and clean—traffic was light as they traversed down Center Drive to the shopping center and back. Paisley was eager to run, so they ran all the way to the family buffet restaurant and walked back to give Paisley time to go to the bathroom.

When they returned to the suite, Mariah sat at her computer and started pounding out notes on the day's events. She emailed the pictures she took with her phone in Chelsea's bedroom to herself, opened her email on her computer, saved the pictures and attached them to her notes. Her eyes grew heavy with exhaustion as she prepared an email with everything attached for Morgan and Riley. Before sending the email, she sat and thought about the small box of letters and the diary she found in Chelsea's closet. Her eyes closed. She drifted off to sleep while sitting at the computer, a swirl of fog filling her dream—a deep growl waking her with a start. She jumped, sat up straight and looked around before she realized she woke herself with her own snoring. Paisley, who had been curled up and sleeping next to Mariah on the sofa, jumped when Mariah did. Mariah couldn't help but laugh at herself.

She closed the laptop, forgetting to send the email to her partners, and reached over to pat Paisley. "Let's go to bed, girl. I'll call Morgan in the morning."

Paisley sat up, stretched, and opened her mouth wide in a yawn, her tongue curling as she made a whining sound. Mariah got up from the couch, set the closed laptop to the side, turned the lights off and headed to bed, Paisley following.

In bed, a deep sadness overtook Mariah for the Dunn family. Mr. Dunn believed he was courageous and compassionate—thinking he was sparing his wife by leaving her so she doesn't have to deal with his failing health—Mrs. Dunn's anger and thinking she was depriving him happiness by not giving him a divorce—the children, all caught in this terrible drama and apparently forced to take sides—and now Chelsea is missing. *This is a crazy world we live in,* she thought, *crazy and terrifying.*

The last thing Mariah remembered before going to sleep was a tear trickling from her eye, across the bridge of her nose to her cheek, and down to the pillow.

TUESDAY IN PORTLAND

Riley stopped outside Morgan's office door.

"Morgan, when's the last time you heard from Mariah?"

"Not since she got down there. I knew she'd be busy, but I'm starting to get worried. Have you heard anything?"

"No, and I don't like it." Riley stepped into Morgan's office and sat in front of the desk. "I don't think she was ready to go off alone on a case like this one. I've left her a couple messages but she hasn't responded. I'm worried."

"I tried to call her a couple times yesterday, and twice so far this morning. No answer on the phone and no response to the text messages. I'm packed and the car is loaded, Riley. As soon as I wrap up this paperwork, I'm headed down there."

"Great. I'll keep an eye on this place, but you call me if you need me. We've got the new secretary starting tomorrow and she is really sharp. Jeri and Janice told me they could come and help her get settled in and keep an eye on this place while we're gone for a day or two, in case I need to come down there too."

"I'll call as soon as I get there and know what's going on."

"Hopefully she's just been busy, but she's usually conscientious about keeping in touch."

"My thoughts exactly. I'm going to ring her pretty little neck when I find her. She's not supposed to worry me like this any more."

"Oh, hey. Remember Albert Caster?"

"Our first case here in Portland?"

"Yeah, the guy who needed us to search for his missing son? We found him shacked up with his coke blowing girlfriend. Remember?"

Morgan nodded. "Yeah. That one. I talked to Albert a couple months ago and he said his son is still clean. He dropped a huge dime on rehab for that kid, but it seems to be working."

"Right. He told me if we ever needed his jet, to give him a call. I can get down there mighty fast if I have to."

"Sure, but by the time you called him and he got the jet fueled and the flight plan approved, you could almost be there by driving."

"Well, there's that."

TUESDAY MORNING IN MEDFORD

Mariah was slow to wake, having slept through the night without any memory of a bad dream. She stretched and reached over in the bed to pet Paisley who was curled up in a ball at Mariah's side.

"How you doing, little girl?" she asked the little dog. Paisley stretched her legs out and rolled on her back to look at Mariah.

"We better get our lazy butts out of bed. I have work today."

Mariah tossed the blanket back and sat on the edge of the bed. She looked back at Paisley who had rolled to her other side and watched Mariah.

"You can stay in bed if you like, but I'm getting a shower."

Mariah grabbed her robe and walked to the bathroom. After her shower she walked back into the bedroom and caught Paisley snoozing.

"You bum!"

Mariah chuckled as she bent to get clean clothes from her suitcase. She decided the next order of business would be to visit the on-sight laundry facilities. She was about out of clean clothes. Once dressed, she called to Paisley.

"Come on sleepyhead. Let's go for a walk."

Paisley jumped off the bed and ran to Mariah who was holding her harness.

The pair stopped at the laundry and Mariah started two loads of laundry—one for whites and one for her jeans and shirts. Once the wash was going, she and Paisley took a walk past all the stores and random businesses to the Cafeteria and back. They stopped back at the laundry facility and Mariah put all her clothes in one dryer and got that started before taking Paisley back to their suite.

Mariah fixed herself a cup of coffee and commenced to play tug-o-war with Paisley. When Paisley tired of that, Mariah called Martin.

"Martin Silkeney, please. This is Mariah Jeffries."

"Just a moment please," responded a cheerful, female voice.

"This is Martin Silkeney."

"Hi Martin. This is Mariah. Good morning."

"Oh. Hi, Mariah. I suppose you're calling for those authorizations."

"Yes. Are they ready?"

"Yes Ma'am. You can come pick them up any time."

"That's wonderful. I'm on my way now."

"Good. I'll see you soon."

Mariah ran to the laundry room, gathered her dry clothes and brought them back to the suite. She folded everything and put them back in her suitcase, closed the bathroom and bedroom doors, gave Paisley a treat and left, pulling the door closed and making sure it was locked behind her.

As she approached her car, her phone rang.

"Hello?" Mariah asked into the phone as she opened her car door.

"Mariah?"

"Yes?"

"This is Robert Dunn. Do you have a minute?"

"Yes. How are you, Robert?"

"I got a call from Gayle Webb a few minutes ago. We were talking about the girls and he thought of something that he thinks might be of interest to you."

"He did? What is it?"

"He didn't say. When I asked him what it was, he lowered his voice and told me to meet him at Frisco's Diner and he would explain it to me then. I got the feeling he didn't want to talk about whatever it is in front of his wife, Tawnie. I told him I was calling you and he said that was great. Can you meet us there?"

"Hold on." Mariah closed her car door and started the engine. She grabbed a note pad and said, "Give me the address." He rattled off an address and said it was behind the movie theater in the Medford center.

When they hung up, she plugged the address into her GPS and headed in that direction. A diner sounded wonderful to Mariah, she was starving.

When Mariah arrived, she didn't see any sign of Robert or Gayle. She thought they might be waiting inside, so inside she went to look around the small diner.

"Table for one?" the hostess asked.

"Um, a table for three, please. I'm meeting a couple people."

"Just a moment and I'll seat you."

"Thank you."

The hostess gathered three menus and led Mariah to a booth next to the big front window. She placed a menu at each place setting.

"Would you like some coffee?

"Yes. Thank you. Where's the ladies room?"

"At the end of the hall across from the entrance."

"Two gentlemen are meeting me here. My name's Mariah. Please seat them if they show up while I'm in the bathroom."

"Of course."

Mariah was finishing up in the bathroom, drying her hands, when she heard three pops followed by screams and a loud crash. She grabbed her baby Glock from her purse, and squatted down before opening the bathroom door. People were crowded around the front door, yelling and screaming, trying to push past the crowd to escape the mayhem. Mariah heard a lady on the phone around the corner from the end of the hall saying someone had been shot and they needed the police and an ambulance.

"Two men. Two men were shot out in the parking lot … No. I didn't see anything …"

Mariah tucked her Glock back in her purse, but kept her hand on it. She stepped out of the bathroom and pushed through the panicked crowd trying to reach the two men outside. She knew, without being told, or seeing for herself, that it was Robert and Gayle.

The woman on the phone continued as Mariah pushed passed her.

"Please send the police here, and an ambulance. … I heard these bangs and then people started screaming. I turned around and saw a man fall to the ground. … Then the front window was shot out. … A man and a lady were sitting by the window, and they're bleeding but I don't know if they were shot or just cut by the broken glass …

Mariah made it out the door and heard the sirens blaring in the distance. On the ground were Gayle Webb and Robert Dunn. A gentleman leaned over Gayle trying to stop the bleeding from his head, while talking on the phone to an emergency dispatcher.

"Yeah … he's alive, but he's been shot in the head …"

She moved over to Robert where another man was leaning over him. The man, dressed in cycling shorts and shirt, a bike and helmet on the ground nearby, looked up at her.

"He's alive, but he's bleeding out." His hands were pressed over the chest wound, trying to slow down the flow of blood.

Mariah kneeled next to Robert, his eyes opened and he looked at her. He tried to say something, his mouth moving, but nothing came out. Then his eyes fluttered, opened wide, and his last breath was expelled as his head rolled to the side. The cyclist leaned back, knowing as Mariah did, that Robert had bled out and there was no reviving him.

"Did you see the shooter," Mariah inquired of the cyclist.

"No. Not really. It was some guy on a motorcycle who sped off around the back of the building."

"Did you see the tags?"

"No. I was over there." The cyclist shook his head and pointed across the parking lot to a shopping center. "Poor man. Did you know him?"

"I met him. I'm Mariah. What's your name?"

"Cliff Pieper."

"The police are going to want to talk to you, Cliff. Don't go anywhere, I'm going to check on the other man."

Mariah got up and went back over to Gayle, kneeling down beside him. He was hit once, in the side of his head—entry wound at the front left of the forehead, and he was unconscious, but still breathing.

"Did he say anything?" She asked the man who was holding his t-shirt over Gayle's wound. The t-shirt was soaked in blood.

"No. He was unconscious by the time I got to him.

"What did you see?"

"Nothing. I was inside at my table talking to Faye, the waitress, when the shooting started. As soon as it stopped, I ran out here to see if I could help."

The first patrol car pulled up and stopped, the officer jumped out of his car and ran over to them. An ambulance came down the parking lot behind him, lights flashing, the siren cut off mid-blare.

Crouching down beside Mariah, the officer asked, "What do we have?"

"Drive by shooting. This man is Gayle Webb and he was shot in the head. Over there is Robert Dunn, DOA. He was shot in the chest and bled out just a moment ago. That's Cliff Pieper sitting next to him. He tried to stop the bleeding, but with no success. He said he was riding his bicycle over there, across the lot." Mariah pointed across the parking lot between the furniture store and the movie theater. "He saw a guy on a motorcycle drive by and shoot the two victims and continue on around to the back of the building over there, out of sight."

Officer Day, according to his name tag, stood and waived to the EMT's to come to Gayle's aid. While they pulled a gurney in his direction, he got on the radio to relay the information Mariah had given him.

An unmarked police unit pulled up and a plain clothes officer got out and walked over to them. "Who saw the shooter?"

"The guy over there, sitting next to the body," Officer Day reported as the EMT's started working on Gayle and getting him ready to transport to the hospital. The good Samaritan and Mariah stood and stepped away so the EMT's had room to work. The Detective asked Mariah what she saw.

"Nothing. I was inside, in the lady's room when a bunch of screaming started and there was a loud crash when the front window was shot out. I came out here to see what I could do to help."

The detective turned to the man who had been trying to help Gayle, asking him the same thing.

"Like I told the lady here, I didn't see anything. I was inside talking to Faye, the waitress."

"Don't go anywhere. I'll need to talk to both of you." The detective turned to Officer Day. "Get their contact information and transport them to the station to give formal statements."

He walked over to Cliff. An EMT covered Robert's body with a sheet after checking for signs of life and finding none.

Officer Day turned to the good Samaritan who was naked from the waist up, his flabby belly pushing over the waist of his pants, his salt and pepper chest hairs smeared with drying blood. "Do you have identification on you?"

"Uh, yeah," the man said, wiping his bloody hands on the front of his jeans before he reached into his back pocket with his right hand and pulled out his billfold. His hands were shaking so much he dropped the billfold when he tried to open it, bent down to pick it up and lost his balance. He caught himself with his left hand, picked up the billfold and stood back up. He handed the whole billfold to the officer as tears spilled out of his eyes. "I'm a wreck, man. Here. It's in here, just take it."

"You'll need to take the driver's license out of the billfold and hand it to me."

Mariah watched the exchange and walked over to help. She thought the man was going to faint so she reached for his arm.

"Here. Sit down a moment." She and Officer Day helped him down to the ground. The sickening metallic smell of drying blood permeated the air and the man started to wretch.

"Breath through your mouth, not your nose. Take a couple deep breaths in through your mouth and let them out through your nose slowly," Mariah told him.

He did as she told him and he seemed to calm a little. He hung his head and started to cry. Mariah kneeled down beside him, her hand on his arm.

"Everything is going to be okay. Take another deep breath in through your mouth and hold it just a moment." He did as she instructed. "Now, let it out slow and easy through your mouth." As he exhaled, he started nodding his head.

"Feeling better?"

"Yeah. A little bit. Thanks," he said and opened his billfold taking out his driver's license. He looked up at Officer Day and handed him the license with a still trembling hand and said, "I'm sorry, Officer."

"You're doing great, all things considered. This is just procedure. I'm sorry, but I need you to answer some questions for me."

"Sure. I want to help."

"Verify your name, please?"

"Gage Rhinehart. I live at twelve-oh-one Crestland Place, unit fourty-eight in Phoenix."

"Verify your date of birth"

Gage said he was born December thirteenth, nineteen-seventy-four.

"Phone number?"

Gage gave his phone number.

"And, what about your vehicle. Is it here?"

Gage gave the information requested and pointed to an old blue Chevy pick-up. Officer Day looked at the vehicle, writing down a description and the tag number before returning Gage's driver's license.

"Can you think of anything else that you heard or saw?"

"No. Like I said, I was inside talking to Faye, the waitress, when I heard these pops. People started screaming and jumping out of their chairs, and then the window crashed. I heard some lady say there was a gun fight in the parking lot and two men were dead, so I ran outside to see if I could render first aid."

"Are you a doctor or EMT or something?"

"No. I just thought they might need some help before the ambulance got here. I had first aid training a couple years ago—just basic stuff."

"Okay. Stay where you are and we'll head to the station in a couple minutes."

He turned to Mariah who had her driver's license out and handed it to him.

"I'm Mariah Jeffries. I'm currently staying at the Medford Suites of the Rogue Valley while I'm here on business, but I live in Portland, OR." She verified her address in Portland, her date of birth, phone number, and gave him a complete description of her vehicle including the license plate number.

His eyes squinted at her. "You sound like a cop."

"An ex-cop," Mariah replied. He wrote that down in his notes and grunted.

"Stay here," he said as Detective Cleveland walked toward them and Officer Day stepped away to meet him. They had a brief conference, taking turns nodding in Mariah's direction and looking at her like she was a criminal, before he walked back to her. "Anything else?"

"I was here to meet both victims."

Detective Day raised an eyebrow. "Both of them? Why?"

"My agency was hired to investigate the missing girls. Robert is the father of Chelsea Dunn, and Gayle is the father of Tina Webb."

"Oh, God!" Gage blurted.

"Those poor families," Detective Day said under his breath while writing that revelation in his notebook. "Detective Cleveland is going to want to talk to you."

"Sure. No problem."

"He just left to go back to the station. Let's go."

A uniformed officer walked over to Detective Day and the two witnesses. "Detective, you're needed over there. A woman says she saw the whole thing."

"Sure. I'll be right there." Detective Day turned from the officer back to Mariah and Gage. "I need you two to go straight to the police department. I'll radio ahead to Detective Cleveland that you're on your way."

Mariah nodded. "I'll go straight there."

"Me too," Gage added.

"Are you going to be okay to drive, Mr. Rhinehart?" the detective inquired.

"Yeah. I'm better now. Thanks."

Mariah got into her car, locked the doors, put the key in the ignition and turned, the engine coming to life. She pulled her phone from her back pocket and punched in a number.

"Hi Norela. I have a job for you."

"Do you need me to come out there?"

"Oh no. You don't need to come out here …"

"Because I can if you need me. We've been kinda slow around here."

Mariah laughed. "Although I would love to see you and Jewel, it's not necessary for you to come out here to do this job. But, if you need to get away ..." Mariah was smiling.

"Okay. What's the job?"

Mariah gave Norela the rundown of the missing girls. She told Norela about the call from Robert Dunn saying Gayle Webb thought of something he didn't want his wife to know about.

"And, Norela, before we could meet to find out what he remembered, the two men were gunned down in the parking lot. Robert Dunn was killed and Gayle Webb was shot in the head. He's unconscious."

"Well, damn girl. You never got to talk to either one of them to find out what it was?"

"No. I never got to talk to either one of them and Gayle Webb may not come around. It doesn't look good. Could you do a deep background check on him for me?"

"Sure. Just send me all the information you have on him and I'll get right on it."

"I'll email you his dossier along with a contract for the job as soon as we hang up. Send me everything you can on him."

"No problem. How are you doing these days?"

"Me? I'm doing great." Mariah saw no need to worry them about her nightmares.

"Uh huh. And how are you *really* doing?"

Mariah laughed. "I'm fine, honest ... now. How's Jewel?"

"Oh my God. She's found herself another boyfriend. They had only been out on two dates and then took off to Vegas for a long weekend together."

"What? Jewel? Isn't it a bit soon for her to go on a long weekend trip with the guy?"

"Yeah. Not like her at all."

"Well, you background checked the guy first for her, right?"

"Yes, of coarse! I didn't find any arrest reports or anything like that—no red flags. He's not an ex-con or suspected drug runner or murderer, I don't think he's dangerous, but he's so annoying—Very arrogant and pompous. I can only stand to be in the same room with the guy for a few minutes before I'm bored out of my mind."

"She's not in love with this guy, is she?"

"No. She said she's just having fun."

"Did you tell her you don't like the guy even though he checked out clean?"

"Sure, but it's her life. If she enjoys hanging out with the guy, then who am I to tell her not to?"

"Yeah. You're right. Just call me if I need to come and kick some butt." They both laughed.

"I will. If he hurts our Jewel, we'll take him out into the mountains and make him hold the shovel on the way."

"That's right. And tell her if she ever does get married, she better be telling me about it before the fact."

"Oh, you know Jewel. She'll never remarry."

"Anything is possible when it comes to Jewel."

"I suppose she may marry one day, but I doubt it."

"Right. Okay, call me as soon as you can with whatever you find. We gotta find these girls fast."

"Will do."

"Oh hey, wait. I'm thinking, maybe you should do the same thing on his wife, Tawnie, too. Maybe she has a lover or ex-boyfriend or something."

"Right, good idea."

"Okay, I'll send hers along too. Good night. Talk to you soon."

Mariah pulled up the Cloud to find the file on the Webbs. She attached it to an email and then found the standard contract. Filled in the pertinent information, saved it to her files and attached that to the email as well. She sent it all to Norela before she put the car in drive and headed to the Medford Police Department.

"As I told Officer Day, I'm here on business." Mariah told Detective Cleveland.

"Yes, we know. I just checked you out," Captain Spencer said behind her as he entered the room and tossed her I.D. and credentials on the table. "I found quite an impressive background and history on you from what I could tell scanning the information. I'll be reading up on you tonight." He paused and looked her over. Mariah wasn't intimidated and stared back at him.

He looked at Detective Cleveland and said, "I'll take it from here."

Detective Cleveland stepped to the door. "Yes, sir." He left the room, closing the door behind him.

"I don't suppose there's anything I can say to convince you to stay out of this case, is there?"

"The shooting? I'm not here to look into a random shooting at one of your local diners. I just happened to be a patron at the establishment when the shooting occurred."

Sitting backwards on the chair across the table from Mariah, and crossing his arms across the back of the chair, Captain Spencer asked, "What did you see?"

"As I already told Officer Day at the scene, I heard the gun fire, and the screams, and then the crash from the window while I was finishing up in the bathroom. I drew my weapon and came out of the ladies room to find the patrons standing around, trying to push their way out the door, or sitting on the floor in a daze. A lady on the phone was telling dispatch about the two victims stretched out on the pavement in front of the building … spilling their blood."

"Prior to the shooting, did you see anything, or anyone suspicious that could lead us to the shooter of the two victims?"

"Mr. Dunn and Mr. Webb? That's their names. And no. Do you have any suspects?"

"I thought you said you're not here to investigate the shooting?"

"I'm not. I guess my investigative instincts are kicking in." Mariah gave him a sweet, innocent smile.

Captain Spencer grunted, nodded his head and said, "Sure. That's what it is." He smiled back at her, absent the humor. "Did you see anything before the shooting occurred?"

"No, sir. I did not."

"What were you doing there?"

"This has been a tough week. I was hungry and stopped in for lunch."

"Why are you here, Ms. Jeffries?"

"Jeffries. Just call me Jeffries, please," she said, shaking her head. "I'm here because Officer Day said you would want to talk to me."

She realized she was dancing around the issue with Captain Spencer instead of getting straight to the point. She was in an ornery mood and felt defensive for no apparent reason, and it took her a moment to realize he reminded her of her old Sergeant back in Albuquerque. That man drove her crazy while she was a patrol officer. He was a crusty and cantankerous old jackass—badge heavy, arrogant, impatient, and gruff. She wasn't about to give the old bastard a reason to fire her, so she kept her smart mouth on good behavior around him. Captain Spencer didn't have that power over her. *Perhaps*, she wondered, *this was a passive aggressive way to get back at the old fart.*

"What did you tell him that made him so sure I would want to talk to you?"

"Well, that's a good question. Isn't it? I just told him what I told you."

"I think not. Why are you in town. You don't live here. Your P.I. firm is in Portland. So why are you here, in Medford? What are you investigating?"

"I was hired to do an investigation and was at the diner to meet with the two victims."

"Who hired you?"

"That's confidential information, Captain."

"What are you investigating?"

"A stolen car."

"A stolen car?" he responded in disbelief, eyebrows raised in skepticism.

"Among other things."

"Look, Ms. Jeffries."

"Jeffries."

"Look Jeffries. Let's not play twenty questions."

"Fine with me. Quite asking them!"

Captain Spencer hung his head and sighed. When he raised his head and looked her square in the eyes he said, "I don't want to find you snooping around the kidnappings either."

"Look Captain Spencer. You and the FBI are getting nowhere in that case." Mariah leaned forward and pointed at the Captain. "A concerned citizen, not related to any of the victims, hired my firm to look into the kidnappings." She leaned back in her chair and crossed her arms. "What's it gonna hurt for another group of very well qualified and connected investigators to run their own investigation and chase down leads? The bottom line is to find out what has happened to the girls, recover them safely if possible, and stop any other children from disappearing. Am I wrong about that?"

"No Jeffries. You're not wrong, but I can't be sharing evidence with you."

"I don't *want* you to share your evidence or notes on the case. We need to look at this from a completely new and different angle—start at the beginning. Maybe, without your information something new will turn up—some little lead that you or the FBI overlooked because of a bigger lead. We're going to start from scratch, do our own interviews, check our own leads, and run our own timeline. With any luck, we'll uncover something that can bring those girls home and end this nightmare for your community."

Captain Spencer stared at her for a good ninety seconds without saying a word. She let the silence hang between them, and it seemed like a stand-off until he nodded his head and said, "Okay. Like us, I guess you suspect this shooting is related to the kidnappings."

Mariah looked him in the eyes and popped off with, "You think?" She shook her head and sucked in her breath.

"I'm sorry." She sighed. "I was afraid of that. Do you have any suspects?"

"No. The FBI are worried about the families of the other missing girls, but we can't find a common denominator for the violence except the kidnappings. Did you talk to either of the men before the shooting?"

"No. They must have just gotten there when they were shot. I had just walked in myself, and went to the restroom—couldn't have been more than two minutes. I didn't notice anyone suspicious."

"What were you meeting them about?"

"Apparently Gayle called Robert and said he remembered something that might be relevant to the case. Robert called me to meet them with Gayle's consent."

"Did Robert give you any hint as to what it was?"

"No. He didn't know. Gayle was going to tell us both at the diner. Robert got the impression that Gayle didn't want to talk about it with his wife around—whatever *'it'* was."

Captain Spencer got up from his chair, opened the door and yelled out, "Pettigrew, tell Clever Cleveland to come in here."

"Yes, sir," a man reply before Captain Spencer closed the door.

"Why did you call him Clever Cleveland?" Mariah asked. "That's not his real name, is it?"

"No." He grinned. "Saying his full name, Eisenhower McKinley Cleveland, is like taking a long trip across consonants and vowels—too much of a mouth full. Besides, he's a smart guy and I like the sound of Clever Cleveland. He doesn't seem to mind it, either."

When Detective Cleveland came into the room, Captain Spencer told him to take Mariah's statement about her phone call from Robert. "After that, you can go, but please call me if you come up with any leads."

"I will Captain. As a courtesy, would you let me know if you find any leads on the shooting?"

"You're not here to investigate a shooting. Remember?" he said with a sideways grin. In spite of his comment, she suspected they were going to work well together.

TUESDAY P.M.

When she finished at the police Department, Mariah went straight to the hospital to check on Gayle. He was still in surgery and she found Martin Silkeney in the surgery waiting room.

"Hi Martin," she said as she walked into the waiting room.

"Mariah," he said, with a nod of his head. "What happened?"

"I don't know. Yet! Robert called me and said Gayle wanted to meet. He told Robert he thought of something that might be relevant to the investigation. It was Robert's idea to call me in on the meeting. That's all he told me."

"And they were shot before you could meet with them?"

"Yes—before they even got into the diner."

"Did Robert say if Gayle told him anything before the shooting?"

"When I got to him, he tried to say something, but nothing came out. Gayle was unconscious on impact from the bullet."

"And Robert was killed instantly?"

"No. He … bled out fast."

Martin was in shock and Mariah had to repeat herself.

"When I got to him, he was still alive, but bleeding out. He opened his eyes and tried to say something to me, but nothing came out. His mouth was moving, but he couldn't say anything. Then he died. Nobody knows what Gayle may or may not have told him."

Martin sighed.

Mariah sat down in the chair next to him. "Has anyone contacted their families—Mrs. Dunn and the boys?"

"The police are taking care of that."

"How about Gayle's family?"

"The police."

"I'm going to have to go and check on Mrs. Dunn when I leave here." Mariah sighed and shook her head. "I feel so bad for all of them."

As if on cue, Mrs. Dunn came into the waiting room on the arm of a much younger version of Robert. She was sobbing so hard, she could barely walk and her son was supporting her until he got her to a chair. She sat and he sat next to her, wrapping his arm around her. A few minutes later, two more young men resembling Robert came in and took seats directly across the room from Valene. After a few minutes of uncomfortable silence, one of them spoke.

"Curtis, is there anything we can do for her?" The young man holding Valene shook his head no without uttering a word. They all sat in silence, absorbed in their own thoughts.

Mariah got up and crossed the room to the two men sitting across from Curtis and Valene.

"Hi. My name's Mariah Jeffries. I'm guessing you are Roberts sons?"

The younger looking of the two nodded his head. "Yeah, I'm Vince and this is Bobby. That's Curtis, our youngest brother, with mom."

"I just wanted to say I'm very sorry for your family."

"Yeah. Dad told us you were looking for the girls and that he talked to you. He said you might come looking for us to talk to us too," Bobby said.

"I was going to. I would ask if you could think of anything that might help. Your thoughts on her friends, boyfriends, where she goes and hangs out—that kind of stuff. I don't want to bother you with it now. But think about it when you can. Here's my card. Any one of you can call me at any time."

"Thanks," Bobby said, taking the card. "We will if we think of anything."

Mariah turned to Valene and took her hands.

"I'm so sorry."

Valene squeezed Mariah's hand. "Thank you."

Mariah went back to her seat beside Martin. They all lapsed back into silence—the only sound was Valene's soft crying.

After a few minutes, she wiped her eyes and looked around the room before saying to the men across from her, "Thank you for coming. I've missed you both so much."

Bobby and Vince both stood at the same time and crossed to Valene as she stood. She hugged Bobby who reached her first, murmuring her love for him, and then Vince.

"We missed you too, Mom. We thought dad needed us more at the time. You had Curtis and Chelsea."

"I know, but I needed you both when Chelsea went missing. I'm glad you were there for your Dad, but I was hurt thinking you sided with that bitch he left me for."

Bobby and Vince looked at each other and then just hugged her. Vince said, "Mom, we'll never side with another woman who might try to take your place in our lives. We're here now."

She held Vince out at arms length and said, "Vincent, you finally got your hair cut. It looks so good. I never liked that shaggy mess you had before. It hid your beautiful eyes." And then she hugged him again while at the same time reaching for Bobby.

"And Robert, how's the job? Your father and I are so proud of you for starting your own business."

"The business is good Mom—growing slow, but steady."

Valene and the boys sat together—their conversation a quiet murmur.

Martin and Mariah walked to the cafeteria for something to eat and to give the Dunn family some privacy. Mariah was famished and got a burger and fries. Martin got a large salad with grilled chicken. Mariah eyed it with somber consideration, but decided she was in need of some serious carbs. When they finished eating, they grabbed some sandwiches and bottled water to take back to the waiting room for Valene and the boys.

When they returned to the waiting room, Tawnie was sitting in the corner with another woman. They were holding hands and staring into space. Mariah and Martin gave the food they brought back to Valene and the boys, then stepped over to Tawnie and expressed their sorrow for her and her family.

"He's gonna be alright. I know he is," she said and introduced them to her sister, Kathleen.

The doctor came into the waiting room two hours later and told them Gayle made it through the surgery. "He's in a coma and it's going to be touch and go for a while. He may not make it through the night." He offered to show Tawnie and her sister to the ICU waiting room. "Once Gayle is settled in his room, you can have a short visit," the doctor told Tawnie.

Martin and Mariah followed the doctor, Tawnie, and Kathleen to the ICU waiting room. The Dunn's hugged Tawnie and told her to call them if she needed anything and then left to deal with their own grief and loss.

It was six by the time they left the hospital with Tawnie and Kathleen. Martin and Mariah stood in the parking lot and discussed the events before they headed over to the Webb's at Kathleen's request. Mariah dreaded the visit. With her daughter missing without a trace, Mariah couldn't imagine what this was like for her, but if Tawnie wanted them there, she wouldn't let her down.

The street outside the Webb residence was lined on both sides with parked cars. Mariah found a parking place at the far end of the block, Martin pulling into the last parking place right behind her.

A lot of people were milling around in the living room when they walked in. Mariah asked the first person she came to where Tawnie was. The gentleman, holding a paper plate with a fried chicken leg and potato salad, tilted his head toward the kitchen. In the kitchen Mariah found an older woman who said Tawnie was in the living room. In truth, there were so many people socializing, that there was no telling where Tawnie was. The place had more of a party atmosphere instead of grief and support for the family. Mariah didn't understand how this was comforting to the family. She would leave the crowded house and go off on a run by herself to deal with her emotions, if she lost a loved one. The last thing she would want was a house full of partying people.

Martin and Mariah went back into the living room and failed to find her there, so they walked through the house to the back door and out into the back yard. Tawnie was standing alone looking up at the stars.

"Hi Tawnie," Mariah said as they approached her from the side. "Martin and I just wanted to stop by and see if there was anything we could do for you."

She turned and looked at them. "There are so many people here to help and so little anyone can do. Thank you for asking, though. I have a wonderful church family and I won't want for anything for the next couple of weeks." She started to cry softly and Mariah wrapped her arms around the distraught woman, Martin standing awkwardly beside them.

He cleared his throat and said, "I'm so sorry Tawnie."

"Thank you, Martin. Thank you for everything." She reached out and took his hand. "I know this is hard for you too. You and Gayle have been friends for a long time."

Martin struggled valiantly to try and hold back his own tears.

"How's Trevor doing?" he asked.

She wiped her eyes with a tissue that she had in her pocket and then blew her nose. "He's confused and scared. How do I tell him that not only has he lost his big sister but his father may never come home again either?"

Martin shook his head. "Does he know what all these people are here for?"

"Not really. I told him his dad was in an accident. That's all I got out before Kathleen and mother arrived and I left for the hospital. Word got around—mom called the prayer chain at church—and people started showing up. He cried for a bit, mom said, and then his friend from Sunday School showed up and they ran off to his bedroom to play, the crisis forgotten."

Mariah cleared her throat. "Tawnie, Gayle and Robert Dunn were meeting me at the diner. Gayle told Robert he thought of something that might be relevant to the girls disappearance. Do you have any idea what that might have been?"

Tawnie closed her eyes before answering. "Oh God. I wish I did, but … I've wracked my brain trying to think of what it could be."

"We'll figure it out, Tawnie. We'll find who did this."

"Thank you."

"If you can think of anything that I can help you with, just give me a call," Martin said.

"Me too," Mariah added. "In the meantime, I'm going to be looking for Tina and the rest of the girls. Don't give up on me, Tawnie."

She aimed a weak smile at Mariah. "I hope you find them, Mariah. Thank you for coming."

Martin and Mariah left her standing in the back yard and weaved their way back through the house. They stopped in the living room to thank Kathleen for inviting them and said their goodbyes. They walked to their vehicles together, stopping at Mariah's driver's door.

"You were close to them, Martin?"

"Yes. Of all the girls missing, the Webb's were close family friends. Robert Dunn and I were once good friends, too, but we had a falling out years ago on a fishing trip. How much more can these people take? I'm broken hearted for these families, and I miss my girls, but no way am I bringing them back right now."

"I'm sorry. You should go home to your wife and call your girls. Maybe you could take a few days off to go down and visit them."

"My wife went down yesterday. I'll call her and tell her what happened, but I can't leave now. Not with Gayle in a coma and Robert dead. If nothing else, I want to be here for Robert's funeral."

"Did you know that Robert was dying?"

Martin, who had turned to walk to his car, stopped, and turned back to Mariah.

"What do you mean, he was dying?"

"You had no idea they were separated and that there is another woman living at his place?"

"What? No," he said, shaking his head. "Not Robert. He adored Valene. He wouldn't leave her and certainly wouldn't be involved with another woman. What about him being ill?"

"Valene doesn't know and he didn't want her to. I doubt there were very many people who knew the truth."

"Tell me."

"He was diagnosed with ALS and he was failing fast. He told me it wouldn't be long before he was in a wheelchair permanently. His two oldest boys knew, but not Curtis or Valene, … or Chelsea."

"Oh my God. I had no idea. Who's the other woman?"

"A nurse he hired to help him. Valene thinks he's in love with the woman and she is withholding a divorce to punish him. He, of course, has not filed for a divorce, but he wants her to think she's punishing him if it makes her feel better. He just didn't want her to see him waste away."

"How sad. I had no idea."

"I'm sorry, Martin. I doubt he told very many people the truth. I find it quite unselfish of him to want to spend the end of his life without his love beside him just to spare her the anguish of watching a terrible disease riddle his body, but in another sense – how selfish of him. I don't know." Mariah shrugged. "I guess they will fill her in now. Maybe, in some small way, that will bring her some peace—knowing he didn't really cheat on her and he never stopped loving her."

"Maybe. Good night, Mariah. Go get some rest."

"You too, Martin. Talk to you later."

TUESDAY NIGHT

It was a quarter to eight and Mariah was exhausted, hungry, and anxious to reach the suite and Paisley.

Poor little girl has been cooped up by herself all day without a chance to go out and potty.

Mariah always left a light on for Paisley when she knew she would be out after dark, but this time, she expected to return before noon when she left, so the suite was dark upon her return.

The hair at the back of her neck stood on end when she opened the door and entered.

Something's not right.

She reached into her purse and drew out the Glock while closing the door and crouching down without turning any lights on.

The music is off and Paisley's being quiet, she thought.

Mariah crouched low, putting her purse on the floor to the side of the door with precise care, and waited for her eyes to adjust to the dark. She listened, but didn't hear anything. It didn't take long for the outside lights filtering in through the drapes to help her make out the shapes in the room. Everything seemed to be in place except that Paisley had still not made a sound. Her heart pounding, she crept over to the dining table where she last remembered placing her flashlight. She grabbed it, and turned it on.

"Paisley," she whispered and swept the dining room, living room, and kitchen, her gun pointed where the light shined, ready to fire. She swept the crate and found the door was open, the crate empty.

Damn!

"Paisley," she called a little louder, her heart sinking. If she were able, Paisley would be at her side. Fear for her little fur baby was spreading in her gut.

She started down the hall, heart in her throat for fear something had happened to Paisley. She tried to keep her panic in check and opened the bathroom door. She swept the room with the flashlight, gun pointed and ready. The shower door slid open on silent wheels when she pushed it to the left.

Nothing!

Memories of Jerry ambushing her in her home and the horrible aftermath of that attack assailed her.

Breathe Mariah.

She turned from the tub, but didn't dare close eyes as she drew three deep, calming breaths to quell the panic. Crossing the hall, she opened the door to the first bedroom and checked it out.

Before she got back to the doorway to return to the hall, the front door opened and the jingle of Paisley's tags rang out. Mariah switched off the flashlight, but not fast enough.

A deep voice called out. "I'm armed and I'll shoot. Come out with your hands up."

Mariah raised her hands with the flashlight in her left hand and the Glock in her right. She stepped into the hallway with a wide smile on her face. Paisley came bounding down the hall to her, still on the retractable leash. Morgan stopped her and pulled her back to him, unhooked the leash and let her go. She ran to Mariah and, just before she reached her favorite person, she jumped up, rebounded off Mariah's bent knees and propelled herself into Mariah's arms.

"Hi baby girl," Mariah said as she caught and hugged the little dog.

"What the hell are you doing skulking around in the dark," Morgan hurled as he put his gun back in its holster. "You could have been shot."

"What the hell are you doing here," Mariah spit back with equal vehemence and putting Paisley down.

"Riley and I have been trying to reach you for two days. When I talked to Martin yesterday, he said he hadn't talked to you in a day or two. He was going to call you this morning and tell you to call us. I tried calling both of you all day, but neither one of you answered."

"Is something wrong? Why the urgency?" Mariah hurried down the hall to Morgan's side.

"Well, hell. Not now, but until just a few minutes ago, nobody could reach you." Morgan reached out and bear hugged her. "You had me scared and I told you before that you were not allowed to do that anymore. You can't go off on a case and not keep in touch with me and Riley, Mariah. We care about you."

Relief rushed through her. "I'm sorry. I've just been working my *ass* off. I'm glad you're here though—things are heating up." They walked into the living room and sat down.

"When I got here, Paisley had obviously been here by herself for quite a while. I had to clean up her mess and then I took her out for a walk. It just reminded me too much of when you were kidnapped in Albuquerque. Scared the daylights out of me, Mariah."

Morgan pulled out his cell phone and pushed a button before putting the phone to his ear. Mariah could hear the rings—one … two …—a man's voice answering but she couldn't make out the words. "Yeah. She's alright, she's just been busy. She said we need to be here, things are escalating." … "Okay. Sounds good." … "I'll call you in the morning with details of what's going on." … "Yep." … "Will do." Morgan disconnected the call.

"I'm sorry, Morgan. I was going to call you and Riley this morning after interviewing the last family, but then I got a call to meet two of the fathers about something that one of them remembered or … thought of. Then both the fathers were shot at our rendezvous before I even got a chance to talk to them. The rest of the day has been all about that."

"Are they going to live?"

"No. Robert Dunn was killed, hit in the chest and bled out in the parking lot. Gayle Webb was hit in the head and is in a coma at the hospital."

"Damn. What the hell's going on down here?"

"I have no idea, but I intend to find out."

"Well, I'm here to help. Tell me everything you've learned so far."

"Can I eat first. The only thing I've had all day was a burger from the hospital cafeteria."

"Sounds good to me. I'm starved."

"I've got sandwich fixings. Ham or turkey?"

"Ham. Got any beer?"

"No. You'll have to go out for that."

"I'll wait."

Mariah fixed sandwiches and opened a bag of potato chips. After eating, Morgan and Mariah sat until two in the morning going over everything about the case. He read and re-read the notes and material she had gathered so far. Mariah didn't bother to tell him about the chance encounter with Erick at the dog park. She didn't feel that it had anything to do with the case.

"I'm beat Morgan. It's been a really, *really* long day," She said, yawning, barely able to keep her eyes open.

"You look it. Take your pain-in-the-butt dog and go to bed. I'll go get my gear out of the car."

"Pain-in-the-butt? You love her and she can sense it." Mariah chuckled. "She loves you too."

"Yeah, but she didn't come running and jumping right up into my arms when I came in. I think she loves you best."

Mariah grinned, looking down at Paisley stretched out on the couch beside her. "Yeah. She does. But, she can't very well run to you when she's crated," Mariah retorted.

Morgan stopped and turned to her. "She wasn't in her crate when I got here. Did she learn to open it and let herself out?"

"What? I always … oh, right. I guess I forgot to crate her this morning. I was running late—now I remember."

Morgan reached over and ruffled Paisley's fur. "You're a good girl, Paisley." Then he looked at Mariah and said, "I'll see you in the morning. What time do you want to get up?"

"I'm free in the morning, so I think I'll sleep in until I wake."

"Alright. Sweet dreams. I saw which room you took when I came in earlier, so don't worry about me walking into the wrong one by accident. See ya in the morning."

As Mariah stood, Paisley raised her head and watched Mariah hug Morgan.

"I'm glad you're here. See you in the morning." She turned and headed to her bedroom, Paisley jumping down from the couch and following.

"Good night," Morgan said as Mariah closed the bedroom door behind her.

****

I'm drying my hands when gunfire erupts on the other side of the door. I duck and reach for my weapon, but the only thing I find is a piece of paper. It reads, YOU ARE GOING TO DIE! My heart pounds and I break out in a cold sweat. People on the other side of the door are screaming and crying. I want to help them, but I'm frozen in fear.

"Get a grip," I tell myself. I start taking some calming breaths and tell myself that I must help them. I can't just cower in

this bathroom. After most of the noise subsides, and with shaking hands, I open the door. Bodies are everywhere. The blood is so think I keep sliding in the viscous mess. I fall and a blood-streaked face of an anonymous woman is staring sightlessly back at me, her mouth open in a silent scream. I push myself up, gagging, and crying. 'My God! What happened?' I wonder. I walk and slip-slide around the room looking for survivors, but everyone is dead.

"No! No!" I scream as sobs rock my body. It was my fault. If I had come out of the bathroom, they would all be alive. It was me that should be dead.

I make it to the door and frantically push a body out of the way so I can open it. Outside at last, I start to run.

I'm running across rooftops and someone is chasing me. I keep looking back but I can't see anything. I can, however, hear them. They are behind me, so I run faster except the blood from the killing room makes it slippery. I lose my balance and start to slide down the side of a roof and plunge over the edge. I spread my arms in reflex and begin to fly, but even flying, whoever is chasing me is right behind me. I can't allow myself to be caught. I have too much to do. The girls. Where are the girls? Now that I can fly maybe I can find the girls.

My pursuer is gone and I'm looking down—looking for Tina, Chelsea, Savannah, and Duskie. I'm flying over a forest—there are trails everywhere.

I spot Duskie running from something or someone. "Run Duskie. I'm coming to help you!" I shout. She runs into a heavy grove of trees up against the side of the mountain and I can't see her anymore. She doesn't come out. I land right in front of the trees where she entered and I look back in the direction she was running from. I don't see any pursuers and I don't hear anything. I enter the dark wooded area.

The trees filter out most of the daylight, and the resulting gloom and quiet under the trees is oppressive. No sound penetrates the gloom, not even the sound of birds or the buzzing of insects. It seems as though I stepped into a deep dark cave, and if I go any further, I won't be able to find my way without a flashlight.

"Duskie," I yell waiting a few seconds for a reply. "I'm here to help you. Don't hide." I wait again, but no response comes back to me.

A sense of dread rolls over me like a fog bank and my heart quickens. I start to back step toward the light. As I do, a shadow emerges from the dark. "Leave me alone," I say to it. "Why don't you leave me alone?" I decide that the shadow will not scare me off because Duskie needs me. I square my shoulders and take a step forward but inwardly I'm cowering in terror. "What do you want?" I ask with quiet resolve, trying to put steel in my quivering voice. It doesn't answer, but continues to advance, slow and steady. I detach from my fear and study the shadow. It's murky and dark. "Who are you," I scream, panic rising up inside of me again. "Who the hell are you," I yell again when it doesn't answer. I can't find any discernable features with the exception of a little darker grey where you would expect eyes and a mouth. The shadow has the basic shape of a person with arms and legs—almost like the Pillsbury Dough Boy but less friendly. "Say something, damn it," I scream, my fear growing. The shadow advances and I retreat. "I'm not afraid of you. I'm not," I cry out, trying to convince myself as much as the shadow. I'm back stepping and the shadow continues to advance. My heart is bouncing around in my rib cage like a marble in a pinball machine. I'm gasping for breath, terrified. I can't tear my eyes away from this … THING. The grey spot where the shadow's mouth should be turns black and grows larger, filling most of the head as if the mouth is opening on wide hinges. Then I hear a loud piercing word, "MARIAH!!!"

I start screaming and I turn to run but trip, falling on my face. I roll to my back and the shadow is hovering over me. I can't stop screaming. I roll to my side to get up and run away when I spy the paper from the bathroom, in the shadow's hand—YOU ARE GOING TO DIE!

Hearing her screams, Morgan came into the room, gun in hand, not knowing what to expect. Mariah woke to Morgan leaning over her, shaking her awake.

"Mariah, wake up. Mariah."

Once out of the throes of her nightmare, she threw her forearm over her eyes and cried. Morgan, clad only in sweat pants, sat on the edge of the bed and watched Mariah, sprawled on the floor where she landed during the dream.

"Are you okay," he asked after her sobbing subsided.

She nodded her head before saying, "I will be. I'm sorry I woke you."

"What were you dreaming?"

"Just the same thing." She shook her head. "The shadow attacking me, that's all it was."

Morgan leaned down and wiped a tear from her cheek.

"You were yelling, 'Who are you? Who the hell are you?' I knocked on the door and called your name. When you kept yelling, I came in. You were screaming and thrashing about. I saw you fall and land on your face—you were quick to push yourself over to your back. That's when I grabbed your shoulders to wake you up, you cried out, 'You are going to die.'"

"It's part of the dream." Mariah wiped her eyes.

"I thought the dreams were getting better." He reached his hand out to help Mariah off the floor.

"I thought so too." She took his hand. "The last one was better, but they're bad again, I think because of yesterday's shooting. If anything, they're worse now. Instead of just hovering over me and waking me right away, it doesn't rush in as quickly ... but it's more threatening. Quite frankly, Morgan, I'm exhausted. I'm lucky if I sleep two or three hours each night, and the days are crazy busy."

"Well, I'm here now and Riley will be here tomorrow night. If you want to go home, we can take over here."

"Oh. Hell no," Mariah shouted. "I am not going to abandon the people I've met here. I'm in this until we finish the investigation. I am finding those girls."

Morgan raised his hands in defense. "Calm down, woman." A slow grin spread across his face before he laughed out loud. "That's my Jeffries. I'm glad your feisty self is still alive and well. What can I do to help?"

"For starters, you can leave my bedroom so I can go back to sleep."

"Fair enough. If you start screaming again, I'm coming back in here. I'm not going to let anyone torment my little sister, not even a phantom in your dreams."

Mariah sighed. "Thanks Morgan." She got to her feet and gave Morgan a sheepish smile. "Goodnight."

"Night," he said and turned at the door. Just before closing it he murmured, "Sweet dreams this time."

****

After Morgan closed the door, Mariah remade her bed and then sat on the floor in the lotus position, thankful she put on sweats and a baggy t-shirt to sleep in. She took several cleansing breaths and started relaxing her muscles, starting at her toes and working up to the top of her head. She concentrated on her breathing and released everything else from her mind. She had to clear her mind and try to release the bad vibes from the dream or it would come back when she went back to sleep. She concentrated on the tension draining from her body as she drifted in meditative rest. An hour later, she took a deep breath and opened her eyes. Much of the tension and anxiety was gone. When she laid her head back down, she dropped off to sleep as soon as her head hit the pillow.

I'm sitting at the bar and Jeffrey is sitting next to me. He nods over his shoulder and asks me, "See that guy with the long black ponytail?" I look and then nod my head yes. He says to me under his breath, "He's a shadow. They call him the ghost!"

"What?" I ask, incredulous.

Jeffrey winks and smiles before everything around me vanishes into thin air, including Jeffrey.

I do a three hundred and sixty degree turn but there is nothing. It's as though I'm in white light, no walls or ceiling. Even the floor is only discernable by the touch of my feet—and it seems to go on forever.

"Hello," I call out, but only the echo of my call comes back to me. "Where am I?" No answer comes.

I figure I'll run into a wall or a door or something, so I start walking.

It seems like I've walked miles without encountering any barriers. The air is still, no breeze, no sound, no smell. I'm in a void.

"Am I dead," I ask no one and receive no answer.

I sigh in a huff and turn around trying to see something, but find only white light.

"Do blind people see light," I ask myself, "or only darkness?" I decide to sit down and meditate. "What better time and place to meditate than in a void," I think to myself. As I squat to a sitting position, I hear a loud piercing screech call my name— "MARIAH!!!"

"Ah CRAP," I say, irritated. "There's that pain-in-the-ass shadow again." I'm surprised to realize I'm not afraid anymore. I'm supposed to be afraid.

"No," I think. "I'm too damned mad and tired. I'm going to ignore it and go to sleep."

I lay down and close my eyes, shutting out the endless light.

I feel my body start to swirl and I get dizzy. I put my hand out to grasp at something to make it stop, but I find no handhold. I open my eyes to find I'm staring straight into the open maw of the shadow, and I'm being sucked in. I can do nothing ... but ... SCREAM!!!!

Morgan grabbed his gun and charged back into Mariah's room.

"Jeffries. Jeffries. Wake up." He shook her awake.

She reached out and grabbed Morgan around the neck like he was a life raft. She couldn't control her sobbing—her breathing more like a wheeze, and her chest hurt from her thundering heart. Morgan held her close, patting her back and repeating soothing words to her.

"Everything is going to be okay. You're safe now. I won't let anything happen to you. You're okay Mariah. You had a bad dream. You're okay."

He was rocking her in his arms, patting her back like she was a small toddler. She relaxed in the comfort of strong arms a moment and then pushed back and wiped her face with her hands.

"I'm so tired, but I don't dare go back to sleep," she said and started crying again.

"I'm not sleepy at all. Let's go find something on TV," Morgan suggested.

"That sounds good. I think I'll fix myself a good stiff drink while I'm at it. You want one too?" Mariah got out of bed and threw a robe on over her sweat pants and t-shirt.

"No thanks. You go ahead. I just fixed a pot of coffee."

A loud knock sounded from the front door as Mariah pulled a glass out of the cabinet.

"Riley?" Mariah looked at Morgan. He shook his head no and headed to the door, his gun in hand.

"Who is it," he barked with authority.

"Police. Open up."

Mariah grabbed Paisley and picked her up as Morgan put his weapon on the table and opened the door.

"Hello officer," he said as he opened the door. "Did someone call in a disturbance complaint, Officer ..." Morgan leaned over to read the name tag, "... Pettigrew?"

The officer stepped into the room and looked around. Mariah was standing in the hallway and his eyes settled on her.

"Are you okay, Ma'am?"

"Yes. I suffer from extreme nightmares. PTSD. I'm very sorry for any disturbance I caused," she said, stepping into the living room.

A second officer, female, walked in after Pettigrew.

"May I see some ID for both of you," Pettigrew asked.

"Sure. Mine's in my bedroom. I'll go get it," Morgan said.

"I'll follow you. Yours Ma'am?"

"In my bedroom."

He nodded and the group started down the hall to Morgan's room, Officer Pettigrew following Morgan. Mariah followed the two men and the female officer followed Mariah. Morgan got his billfold from his nightstand and pulled out his PI license and his Driver's License and handed them to the officer. They left Morgan's room and went into Mariah's room. She handed Paisley to Morgan and got her ID's from her purse and handed them over.

Looking at Mariah's ID's, Officer Pettigrew looked up and said, "Mariah Jeffries?"

"Yes."

"I heard about you. You were at that shooting yesterday." He handed Morgan and Mariah's ID's to the female officer. She went back into the living room to run a check on them both.

"That's right."

"Awfully soon for you to be diagnosed with PTSD, but I'm sure that scene could give anyone nightmares."

"I have PTSD from a prior incident."

"Trouble follows you?"

"Hey! Wait a minute," Morgan said in a huff.

"I'm sorry," Officer Pettigrew replied as Mariah tugged on Morgan's arm to encourage him to calm down.

"One of the tenants called in a complaint and said a lady was being beaten or killed. I'll make a report of what you said. Keep the noise down, will ya," the office said as he backed out of the bedroom, down the hall, and back to the living room. Morgan and Mariah following him.

"We will," Mariah said as he reached the door and opened it.

The female officer handed the ID's back to Mariah.

"I hope you feel better soon." Officer Pettigrew told Mariah and turned to followed his partner out the door. Morgan closed the door behind them and turned to Mariah.

"Wow," he said with a mischievous grin. "I never realized you were a screamer."

Mariah punch him in the gut. "Oh, shut up!" She turned her back on him to hide the smile on my face, but she couldn't hold the laughter back. Morgan clapped her on the shoulder.

"The neighbors are going to be talking about the crazy woman in the room next door for days to come. Maybe longer." He laughed as he picked up his mug of coffee from the kitchen counter.

Mariah sat on the couch and stared off into space, wondering if she would ever be able to sleep a full night again. Morgan sat in the chair next to the couch and turned on the TV. They settled on a Criminal Investigation Services marathon, forgetting about the stiff drink and settling in to wait for sunrise.

"I'll call Velia in the morning and check if she has time for me to have another session."

"You found a therapist down here?"

"Yeah. Well, not a counselor or psychologist. She's a past life regression therapist."

"Oh, right. Was that helping?"

"I thought so. We figured out that the shadow represents fear. I just don't know how to stop being afraid. I even stood up to the shadow in my dreams ... or tried to."

"A particular fear, or fear in general?"

"Fear in general, I think." Mariah shrugged. "I'm not sure, Morgan." She shook her head, " … I don't know."

They sat in silence, watching the marathon. The last thing Mariah remembered watching was Grady slapping Tom on the back of the head after he made a smart-aleck remark.

WEDNESDAY

The tinny default ring of a cell phone woke Mariah. She had fallen asleep sitting up on the couch, her head leaned back and her mouth hanging open. Mariah's throat felt like sandpaper and she needed a drink of water.

Morgan jumped up from his chair and grabbed the phone off the dining room table.

"Morgan," he said, almost in a whisper trying to keep from waking Mariah. "Yes, Martin. I understand. ... When I didn't hear from you or Mariah, I came down. ... Right."

Mariah sat forward on the couch, elbows on her knees and rubbed her face with both hands.

Morgan turned to check on Mariah. "I'm here with Mariah now. She explained it all to me. ... I called Riley last night and he'll be coming down today so we'll be here to help with the case. ... Right. Mariah has done a great job with the ground work. ... Okay. ... Talk to you later this morning."

"How long was I asleep?" Mariah stretched her neck and yawned.

"About three hours."

"Wow."

"Once you started snoring, I turned the TV down so the commercials wouldn't wake you and then I kept an eye on you for any signs of a nightmare."

"I want to go back to sleep, but … I better not test my luck. What time is it?"

"Seven. Want some coffee?"

"Yes, but first I'm going to shower. Then I'll cook you some breakfast."

"That sounds good. I'm starving."

Mariah stood, patted Paisley who had been sleeping next to her on the couch, and walked to her bedroom. She closed the door and Morgan stretched and walked to the couch.

Thirty-five minutes later, Mariah, dressed and combing out her wet hair, found Morgan lying on his side on the couch, snoring softly, with Paisley curled up behind his knees.

"Come here, girl," Mariah whispered. "Let's go for a walk."

Paisley stood and stepped over Morgan's legs, jumping to the floor with a gentle thud. Morgan stirred, but didn't wake.

Mariah wrote him a note and left it on the kitchen counter in case he woke before they got back. Mariah and Paisley walked up to the shopping area, and back. It was an hour walk with Paisley's stop and go habits. Since the little Jack Russell had been cooped up the whole day before, Mariah felt it was only fair to let her do some exploring while they walked. That included stopping and sniffing every twig, bush, tree, and post they came to. Of course, after thoroughly sniffing something, it was the exception for Paisley not to pee on it.

Morgan was still asleep when they returned until Paisley went over and sniffed his face. He woke with a start, yawned, sat up, scratched his abdomen with his left hand, and rubbed the back of his head with the right.

"How long was I asleep?"

"About an hour and a half. Why don't you go lay down on your bed and get some real rest while I fix breakfast?"

"No. I'm going to meet with Martin and get the authorizations to talk to the girl's teachers. That should free you up to de-stress. When's your next counseling session?"

"I don't have one scheduled, but she said I could call her if I needed to and she would work me in."

"That's great."

"Yeah. She's helped me to see things in a new light. I'll give her a call. You'd like her, Morgan. I sure do.

"I'm glad. Maybe she can help you calm your psyche back down. You said last night, you thought she was helping, right?"

"Yes. I thought it was getting better. Not a lot, but it gave me hope. After last night … not so much."

"Hmmm. Give her a call. Can't hurt," Morgan said, getting up from the couch. "Coffee?"

"Sure."

Morgan walked to the kitchen and started fixing a fresh pot of coffee. Mariah followed him into the kitchen to start some sausage and eggs. While the coffee brewed, and Mariah started cooking, Morgan excused himself to go to the bathroom and clean up.

*****

Morgan left at nine to meet with Martin. Before leaving he told Mariah to take the whole day off and regroup.

Easy for him to say, Mariah thought. She sat down and started typing out a report of yesterday's events. When she finished at ten thirty she decided it was late enough to make some calls. Her first call was to Velia who picked up on the second ring.

"Mariah. I've been waiting for your call."

"You have?"

"Of course. You want to come out today for another session."

"Yes. I do. How did you know?"

"I have my ways."

"Um, okay. Velia, I thought I was on the verge of a breakthrough until last night."

"What happened?"

"Did you hear about yesterday's shooting? … Velia? Are you there?"

"Yes. I'm here and I did. You were with them, right?"

Mariah nodded her head as if Velia could see her through the phone. "The two men that were shot, they were there to meet with me. They were fathers of two of the missing girls."

"I'm sorry."

"Me too. Do you have some time available for me today? One of my partners is here to help with the investigation …"

"Morgan," she announced.

Mariah paused, wondering how she knew.

"Yes. His being here frees me up a little more. My dreams are as bad as … no … they're worse than ever and I don't have a clue what my regression has to do with them, but I'm convinced there is something."

"Of course I have time for you. Can you come out now?"

"Thank you, Velia. I'll be there in 30 minutes."

"You're welcome. See you soon."

****

"Hi Mariah. Come on in. You made good time."

"I was anxious to see you. I hope my visit isn't an inconvenience for you."

"Of course not. I always have time for a friend."

Mariah smiled.

"I had a snack sent up in the studio. We'll talk first and if you need another regression, we'll do that too."

"Thanks. That sounds wonderful."

The elevator transported them to the third floor with a quiet whoosh.

"You look great. How have you been, Velia?"

"Good. My doctor gave me a new medication and it seems to be working well. I still have to take it easy, but the pain is much less than it had been, and I'm sleeping better than I have in years."

Mariah pulled open one of the big wooden doors and held it open for Velia.

"I'm glad to hear that."

"I'll pour the wine while you fix a plate," Velia said, sitting in her favorite chair. She picked up the open bottle of wine and a long stemmed wine glass.

After Mariah's plate was full and the wine poured, Velia sat back.

"Tell me what happened that prompted you to call."

"It was awful. I felt stronger ... like I could let the fear go, but after the shooting ..." Mariah shook her head. "It was awful, Velia."

"Maybe you have more than fear to overcome. Maybe you're dealing with anger, too. After Jerry betrayed you the way he did, I suspect you have a lot of anger, as well as fear from the attack. Yesterday's shooting would cause anyone to be fearful, but you were also betrayed by the shooter. Am I right?"

"I'm not sure about betrayed, but denied the interview that might bring those girls back ... sure."

"Cheated then."

"Yes. Cheated."

"How does that make you feel?"

"Angry ... and frustrated, of course." Mariah took a bite of sausage and chewed. She swallowed and said, "I understand what you're saying. But still, how do I overcome this?"

"Everyone deals with these things in different ways. You must find what works for you."

"Joseph told me that fear will always chase after me until I learn to let go of it. I suppose that can be true of anger, too."

"Makes sense."

"That's why Paul has been coming to me. He was Joseph in that life. Did I tell you that?"

"Yes. You did."

"So, how do I let go of it ... anger and fear? I can't just pretend that nothing happened. What I experienced in this life was deadly stuff. People wanted me dead. They were trying to kill me and Jerry damn near did. He came within the speed of a bullet from accomplishing it. It took me more than a year to recover from his physical attack and return to my prior health and strength. How do I get over that?"

"How do you think?"

Mariah took a sip of wine and stared out the big windows to the azure blue skies meeting the mountains in the distance. A bird she couldn't identify glided past the window in front of her.

"Now I have a starting point. It's not just some random haunting. Apparently, in my past lives I let fear rule my life and if I'm not careful, anger will rule this one."

"So where do you think you need to start?"

"Well," Mariah said, looking from the window to Velia, "I don't know. ..." Mariah shrugged her shoulders and leaned forward to put her plate on the table.

"Do you think I need to try to visit other past lives?"

"That's up to you. What do you think?"

"I think I got my answers." Mariah sat back on the love seat. "In a lot of ways, Caroline was a strong woman. She was young and it was normal, I think, that she deferred to her parents wishes at first. But once she was old enough and more mature, she stood her ground against them and the social structure she was raised in. She did what was right for her. She married the man she loved knowing society would frown on the union. She made a life with him—had a family. It's just too bad that she lost her first born over it."

"But how did that impact the rest of her life?"

"I think in spite of her strength and determination, she lived in fear of making the wrong decision again."

"And how does that relate to what you've been experiencing?"

Mariah sat in pensive thought, sipping her wine and staring out the windows.

"I think ..." she said, and placed her wine glass on the table before standing. She looked at Velia before walking to the large windows overlooking the valley below. "It's a warning for me to face each day with renewed courage and centeredness—to consciously release the fear and anger on a daily, sometimes more frequent, basis."

Velia turned in her seat to watch Mariah.

Mariah turned from the window and looked at Velia.

"How do you plan on implementing that in your life, now that you have a strategy in place?" Velia inquired.

Mariah walked over to the massive fireplace at the end of the room. She reached out and traced creatures carved into the totem scroll that supported the left side of the mantel. A rabbit was sitting up on his hind legs, ears standing straight up, front paws curved in front. His nose was lifted as if it were sniffing for danger. Above that was a tree trunk, a buck coming out from behind it, his head facing out toward the room, a six point rack held high on his head. Beside the rabbit was a turtle, head craned, looking out from his wooden prison. Below that was what looked like a large fern, an intricate spider web spread from a branch to a tree trunk to the right of the bush.

She moved to the eagles that made up the mantle. Screaming eagles is what came to mind when she looked on it.

They are so beautiful—so fearless—so strong, she thought.

Mariah turned to face Velia, sitting at the other end of the studio, her right elbow resting on the armrest, her hand holding the wineglass.

"I am going to be an eagle," Mariah said. "I am going to soar above the storm, fearless and strong. I am going to fight for those who can't fight for themselves—root out the evil for my clients and if I'm lucky, I will be a good and positive influence on others. I hope to teach others to put fear and anger behind them and stand strong in the face of adversity no matter how big or how small that adversity is. I am going to be an eagle.

"I know how to let go now. It's through meditation and I've been doing it my whole life. I've let fear interfere with my meditations and sleep since the attacks, but not anymore. Now that I understand what the problem has been, I can overcome it.

"I will speak only of courage and love like I was born to it … like the eagle is born to soaring above the storm. I will speak only of love and forgiveness … strength … and courage. The past couple years, when going into a meditative state, I was fearful of the shadow appearing—because I thought of it … feared it, I gave it dominion over me. Fearing the shadow, and being angry because of the shadow, has given it power and strength. I will not give it thought anymore. I will think of love and gratitude, courage and strength before sleep and meditation. In doing that, I will suffocate fear and anger out of my life. That's what Uncle John taught me, but I've forgotten that lesson."

"I think you have found the answer to your questions. It won't always be easy, but …" Velia smiled. "Let's drink to your breakthrough. If anyone can accomplish this, it is you."

Mariah crossed the room, and sat on the love seat. She picked up her wine glass and they clinked glasses before draining them.

Velia winced as she leaned forward, reaching for the bottle.

"Here. Let me," Mariah said. "Pain coming back?"

"No, I just moved wrong."

Mariah took a sip of the wine. "Mmm, this is good."

"Thank you. This wine is from a local vineyard. The owners are very good friends of mine."

They sat, letting the quiet fill the room, lost in their own thoughts, and sipping wine. Mariah broke the silence.

"I can't tell you how much I appreciate your help."

"I'm glad I was able to help you."

Mariah's phone dinged to notify her of a new email. She pulled it out to see if it was important and noticed it was two o'clock.

"I should go. I have cash for my session, or I can write you a check."

"This one's on me. I'll charge you for the next regression if you do that again." She smiled again and set her empty wine glass on the table.

Mariah stood. "Thank you, Velia."

"You're welcome. Call or come out any time. I enjoy your company."

"I would like that. I'll keep in touch. If you don't mind, I'll let myself out. No need for you to get up."

"Thank you. I'll just sit here, enjoy the view, and sip another glass of wine."

As Mariah got into her car, her cell phone started ringing.

"Mariah Jeffries."

"Hi, Mariah. This is Alexis."

"Hi Alexis. How are you doing?"

"Good. I was wondering if you wanted to go for a run today?"

"I would love to. In fact, I want to take Paisley to the Old Forest. Do you want to ask your dad if you can go with me?"

"Dad's out on the road. I'll ask Mom. Hold on."

While Mariah waited, she started the car, backed out of the parking space and started through the open gates when Alexis came back on the phone.

"She said I could as long as I stayed with you."

"Okay. I just finished with an appointment so I'll go pick up Paisley and then head to your house. Give me an hour."

"I'll be ready."

Mariah hung up the phone and called Morgan, getting his voice mail.

"Hey Morgan. I had a breakthrough with Velia. I'll tell you about it later. Right now, I'm headed to the suite for Paisley. I'm taking her out for a run with Alexis. I think I told you about her. … Alexis? If not, I'll talk to you later and catch you up."

At the bottom of the mountain, the usually sparsely traveled road was backed up with traffic. Mariah waited for three cars to creep by before she turned left and headed back to highway OR-140. The reason for the back up was evident when she approached the first big curve. A Ford F-150 hit the curve too fast and rolled over several times, taking out a barbed-wire fence. The police and an ambulance were already on scene, working the accident. A young guy sitting up on a gurney, waited to be loaded in the ambulance.

He doesn't look to bad considering the looks of the accident, Mariah thought.

A wrecker arrived to haul away the wreckage as she was directed past the scene by a deputy sheriff.

****

Mariah noticed Riley's car in the parking lot when she pulled in at the Medford Suites. She grabbed her purse and water bottle, exited the car, and closed the door. When she turned to walk to the suite, Riley and Paisley stepped out from around the corner of the building. Paisley heard the car door slam, looked up and spied Mariah before Riley did, and she started running into the parking lot toward Mariah.

Mariah screamed, her heart in her throat as a car came speeding through the parking lot toward Paisley. The driver slammed on his brakes, and Riley locked Paisley's retractable leash, jerking her back out of the way just in the nick of time. The driver of the car eased passed Riley and Paisley while Riley yelled at him to slow down.

Mariah rushed across the parking lot and once close enough, Paisley jumped up on Mariah's knees and into her arms. Mariah held the little dog close and rested her head on the side of Paisley's chest. Paisley let out a soft, but audible sigh before Mariah reached around and hugged Riley.

"How was your trip down?"

"Uneventful. I just got in about an hour ago. Morgan's out interviewing teachers. He should be here to meet us for diner by six."

They walked to the suite together.

"I'm glad you made it in alright. There is so much to tell you guys."

"You look different—happy. I don't think I've ever seen you this at ease. You're projecting a different energy, Mariah. The regressions worked."

She smiled. "You're not going to believe what I've been through but there isn't time to go into it now. I promised a young lady that I'd pick her up and go for a run." Mariah filled him in about Alexis as they walked into the building to go to the suite.

"How do you like the accommodations? Nice, huh?"

"Yeah. A lot better than the last time you guys were holed up somewhere."

"Yeah, right?!"

Mariah laughed and put Paisley down. She grabbed her backpack, put a couple apples, two small baggies of mixed nuts, and four bottles of water inside. She zipped the backpack closed and set it down by the door.

"Excuse me a minute. I've got to go to the bathroom."

When she came out of the bathroom, Riley was sitting on the couch, legs crossed, reading something on his phone.

"What are your plans for the rest of the afternoon?" Moriah asked him.

"I don't have any. You?"

"I'm picking up a young lady and we're going for a run with Paisley. Want to join us?"

"Nope. I think I'll relax for a while. You'll be back in time to go to dinner won't you?"

"Yes. We won't be that long."

Riley got up from the couch and started down the hall.

"See you when you get back, then."

Mariah picked up the backpack and grabbed Paisley's leash from the floor.

"Come on, girl. Lets go check out the Enchanted Forest."

"The *what*?" Riley barked turning from the bathroom door and staring at her, open mouthed.

Mariah laughed. "Not really the Enchanted Forest. It's a forest outside of Jacksonville with running trails that I heard about. I'll tell you about it tonight. Catch ya later." With the backpack slung over her left shoulder and Paisley's leash in her right hand, she told Riley she would see him in a couple of hours and pulled the door closed behind her.

Mariah eased across the school parking lot entrance and made a u-turn, pulling up at the curb in front of Alexis' home. Alexis turned where she was standing on the front porch, stuck her head in the front door of the house—to say good-bye, Mariah guessed—and bounded to the car, all smiles and swinging pony tail. As she tossed a hoodie in the backseat and buckled up, her mother opened the front door of the house and peered out. Mariah waived and Twila waived back before ducking back into the house.

"How was your day?" Mariah asked as she put the car in drive and eased out into the street. Alexis flashed a great big, pearly white smile.

"You got your braces off!"

All she could do was smile and nod her head. It was clear she was thrilled.

"You look beautiful."

"Thanks, and Tommy called yesterday and asked me to go to the movies with him next weekend. My dad said 'yes'! I'm so happy and excited I can't sit still for more than a minute."

"Your dad said yes? Wow. I'm surprised."

"Yeah, well he gave conditions, but Tommy was okay with it."

"Ah! I see. Which way do I go?" Mariah glanced at Alexis as she came to the intersection at Stewart from Peach.

"Oh. Turn right and just keep going until you come to the 'T' and then turn left. That will take you straight into Jacksonville, then we turn right on California and keep going. There will be signs the rest of the way."

"So, what are the conditions you're father made?"

"Well, at first Tommy asked me to go Friday night, but my dad said,"—she lowered her voice to mimic her father's tone—"'no way, but if he wants to come over Saturday and spend about an hour with us so I can meet him, then you can go to a matinee.'" Back in her normal voice she continued, "I just have to be home before dark."

"What did Tommy say when you told him?"

"He said he understood and that he would like to meet my parents. Can you believe that?"

"Well, I would say that wanting to meet your parents is a bit unusual, but it implies that he is a respectful and confident young man. That's a good start."

Alexis just looked forward with a huge smile on her face and nodded her head.

"When did you get your braces off?"

"This afternoon. Mom took me out of school at one o'clock for my appointment. It feels weird … but good. I can't stop running my tongue over my smooth straight teeth and smiling."

Mariah smiled at her and nodded her head.

"I've never been out this way. It's a beautiful drive."

"My mom told me to warn you about the cops in Jacksonville. They like to write tickets so be careful of the speed limits."

"That's good to know. Thanks."

Heeding Mrs. Givens' warning, Mariah paid close attention to the speed limit and adjusted her speed accordingly. Passing down California street, the downtown area appeared to be a quaint little town. She could picture it with actual board walks instead of the paved sidewalks she was observing as she passed through.

When they reached the trailhead, Mariah parked in the small gravel lot with a motorcycle, on the driver's side and an empty space on the passenger side. Across the small lot was an old yellow Honda Civic and one space over from that was a silver Subaru with a bike rack on the back. Before getting out of the car, she reached into the backpack, handed Alexis a bottle of water, and put another one in her own lap. She extracted two apples, offering one to Alexis.

Alexis took the apple and reached for the door handle.

"Oh. I almost forgot. Mom invited you for dinner when we get back."

"I would love to, but I can't. My partners are in town and we have a conference planned this evening. Maybe another time though. I would like that very much."

"No problem. I'll let her know."

They reached the trailhead at 4:30, the sun was already low in the sky.

Mariah pulled Paisley back who was pulling and anxious to explore. "We won't be able to go far. I'd forgotten how early the sun sets this far north, and with the mountains in the way, it will get dark even earlier."

"Okay. So you want to do thirty minutes in and thirty minutes back?"

"That's going to make it well past dark by the time we get back to the car, and I only have the small flashlight on Paisley's leash. Let's just play it by ear."

"Sure."

After a quick stretch, they began their run, Paisley leading the way. The darkness encroached around them fifteen minutes into their run, making it more difficult to follow the trail. To make matters worse, a heavy fog was moving in. Mariah reached out for Alexis' arm, slowing down and stopping.

"We better turn back. We'll come back sometime when there's more daylight. I would like to see more of the trails out here."

"I'm ready. It's kinda spooky out here in the dark and the fog." A light mist was forming droplets of water on their faces.

As they turned back toward the trailhead, the sound of someone dragging a heavy load over rocks and dirt seemed to be coming from in front of them. Paisley crouched, looking toward the trailhead, a deep rumble emanating from her chest.

"Shhhh girl." Mariah said in a hushed voice, crouching down to put her hand on Paisley's back. She reached for Alexis' hand and pulled her down beside her. "Stay down and back off the trail a little. Stay behind me."

Mariah reached into her jacket to her shoulder holster and gripped the FN. A man's faint voice drifted through the mist, but Mariah couldn't make out all the words.

"… better her … sick … care … damned girls … tired … this shi …"

A man's coughing faded off to the right of them.

"Did you hear that?" Alexis whispered.

"Yes. Take Paisley and stay here."

Alexis grabbed Mariah's arm. "No. I promised my mom. I'm scared."

Paisley growled.

"Shhh. Quiet!" Mariah admonished.

Mariah, torn between wanting to investigate who was out there talking about 'girls', and keeping Alexis safe, nodded.

"Okay, stay behind me a little bit and keep Paisley back." She reached down to Paisley and unhooked her collar leaving the harness on. Mariah put the collar with Paisley's jangling tags in her pocket before starting forward, listening for more sounds. They reached a cross trail going from left to right and Mariah eased down the trail to their right. Paisley growled and Alexis tried to shush her, but the little pup dashed off toward the underbrush at the side of the trail, snarling and barking, almost pulling Alexis off her feet. Mariah grabbed for the leash and pulled Paisley back, picking her up and holding her.

"Shh, shh. It's okay." She cuddled the muscular little dog, who was trembling with excitement. Alexis squatted beside them. Mariah put Paisley back on the ground, but kept her hand around her side. The scraping noise had stopped. They stayed still and listened for it to start again.

Behind them, on the main trail to the parking lot, a woman laughed. Alexis drew in a sudden breath and clapped a hand over her mouth. Paisley jumped and faced the noise, barking and growling.

A woman spoke.

"That was great. I love sex in the outdoors." Her voice was sultry.

A man's voice responded.

"You wanna do it in this fog? It'll be like we're fucking on a cloud."

The woman's laughter was a light twitter.

"Next time, big boy. I'm getting cold and wet."

"Oh baby. You were already wet."

The man laughed. Their voices faded as they continued their seductive banter. Mariah waited half a beat and then stood. "Let's go. We're not going to find anything in this soup." She pushed Alexis ahead of her, guarding her back.

A motorcycle started up as they reached the trailhead and the two women watched as a car's tail lights turned right toward Jacksonville behind the bike. The yellow Civic was already gone, but an old, white utility van was parked in the spot nearest the trailhead.

They got into the car and Mariah locked all the doors, put the key in the ignition and eased out of the parking space.

"Who do you think that was?" Alexis wondered as Mariah turned the car toward Jacksonville.

"I don't know. Probably just someone out walking. Maybe a homeless person—could be anyone."

"That was scary. Paisley sensed something."

"Oh, she could have been growling or going after some rodent, but she was definitely on alert for something." They were quiet for a moment.

"What did you hear?" Mariah was curious if Alexis heard the same thing.

"Well, there was a dragging or scraping sound and then a man's voice saying something about 'her being sick' and that he was tired. What ever that meant. Oh and the couple talking about sex."

"Did you hear the first man say anything else?"

"No. Just 'her', 'sick', and 'tired of this shit'. That's all I heard."

They drove in silence for a while.

"Do you think people really go out there to have sex?" Alexis laughed nervously.

"Yeah. I wouldn't doubt it. People have sex in all kinds of places. Some people get off on the possibility of getting caught—thrill seekers. But they can be arrested for indecent exposure or worse if they're not careful, so don't get any wild ideas."

"Me? No way. I would die if someone caught me having sex. How embarrassing. It's just so … personal and all. Not for someone else to be watching, that's for sure."

A slight smile formed on Mariah's lips, but she didn't say anything. She was keeping her eyes on the road directly in front of the hood of her car because that was as far as she could see.

"That's how I feel about it anyway."

"Well that's not a bad way to feel, Alexis. You're right. Sex is very personal and it's a natural part of life. Sex isn't something to be ashamed of or embarrassed about though, especially when it's with someone you love."

"Did you ever have sex outside?"

"Sure. My late husband and I used to go camping and hiking a lot. We would make love in our tent."

"I mean OUTSIDE, outside. Where people could walk up on you or be spying on you."

"One time," Mariah smiled, "we were hiking and came upon this small spring fed pond. It was very isolated and beautiful up on top of Sitting Bull Falls. We went skinny dipping and then made love on the grassy bank with the sun glinting through the leaves and onto us. It was beautiful." Mariah sighed. "A great day."

"Where's Sitting Bull Falls?"

"In New Mexico. That's where we lived."

The fog was thick. They passed through Jacksonville in silence and when they reached the outskirts toward the Medford turn off, Alexis asked, "How did he die? Your husband?"

Mariah paused before answering, trying to decide how much she wanted say. "It was a freak accident. He was a Naval fighter pilot."

"I'm sorry."

"Me too."

"It's eerie driving around in this fog." Alexis shivered.

"Yes it is. Help me watch for deer."

They were quiet until they reached the edge of town where the street lights started.

"Has there been any gossip about the girls who have gone missing?"

"Well, yeah. Everyone is talking about it. A lot of the girls at school are scared. You know, like ... who's gonna be next ..."

"I hope we can stop the kidnappings before there is a next. You just keep your eyes peeled for anyone suspicious and be careful."

"I will."

Mariah pulled up at the curb in front of the Givens' house and put the car in park.

"Do you want to work on your Tai Chi exercises in your front yard for a few minutes before I go?"

"Yeah. That would be great." Alexis' enthusiasm was evident in her voice.

"Is your fenced front yard secure? We could let Paisley loose while we exercise."

"Yeah um ... the front yard is. I'll make sure the gate to the back yard is closed—I'm not sure the backyard is safe for her, but I think she'd be okay in the front yard."

"I'll walk the perimeter and take a look before I let her off the leash."

They entered the front gate and Mariah suggested that Alexis let her parents know she was back and what they were going to do. While Alexis was inside talking to her parents, Mariah walked the perimeter of the fence, checked the gate to the back yard to make sure it was latched, and was satisfied the yard was secure with no holes or gaps.

"I told mom you couldn't stay for supper this time." Alexis closed the front door and came down the steps just as Mariah was unhooking Paisley's leash. Paisley bounded away to check out the yard and the two women began their stretches in the middle of the yard.

"Have you been practicing the moves I taught you?"

"Uh huh. Going through the movements is peaceful and relaxing. I tried to go into the backyard in the morning to practice, before I left for school, but it's been too cold, so I did them in the living room. Mom liked watching me."

"That's good. Now, step in front of me, your back to me so I can watch you go through the exercise while we do them. That way I can correct any mistakes you might be making in your form." Alexis positioned herself in front of Mariah and they started the Beijing short form moves. She was great on the Commencement, and Parting the Wild Horse's Mane, but when they got to Brush Knee, Hand Strum the Lute, and Step Back and Repulse Monkey, Mariah had to make some slight corrections to Alexis' stance and movements. Alexis was very open to critique and correction and made the proper adjustments.

"I recommend you practice those moves in front of a mirror if you can, to make sure you're doing it right. Do you have a full length mirror in your bedroom you could practice in front of?"

"Um, not really. There's not enough room in there. I guess I could take my free-standing full-length mirror into the living room if mom will let me. It's an heirloom though, so I'm not sure she would like me moving it around."

"Let's run through them again and when you practice alone, you'll need to be aware of your form and pace."

They went through the moves again and Alexis performed them with perfect precision.

"Great job. Do you want to learn one more move or practice those more before we add another one?"

"Oh, please teach me another one. That would be great."

"I'm actually going to show you two. Grasp the Sparrow's Tail left and Grasp the Sparrow's Tail right. So watch me do them first."

Mariah went through the exercises while Alexis watched.

"Now, I'm going to start from Step Back and Repulse the Monkey and go into the two Grasp the Sparrow's Tail movements."

Mariah transitioned from Step Back and Repulse the Monkey into Grasp the Sparrow's Tail left.

"Do you see how that transitions?"

"Yes. I think so."

"Your turn. I'll watch for form."

"Do you want me to start with Step Back and ..."

"Yes, that way you can perform the transition."

Alexis placed her left foot in front of her body, resting her foot on her toes. She kept her right foot about a foot-and-a-half behind, bent both knees, and turned her torso slightly to the right. She continued the movements and Mariah made suggestions and corrections as she went into the two new moves.

"That looked wonderful." Mariah told her when she finished. "Let's do them together. I'll stay in front of you so you can watch me."

They ran through the last three moves together.

"What do you think?"

"I think I have it. Can we do the whole thing from the beginning?"

"Sure. You stand in front of me."

Alexis moved back in front of Mariah and they started from the beginning. When they finished, Mariah told her to keep practicing and then called Paisley. She gathered the leash from the porch, hooked it on Paisley's harness, hugged Alexis and headed to the car.

"Bye Mariah. Thanks for taking me with you."

"My pleasure. Keep practicing and we'll get together again as soon as I have some free time."

"I will."

As she was getting out of the car to meet with Morgan and Riley in their suite, Mariah realized that Alexis had left her hoodie in the backseat. She gave brief consideration to running it back over to Alexis, but decided to wait and give it back to her the next time they went running.

Mariah opened the door to the suite. Morgan, standing at the kitchen counter, stopped what he was doing and turned his eyes on Mariah. Riley stepped out of the bedroom.

"Ah. There you are," Morgan said. He pushed the pad of paper back and set the pen down beside it.

"I was just writing you a note that we're going to dinner and to call us when you got in."

"Where'd you decide to go?"

"The Roadhouse."

"That sounds wonderful." Mariah unhooked Paisley and took her harness off. "Oh, great!" she explained.

"What?" Morgan stepped up next to where Mariah was squatted down with Paisley.

"One of the hooks on Paisley's harness tore away and the second one is loose. I need to buy her a new harness. I don't think this one will hold up to another strong tug from her."

"Let's see." Riley took the harness and looked it over while Mariah put down fresh food and water for Paisley.

"Yeah. It ripped right off. What was she chasing?" He turned it over in his hands, inspecting it. "She must have pulled pretty hard to tear it loose."

"Oh, it was getting worn but I didn't think it was that bad. I'll tell y'all about it at dinner. Let's go. I'm starved."

"You're always starved." Morgan quipped.

"Yeah? Look who's talking, Mr. 'Molly's got supper on the table so I better go.'"

Riley laughed, "You're both a couple of chow hounds."

Mariah put Paisley in her crate and the partners walked out the door. Morgan pulled the door closed behind them, making sure it was locked and followed Riley and Mariah to Riley's car.

At the restaurant, Riley filled Mariah in on the interviews for office help before Mariah told the guys all about her regressions and the day's session with Velia. She followed up that information with her run in the forest.

"Do you think he was talking about the missing girls?"

"I'm not sure. I thought he said 'girls', but when I asked Alexis what she heard, she didn't mention that. I guess I could have been hearing what I wanted to hear, but I don't think so. I had this gut feeling … you know?"

"Yeah. I know what you mean," Riley responded.

"I have a couple appointments to meet with friends of the girls and their families. Maybe we can divide them up in the morning, and then go out to the Old Forest to check things out in the afternoon," Morgan suggested.

"What time are your appointments?" Mariah asked.

"One is scheduled at ten to meet with the AAU basketball team, the coaches, and any parents that are there. It might be helpful if you go with me to that one, Mariah. Riley, you could call Heidi Kirschner's parents—she's a friend of Tina Webb, and Julianna Strobel who's a friend of Chelsea Dunn's, to ask if you could meet with them in the morning. I'll take the eight o'clock appointment with Xander Ferguson—he's Duskie Banks' ex boyfriend."

"The whole teams meeting at ten on a school day?" Riley was incredulous.

"Yes. Apparently, the team has some kind of big tournament and the girls are excused from school to attend. I have about thirty minutes to talk to them before they load the bus and head out to Salem. Xander Ferguson has study hall first thing in the morning, and Heidi and Julianna's families are keeping them home until this is over."

"Sounds like a plan. Just give me the address where you're meeting the team and I'll meet you." Mariah took a bite of her salad.

"Why don't you go ahead and call the other two since you've had first contact, and check with them about me seeing them instead—the earlier the better." Riley told Morgan.

Morgan pulled his phone and a notepad out of the breast pocket of his jacket. He flipped several pages in the notepad, found what he was looking for, and then punched in a phone number.

"Mr. Kirschner? ... Hi. This is Morgan Sellers. ... Yes, sir. My partner, Damion Riley got into town to help with the investigation and I was wondering if he could do the interview with your family tomorrow morning? ... Yes, sir. I'm meeting with the girls basketball team and we have some locations we want to check out tomorrow afternoon. ... Nine-thirty?" Morgan looked at Riley. Riley nodded his head in the affirmative and Morgan continued, "That would work just fine. Thank you for being so flexible with us. ... Yes sir. We appreciate it. ... You too. Good night."

He hit the end button on his phone, referred to his notepad and then punched in another phone number.

"Hi. Mrs. Strobel? ... Hi. This is Morgan Sellers again. My partner, Damion Riley got into town today to help with the investigation. I overbooked some interviews for tomorrow so I was wondering if you would consider scheduling an interview with Damion for tomorrow morning instead of tomorrow afternoon? ... It would? ... He's right here, I'll let you talk to him. ... Okay, here he is." Morgan handed the phone to Riley.

"Hello, Mrs. Strobel. ... Yes. I have a nine-thirty appointment but I should be done by ten-fifteen or ten-thirty. Would it be alright if we plan on eleven? ... Oh. I see. I'll see you tomorrow, at ten-thirty, then. ...Yes Ma'am. I can make that work. ... Thank you. ... I look forward to meeting with you. Bye now."

Riley handed the phone back to Morgan who put it back in his pocket. "I have interviews with the girls teachers for the next afternoon, after classes. We can split those up between us later."

Riley nodded as he chewed on his steak.

"Sounds like a plan." Mariah responded.

They finished their meal, Riley paid the bill with the company credit card, and they went back to the suite.

Mariah let Paisley out of her crate when they entered the suite, and the little white, four legged partner ran around to everyone in the room trying to encourage them to play with her. Riley picked up one of her toys and played keep away. Paisley jumped up and succeeded in grabbing the toy after several attempts. She tried to tug the toy away from Riley, pulling and hooking her front paws over the top.

Morgan ignored the play, went into the kitchen, and took a tumbler out of the cabinet.

"Anyone want a drink before bed?"

Riley was laughing and playing with Paisley failing to hear Morgan's question.

"None for me. Thanks."

Mariah stopped in the doorway to the kitchen.

"You think you'll be able to sleep tonight?" Morgan asked.

"I hope so. … I think I'll be able to. … I guess we'll see." She smiled at him. Riley abandoned the play with Paisley and came into the kitchen.

"Hey, fix me a drink too while you're at it."

Morgan handed his cranberry and rum cocktail to Riley who put the drink on the counter.

"Hell no. I'm not drinking that foo-foo drink. Fix me a Crown and coke, why don't ya?"

"Bitch, bitch, bitch. Is that how you ask Jeri for something? It's a wonder you're still married."

"I happen to love Jeri and she knows it, buster."

Morgan poured two fingers of Crown in a clean glass and reached for the cap when Riley tipped the bottom of the bottle to splash more crown into his glass. "Don't be so damned stingy with the whiskey, man."

"Well here. Fix your own drink, you old grump!"

"Can I go to bed, or do I need to stay here and referee?" Mariah smirked at both of them, before giving them her sweetest smile and laughing at their friendly banter. "You two sound like an old married couple."

"Go on to bed, Mariah." Morgan stepped into the living room with his drink in hand. "We'll be fine. Won't we, old man?"

"Yeah, I suppose so dawlin," Riley drawled, coming out of the kitchen with his drink. "As long as you stop holding back on the booze, sweetheart."

Mariah laughed and Morgan cuffed Riley on the back of the head.

"Come on Paisley, let's go to bed. Night, boys. Play nice!"

"Good night, Mariah." Riley and Morgan chimed together.

"Sweet dreams, Jeffries," Morgan added.

****

Sweet dreams. I hope so, Mariah thought, a little apprehensive that the shadow would return and she would fail to be fearless in its presence. She resolved to meditate, in spite of her fatigue, and release her fear and anger. She sat on the bedroom floor, crossed her legs, ankles over knees, and closed her eyes. She immediately slipped into a meditative state, able to clear her mind and drift in the present, quiet moment. She gave thanks for the regression therapy, her partners, her job—everything she could think of including the wisdom to be at peace and sleep a full night without a disturbance. She reminded herself how strong and courageous she has always been and would continue to be. When she ended the meditation, she felt cleansed and at peace.

She gathered her clothes, and went back into the living room to make sure Morgan or Riley didn't need the bathroom before she occupied it for a hot shower. Paisley followed her into the living room, jumped up on Morgan's lap and stretched out the length of his thighs with her head resting across his right knee.

In the shower, Mariah turned the water as hot as she could stand it. The warmth seeped into her, further relaxing her muscles, as the steam swirled and coated the surfaces of everything in the small room. She became so relaxed her legs didn't want to hold her weight anymore, so she sank down and sat, leaning back with her head against the wall. She closed her eyes and sighed, enjoying the spray of the warm shower raining down on her like a summer storm. Mariah visualized herself standing strong in front of the shadow, with a heart full of courage, confidence, and love.

After the visualization, her relaxation complete, she gave quiet thanks for Morgan and Riley. She realized she had renewed purpose in life through a beautiful young woman who was smart and funny, who looked up to her as a mentor and wanted to spend time with her, learning her craft. She sent up a silent prayer for Gayle Webb and his family, for Robert Dunn's family, and for the rest of the missing girls. She sent heartfelt thanks for everyone else she'd met in Medford; Velia, Jeffery, Katherine, Cliff Pieper, Gage Rhinehart, Captain Spencer, Detective Cleveland, Officer Day, the families of the missing girls, Erick, and Martin Silkeney. She was falling in love with this beautiful valley and was beginning to bond with some of the people she had met. Even though the circumstances of the team being in Medford was horrible, life was good for her at that very moment.

Mariah stood after relaxing in quiet reflection and finished washing. She turned off the water as the temperature cooled, and stepped out of the shower.

Dressed in sweat pants and a baggy t-shirt, she went into the living room. Paisley was stretched out next to Morgan who was watching an old black and white rerun, the volume turned low. Riley was in the chair, his feet up on the coffee table, head back, mouth open, and snoring like an old bear.

"You going to sit up for a while?"

"No. I was waiting for you to finish in the bathroom. I suppose you used all the hot water." Morgan stood from the couch.

Mariah just nodded her head and grinned. "And I'm so relaxed."

Morgan smiled. "You brat!"

Riley stirred, sat up straight, and rubbed his face. "Why don't you two go to bed. I want to pull the couch out and get some shut-eye."

"We're doing just that. I'll see y'all in the morning." Morgan walked down the hall to the bathroom.

As the bathroom door clicked closed, Paisley jumped from the couch and walked to the bedroom, tags jangling. Mariah followed.

"Night Riley," she called before entering her bedroom and closing the door. Paisley jumped up on the bed and snuggled up next to Mariah as soon as she got settled. Mariah patted her and smoothed her fur from her head to her tail.

"I love you little girl. Night, night," she whispered.

Mariah was asleep before she knew it.

I am in a fog bank and can't see anything. Suddenly there is a scrapping/dragging sound. I know no fear, just caution and confidence as I draw my weapon and crouch down to listen. I creep toward the sound and as I draw closer, the fog clears and I can see the forest around me. I walk down a trail and stop at a cross trail. The shadow moves out of the last vestiges of the diminishing fog and blocks the path in front of me. I stand, my back straight and unyielding, as I drop my gun hand to my side. We face off with each other, the shadow and I.

"Go ahead. Take your best shot," I state with quiet calm. "You can't hurt me any more. I'm not angry anymore. The attack and betrayal made me stronger ... smarter. I'm confident, not fearful. I know what I'm doing now. If I make a mistake or a bad choice, I will deal with it. You can leave now. You don't scare me anymore.

The shadow bows its head and dissolves into nothingness. I am alone and the fog swirls in around me, peaceful and quiet. I close my eyes and begin to meditate.

THURSDAY

Mariah woke with the sunrise and an urgent need to pee. She got out of bed and padded to the bathroom, took care of her morning ablutions, poked her head into the living room, and saw Riley was still asleep. She went back to her bedroom turned the knob and pushed the door closed, making sure it latched without making a sound.

Paisley, who stayed curled up under her own blanket on the bed, quietly yipped and twitched, her little feet jerking as she chased something in her sleep. Mariah climbed back into bed and laid down. She was in awe. Except for that brief dream in which she released the shadow, she had no recollection of dreaming during the night. She felt refreshed and relaxed when she woke, and she was elated. She yawned and stretched, reached over and patted Paisley, and closed her eyes. She was asleep again before she knew it.

Paisley's scratching at the bedroom door woke her an hour later. She threw the covers off and got out of bed. Before she got the bedroom door open, she could hear the murmur of Morgan and Riley's conversation. Paisley ran into the living room and Mariah followed.

"Good morning," she said entering the room. Riley already made up the couch and was sitting at one end, a cup of coffee in hand.

"Morning, Jeffries. I was just about to come wake you. We've got a busy day."

"Yeah, it looks like you were about to come wake me." Mariah grinned.

Morgan looked up from the kitchen sink where he was rinsing out his coffee cup.

"How'd you sleep?"

"Great. I feel wonderful … happy … rested. I haven't felt this good in a long time."

"So it worked?!" Riley took his feet off the coffee table and leaned forward.

"Seems so. The shadow came to me right off and I just told him he could go because I wasn't angry or afraid anymore, and then he just dissolved."

"Wow. What a breakthrough." Morgan sat in the living room chair, a kitchen towel draped over his left shoulder.

"Yeah. It really is. I slept so well through the rest of the night. Do you know how long it's been since that happened?"

"Yes. I do." Riley got up from the couch, put his arm around her and kissed her on the forehead.

"I'm glad you're doing better."

Riley ambled off to the bathroom.

Mariah went into the kitchen and poured herself a cup of coffee. She set it down on the counter, put some fresh food and water down for Paisley, picked up her coffee and walked into the living room to sit on the couch.

"I'm more relaxed than I've been in a long time." She took a sip of her coffee.

"Take your time and enjoy the morning. I'm going to meet with Xander. I put the address where I'm meeting the AAU team on the kitchen counter. Don't forget to meet me at ten." Morgan stood and donned his shoulder holster. He seated his Kimber 1911, and tugged on his jacket.

"I won't forget, Morgan. I'm going to drink my coffee and then take Paisley out for a run. I'll meet you at ten."

As Morgan was closing the front door, Riley came out of the bathroom, the top of his bald head still wet from his quick shower.

"I don't know how people take a three minute shower." Mariah rolled her eyes and aimed a wide grin in his direction.

"Obviously, since you need at least twenty minutes for yours."

Mariah stuck her tongue out at him.

"You want me to take Paisley for her walk while you relax a few minutes?"

"Oh, I would like that very much. I'm just not ready to get up and move yet."

"No problem. Come here girl. Let's get your leash on."

Riley snapped her harness on.

"Don't forget to buy her a new harness today."

"Yeah. I know. I don't think she would run far, but if she saw a cat or something across the road, she might run off in front of traffic after it, and I wouldn't like that."

As Riley and Paisley went out the front door, Mariah pulled her laptop into her lap to go over notes on the case. She pulled up the pictures on her cell phone and started with the note she found in Savannah Massey's jeans that was from Tina Webb. She then read Chelsea Dunn's love letters from Lucas, and Chelsea's diary. She had forgotten about those items.

She read the note from Tina Webb to Savannah first.

Tell coach Jones that I'll be late for practice today. I have an eye appointment right after school. Gigi said she would take me to run on the Old Forest trails tomorrow after practice, but don't tell anyone. My dad would go crazy, he won't let me do anything fun! You can come too if you want. Thanks.

The note was dated two days before Tina went missing. *I'll have to find out who this Gigi is,* Mariah thought.

Next were the love notes and letters she found at Chelsea Dunn's. They were all from this Lucas kid and pretty innocent—he loves her, why was she mad at him, please don't break up, had a blast last night, he'll never forget her and good luck at Ashland High. There were no threats or intimidations—just teenage angst, it appeared.

She put those all aside and studied Chelsea's diary. She read through the first fifteen pages without anything of interest catching her eye. On page sixteen references to a Mrs. Dailey, who was on staff at the school, started popping up. Mariah jotted down notes in the order of the references to her.

Mrs. Dailey

1. *New attendance secretary at South Medford High School*
2. *Pretty*
3. *Widowed*
4. *Friendly*
5. *Asking a lot of questions about Tina and her teammates*
6. *Tina said she likes her too, but thinks she's kind of weird*
7. *Alexis said she gives her the creeps*
8. *She chaperoned several AAU basketball trips*
9. *She quit or got fired*
10. *Rumor is she got married and moved away*

Aside from references about Mrs. Dailey, Mariah didn't find anything else of interest. Mariah made a mental note to contact Alexis and find out what she knows about the woman as well as checking with Robert Beaumond, the principal.

Within twenty minutes, Riley and Paisley were back and Riley sat on the couch next to Mariah.

"Whatcha working on?"

"Notes and stuff from the interviews I did. Look at this. I found this diary at Chelsea Dunn's, buried under some stuff in her closet floor. Most of what she wrote seems normal for a teenaged girl, but … before the kidnappings started, she referenced this women who went to work at the school and befriended at least one of the girls. Sounds like she tried to befriend several of them. I'm going to look into this a little further when we get back from the Old Forest. I'll talk to Alexis first—ask her what she knows."

"Probably won't pan out to be anything. You know how high school kids are. Some of the school staff they like and some they make fun of. Worth looking into, though." He paused just a moment. "Morgan told me about the dreams you had before I got here. Sounds like they were intense."

"They were. Did he tell you that one of the neighbors called the cops?"

"Yeah. I can imagine what they were thinking."

"Me too." Mariah felt the heat rise in her cheeks and chuckled.

Riley turned his head to look her in the eyes. "Do you think the nightmares are really over? Do you feel good about it?"

"I do, Riley. It's kind of hard to believe that it could end so abruptly, but it did. Those nightmares are over. I'm confident."

"I'm happy to hear that. Well, I better go." Riley patted her knee before standing up. "I don't want to be late for my appointment. We'll meet back here after all the interviews and then we'll all go out to the Old Forrest together."

"Yeah, I need to get moving, too." Mariah stood and stretched. "Thanks for taking Paisley out."

****

"Bye mom. Will you be at my game this afternoon?" Alexis called to her mom from the front door of their home.

"I'll be there. Have a good day, sweetheart. I love you."

"Love you too."

She pulled the door closed until it clicked, adjusted her books, and walked down the front steps. She turned left at the gate and turned left again at the next corner. The wind was blowing and it was colder than she expected. *Maybe I should go back and get a warmer coat.* She decided not to take the time.

Halfway down the block, a white pick-up sat idling. As Alexis approached, a woman rolled down the passenger side window and called to her.

"Hi Alexis. How are you doing?"

"Gigi? Where have you been?" Surprised, Alexis stepped up to the open window. "We thought you ran off and got married."

"Nah, I had a family emergency and had to leave, but I'm back. Want a lift? I'm going your way."

"Oh, I don't know." She backed away from the truck.

"Come on. It's freezing out here and I just got my truck warmed up." Gigi got out of her truck and started around to the passenger side.

"You know what?" Alexis said, backing up the way she had come. I just remembered, I forgot my volleyball uniform." She turned and started walking fast toward the corner of her street. "You go ahead. I'll ask my mom to drop me off so I'm not late," she called over her shoulder.

"Alexis wait. You dropped something."

Alexis stopped and turned. Gigi was standing in front of the truck and holding a piece of paper in her left hand.

"I … Oh, thanks." Alexis looked at the stack of books in her arms and walked back toward Gigi.

As she reached to take the paper she thought was homework, Gigi dropped the paper and grabbed Alexis' arm with a fierce grip and pulled her close.

She had her right hand in her coat pocket. "If you yell, I'll shoot you. Get in the truck."

Tears sprang to Alexis' eyes, from both pain and fear.

Gigi walked Alexis to the passenger side of the truck and told her to open the door. She did, her Algebra book falling in the gutter. Gigi pushed her to get in the seat.

"Gigi, please."

Gigi leaned in and pulled Alexis' head down with her left hand while she pressed a cloth she pulled out of her pocket over Alexis' nose and mouth. When Alexis went limp, Gigi sat her up in the seat and belted her in. She closed the door and ran around to the drivers side, climbed in and drove off.

****

Morgan and Mariah got back to the suite at eleven-thirty and began to record their notes on the interviews while they waited for Riley who walked in just a few minutes past twelve.

Morgan looked up from his laptop.

"How'd it go?"

"Fine. Didn't pick up on anything helpful, though."

"You've got a few minutes to make your notes on the interviews before we go. I need to fix something for us to eat on the way out to the park." Morgan reached to close his laptop.

"I'm done with my notes. Finish yours Morgan and I'll fix us all some sandwiches." Mariah folded the top of her laptop down and set it aside before rising.

"Ham and cheese sound good to you guys?"

"Sounds great." Morgan nodded without looking up.

Riley smiled at her and gave her the thumbs up, bent to retrieve his laptop case from beside his suitcase, and sat on the couch.

She finished loading her backpack with two sandwiches apiece, three apples, three baggies of mixed nuts, and nine bottles of water. Morgan went to the bathroom.

Riley stood when Morgan came back into the living room.

"Let's head out."

Mariah harnessed Paisley, hooked her leash and asked Riley to bring the backpack while she took Paisley out to potty.

They took Mariah's car, Morgan getting in the backseat with Paisley since Riley was already in the front. Paisley found Alexis' hoodie in the back seat, sniffed it and rolled it around until she could lay on it comfortably.

When they parked in the gravel parking lot at the Old Forest trail head, Morgan opened his car door and grabbed the backpack.

"Pop the trunk and I'll stow the backpack, unless you think we'll need it on the trail."

"Nope, I don't need it. I have my water. We can come back to the car for food if we get hungry"

Morgan stepped out of the car and Mariah pressed the trunk button on her key fob.

Morgan placed the backpack in the trunk and took out a bottle of water. Riley reached in for a bottle of water also, and pulled out a sandwich before closing the trunk. Paisley jumped out of the car, attached to the leash in Mariah's hand.

Mariah squatted to check Paisley's harness. "We forgot to stopped and buy a new harness. Do you think this will hold?"

"Yeah. She didn't pull at all this morning. She'll be fine for now and we'll pick up a new one on our way back." Riley crammed the last quarter of the sandwich in his mouth and they started down the trail. He looked around for a trash can but didn't see one, so he wadded up the plastic bag and stuck it in his back pocket.

Mariah pointed out where she and Alexis were when they first heard the noise, and the path they went down to follow the sound.

"Well, the sound could have carried from a different direction and only sounded like it was coming from here. He would have had to be pretty close to you for you to hear even part of his mutterings, though."

Riley walked down the side trail, looking for signs of dragging but found nothing. He came back to Morgan and Mariah, and the group walked down the main trail toward the branch where the fog rolled in on Mariah and Alexis.

"Instead of being at the upper side trail, he could have been in either direction on these two side trails." Morgan pointed down each path when they reached the branch where Mariah and Alexis had stopped their run and turned back.

"But he would have had to pass us to get down either of those before we got here."

"Not if he was ahead of you." Morgan scratched his head and looked past Mariah and Riley.

"The weather was clear when we began. We didn't see anyone in front of us."

Morgan threw his hands up.

"What about the biker couple. Did you ever see them?"

"No."

Riley shook his head. "He could have been coming back up the trail."

"I haven't seen any evidence of something being dragged so far. Why don't we split up. I'll go down this trail," Morgan indicated left, "and you go down that one, Jeffries. Riley, why don't you go back to the path that Mariah and Alexis went down. We'll look for any signs of dragging, or someone going off path into the forest."

They parted, Paisley with Mariah. Mariah was sweeping the path and sides with her eyes for anything that might be suspicious, but found nothing. Paisley was helping out by sniffing and peeing on every blade of grass, every bush, and every tree they came to. About a half mile down the trail, Mariah spotted what looked like drag marks off the side of the trail that went into the underbrush. This section of the forest was covered more in dry patches and low bushes than trees. She pulled her phone out of her pocket to text the guys. Paisley was sniffing around with heightened interest when she suddenly started barking and jerked at the leash, breaking free of the last hook on her harness. She ran off into the forest, barking. Mariah, unable to keep hold of her phone, threw the leash on the path, and yelled for Paisley to stop. The last thing she saw of Paisley was her short, apricot colored tail disappearing into some brush. Mariah snatched up her phone from the dirt path and punched in a quick message to the guys, 'HELP!', before running after Paisley trying not to disturb the evidence of the dragging.

Between Paisley's speed and her build for running through the rough terrain, Mariah knew she didn't have a chance to catch her. Instead of continuing to chase after the little dog, Mariah started tracking her and continued calling her name.

Morgan called out to Mariah.

"Where are you?"

"Follow the dragging marks by Paisley's leash. She got loose."

Morgan caught up to Mariah and Riley came up from behind him.

"I found Paisley's leash. I guess we should have gotten her a new harness before we came out here. Sorry."

"You think?" Mariah snapped at him, frustrated and worried about Paisley.

Morgan patted Mariah on the shoulder. "I know you're worried, but she'll be alright. We'll keep calling her and when she finishes chasing whatever vermin she caught sight of, she'll come back."

"I hope so. She was barking, but she quit."

"Look here." Riley pointed. "Paisley's tracks go off in that direction, but the dragging marks end right here."

Mariah squatted by the tracks. "Yeah. What in the world happened to whatever they were dragging?"

"Picked up whatever it was and carried it from here?" Morgan looked out across the field of short shrubbery and brush.

Riley gripped Mariah's shoulder, "Morgan and I are good trackers. I'll follow Paisley's tracks with you. Morgan, search around here to see if the dragging picks up in a different direction. Look for any foot tracks carrying a heavy load."

Riley and Mariah followed Paisley's tracks and called her name, while Morgan moved off in the opposite direction. Paisley's tracks continued deeper into the forest, never crossing another trail. None of them heard her yelp in pain, but she wasn't barking either. Mariah thought she had finally run whatever she was chasing to ground and caught it or was digging for it.

They heard Morgan moving closer, calling Paisley's name.

"I picked up some dragging marks again," Morgan called as he approached Riley and Mariah.

The two tracks merged. Paisley's continued but the dragging marks stopped again.

"They seem to have petered out. I didn't find any other dragging tracks," Morgan announced when he stopped next to Mariah. "As you can see, Paisley seemed to have run around in circles, sniffing the ground before she ran off in that direction."

"Where is she?" Mariah asked, apprehension growing. "She should have come back to us by now." No one answered, they kept calling her name as they continued to follow her tracks. Her prints ran into heavy underbrush and they couldn't find any place where they came out, but the underbrush covered a very large area. It took them fifteen minutes to circle it.

"She must be in that tangled mess, somewhere." Riley called her again. "Paisley! Come here, girl!"

"I don't hear anything moving around in there, and I don't hear her tags jingling. If she were in there, we should hear something. She barks when she has something cornered." Mariah slapped her thigh and called Paisley's name.

"Keep calling her." Morgan stepped back to where the paw prints entered the brush. "I'll start crawling in at her point of entry and follow her tracks."

"I'm smaller than you guys. I'll go in." Mariah followed Morgan back to the last visible tracks.

"Keep calling her name," Riley yelled after her and continued to circle a second time looking for exit prints. Morgan watched Mariah as she got on her hands and knees to crawl in.

"Wait a minute." He squatted down taking his .38 Chief Special out of his ankle holster and reached it toward Mariah as she lie halfway under the brush. "In case you come across anything that needs killing."

"Good idea, but I brought my baby and it has more rounds." Mariah leaned up and pulled the weapon out of her shoulder holster under her jacket.

"Be careful. I'm going to circle around this way and meet up with Riley. Call if you need us."

Mariah turned back and crawled into the tangled underbrush on her belly. After about ten feet, she could rise up on her hands and knees except for a few places where she had to drop back down on her belly.

"PAIIISSSLEEE. Come here girl."

Riley and Morgan continued calling her too.

The stirred up cloud of dust and dirt choked Mariah. She had to stop between calls for Paisley and cough.

"Are you alright, Jeffries?" Morgan called from Mariah's right.

She coughed again.

"Yeah. It's just really dusty down here." She called Paisley again. Another twenty feet and she had to lie back down on her belly and crawl along. Eight feet after that, she reached a rock ledge with little growth but surrounded by the brush. She stood and looked around. Morgan was searching the ground on the far side of the area to her right and Riley about ten feet in front of her. "The ground is rocky here and I've lost her trail."

"You followed her to the edge of that open area?" Morgan coughed.

"Yes, but I can't find prints here It's solid rock."

"Search around at the edges and see if you can pick them up. She had to run across there, somewhere." Riley sneezed.

Mariah's cell phone rang before she could duck back down and start searching the edges. She answered it, "What?"

"Mariah?"

"Yes."

"This is Twila Givens. Have you heard from Alexis?"

"No." A chill ran through Mariah's body. "What's wrong?"

"Oh God." Twila's voice quivered. "She never made it to school."

"Oh no," Mariah sank to the ground. "Has anyone seen her since she left the house?"

"What's wrong, Jeffries," Morgan called. "Jeffries?"

"I called everyone I could think of since the school called me at eleven to ask why she wasn't there. Bruce was in Sacramento when I got hold of him and he's on his way home."

"I'm so sorry."

Mariah wiped her face with her dirty hand and suppressed a sneeze.

"Mariah?" Riley walked to the edge of the clearing. "Are you alright?"

Mariah waived him back.

"Can you come over? The police are here, but I would feel better if you were here too."

"I'm um. ..." Mariah looked around. "I'm in the middle of something important, but I'll ask one of my partners to come over and help with the search."

"Thank you." Twila's voice was choked with fear.

Mariah disconnected the call and rose on weak legs. She couldn't stop the tears pooling in her eyes from falling down her cheeks.

"Jeffries!" Morgan started to push through at the edge of the underbrush to reach her. "What is it? Is she hurt?"

Mariah shook her head and wiped her eyes.

"Stop Morgan. You might mess her tracks up. That was Alexis' mother. Alexis went missing today. She never made it to school."

"Son of a bitch!" Riley whacked a stick he was holding against a nearby tree trunk, breaking the stick in two.

"I'm going to stay here until I find Paisley. One of you has to go to Alexis' house and help with the search."

"We can't, Mariah."

Riley stepped toward the edge of the underbrush.

"Yes, you can. One of you has to."

"Jeffries, we came together in your car."

She sank to the ground and looked around the edge of the rock ledge for Paisley's tracks running out of the clearing. She wiped the tears from her eyes so she could see.

How could things go so far off track? She was scared now for Paisley *and* Alexis. She finished the circuit of the clearing and stood. "I can't pick up her tracks." Mariah cupped her hands around her mouth. "PAIIISSSLEEE" She cried out Paisley's name, repeating the fervent call.

Morgan pushed through the brush and came to her, taking her into his arms and holding her head against his chest.

"Shhh, shhh." Morgan gave her a gentle squeeze, then held her out at arms length. "Everything is going to be alright. We're going to find them both. It's okay, Jeffries. Everything is okay."

She pushed away and wiped her eyes. "I'm not leaving without Paisley." She dug her car keys out of her pocket and handed them to Morgan. "Go to the car and bring back my backpack. There are sandwiches and some apples, nuts, and water. I'll stay out here tonight and keep calling her while you and Riley go into town and help with the search for Alexis."

"No, Mariah. We're not leaving you alone out here." Riley tripped through the underbrush in her direction. "We're losing daylight and you're not going to find her. You might even obliterate her tracks."

Mariah cupped her hands around her mouth again. "PAIIISSSLEEE."

"We'll come back out at first light tomorrow and pick up our search. We need to go check on Alexis."

"Riley, Paisley is my girl. She's *my* child! I'm not leaving her out here."

Riley reached her and grabbed her arms. "Mariah, she's not barking, she's not whimpering or yelping in pain. She's not coming back to you. She may be hurt or …"

"No." Mariah shook her head. "She's not dead, but if we leave her out here all night, she might not make it. If she's hurt she's more vulnerable to any wild animal. I have to keep looking for her."

Morgan turned Mariah back to face him. "Do you keep a flashlight in your car?"

She nodded her head. "In my trunk—maybe two."

"I'll stay out here with her, Riley. You take the car into town and help with Alexis." Morgan tossed the keys to Riley. "Let's get out of here and back to the edge of this clearing."

"Be careful you don't trip and hurt yourself. The undergrowth is pretty dense." Riley led the way.

"Morgan you go back to the car with Riley and get the backpack and the flashlights. I'll stay here and keep calling her and looking."

"It's getting too dark for you to be going out into the forest any further. You might miss her tracks or worse … destroy them. Come back to the car with us and you and I will …"

"No. You go. I'll be real careful. I can use the flashlight feature on my phone if I need to, … or the little one on her leash."

"How's the charge on your phone?" Riley asked.

Mariah checked. "Seventy-five percent. Grab the emergency charger in the front console, Morgan, in case we need it. It will charge one phone twice or two phones once. I just charged it yesterday, so we'll both be able to get a good charge if we need it."

"Okay. Let's go." Morgan pushed Riley back toward the trail. "Don't go wandering off and get lost yourself. I'll call out from the trail when I get back and you can let me know what direction to head in."

"Okay. Hurry."

****

Mariah hadn't gone very far, because there were no tracks that she could follow. While Morgan was gone, she remained where he left her and called Paisley.

"I found a light jacket for you in your trunk along with this wool army blanket. It's going to be cold tonight."

"Yeah, thanks. I'm worried sick, Morgan."

"I know hun. Let's go back to the trail so we can move easier. We can't do any good out in this brush."

They reached the trail and sat down on a large flat rock that was off to the side. Morgan fished out a sandwich and a bottle of water for each of them. He handed Mariah a sandwich and placed a bottle of water beside her on the rock.

"Eat," he ordered her.

"Am I being stupid staying out here, Morgan?"

"No. We'll find her."

"I realize she could be hurt or … or … you know, maybe … I can't think of that. We just have to find her, Morgan."

"I know. We will."

They sat in silence while they ate. Morgan took the empty baggie from Mariah and handed her the water.

"Drink something."

Mariah drained the bottle of water and handed the empty to Morgan who stored it in the backpack with the rest of the trash.

"Well, let's go. Maybe we'll find her a little further down the trail."

Mariah stood with Morgan and put the jacket on he brought back for her. She reached for the backpack, but Morgan grabbed it first.

"I'll carry this." He stuffed the blanket inside the backpack and swung it onto his shoulder.

They started down the trail calling Paisley and came upon two men in jogging tights running in their direction.

"You guys lose someone," the taller of the two men asked.

"Yes, my Jack Russell Terrier. Have you seen her?" Mariah showed them a picture of Paisley from her cell phone.

"No. Sorry." They both shook their heads.

"Thanks. If you see her and can catch her, her name's Paisley. Would you tie her up to the black Toyota corolla in the parking lot? If we don't find her, we'll check the parking lot for her."

"Uh, sure. If we find her."

"Thanks." Mariah turned and continued down the trail calling Paisley.

Morgan caught up to her and grabbed her arm, turning her to face him. "Your car is gone."

"What?"

"Your car is gone. You told those guys to tie her up at your car, but Riley took it back to town."

"Oh. Yeah! I forgot."

"She won't go to them anyway."

"Right. She won't."

They stopped every twenty feet or so to listen for the jingle of her tags, or her barking, or crying … anything. There was nothing. After about an hour, as they approached the edge of the forest that backed up to the mountain, the fog started moving in.

"Oh great!"

"Maybe we'll be able to hear her better with the fog. I've been in heavy fogs before and it seems like sound is amplified, Mariah. Or maybe it travels better, I'm not sure."

"We can hope."

They continued on the trail which curved around past the side of the mountain to the back side of the forest, calling Paisley and stopping to listen for her.

"We should head back the way we came and see if she comes back to the spot you lost her. That's where she'll show up."

"That's what I was thinking. She could be anywhere."

By the time they got back to the flat rock where Paisley ran off, Mariah was shivering from the damp cold. Earlier,

Morgan pulled the blanket from the backpack and wrapped it around his shoulders.

"Jeffries, I'm calling Riley to come pick us up."

"N-n-n-ooo, Mo-mor-g-gan."

"If necessary, I'll pick you up and carry you out of here kicking and screaming, which you can't because you're too damned cold." Morgan pulled his phone out of his pocket and dropped it because his hands were so cold. He picked it up, and punched in Riley's phone number.

"Hey. Can you get away to come pick us up? We're freezing out here, especially Mariah. She's about half frozen. ... You are? ... Thank God. We're headed that way. ... What? ... No." Morgan shook his head and turned concerned eyes on Mariah. "Nothing. ... Yeah, we'll be there in a few minutes if I can keep her upright and moving. She's on the verge of hypothermia. ... Thanks man."

They continued to walk as Morgan talked on the phone and was almost at the intersection to the main trail. As they approached that intersection, a man approached out of the fog from the opposite direction. Morgan pulled his pistol, but couldn't hold on. It thumped on the ground at his feet and the other guy raised his hands. "Hi folks. You lost?"

Morgan bent to retrieve his pistol.

"Er-Er-Erick? Is the-that ya-you?"

"Why, yes ma'am. It sure is. Why, you're the woman I met in town, doin' that pretty dance at the dog park."

"Yes. Ma-ma-ri-ah Jef-ef-er-ies."

"You were very kind to me." Erick took the blanket from around his shoulders and wrapped it around Mariah.

"Ma'am, you need to get out of this damp cold."

"N-n-no. Pai-ai-slee-ey is m-m-mis-s-sing."

Erick leaned closer and with genuine concern asked, "That young lady that was with you the other night?"

"No, her dog. A Jack Russell Terrier. Have you seen her?" Morgan put a protective arm around Mariah's shoulders.

"No. I'm sorry, but why don't you folks go ..."

"Morgan, Mariah," Riley called as he appeared out of the fog.

"Hello. I'm Erick. I hope you're here to get these folks out of the cold."

"Nice to meet you Erick and I sure am. Why don't you come with us. It's only going to get colder."

"No, thank you. I know how to stay warm, but this young lady needs to warm up. I'm getting worried about her.."

"I'm doing just that." Riley scooped Mariah up in his arms. "There's room. Sure you don't want to come with us? We'll get you something hot to eat and a warm bed."

"I'm sure."

"Wa-wa-wai-ate-ta. Y-your ba-ba-blan-k-k-ket," Mariah stuttered, trying to release it. Even in her frozen state she knew that Erick would need it if he stayed out in the elements.

Morgan took the blanket from around her, gave it back to Erick, and took Mariah's blanket from his shoulders and wrapped it around her.

"Thanks Erick. If we can do anything for you, please don't hesitate to call. Here's my business card."

Morgan held out the card with a five dollar bill. Erick took the card, but refused the money.

"No problem. I'll keep a look out for your little dog. If I come across her, I'll wait at the trailhead with her in the morning."

"Thanks." Riley turned and started jogging with Mariah in his arms, up the trail to the car.

At the car, Riley told Morgan to climb in the backseat with Mariah and keep his arms around her for warmth.

"I threw my sleeping bag in the backseat before I left. The rating is for minus 30 degrees. Wrap it around both of you. Your combined body heat will help you both, especially under the bag."

Morgan opened the back door behind the driver and ran around to the other side as Riley placed Mariah on the seat. Riley pulled the wool blanket from around her shoulders as

Morgan slid in beside her. Morgan unzipped the sleeping bag, leaned her forward, and tucked the long edge behind both of them. He pulled her close. Riley grabbed both of Mariah's hands and looked at them under the light in the car. He rubbed each hand quickly between his own to get the blood circulating. When Riley let go of Mariah's hands, Morgan wrapped the rest of the bag around them both, covering them from thighs to heads. Riley wrapped Mariah's feet and legs in the wool blanket after he stripped her shoes and socks off, inspected her feet, and rubbed the circulation back into them. The car doors slammed closed, rocking the vehicle. Riley started the vehicle and backed out of the parking space, pulled onto the highway, and left the Old Forest, leaving Paisley behind.

Mariah leaned into Morgan and softly cried.

"Do we need to take her to the emergency room?" Riley ask after a short while.

"N-no. I'm g-getting warm-ma-mer. J-just go t-to the suite."

"I think she'll be okay. She's not shivering as bad. I think she's warming up."

"The heater's going full blast. Can you feel it back there?"

"I'm f-feeling w-warmer."

"Yeah, thanks man." Morgan took Mariah's hands and started rubbing them, then rubbed up her arms to her shoulders, stimulating her circulation. "Feeling better?"

Mariah nodded her head.

Morgan threw the sleeping bag off himself and wrapped it further around Mariah, tucking it in around her legs and feet. "Just stay under that for a while."

He wrapped both his arms around her and pulled her close.

"Are y-you w-warm enou-ough?" Mariah asked Morgan.

"I'm warmed up. I didn't get as cold as you did."

"How you doing, Mariah?" Riley looked back at Morgan.

"B-better. Tha-thanks."

By the time they came out of Jacksonville headed to Medford, most of the shivering had subsided. "First thing in the morning. You promise?"

"Yes. We'll come back at first light." Morgan gave her a gentle squeeze and she leaned her head into his chest as her eyes leaked like an old rusty faucet and her breath shuddered.

They made it to the suite and Mariah started to climb out of the car to walk into the suite on her own.

"You're barefoot. I'll carry you. Stay wrapped up." Riley reached into the backseat and started pulling her out.

"I can walk."

"It's twenty-three degrees out here, and you're just starting to warm up. You're not going to walk out here barefoot. Morgan grab her shoes, will ya."

As soon as they got inside their apartment, Riley put Mariah down. She tripped and fell trying to step out of all the blankets wrapped around her. She rolled to her back and threw a hissy fit, thrashing about, arms and legs flying everywhere to disengage the blankets before she got to her feet. She snatched the sleeping bag and pulled it back around her shoulders.

Riley picked up the wool blanket where she left it crumpled on the floor.

"Feeling better now?" He aimed a crooked grin at her.

"Yes."

She went over to the couch where she sat, pulling her feet up under her, still wrapped in the sleeping bag. "Thanks Riley. I know I was stupid to stay out there."

"I understand why you did, Mariah. Glad you're alright."

"Coffee?" Morgan asked from the kitchen as he started fixing a pot.

"Yes, please." Riley and Mariah both sang out.

Morgan brought a cup of coffee to each of them, both laced with Crown Royal. Mariah took a sip and nodded as the warmth from the coffee and the fire from the whiskey raced down her throat, warming her blood.

"Who was that Erick guy?" Morgan sat next to Mariah on the couch.

"He's a homeless guy that Alexis and … Oh my God. Alexis! Did you find her? Anything?"

Riley shook his head. "We found one of her textbooks in the gutter around the corner from her house. The cops and the FBI are looking into it now."

"Erick," Morgan pressed.

"Yeah, um. Alexis and I ran into him at the dog park one night." Mariah drained her coffee and got up from the couch.

"We were leaving and he stepped out in front of us."

She walked to the kitchen, the sleeping bag trailing behind her, and refilled her cup.

Morgan and Riley both watched from where they were seated, and grinned at each other. She walked back to the couch.

"We chatted while we walked to my car and I gave him some change and some food. I think he's a good guy. I think that he saw us in that park after dark by ourselves, and was watching out for us. Making sure we made it to the car safe and sound. I got a sense of protection from him." Mariah sat back down on the couch.

"He's ex-military. I could swear by it." Riley kicked off his shoes.

"I thought so too," Morgan added.

Mariah took a swig from her mug and made a face.

"What's the matter?" Riley was holding his laughter in and tears were rimming his eyes.

Morgan guffawed.

"Too much whiskey." Mariah shook her head and shivered. "What'd I do?"

"You don't remember?" Riley asked.

Mariah shook her head.

"You poured the rest of the Crown in your mug and added a touch of coffee. I think you need to drink it, too. It would do you a world of wonders." Riley wiped his face, still chuckling.

"I will. Anyway, he told us that Uncle Sam taught him how to survive the elements when I encouraged him to go to a shelter. I hope he'll be okay out in the cold."

"He had an extreme-cold-weather sleeping bag on his pack. I recognized that," Riley commented.

Mariah sipped her drink.

"I think he'll be fine. Hopefully, he'll find Paisley and be waiting for us at the trailhead in the morning." Riley put his feet up on the coffee table.

"I hope so." Mariah stared off into space as she sipped her coffee laced Crown Royal. They sat in silence sipping their drinks until Riley started snoring. Mariah got up and put her almost empty mug on the counter.

"I'm going to take a hot bath and go to bed. Y'all be ready at first light or I'm going back by myself."

"Yes ma'am." Morgan nodded at her.

Riley startled awake. "Good night, Mariah. Do you want me to throw the sleeping bag on your bed in case you need more blanket tonight?"

Mariah stumbled exiting the kitchen and caught herself. "No. I'm fine now, Riley. Thanks though. Thanks for saving my stupid ass."

"You're not stupid. You love that pup. She's your family just like we are. We look out for each other."

"Would you have left if I was the one missing?"

"Mariah ..."

Her eyes started leaking again. "This is all my fault," she slurred. "I knew her harness was worn and I should have gotten her a new one before we left town."

Riley came to her and held her by the shoulders. "None of us thought it was that worn. I looked at it too. I'm sorry Mariah. We'll find her tomorrow."

FRIDAY A.M.

Morgan shook Mariah awake. Bright sunlight sifted in around the dark drapes. "How you feeling, Jeffries?"

"Ready to get an early start. What time is it?" she mumbled.

"Eight-thirty."

She bolted upright. "Eight-thirty? I said first light! You promised."

"It was too cold. The temperature is just now creeping above thirty degrees. Let's eat and get on the road. It should be up to at least thirty-five by the time we reach the forest."

Mariah threw the covers off and got out of bed. "Damn it. You guys promised me."

"Jeffries," Morgan bellowed. "It was too damned cold. Now, get over it and get dressed so we can go."

She glared at Morgan. Riley stepped into the room behind him.

"It's too damned cold," she sneered. "Well Paisley is out there in the 'too damned cold'—maybe hurt. Probably frozen to death by now. But it was too damned cold for us to go out at first light after a good night's sleep in a warm bed and look for her?" Morgan and Riley shimmered in her tear blurred vision. She had to clamp her jaw down to keep it from trembling.

Morgan threw his hands up, turned around and started out of the room, pushing past Riley.

"We can't win, Riley. She's pissed and if we don't find Paisley alive and well, she'll always blame *us* for it. All because we didn't let *her FREEZE* to death looking for Paisley."

Riley stood in the doorway and stared at her. Mariah covered her face with both hands and drew in a deep breath. "I'm sorry. I don't blame you guys. I don't. I'm just sick with worry and fear for Paisley."

Riley walked over to Mariah and put his arms around her, his hand on the back of her head, holding her close. "Did you have nightmares last night?"

Mariah shook her head no. "I slept like a rock and I feel so guilty that I did. I didn't even dream of her."

"Morgan and I know how much you love that crazy, sweet, little dog, Mariah. We're worried too, and not only about Paisley. You scared the crap out of us last night. You were near hypothermic."

She just nodded her head against Riley's chest and reached up and wiped her eyes. "I need to get dressed. Will you poor me a cup of coffee?"

"Sure. We'll be in the kitchen. Don't take too long."

She dressed in layers—Under Armor leggings and shirt, wool socks up to her knees, jeans, t-shirt, and a pull-over hoodie. She sat on the bed and pulled on her waterproof, thick-tread hiking boots, before she pulled on her holster for the FN Five-seveN that held two additional magazines. She pulled the FN from the bottom of her suitcase and slid it into the holster.

Morgan was standing with his right hip leaning up against the counter, talking to Riley and drinking his coffee. Mariah walked right up behind him and put her arms around his waist and hugged tight.

"I'm sorry. I'm not mad at you. Really. I appreciate that you care about me," her voice muffled against his back.

He put his coffee mug on the counter, turned and wrapped his arms around her, kissing the top of her head.

"I know you're worried. I am too. I love that little dog too. My whole family sees her as a family member." He murmured against the top of Mariah's head. "How am I going to go home and tell them she's gone?"

Mariah leaned away and stepped back. Riley handed her a cup of coffee and she took a sip, testing the heat. She swallowed, afraid that anything she said would put her over the edge and she couldn't afford that now. She needed to find Paisley. Finally, her emotions under control she said, "We're not going to tell them that. We're going out there and we're going to find her ... alive."

"Okay."

"Let me make some sandwiches to get us through the day."

"Already done," Riley said. "Drink your coffee. Here's an egg sandwich for breakfast. Let's go, you can eat in the car." The sandwich was wrapped in a paper towel. Mariah's stomach growled at the aroma of whole grain toast, bacon, cheddar cheese and fried egg.

"What did you pack?" she asked, setting the sandwich down on the counter and taking a drink of coffee.

"Sandwiches, water—Riley and I had our camelbaks in the car, so we've got those too. You can have mine if you want, and I'll carry the backpack with the food and bottled water." Morgan said.

"I made the sandwiches and Morgan mixed some of your nuts and put those in baggies. I tossed in the last two apples and three oranges—a banana too. We've got plenty to eat," Riley said. "I know what chow hounds you two are."

Mariah nodded with a smile and drained her coffee cup. She put the mug on the counter, reached for an empty baggie and scooped out some kibbles, filling the baggie and sealing it.

"I already put food in the pack for Paisley," Morgan said.

Mariah glanced at him with a small, weak smile and nodded her head, putting the filled baggie on the counter.

Morgan picked up a camelbak and a travel mug and handed them to Mariah. "Your second cup and extra water."

"Thanks." She took the egg sandwich from the counter with her free hand, walked to the door, held the sandwich in her mouth and laid the rest on the floor. She grabbed her down stadium jacket she'd left at the suite the day before. She pulled the watch cap and gloves out of the pocket and put them on, then the jacket, grabbed the travel mug and camelbak, took the sandwich from between her teeth, and headed out the door, Riley and Morgan following behind with the rest of their gear.

They pulled out of the parking lot and Riley drove around to the big box grocery store, pulled into the parking lot and unhooked his seatbelt.

"What are we stopping for?" Mariah asked, irritated.

Riley got out of the car, turned to her in the backseat and smiled. "A new harness for Paisley. We'll need it when we find her."

"Oh. Yeah."

Morgan and Mariah got out of the car and followed Riley into the store. They found the pet supplies and found the harnesses. The selection was slim but they found one that would fit her, purchased it and left the store.

A yellow Kia was in the parking lot as they pulled in at the trail head, but no one was in sight. Mariah had been hoping Erick would be there with Paisley. He wasn't. She sighed as they started down the trailhead.

"I'm going back to the area where we lost her tracks. Morgan, why don't you go on around the trail that I lost her from—where it curved around to the back by the mountain's edge. Riley, maybe you should take the trail that is just above and parallel to the trail that I lost her from. She ran off in that direction. I have a feeling she is in that quadrant somewhere. We'll all head in an easterly direction and meet around the back end of the forest."

"Sounds like as good a plan as any," Riley said.

****

At the overgrowth of short shrubbery and brush where Paisley's tracks were last seen, Mariah circled around to the east, her eyes sweeping the ground for any signs of her little furry, white friend. The call of Paisley's name rang out from Morgan to the south and Riley to the north of her.

Mariah had been walking through the forest for close to an hour, approaching the base of the mountain, just before it started a steep rise when she saw a flash of white in her peripheral vision to the right. She turned her gaze in that direction and there was Paisley, running toward her, something flapping from her back. Mariah opened her mouth to call Paisley when a man came into view chasing her, a pistol aimed at the little dog. Time slowed to a crawl as the man's arm jerked up from the recoil, and a boom rang out from the fired gun. Paisley jumped a bush when the shot rang out, and yelped when she hit the ground on the other side, tumbling three or four times out of Mariah's line of site.

"N O O O O," Mariah yelled as she pulled her FN. All she could think was, *I can't shoot him. To the law, she's just a dog. I can't use deadly force.* But to Mariah, she's not just a dog—Paisley is her child, her family.

He was a short, squat man with a round face and torso—clearly out of shape. He stopped just inches from where Paisley went down and stared at Mariah, huffing, the Smith and Wesson .357 in his hand. She still had her gun up and pointed at him. Time sped up, back to normal.

"Don't you touch her." Mariah growled through gritted teeth, seething with rage. He took three steps forward and started to bend down to grab at Paisley. In that instant, Morgan came running from behind a tree to the man's left and tackled him, driving him into the ground.

Mariah holstered her gun and ran to Paisley. She was laying on her side, her legs sprawled, eyes closed, tongue hanging out. Mariah squatted and reached for the dog, blood starting to show in her white fur just above her hind leg. Paisley's eyes opened and she peered up at Mariah without moving a muscle. Mariah started to ease her hands under the little terrier to pick her up, when Paisley scrambled to her feet and into Mariah's arms. She licked Mariah's face, wiggling in joy and emitting little joyful whines, her tail a blur. Mariah laughed, hugged her little dog, and checked for the wound.

Paisley didn't yelp or pull away when Mariah rubbed her hands over Paisley's body, but the blood that came away on Mariah's hands told her what she needed to know. In a panic, Mariah parted Paisley's coat until she found a superficial flesh wound on the top of the Paisley's left hind leg. Mariah blew a breath of relief.

"Playing dead. Smart girl. You were playing dead." Mariah laughed and hugged Paisley until the little dog squirmed to get free. She extracted the one armed jacket, with an obvious bullet hole through the back, from around Paisley's head and gasped. Mariah stood, Paisley in her arms, and called to Morgan.

"He knows where the girls are. Paisley was tangled in Alexis' jacket. One sleeve has been ripped off."

Riley burst on the scene from Mariah's right. "Where's that son-of-a-bitch?"

"Over here Riley." Morgan grabbed the man by his jacket lapels and jerked him up into a sitting position after having cuffed his hands behind his back.

Riley got there and the two of them pulled the man into a stand.

"Where. Are. The. Girls?" Riley spit out like bullets fired from his Kimber 1911. The man was shaken and could barely stand, blood racing tears down the left side of his face and from his nose.

Morgan, who held the man by his right shoulder, gave him a violent shake. "Tell us. Where. The girls are. NOW."

"Man, I'm bleeding. I need help," the man squealed. "Get me a doctor."

Riley let go of the man, shoving his shoulder. If not for Morgan's hold on him, the man would have been tossed to the ground again. The ragged edges of Riley's furry radiate from his body as the muscles in his neck, back, and shoulders bunched and his hands fisted.

"Don't kill him, Riley. He knows where the girls are. He has to tell us," Mariah shouted.

Paisley pushed at Mariah, trying to get out of her arms. Mariah squatted down, took the old, broken harness off Paisley, and put the new one she carried in her pocket, on the little dog. She adjusted the fitting and clipped her leash to it. She stood and strode over to the quivering man, Paisley pulling and whining to go back the way she came.

The stranger looked at Mariah and then Riley. He knew fury when he stood in front of it, and he didn't like the penchant for justice in Riley's eyes waiting to be unleashed on him. He cowered.

"Lady, help me. Don't let him kill me."

She glanced at Paisley and then to the man. With deadly calm, looking him square in the eye, she spoke.

"I've changed my mind, Riley. Kill the weasel. Paisley can lead us to the girls." She turned her back and started to give Paisley the leash, following her. After ten paces, she stopped and over her shoulder, snarled, "He's worthless."

Riley started to reach for the man when the guy started groveling.

"Wait," he cried. "Wait. I'll tell you. I'll tell you everything. Just don't kill me. Please.

"Start talking." Riley growled. "What's your name?"

"Hershel."

Mariah stopped. Paisley tugged at the leash and whined to continue.

"Last name." Morgan gave the man a violent shake.

"Hoffman. Hershel Hoffman. It was only supposed to be one girl, but she got greedy. My, my wife's sick or I would never, NEVER have agreed to taking care of the girls. I promise. I needed the money for my wife's medicine. She's gonna die without it."

Mariah looked back at Hershel. Paisley sat at Mariah's feet and whined.

"So your wife told you to take the girls?"

"What? No lady! Not my wife. She doesn't know anything about this. This is Gigi's scheme."

"Who the hell is Gigi," Morgan yelled at him, shaking him again. Hershel physically shrunk in on himself and stammered.

"Gi-Gi, Da-Daily. She pay-paid me five thou-thousand da-dollars to come out here and take … take care of the ga-girls until the uh, traffic, uh traffickers from San-San Francisco could come co-co-collect them." He stopped and took a deep breath, and stood a little straighter. He swallowed and said, "It was just, just supposed to be Tina, Tina Webb, but when the guys … the traffickers were delayed in collect, collecting Tina, and Gigi realized how mu, much she could make off them, she … she decided to take some more. More girls." He took a deep breath. "She said it would help throw the cops off too, because … it, it would be harder to, you know … figure out who ta-took them and wha-why. It was working, too—until you ca-came to town."

Mariah's phone dinged, indicating she had an email. As she pulled it out of her pocket to take a look, it chimed with a text message. She peered at the screen and saw that it was from Norela. **Call me. Can't wait to tell you what I found** it read. Mariah knew it was something that could wait and put the phone back in her pocket.

Morgan, with clenched teeth, shook the man again and articulated in a quiet rumble, "Where-Are-The-Girls?"

"I, I'll take you. Follow me," Hershel said and started to pull away from Morgan.

Morgan pulled him back. "You're not getting out of my grasp. Get moving," Morgan barked at Hershel. The two men followed Mariah and Paisley who was in the lead. Hershel stumbled and then started forward with his hands cuffed behind his back, Morgan holding tight to the man's upper right arm.

"You're hurting me, man. I'm not going anywhere. Got no where to go. You know who I am and I won't run off without my wife. She's too sick to leave, so …"

"Ease your grip, Morgan," Riley seethed. "If he tries to run, I'll shoot his knees out. He won't get far."

They discovered they weren't far from the girls' location. It was off the path by fifty yards and slightly up the side of the mountain. They came to a heavy brush area next to a run off ditch.

Hershel stammered, "Be-behind, the, the dead bu-bush. There's an old, old abandoned ah, ah, gold mine. Lo-long forgotten."

Riley and Mariah pulled the bush back and sure enough, there was a small cave mouth. Just inside the opening sat two large flashlights. They each grabbed one and clicked them on shining them into the cave. It was empty.

Stooping to enter, they didn't see anything but rough rock wall with a four foot tall ceiling. Riley backed out and turned on Hershel, grabbing the front of his coat. He jerked Hershel up to within an inch of his face, feet swinging in the air.

"What kind of game are you play?"

"In, in there. I'll show you," Hershel squealed.

"If you don't tell me where those girls are right now, I'm going to stomp your worthless, sorry ass into the ground, right here, right NOW."

While Riley threatened to leave Hershel in the dirt, broken and bleeding to death, Mariah followed Paisley into the cave. Toward the left side, in the back, she found a small open space concealed by an overlap of rock wall.

Paisley jerked forward, the leash jumping out of Mariah's hand as she shined the light in the opening. Mariah noticed the path went back and curved to the right.

Hershel's voice drifted toward her. "There, they're in there. The cave curves off to the left, goes back a few feet and curves to the right with a slight incline. They're in there. I'll lead the way."

Paisley, leash dragging in the dirt, disappeared around the curve, barking.

Mariah turned back to the mouth of the cave and called out, "Back here, guys." She turned back to the passageway and followed Paisley.

Morgan pushed Hershel forward and he stumbled, hitting his head on the cave opening before falling on his side, unable to brace the fall with his hands since he was handcuffed. He grunted, and then groaned.

"Easy man. I said I'll take you to them." Hershel rolled around on the ground trying to get up. Riley reached down and pulled him to his feet. Morgan entered the cave, followed by Hershel and then Riley.

"Let's go. You better not be playing any games." Riley said. "And don't think you're going to get away. Just try to run and I'll shoot. I don't miss."

As they turned into the tunnel created by the rock overlap, the stench of human waste became nauseatingly thick. Twenty paces down the tunnel, the cave opened up, and to the left, up on a rise of dirt were the five young girls, each bound to a stake in the ground, hands behind their backs, and gagged. Two of them were laying on their sides, curled up in a ball. Down and to the right, in front of a small pool of water was a fire pit with a nice, moderate fire burning, keeping the chill at bay for the girls. It was a little smoky, but Mariah noticed a lot of the smoke drift back behind the pool and up into fissure's in the rock.

Paisley was in Alexis' lap, licking the tears from her face. Mariah ran to Alexis, hugged her, and took the gag off just as the men entered the cave.

"Mariah. I knew you would come and then when Paisley found us …" She started to sob as Mariah untied her hands from behind her back. Alexis rubbed her wrists while Mariah untied her feet. The two women hugged, Alexis holding onto Mariah with a death grip.

"It's okay. You're safe now. Let me help the others and we'll talk later."

Paisley ran to each of the girls to checked on them, her tail a furious blur from wagging. She licked each girl's face before she went back to Alexis and crawled in her lap.

Morgan had gone to one of the girls that was laying down. And then scooted over to the other one. "These two need medical attention fast."

Riley pushed Hershel to the ground and told him not to move, before going to the other girls to untie them. Mariah pulled her cell phone from the pocket she had stuffed it into, but had no reception.

"I gotta go outside to call the cops. I'll be right back."

Outside the cave, Mariah called Captain Spencer. "Captain," she said when he answered. "This is Mariah Jeffries. We found the girls. … Yes. All five of them. Two of the girls need medical attention as fast as possible. The other three look to be in pretty decent condition. … We're out at the Old Forest outside of Jacksonville. … From the trailhead … shoot … one of us is going to have to meet you at the trailhead and guide you to the cave. Otherwise it will take you too long to find it. … Um, no. Not real close. Maybe they could touch down on the road in front of the trailhead and then pack in. … about twenty, thirty minute hike. … Yeah. I can send Morgan or Riley to meet them there. I'm staying with the girls until they're all out. … See you soon."

Mariah went back into the cave. "Captain Spencer is going to have a rescue chopper set down at the parking lot. I need one of you guys to meet them there and show them to this cave. I'll stay here with the girls."

The three stronger girls huddled together—arms wrapped around each other. The soft murmur of their console to each other filled the cave with a quiet hum. Mariah took her coat off and wrapped it around the three girls as best she could. Morgan had covered Tina Webb, one of the girls who was laying down, with his coat and administered to her. Riley covered the other girl, Duskie Banks, and had her sitting up.

Her loud wheezing and coughing concerned Mariah. Hershel hadn't moved from his spot—his head down, he stared at the ground.

"I'll go," Riley announced. "Mariah, come sit with Duskie and try to keep her calm."

Hershel looked up as Riley approached him. "I won't try to run. I'm glad it's over. I don't care what happens to me. I'll tell the cops everything I know. I know I deserve everything I get."

"You're coming with me. Come on." Riley took Hershel by the arm and lifted him to his feet.

Hershel pulled away. "No. You'll get me out there away from everyone and kill me with no witnesses. I'll stay here and wait for the cops."

Riley chuckled. "Killing's too good for the likes of you, Hershel. You're coming with me so you don't interfere with them helping the girls. I'll turn you over to the cops when they get here. Now, let's go."

Riley grabbed Hershel's arm and pulled him forward, into the tunnel leading to the cave mouth.

Morgan lifted Tina, layered in her own body waste, into his arms and carried her down closer to the fire. Mariah told the other three girls to follow and sit with Tina before she went to Duskie and asked her if she could walk. She had pushed herself up halfway to a standing position, but started coughing and hacking violently. Mariah grabbed her before she fell and started to ease her back to the ground. Morgan came and lifted her into his arms and carried her to the fire, setting her down next to the other girls.

"Morgan, Duskie needs to get outside to fresh air. It's too smoky in here for her."

"I want to wait outside too," Alexis said.

"Me too," the other two girls echoed.

Morgan scooped up Duskie in his arms. "Alexis, y'all come with me. Bring Paisley."

A few minutes later, Morgan came back for Tina and picked her up. "Let's get out of here. We'll stay in the outer cave, there's fresh air there."

Morgan sat Tina on the ground with care, next to Duskie. The other three girls bookended them for protection and comfort.

"Are you girls hungry or thirsty? Four girls nodded their heads, Tina didn't respond, her eyes wide open, starring sightlessly. Mariah nodded toward Tina and Morgan told her under his breath, "Shock."

She picked up the backpack that Morgan had discarded and the camelbak she'd been carrying and took them to the girls. She gave Duskie the camelbak and showed her how to drink from it, then pulled out a bottle of water for each of the other girls, tossing one to Morgan who twisted the cap off and then sat Tina up and helped her to swallow a little bit of water. He sat down next to her and pulled her into his lap, wrapped his arms around her, rocked her, and mumbled soft comforting words to her. She laid her head against his chest and started weeping.

The girls emptied their water except for Duskie who's camelbak held twelve times the volume. She also had to stop and cough every few sips. Alexis took Mariah's coat from her shoulders and wrapped it around Duskie for added warmth.

Mariah pulled out the sandwiches and handed them to the girls. Duskie laid hers in her lap, too week to eat. Mariah extended one to Morgan for Tina, but Morgan shook his head.

"Are any of you hurt?" Mariah asked.

Alexis said no and the other two girls shook their heads.

"Can-can't breath," Duskie wheezed.

"I know. We're getting help. Just hold on." Duskie pulled the coat around her and laid down, her head tucked inside. Mariah kept her hand on the girl's back, afraid she would stop breathing.

"Did he, did anyone touch any of you … inappropriately?"

"No," they responded in a chorus.

"How did they take you without anyone seeing anything?" Mariah asked.

"It was Mrs. Daily," Alexis said. "She was in a white pick-up truck. I heard someone call me while I was walking to school. I saw Mrs. Daily sitting in her truck and went over."

"How do you know her?"

"She used to work at the school, a secretary. She was nice to all of us, like she wanted to be best friends or something. She helped chaperone some of our basketball trips. We all thought she was okay … a little weird. That's all. But we didn't make fun of her or anything. We weren't mean to her at all. Anyway, she wanted to give me a ride to school, but it felt funny, so I told her I forgot something at home and started walking away. She got out of her truck and said I dropped something. I thought it was my homework, so I walked back to get it and she grabbed me. She said she had a gun and she would shoot me if I didn't get in the truck. When I got in the truck, she pushed my face into a rag in her hand and held it there. I couldn't breath. The next thing I remember was being here, tied up."

"That's pretty much what happened to me, too," Savannah said.

"Me too," Chelsea chimed in.

Duskie's breath was even but the deep vibration in her back produced a loud wheeze with each breath.

Paisley, curled up in Alexis' lap, licked Alexis' hands, then her own front paws, before she laid her head down across Alexis' thigh and sighed, closing her eyes. Mariah sat close to Alexis, one arm around her, holding her close. Her other hand she kept on Duskie's back.

"Paisley found us yesterday. She came and laid in my lap when I didn't get up to follow her. She stayed all night and only left when she heard Hershel coming. My jacket sleeve got ripped off when I tried to escape one time, when Hershel took me to the bucket to pee. Paisley had curled up in my jacket that I took off before he tied me back up and the armhole got hung up around Paisley's head. She skittered to the dark edge of the wall before he came in and tried to sneak out of the cave after he got past the opening. He saw my jacket moving and raced after her."

"That's how we caught him. We were out looking for Paisley and when we saw her, Hershel was chasing her. She was running to us and I couldn't tell what was flying like a cape over her until I picked her up. He tried to kill her. If it wasn't for Paisley, we wouldn't have known that Hershel had you girls. She found you and led us to you."

"Thank you, Paisley." Alexis picked up and hugged the heroic Jack Russell Terrier.

"Your families have been so worried about you girls. They're going to be so happy to see you. We've been looking frantically for you."

"When that man would come to give us food and water, he wouldn't tell us much, but he did tell us that we would be women soon," Chelsea said quietly. "He said that we would be taken to our promised husbands and have good lives. I told him that I wasn't promised to anyone and I didn't want to get married. I told him I was going to college, but he just shook his head. He said," she choked up, "he said my parents sold me to a man in Saudi Arabia, to be his wife and have his babies. I didn't believe him. I knew my parents wouldn't do such a thing." She sat, sobbing, when she finished.

"What did he tell you, Savannah?"

Savannah, bowed her head and shook it before saying, "He just said, …" she stopped and shook her head.

"It's okay. You don't have to talk about it right now."

They sat in silence a few minutes when Mariah finally asked, "Do you girls need anything?"

"I need to go to the bathroom," Alexis said, lifting Paisley and handing her to Mariah. She started to walk back into the cave, but stopped and turned to Mariah.

"Can I go outside?"

"Yes. Of course. Do you want me to go with you?"

"Yes. Please."

Mariah put Paisley on the ground and stood. "Anyone else need to go?"

Savannah pointed to the tunnel. "He had a bucket with bags in it for a toilet. He would come and take us to it one at a time, twice a day. Once in the morning and once in the evening. He would stand there and watch us, keeping a flashlight on us so he could see. It was disgusting. Then he would tie us back up. Tina never got up to go. She couldn't."

Paisley started for the mouth of the cave, Mariah and Alexis following.

"We'll be right back. Then I'll go out with any of you who need to go out, one at a time."

When they came back, Paisley curled up in Mariah's lap.

"Is there any more water? He barely gave us enough to keep us alive. Food too."

"Yeah." Mariah leaned forward and grabbed the backpack.

"Here's two more sandwiches. Ya'll can share. And I have some fruit and nuts, too."

Duskie pushed her sandwich toward Chelsea. "You can have mine." she wheezed.

"You sure, Duskie?" Chelsea whispered. Duskie nodded her head, too exhausted from trying to breath to say more.

Chelsea took Duskie's sandwich and opened the baggie. Mariah handed the other two to Alexis and Savannah. They ate in silence while Mariah pulled out the last three bottles of water and handed one to each of them.

She pulled out the baggie of kibbles for Paisley and scooped some out in the palm of my hand, offering it to her favorite little dog. Paisley ate with gusto until Mariah's hand was empty. She aimed her stare at the bag of food first, then at Mariah, asking for more and Mariah scooped out another handful. They did that several times, before Paisley sat down in front of Mariah and put her paw on an empty water bottle. Mariah got up and retrieved Riley's camelbak and opened the collapsible bowl she kept on Paisley's leash for their runs. She squeezed water into the bowl and put it down for her. Paisley lapped up the water and Mariah provider her with more until she was sated.

Mariah sat back down and Paisley crawled into her lap and fell asleep.

Finished eating and drinking, Alexis laid her head against Mariah's shoulder.

"How much longer before they get here to take us home?"

"It shouldn't be too much longer," Morgan answered.

Savannah laid down, putting her head in Chelsea's lap who sat on the other side of Duskie.

They sat in silence, watching the shadows at the mouth of the dark cave.

"Morgan, let's get the girls out of here and into the sunlight."

"It's warmer in here at the moment. I think we should wait until the paramedics get here."

"Duskie might breath better outside."

Morgan shook his head. "It shouldn't be much longer and they'll be here. Let's wait."

****

An air-ambulance touched down at the entrance of the parking lot, blocking the highway in both directions. A moment later a State Police unit pulled up on the west side of the ambulance and two uniformed officers exited the vehicle. They walked to the trunk of their unit to remove equipment, and the driver of the unit started walking back down the road in the direction they had come, a fistful of flares in his hand. The other officer walked up to the air-ambulance and spoke to the two EMT's before walking east on the road. He also carried a bundle of flares.

Riley was in the parking lot, talking to two men who had stopped to hike, Hershel sitting at his feet.

"Look man, I'm sorry for the inconvenience, but this is an emergency. You guys are going to have to talk to the police when they get here. No one is allowed out here until we finish the investigation."

"Let me see your badge," the shorter of the two men demanded.

Riley reached in his back pocket and was pulling out his ID when Captain Spencer came to a screeching halt in front of the helicopter.

"Ah, here comes Captain Spencer. He'll confirm everything."

"What's going on, Riley?"

"Just clearing the area. We need to keep everyone out of here." Riley arched an eyebrow. "Everyone, including any media, until we know what we're dealing with."

"I agree. Who are these two gentlemen?"

"A couple guys who want to hike. I told them they have to leave."

"They want to hike, huh? How do we know they aren't part of the problem?"

"Hey! We're just here to hike."

"We need to make sure. Is that your vehicle?"

"Yes, sir."

Captain Spencer escorted them to one of the deputy sheriff's vehicle as another ambulance arrived.

"Joe, put these two guys in your backseat. They need to be transported to the station for questioning. They talk to no one until I have a chance to question them."

The deputy nodded.

As the two men, now handcuffed, were encouraged to sit in the police unit, Captain Spencer spoke to another officer.

"Don't let anyone talk to those two."

"Yes, sir."

Captain Spencer walked back up to Riley.

"We need to keep this out of the media for as long as possible," Riley told him. "We don't have everyone involved, except Hershel here," Riley pointed to Hershel who was sitting on his knees at Riley's feet, "and if it gets out that we have recovered the girls, we'll lose the upper hand in this investigation."

"I agree. We're working on a cover story, but we need to get those girls out of here and to a hospital."

"If you get one of your officers to collect Hershel and lock him up, I'll show you the way."

Captain Spencer got one of his officers to lock Hershel up in another patrol car and keep watch over him until they were ready to go.

Riley rounded up the rest of the EMT's, police, and FBI who arrived, and led everyone to the girls.

"My God," Captain Spencer muttered as they left the path and started up the hill. "How did you find them?"

"Hershel," Riley said. "Let's get them out of here and to the hospital. I'll fill you in once they're all safe."

Approaching the cave, Riley's voice drifted inside. The occupants of the cave looked to the opening when Riley announced, "This way."

He stepped into the cave with two EMT's following behind. Entering behind them was Captain Spencer and then three FBI agents. Chelsea, Savannah, Alexis and Mariah rose to their feet. Duskie raised her head. Morgan remained on the ground with Tina Webb in his arms.

Mariah gave Paisley's leash to Alexis and asked her to hold it. She bent down next to Duskie and asked her if she could stand. She shook her head, pushing herself to a sitting position. Through her wheezing, she said, "I don't think so."

Riley went over to Morgan and took Tina from his arms while Morgan got to his feet.

While holding Tina, Riley nodded his head to the FBI agents toward the back of the cave.

"There's a gap in the wall back there that leads to a bigger cave where the girls were being held."

Once Morgan was standing, he retrieved Tina from Riley and headed out of the cave. Riley came over and picked up

Duskie and followed Morgan. Captain Spencer and Mariah ushered the other three from the cave.

****

As the team exited the cave with the girls, additional FBI agents arrived with forensic equipment to examine the hiding place. They already had the path to the cave marked off with yellow crime scene tape.

Two more EMT's were waiting outside the mouth of the cave with stretchers ready for the two weaker girls. Morgan refused to put Tina down, telling the EMT who reached for her that he would carry her himself.

The EMT, with Morgan's help, draped a blanket around Tina, swaddling her like a baby and covering her head to keep the now bright sunlight out of her dark accustomed eyes.

Riley placed Duskie on a stretcher and one of the EMT's put a mask that was hooked up to a portable oxygen tank over her mouth and nose before he opened the valve and checked the level that was going to her. Another EMT asked her if she was allergic to anything and she shook her head no. He prepared an injection of Epinephrine and administered it.

"This will help you breath easier while we get you to the hospital," he told her, and patted her shoulder when he heard a muffled "Thanks."

She nodded her head and closed her eyes.

He ripped a plastic bag open and took out another clean blanket and draped it over her, tucking it in all around her. He placed the oxygen tank between her legs. The two EMT's strapped her to the stretcher before they picked it up and started out of the woods and away from the cave.

Morgan fell in behind them with a third EMT staying close to his side to monitor Tina.

A fourth EMT pulled out clean blankets for the other three girls. Each of the girls clutched the blanket like a lifeline, wrapping them around their shoulders.

Riley put his arm around Chelsea and walked with her behind Morgan. Captain Spencer had his arm around Savannah and Mariah was holding Alexis' hand as Alexis held Paisley's leash with her other hand. Paisley was walking beside Alexis only stopping three times to pee and once to poop.

When they got to one of the hard packed trails, the head FBI guy, Agent Machado, was waiting for them.

"Riley, good to see you again."

"You too Paul,"

"Excellent job finding the girls. We'll handle the mop up from here."

"Thanks."

The entourage made it to the trail head and the waiting rescue chopper. The EMT's loaded Duskie into the chopper first, and Morgan climbed in with Tina in his arms.

Captain Spencer got a call on his cell phone, then went and talked to each ambulance driver.

The two EMT's in the rescue helicopter helped them all get strapped in. The pilot nodded once everyone and everything was secured, but before the door closed, Captain Spencer jumped in and one of the EMT's got out. The pilot started up the rotors and they took off toward Medford and the Rogue Valley Hospital.

There were three ambulances parked out on the road, one for each of the remaining girls. Riley and Chelsea walked with Savannah to the first ambulance. As an EMT started to help her into the back, she pulled away, turned and, with fear laden eyes aimed at Riley, said, "Not alone. Can't someone ride with me?" Tears pooled, as she reached for Chelsea's hand.

"Me too," Chelsea replied, looking at Savannah and then Riley. "I don't want to be alone with strangers any more."

The EMT with Savannah looked at Riley who shrugged.

"This is your call. What do you think? They've been through a lot and if they feel safer together, can they ride in one ambulance?"

"We can only take two per ambulance."

"That's okay," Mariah said, having walked up to the group with Alexis. "I'll ride with Alexis."

Chelsea smiled and hugged Savannah before they both climbed into the back of the ambulance. Two EMT's climbed in behind them.

"Don't let them out of the ambulance until we know there are no witnesses, including press," Riley said and slammed the doors closed, banging on it with the flat of his hand, twice.

The engine roared to life and the vehicle eased out onto the road toward Jacksonville.

Riley took Paisley from Alexis before she and Mariah climbed into the next ambulance.

"I'll take Paisley to a vet and have her checked over before I meet you at the hospital."

Mariah nodded her understanding as he stepped back and let the two remaining EMT's climb in and close the doors. Their ambulance started up and they followed after the first one.

Riley took Paisley to his car and followed the empty ambulance. As he passed one of the State police cruisers, he could see Hershel sitting in the back seat, head down, waiting to be transported to the station.

On the ride to the hospital, the EMT's monitored the vitals of each girl and asked questions about how they felt, and if they suffered any injuries. Tina continued to be unresponsive, Duskie reported she was not injured and was breathing easier with the oxygen and injection they gave her. Chelsea and Savannah, in the first ambulance, reported that they were not injured, and Alexis, in the second ambulance showed a vibrant bruise on her arm where she had been grabbed.

While Tina and Duskie were being administered to by the EMT's Captain Spencer filled Morgan in on the plan.

"I've instructed the pilot and the two ambulance drivers to go straight to the airport. The FBI has a jet fueled and ready to take the girls to a hospital in Portland."

"The press is going to be all over that when no one shows up at the hospital."

"Nope. The FBI already have people who will board the emergency vehicles as victims of a traffic accident for transport to the hospital. That's going to be the story. It will explain why the road before and after the trail head is blocked off."

"That's great, Captain. We need to get more information out of Hershel so we can round up the whole organization."

"I agree."

"Just so you know, I'm going to Portland with the girls. I'm not letting go of Tina until here family is with her. She's been traumatized enough and I want her to know she's safe."

"Fine with me, but for the record … " Captain Spencer leaned in close to Morgan and whispered, "… you stink to high heaven."

Morgan grinned. "I know, but it can't be helped. Poor kid. I hope they're able to bath her as soon as we get her to the hospital."

"This is a good place, Morgan … with good doctors. They'll all be taken care of."

The helicopter landed at the Medford airport, near the maintenance hangers where Tina and Duskie were transferred to a private jet with doctors waiting on board.

As soon as they were on the ground, Morgan dug his cell phone out of his pocket and made a call.

"Molly, hi babe … good. How's everything? … Good. I'm calling to let you know I'll be in Portland in an hour. I need you to bring me a clean change of clothes … Yes, everything … No. I don't need clean shoes." Morgan laughed. "… Yeah. Everything's fine … No … No, babe. I haven't been hurt, I'm just very, uh, smelly … I'll explain everything when I see you. If you can get my clothes together, I'll call you and let you know where to bring them … No. I don't even know that yet. I'll call you. I gotta go. I love you … Okay. Love you too. Bye."

Once the girls were off-loaded from the helicopter, two dummy victims ran on, taking their place, and the chopper took off for the hospital. Each ambulance, in turn, stopped at the airport, off-loaded their real victims and took on fake ones made up with blood, burns, and gore.

Captain Spencer met each ambulance to explain to the girls what was going on and why they were flying them to Portland.

"But my parents," Savannah wailed.

"We have another jet ready to transport each of your parents. You'll see them soon. I promise."

Mariah helped Captain Spencer usher the girls to the jet and joined Morgan on the plain.

Once all the passengers were loaded, Captain Spencer boarded the last ambulance and left the airport for the local hospital. The jet with the girls taxied from it's private loading area and prepared to take off. The second jet standing by for the girls' families, taxied to the private loading area as soon as the girls were in the air.

In the meantime, at the hospital, the FBI and local police were holding everyone back since the press had gotten wind there was a situation and were pressing for information.

At the same time the jet lifted off from the airport, the Chief of Police called a press conference. He announced the closure of highway 238 at Reservoir Road due to a head on collision at ten-seventeen in the morning at Jacksonville's Forest Park. Because of the accident, he announced, the highway will be shut down for several hours. He also stated there were currently no casualties, and names of the victim's, who are being transported to the Medford hospital, would be announced after families were notified.

As the fake victims arrived at the Medford hospital, the medical staff rushed them from the emergency vehicles into private examining rooms off the emergency room floor.

The girls were met by ambulances at the Portland airport, and transported to the small, private hospital in Portland the FBI arranged for. Tina and Duskie were wheeled into the emergency department on gurneys and put in a private room down the hall with two screened off cubicles, and guarded by an FBI agent who had been standing by. The other three girls, walking in under their own power, were ushered into a separate room with three screened in cubicles—an FBI agent standing guard outside.

Morgan got the name and address of the hospital and called his wife.

Once Chelsea, Savannah, and Alexis were settled, they asked Mariah to push the screens back so they could see each other from their beds, and talk to each other. That done, they expressed their frustration at being locked up and whined how they wanted to see their families.

"Do my mom and dad know that I'm alright?" Savannah asked.

"Yeah, have my parents been told that we were found? My mom's probably been freaking out," Cheslea exclaimed.

"Yes. I'm sure all of your families have been notified by now, and I know they are just as anxious to see you. In my investigations, I talked to all of your parents, and they were terribly worried," Mariah responded.

"When will we get to see them?" Alexis asked.

"Soon, I'm sure. I'll check and let y'all know something definite as soon as I can."

Mariah left the girls and walked up the hall to check on Duskie and Tina.

"How's Tina?" she asked Morgan as she approached him standing guard outside the girl's examination room with the FBI agent.

"About the same. They're bathing her now. Duskie is holding her hand in my place. I told her not to let go for any reason. I think she needs physical contact with a friend, someone she trusts."

"That's why you carried her all the way to the air ambulance?"

"Yeah. She may not have been able to talk, but she clung to me, Mariah."

"I saw that. I hope she'll be okay."

"Me too."

The nurse came out of the room wheeling an industrial laundry cart with smelly, dirty laundry.

"You can go in now."

"How is she?"

"Poor thing. Her skin is raw, and in some places infected from the filth. She's going to be okay, though. The doctor will be in soon to examine her and start a treatment plan."

"Thanks. Her mother should be here soon. I hope that will help her."

"Me too." The nurse turned and wheeled the stinking linen cart down the hall to be disposed of.

"Do you think I can come in and see her and Duskie?"

"I don't see what it would hurt. Come on."

Morgan and Mariah stepped into the room and saw Duskie resting on a gurney pushed up next to Tina's, the two girls holding hands. Duskie was singing a soft lullaby to Tina.

Back in Medford, Riley arrived at the Medford hospital where he was met by Captain Spencer.

"Hi Riley."

"Hey. How are things going?"

"Good, so far. Let's step into this examining room, and I'll fill you in."

FRIDAY P.M.

"So, you're saying Hershel won't talk to anyone except Mariah?"

"That's right."

"And, Mariah is in Portland with the girls."

"Yep. The FBI have a jet there, the one that transported the girls. It's re-fueling and they'll bring her back. Will you talk to her? I don't think I want her ripping me a new one right now."

Riley stood with his hands on his hips, leaned his head back and bellowed a laugh.

"Hey, it's not that funny." Captain Spencer was pink with embarrassment.

"Yeah. It is, but I know the feeling. I'll call her."

"Tell her an agent will drive her to the airport."

"Sure. No problem."

Riley pulled his cell phone out of his shirt pocket and dialed.

"Riley! What's going on there? We're stuck …"

"Yeah. I know. I'm calling …"

"… in Portland and the girls are anxious to …"

"We have to keep …"

"see their parents. When will …"

"Mariah!" Riley roared. "Listen to me."

Captain Spencer grimaced at what he thought Mariah was saying.

Mariah sighed. "I'm sorry! So, what's going on?"

"We have to keep their rescue dark so we can try to catch the rest of the people involved, including the sex traffickers."

"Okay, I know that. But, couldn't they do that without shipping everyone across the state?"

"This is the best plan they came up with at the last minute. The FBI didn't expect the girls to be found alive."

"Well, they were and they're anxious to see their families. What's the plan for that?"

"The FBI had fake victims board the ambulances and the Chief of Police announced a major traffic accident out there to get the media off the scent. So far, it's working."

"That's great, but what about the families? These girls need to see their parents."

"The jet with the families, just took off. They'll be there within the hour."

Mariah sighed in relief. "I feel much better knowing that. Once the parents get here and get settled with the girls, I can run to the house, shower and get clean clothes—Morgan too. He stinks to high heaven. Molly's on her way here with clean clothes for him."

"Mariah, we need you back here ASAP."

"Oh my God. Paisley?"

"No. She's fine. Hershel won't talk to anyone but you. We need you to come talk to him so we can set up a trap for the traffickers and this Gigi gal."

"Crap!"

"I'm sorry, babe."

"I know. I'll call the airport and catch the first flight down."

"No need. An agent will take you to the airport and you'll catch the private jet that flew you up there. It's refueling and getting ready now."

"Well, that's nice of the Feds."

"Everyone wants to get this wrapped up."

"Me too. What about Morgan?"

"He can come back with you if he wants, or he can stay there and take care of the office. We'll have to figure out how to get his vehicle back."

"Come on, Riley. Morgan won't want to sit this part out. I'll …"

Riley laughed. "You're right."

"I'll go find him and let him know. Where do I find this agent?"

Riley turned and called to Captain Spencer. "Hey Captain? Who's the agent who's driving Mariah to the airport?"

"Agent Gletch. He's waiting at the end of the hall for her to finish the call. He's got eyes on her."

"Did you hear that?"

"Yep. I see him. I'll go get Morgan. See you soon."

"Good. See you when you get here."

Mariah disconnected the call and walked to Agent Gletch. "Give me a sec—I've got to find Morgan. He'll want to come back with us."

"I'll follow you if you don't mind. We expected Morgan would be coming back with you."

They walked together to the room where the three girls were being treated and Mariah asked Agent Gletch to wait outside. She announced to the three that their families were on their way and should arrive in about an hour. She explained to them that she had to go back to help catch the rest of the people involved in their kidnapping and told them goodbye, hugging each girl.

"I'll see you soon. I wish I could be here to see your reunion with your parents. They're going to be so happy and relieved."

She left that area and went to the private examination room where Tina and Duskie were and explained the same thing to them. Duskie smiled and said thank you. Tina, flat on her back on the gurney, a pillow under her knees, was unresponsive. Morgan, who had been by her side since they found the girls, was standing beside the gurney, holding Tina's hand. He leaned down and spoke softly near Tina's ear.

"Tina, you're safe now. You're at the hospital and your parents will be here soon. I wouldn't leave but I have to go get the bad people who did this to you."

Tina blinked her eyes and turned her face toward Morgan.

"Do you understand?"

Mariah could see her squeeze Morgan's hand.

"I'll check back in on you as soon as I can. Okay? Squeeze my hand again to tell me you understand."

She squeezed his hand again.

"Will you stay with her and keep in physical contact with her, Duskie? Don't let go of her hand until her parents are here. Not even to hug your parents if they come in first. Can you do that? She needs that contact to stay grounded."

Duskie nodded. "I'll take good care of her, Morgan. You can count on me," Duskie wheezed.

"I know I can."

Duskie took Tina's hand. "I'm here with you Tina. I'm not going to leave you." Tina turned her head toward Duskie's voice, closed her eyes and squeezed her hand. Morgan let go of the hand he was holding.

"We'll be back as soon as we can."

Morgan followed Mariah out of the room.

Agent Gletch met them as they stepped into the hall. "We need to be going."

"Let's go then," Morgan said, walking toward the exit and pulling his cell phone from his pocket.

"Morgan!" Molly called from down the hall.

Morgan stopped and turned to watch his two kids and Molly run down the hall toward him.

Agent Gletch and Mariah stopped and watched as Morgan jogged to meet them, sweeping his family into his arms. He gave Molly a passionate kiss, kissed Mia on the top of her head and ruffled Max's hair.

"Ewe!" Max exclaimed, wrinkling his nose. "You smell like shit."

"Max! Watch your mouth," Molly chastised.

"Well, he does!"

"I'm sorry, guys. Long story and I don't have time to explain. I gotta catch the jet back to Medford."

"Already?" Mia asked.

"Yep. Things are happening fast. Got my change of clothes, Mol?"

"Right here." Molly handed him an overnight bag.

"Everything alright with everyone?"

"We're fine." Molly hugged him. "We just miss you."

"Miss you too. I'll call you as soon as I can and fill you in. In the mean time …" he placed his left hand on Mia's shoulder, his right on Max's, "… do NOT say a word about this to anyone. Top secret stuff going on. Even the hospital staff here has been sworn to secrecy. Catching the bad guys depend on it. Do you understand?"

"Sure Dad," Max answered as Mia nodded her head. "Not sure what *this* is anyway."

"If anyone asks, I'm still in Medford looking for the missing girls." Morgan kissed Molly one last time, waived goodbye and jogged back to Mariah and Agent Gletch.

"How ya doin?" Morgan asked Mariah.

"Good. How about you?"

"Feeling accomplished. Riley gonna meet us at the police department?

"I guess. I want to find out more about what Hershel was alluding to. He obviously wasn't the master mind of this production. And who's this Gigi woman … and why was she targeting Tina … oh, and I wonder if she had something to do with the shootings."

Morgan smiled. "We'll get our answers."

"Yeah. Will you do me a favor?"

"Sure. What's that?"

"Will you step into the bathroom on the jet and wash up? You're making me nauseous."

Morgan grinned. "I can't wait."

Riley and Captain Spencer were waiting for Mariah and Morgan as the jet touched down and taxied to the gate.

Mariah waived to the two waiting men as she walked toward them.

"How's Paisley?"

"Well, hello to you too." Riley grinned and Mariah gave him her, 'don't-mess-with-me' look.

"She's fine. The vet checked her over and reported she wasn't hurt. The wound was superficial and didn't need stitches. I think the bullet only grazed her as it tore through the jacket. The force of the bullet ripping through the jacket and pulling her off balance is why she rolled. Pretty smart of her to play dead. That's what I think."

"I taught her that," Morgan interjected with a proud smile.

"We know, Morgan." He clapped Morgan on the shoulder. "Great trick. It served her well this time."

Mariah nudged Morgan. "Of course, her being the smartest dog in the world made a huge difference, too."

"Of course!"

They all climbed into the car and buckled up. Riley glanced back at Mariah and continued. "I gave her a quick bath when we got to the room and removed a couple ticks that were crawling in her fur. None were attached. I put down fresh food and water and left her curled up on the couch under that little throw you keep for her. I think she's exhausted and happy to be in a safe place."

"She's due a new flea and tick treatment. I'll take care of that later. You didn't crate her? I hope she doesn't get into anything."

"Awe, she'll be fine."

Captain Spencer pulled out on Biddle toward downtown Medford.

At the police department, the partners were told to wait in the lobby. They took a seat and watched the comings and goings of the police, clerks, and FBI behind the bullet proof glass enclosed counter in front of them. Fifteen minutes later, Detective Cleveland opened a door to the side of the waiting room and called them in. They traversed a long corridor and turned left into a moderately sized interrogation room. Captain Spencer and Special Agent Paul Machado were seated at the table. Captain Spencer swept his hand out.

"Please have a seat."

"How's Hershel holding up?" Mariah asked.

"Before we go into that, let's get your story. What were you doing out there?"

"Alexis and I went for a run out there with my dog, Paisley the other day. The fog rolled in and we heard a dragging sound and some guy muttering some stuff. We couldn't make out much of what he said, but ... Have you ever had a gut feeling about something?"

Captain Spencer nodded his head.

"I don't believe in them." Machado snapped.

Mariah raised her eyebrows and leaned toward Machado. "Well, I do and my gut has saved my life on numerous occasions. My *gut* told me there was something going on out there that warranted further investigation so Morgan, Riley and myself went back out there yesterday with Paisley. I didn't know it at the time, but Paisley got a whiff of Alexis. Her harness was worn and she broke free when she ran to chase the scent."

Morgan jumped in to tell how they went back that morning to look for Paisley. He said he spotted Paisley running with something flapping over her back and dragging on the ground. He explained about Hershel chasing Paisley with a gun in his hand, pointing it and shooting at her.

"He shot your dog?"

"Yes!"

Morgan described how he started cutting across to try to intercept the man and that before he could get to him, Hershel fired at the dog and, it appeared, struck her when she yelped and went down. Before Hershel could hurt her any more, or Mariah, Morgan said he tackled the man and then cuffed him.

Riley stood and picked up the story.

"I already reached the back of the forest trail and was cutting through to meet up with Mariah and Morgan. I heard the shot, Mariah screamed, and I began to run in their direction. As I made the clearing, Morgan had just cuffed Hershel and Mariah was saying Hershel knew where the girls were."

Riley continued with details of the information they got from Hershel and how he led them to the abandoned gold mine and the girls.

Morgan stood from his chair and crossed his arms. "So, did he tell you who this Gigi Daily is or where to find her?"

"He told us that you and Riley tried to kill him and he's claiming police brutality."

"I guess it's a good thing we're not cops," Riley retorted.

Captain Spencer shook his head. "He refuses to talk to us. He said he'll only talk to you, Mariah. He said you kept Morgan and Riley from killing him and he'll only talk to you … alone."

Mariah nodded. "Okay. I'll get what I can from him."

"What is it with you, Mariah Jeffries?" Special Agent Machado asked as she stood from her chair.

"What do you mean?" Morgan squared on him defensively, his chest expanding. Riley straightened in his chair, waiting for a response, ready to jump to her defense.

He looked from Morgan to Riley, and then to Mariah. "You are the luckiest person I have ever heard about. You should have been dead several times over from what I read about you, yet you not only live, you thrive. People respond to you and not only do they give up their secrets to you, but they're eager and willing to do it. You have cleared some remarkable cases, both when you were a cop and since you left the department. I'm amazed."

"I'll tell you, Agent Machado. I don't feel all that lucky. And people don't just offer up their secrets to me. I research, investigate, and interview. I'm good at reading people and I tend to be quite intuitive. That certainly helps, but it's not easy by any means."

"Yeah. I know. I just think you're amazing, and you have some very accomplished partners too."

"Thanks. I think they're pretty amazing as well."

"Well," Captain Spencer stood. "If we're through with this warm and fuzzy chit chat, we have some information to extract. You ready, Mariah?"

"I sure am."

"You guys want to watch the interview with us?" Agent Machado asked Morgan and Riley.

"Yes." Riley pushed his chair back to follow Captain Spencer and Mariah to the door, and out to the hall.

"I'm in too." Morgan followed Riley.

****

Captain Spencer led everyone out of the room and showed Agent Machado, Morgan, and Riley into an observation room where they could watch and listen to the interview from behind a one-way mirror. Once they were in the room, Captain Spencer and Mariah went into the next room down the hall.

"Hi, Hershel," Mariah said as respectfully as she would a friend. "I understand you wanted to talk to me?"

"I'll leave you two alone." Captain Spencer backed out of the room and closed the door behind him.

Hershel was sitting at the small steel table, his left hand cuffed to a heavy loop that was welded on top, his right hand in his lap. His head hung low, his shoulders shook in silent sobs. At the sound of her voice, he reached up with his right hand, wiped his eyes, and dragged his sleeve across his nose, sniffing loudly.

Mariah took a quick survey of the room and noticed it was bare of everything except the table, the chair he was sitting in, and an interrogators chair. There was no hint of audio/video equipment, even though she knew it was there.

"Would you like me to get you some tissue and something to drink?"

"No. I know I don't deserve nothin'. I'm so sorry." A new set of sobs emitted from him.

Mariah went to the door and poked her head out into the empty hall and called out, "would you bring us some tissues, please. And a cup of water, too." She knew Captain Spencer, in the observation room, would hear the request and have someone deliver them. She turned back to the room and closed the door. With measured steps, she walked to the table and took the seat across from Hershel.

"I need you to get a hold of yourself, Hershel. Captain Spencer said you wanted to talk to me. Can you help us find the people responsible for taking those girls?"

Hershel nodded, sniffing. Captain Spencer came in with the requested items and handed them to Mariah.

"Thank you."

Captain Spencer left and Mariah pulled two tissues out of the box and gave them to Hershel who took them and wiped his eyes before he held the wad over his nose and blew with a loud honking noise.

"Are you ready to talk?"

He nodded his head, and Mariah waited letting the silence grow uncomfortable between them.

"I'm so sorry I helped." Hershel shook his head. "I know now it was a stupid thing for me to do. My wife had just had a crisis and I needed money for her blood transfusion. I was desperate and didn't even think about what I was doing.

"After we had little Tina, I wanted to go to the police, but she threatened me when I picked up Tina. She said she'd killed me and get someone else—someone who would hurt her. I decided to take as good a care of her, and the others, as I could for as long as I could."

Hershel didn't raise his head and look at Mariah until he finished his statement. When he did, his eyes held immense sorrow and anguish. "I didn't know what to do by then."

"I understand. Sometimes people make very bad choices out of desperation. But what we need to know *now*, is how to catch these people before they hurt someone else. What can you tell me about this Gigi Daily woman? How did you come to know her?"

Hershel sat with his eyes closed, nodding his head and trying to gather his thoughts.

"We were childhood friends, but she went by a different name back then."

"What was her name?"

Hershel opened his eyes and glanced at Mariah before he dropped his gaze to the table. "Bertha. Bertha Skedro. She was beautiful and funny and nice ... until the ninth grade, when I asked her for a date. She laughed at me and told me she could do a lot better than me. She never talked to me again after that day."

"Then what?"

"In High School, she got pregnant and the guy married her. She lost the baby after a couple of months and left town. That's the last I heard of her until she moved back as Gigi."

"When was that?"

"A year ago, I think. She used to live here, in Medford. She worked at the school—a secretary I think."

"Which school?"

"JFK. I saw her again for the first time in years at the dog park. She had a little mixed breed mutt that she would bring and let loose, and then ignore. That should have been my first clue she's not a nice person. I would take my dobie, Prince, and she would stop and talk to me.

"You don't see very many Dobermans around here anymore." He raised his eyes to Mariah. "People think they're bad dogs, but they're not. There are no bad dogs, just bad owners."

"Where did she live?"

"I don't know." Hershel shook his head. "But I didn't see her anymore for a long time, and then one day she showed up at the dog park again. I didn't see her dog and I asked her where her little dog was and she said she didn't have *it* anymore. Not him, not her, but *it*. So many clues that I ignored." Hershel shook his head.

"She said she came to talk to me and offer me some extra cash under the table for a little job. That was when I was strapped for cash and I told her, 'Sure. Anything.'—like some kind of love sick idiot." He sighed and dropped his head to stare at the table. "I still thought she was that same beautiful, funny, kind girl from grade school. How stupid.

"I just wanted her to like me again. Not romantic … I love my wife. But we were friends once, I thought … and then we weren't and I never understood why. She was always so beautiful—like an angel. And until she broke my heart in the ninth grade, as sweet as an angel, too." He shook his head. "I didn't know what I was getting into. I couldn't believe what she wanted was going to be so horrible.

"She went on to say, if she told me what the job was, I couldn't tell anyone about it or some bad people she knew would come and hurt me real bad.

"I should have walked away then, but the money … I asked her how much and she told me, five thousand."

He snorted and shook his head with a sad smile.

"I was so stupid to even listen to her, but I went ahead with it for the damned money—and the treatment didn't even help my wife. She's dying."

He started crying again. "And I'm going to jail for the rest of my life."

Mariah gave him another tissue and he wiped his eyes and blew his nose. Mariah waited.

"Gigi asked me if I knew of a secret place where she could hide some stuff. I asked how much stuff and she said it would need a ten by twelve enclosed space, at least. Bigger if possible."

"And?"

"I told her I did. She told me she would be in touch when she had the merchandise. So, when she had Tina, she called me and told me to meet her at this abandoned farm by the Table Rocks. When I got there, she had Tina—tied up and gagged. I looked at that little girl and suddenly I realized that I had sold my soul to the devil. I was so sad for her. We carried her to my pick-up and put her in the bed, tying down a tarp over her. I had to wait for night and then I untied her feet and made her walk down to the cave with me. It was only a couple hours after I picked her up from Gigi so she wasn't in the bed of my pick-up for long."

"She didn't yell or try to run away?"

"She was terrified, that's for sure. I could see it in her eyes. I told her I wasn't going to hurt her, but she needed to cooperate or the other people might. I said I would protect her the best I could. She struggled a couple of times on the walk to the mine and when we got to the opening, she pulled back, but I told her it was okay and I had food and water for her. She hadn't had anything to eat or drink, so I knew she must be hungry."

"You already had food and water there?"

"No. When Gigi told me to meet her, she said to bring some portable food and water along. I didn't know what it was for but I had it in a backpack I carried."

"So you took this poor, terrified, young girl into this dark cave, tied her up, and left her there alone?"

Hershel hung his head again and nodded, sniffling. They sat in silence. A minute later he whined, "I know I'm despicable. I don't even know how I sank so low. I would never hurt a child. My wife and I wanted children so bad, but then she got sick and she's been battling Leukemia ever since. I couldn't hate myself more."

"What were her plans for these girls? Why was she taking them and then keeping them in the mine for so long?"

"She was going to sell them."

Mariah stood so suddenly her chair fell backward. She planted her palms on the table, leaned toward Hershel and yelled, "Like slaves? To who?"

Hershel shrank back. "She found this person who said they had buyers in foreign countries who wanted young wives."

"Are you dense? They're sex traffickers! You idiot!" He coward in his chair as Mariah continued her rant.

"*Sex traffickers*, Hershel. You say you always wanted children, but you were willing to not only sit back and allow her to sell these young, terrified girls to sex traffickers, but to aid and abet? You don't deserve to be a parent."

Mariah pounded her fists on the table.

"I know that now," he whined. "But at first she told me that the girl was her daughter, kidnapped at birth. I thought I was helping her get her baby back."

"Hershel. All you were thinking about was that damned money. You didn't want to know the truth. That's why you bought that cock and bull story she fed you. It was easier on your conscience. Didn't you wonder why she would gag and tie her *baby* up, hide her away in an abandoned mine while she waited for *flesh traffickers* to come and take her? DO YOU THINK I'M STUPID?"

"She did. That's what she told me when she handed Tina off to me. The rest of it came out when she took the second girl."

"So what was her explanation for you getting an old abandoned mine set up to hold a captive before she took Tina? I don't get this. None of it makes any sense."

"I know. When I met her for the first package—the only one I expected—she told me the girl was her kidnapped daughter but the girl didn't know and would try to run. She needed time to help the girl understand the truth. I didn't get anything ready before she took Tina. I just told her I knew of a place where she could hide some stuff. She didn't even know where I was taking the girls. She didn't want to know.

Looking back, I should have asked why she didn't want to know where I was taking her long lost daughter, I guess. ..."

"Looking back, my ass. I don't think you cared about any of those girls or what happened to them. You just saw an opportunity for some money. Isn't that right?"

Mariah pounded the table and Hershel jumped.

"And that's all that girl's life was worth to you—*five thousand dollars*? What was she getting paid for the girl?"

"I-I ... I don't know. Probably twice that. I didn't know what she was really going to do until I met her at the old farmhouse. I would never agree to what she was doing if I had known it in the beginning."

"Fine, so you had Tina trussed up and tucked away in a cold, smoky, abandoned mine and left her all alone. Then what?"

"Then she called me ... Gigi did ... and said she had another package for me to pick up—and then after that, another ... then another. That's when I told her I was done. I wasn't going to pick up any more packages from her or take care of the girls if she didn't stop taking them. She-she ... she told me that she would hurt my wife if I didn't cooperate and I knew she meant it. Then she called me to come pick up the last girl from her and then you ... I found your little dog running away from the mine and I had to stop the little dog. That's when you caught me."

"You almost killed my dog! I could kill you for that alone ..." Mariah turned and picked up the chair, slamming it down on all four legs. "Where does this Gigi live now?"

"I don't know. I don't think she lives around here, but she comes to town to meet me or take the girls. They must know her and trust her from the school. How else could she take them without anyone knowing?"

"Did she say when she was going to come collect the girls? That's a bunch of girls to manage all at once."

"The traffickers are coming for them tonight. They'll be in a box van or something. They're supposed to meet me in the parking lot of the park at eleven-thirty tonight and I'm supposed to lead them to the girls."

"How many are going to be there? It's going to take some time to move just one or two girls at a time."

"I'm not sure, but I think there will be two or three men … and-and me. We'll untie their feet and make them walk to the van, their hands still tied up and the gags still in place, even though there is nowhere for them to go and no one to hear them screaming or yelling."

"This is sick on so many levels. I've got to go wretch. I'll be back."

Mariah turned and marched to the door, slamming it behind her. Captain Spencer and Special Agent Machado stepped out of the observation room.

Mariah turned to the two men. "We can use him to lure the men to the old mine and take them there. Maybe they can lead us to Gigi."

"Sounds like a good idea." Machado crossed his arms. "Talk to him Mariah, and let him know that he can get a lesser sentence for cooperating and warn him that he better not try to warn the men or run. He'll be shot on sight."

"That's a bit extreme, isn't it?"

"Just tell him. He's scared enough—with that threat I don't think he'd even consider double crossing us. He's obviously a coward."

"I think he sincerely regrets his involvement and not just because he got caught. He didn't know how to extract himself from the situation without implicating himself or endangering his wife. Yes, he's a coward because he could have stepped up, but people like Gigi know how to twist and manipulate a weaker person to make them do what is demanded."

Mariah went back into the interrogation room and sat. She relayed the message to Hershel, stressing to him the dire results if he tried to double cross them or run. He immediately started bobbing his head.

"Yes. Yes. Please let me help make this right. I'll do anything you say, but could you guys protect my wife? Please don't let her hurt my wife."

"The police will do everything they can to keep your wife safe. I'm going to ask Captain Spencer and Special Agent Machado along with Morgan and Riley, my partners, to come in here so we can devise a plan. I'll be right back."

She stepped from the room into the hall, leaving the door to the interrogation room open. Special Agent Machado met her in the hall just outside the door. Captain Spencer walked up behind him, Morgan and Riley following.

"Whoa. This is an FBI case and you and your team are not going to participate, Jeffries. We'll take it from here. Thanks for your help."

"NO!" Mariah yelled. "You wouldn't even have the girls back, much less know anything about the people involved without our help. I think we should be allowed to follow this through to the end. No disrespect to you, but we've earned this and we're vested in this investigation too." Mariah stopped yelling and took in a deep breath. Heads popped out of doorways along the hall to check on the commotion.

"Not a chance!" Machado turned to the Captain. "Captain Spencer, escort these people out of here."

Machado pushed past Mariah and walked into the interrogation room, slamming the door closed.

Captain Spencer watched Mariah and shrugged, shaking his head. He called down the hall, "Cleveland."

Detective Cleveland stepped out into the hall.

"Sir?"

"Please escort these investigators out." He nodded his head toward Mariah, Riley, and Morgan.

"I'm sorry Mariah. It's out of my hands, as you can see."

"Thanks. Will you keep us posted on the developments? I'd really like to know who this Gigi is and why she targeted these girls."

"I'll do what I can, but this is the FBI's case. My hands are tied."

"I understand. I know the shooting of Gayle and Robert is somehow related. Find out what you can. Please?"

Captain Spencer nodded his head.

"I will."

"Thanks Captain."

Captain Spencer nodded, turned, and walked into the interrogation room, closing the door behind him.

As the team followed Detective Cleveland to the end of the hall, and before exiting to the lobby, Riley asked to use the bathroom. "All that coffee has gone right through me."

"Sure."

The group turned down another hall and Detective Cleveland pointed to a door marked MEN. Riley went in and Morgan asked him, "Is that a one hole-er or a two hole-er?"

"There's three stalls," Riley reported before the door closed. Morgan pushed into the room behind Riley.

"Miss Jeffries?" Detective Cleveland nodded at the women's door next.

"No thanks. I'm fine and please, call me Jeffries. Everyone else does."

After a few minutes, Morgan and Riley emerged and the entourage turned back toward the central hall to the lobby door. As Detective Cleveland was pushing the door open to the lobby, Captain Spencer came running down the hall.

"Jeffries, wait."

They all stopped inside the door, Detective Cleveland allowing the door to swing closed.

"Yes?"

"Wait." He stopped in front of her and huffed to catch his breath. "Hershel refuses to help us unless you're there. Machado is furious, but Hershel is steadfast about it. He said we could lock him up for life, kill him, he didn't care. He's not budging. Without him, we're not likely to catch those guys or this Gigi person. Hershel wants you there, so you and your partners are in."

"Fantastic!" Mariah beamed. Morgan and Riley nodded their heads and made noises of agreement. Captain Spencer smiled.

"Hershel heard the exchange in the hall between you and Machado and he didn't appreciate that you guys were being shut out—well you, Jeffries—after all you've done for the girls. He likes you." Captain Spencer shook his head. "People really respond to you, Jeffries, like nothing I've ever seen before."

She smiled and shrugged her shoulders. "Not sure about that Captain, but if we're allowed to take part in bringing these bad boys down, I'll take it."

"Come on back then. Thanks Cleveland."

They went back to the interrogation room where Special Agent Machado sat glaring at Hershel. Hershel stared at the floor, avoiding the evil eye. Captain Spencer ushered the team into the room and closed the door.

"Okay, she's here. Are you happy now?" Machado snapped before he banged his flat hand on the table. Hershel lifted his gaze and smiled broadly at Mariah. "Yes."

"Alright. So we'll have a car for you a couple miles from the trail head and …"

"No, wait." Hershel turned his gaze from Machado to Captain Spencer to Mariah. "They'll be watching for my truck. It has to be my truck."

"They'll know your truck? How the hell are they going to know your truck? You haven't even met with them yet, have you?"

"Nooooo," he said, the tail end of the word rising an octave. "But, Gigi has and she's supposed to relay to them what my truck looks like and the license plate."

"Where's your vehicle?"

"It's at the trail head. I was arrested at the mine, so it should still be there in the parking lot unless you guys hauled it off."

Captain Spencer opened the door and called down the hall.

"Cleveland!"

Everyone in the room could hear a muffled, 'yes sir'.

"Find out if ..." Captain Spencer turned back into the room, "make and model?"

"Oh, a ninety-eight Chevy S10 extended cab pick-up, faded red. It has some buckets and ropes and a big tarp in the bed."

Captain Spencer turned back to the hall. "A ninety-eight Chevy S10, extended cab, faded red in color—see if it was impounded from the parking lot of the Old Forest Trail Head."

"It was, sir. I took care of it myself," they heard from Detective Cleveland in the hall. Captain Spencer turned back to the room and closed the door.

"Fine, so we'll move YOUR truck out there and take you to it." Machado sighed and shook his head in disgust. "You'll be allowed to drive to the parking lot from the drop off location and wait for the traffickers. That's the plan, right?"

"Yes, but if they get a whiff of any cops or feds around, they'll just keep going, so none of your guys can be in sight."

"They won't be. So when the traffickers arrive, you'll escort them to the mine, right?"

"That's the plan as it was given to me, but these people don't keep with the plans, if you know what I mean."

"Sure. And you're not sure how many men will be meeting you?"

"No, Gigi said two or three of them, but there's no telling."

"We'll play that by ear. Our agents will be in the woods along the trails. It'll be dark enough, you and the traffickers won't see them. What trail are you planning on taking?"

"I usually switch off between the lower trail and turning up toward the mine, and the middle trail and turning down toward the mine. Which one would be easiest for you?"

Machado stood, shoved the chair against the table, glanced up at the ceiling and tapped his chin with his right index finger.

"Let's not get too set on either one. They may not want you to take your usual route. For all we know they know of another route to the cave. We'll be ready either way. Do you know of any other routes?"

"Uh-uh."

"We'll leave about ten tonight and you'll be in place in time to rendezvous with the traffickers. Captain, Hershel can be escorted to a holding cell for now."

"Sure. Come on Hershel. Let's get you something to eat." Captain Spencer unlocked the shackle from the table and helped Hershel to a stand. He then cuffed Hershel's hands behind him and left the room with him. The group heard the Captain call Cleveland and instruct him to lock Hershel up and have the guards fix him a meal.

Special Agent Machado pulled out the interviewer's chair and sat down when Captain Spencer walked back in and closed the door. "I don't want Hershel to be in on the whole plan. Mariah, I want you to go with the officer who takes Hershel to his rendezvous point. We'll post men inside the cave and wait to take them as they come into the mine. It's a narrow 'hallway' from the entrance to the area where the girls were held and that's a good place to trap them. Less room for them to run."

"Where do you want us?" Riley indicated himself and Morgan.

"No disrespect to you, Riley, but I would prefer if you two weren't involved."

"Do you really want to risk Hershel finding out and blowing the whole thing?"

"No. But …"

Riley shrugged his shoulders, "It's your ass on the line, Machado. Remember the Castleberry case?"

"Oh hell." Machado glared at Riley. "Sure. I'll tell the team to let you two tag along but you're going to have to sign waivers in case you're hurt or killed. We don't know what to expect but I wouldn't be surprised if these guys are heavily armed and you'll be in a closed area, possibly under fire."

"Don't you think we've already thought of that? Provide us with vests. We'll be fine. We're both trained in how to handle situations like this."

"Fine! Meet us back here at ten."

"Great. We'll be here. And I want you to issue Jeffries a vest too, even if she's not going to the mine."

"What? Wait!" Mariah glanced from Riley to Machado. "What about me?"

"You'll be with the agent taking Hershel to his truck."

"I want to be at the take down."

"Hershel needs to know that you're part of the plan. You'll be with him and my agent when Hershel leaves in his truck to go to the trail head."

"And then what? Just sit back on the road and wait?"

"The agent will be notified when to meet the rest of us at the trailhead to mop up."

"No way. I'll go to the trail head with Hershel. I can hide in the back of his truck under the tarp and then follow behind them down the trail."

"Don't be ridiculous. You'll blow the whole operation."

Mariah glared at Machado, anger and frustration rising in her like a storm.

"Come on, Mariah. Let's get you out of here. We all need something to eat." Morgan, seeing her frustration, steered her toward the door before she blew up and got them all thrown off the operation.

She released her pent up breath. "Sure. Let's get the hell out of here." The three partners walked to the door, Captain Spencer following.

"See you at ten, Machado."

"Sure thing, Riley. See you then."

****

On the drive back to the suite, Mariah, Morgan and Riley discussed ways she could get away from the Fed and reach the mine once Hershel took his truck to the Trail Head. She had no intention of missing the take down.

"Well," Riley hedged, "you could try to appeal to Machado—talk him into it, but I'm telling you now, he is not likely to back down. He's a badge heavy prick and doesn't want anyone around that he can't threaten with their job to control them. Do you know where his truck will be when they drop Hershel off?"

"Yeah. About a mile and a half up the road past the parking lot—there's a drive, not easy to see by a passing vehicle because of the brush and trees to either side."

"That's great. We can go scope it out—figure out how much woods there is for you to run through in order to reach the take down. You'll have to lose the agent before you head to the cave if he chases you into the woods. That's the best suggestion I can come up with."

"Or maybe," Morgan added, "as Hershel is driving off, run and jump into the back of his pick-up."

"Yeah, but what if the traffickers search Hershel's truck to make sure he's not bringing along a cop?" Mariah shook her head. "Too risky. I realize that's what I suggested to Machado, but it's not the best idea."

"Yeah. I didn't like that idea when you first mentioned it." Riley shook his head as he turned the corner onto Center Drive.

"Well, what else, then?" Morgan sat forward from the back seat as they pulled into the parking lot of the suite.

Riley pulled into a parking space and cut the engine.

"I don't know, but I'm hungry." Mariah sighed. "Maybe I'll come up with something brilliant after I've eaten." She pushed the front passenger door of the sedan open and stepped out. As she pushed the door closed and Riley got out from behind the steering wheel, Mariah heard someone call her name. She searched across the parking lot and spied a woman waiving her hand.

"What the …" she muttered. "Norela? Morgan is that Jewel and Norela?"

Morgan followed her gaze across the parking lot and started waiving. "Hey, you two. What brings you all this way?"

Jewel Diamond and Norela Morales both called back, "Hey, y'all," while waiving and jogging over to them.

"What the heck! You're a sight for sore eyes." Mariah laughed as she hugged first Norela and then Jewel. "What are you doing here?"

"Didn't you get my email?" Norela asked hugging Morgan and then Riley, Jewel following suit.

"What email?"

"I sent you an email and then a text message to call me this morning. I wanted to tell you that we were coming with some interesting information on your folks, the Webbs. I wanted to deliver it in person and go over some possibilities with you, and Jewel wanted to tag along. You know how she can't stand to be left out of *anything*."

"That's right. I'm the boss." Jewel laughed. "Can we go inside? I need to use the bathroom."

"Sure. Follow me." Morgan slung his arm over Norela's shoulder and led the group to their suite. Riley, Mariah, and Jewel following behind, chatting.

Mariah fixed sandwiches and everyone grabbed drinks. They sat at the table and ate while Norela pulled out a half inch stack of papers and started flipping through them and pointing out significant information to the group.

"This was buried deep, but it's very interesting. I'm not sure, but the possibility that she's come back and is taking out her revenge is real."

"Who? What revenge?" Riley asked.

"Here. Here's a marriage license for Gayle Webb and Bertha Skedro. Have you heard of her?"

"Yeah, just this afternoon." Mariah took the documents from Norela. "She goes by Gigi Dailey now."

"I'm not surprised, but this might be what that guy that got shot wanted to tell you about—not sure, but could have been. I did some more digging and it turned out they were in high school when Gayle married her."

"Hmmm. That's starting to make some sense, now," Morgan cut in.

"She didn't have any family to speak of. Her father was a deadbeat and no one seemed to know who, or where he was—her mother was young when she gave birth to Bertha—sixteen. Here's her birth certificate." Norela handed the marriage license and birth certificate to Mariah, who examined them and passed them on to Riley as Norela continued.

"After Bertha was born, her mother got into drugs and the state took Bertha out of the home and put her in foster care. She was shuffled around quite a bit from the age of four until she was fifteen when she went to live with the Cobella family. When Bertha was twelve, her mother was found dead in her apartment from an overdose and the state couldn't find any other family. Anyway, when Bertha went to live with the Cobella's, she was registered in the same high school Gayle was attending and they started dating. She got pregnant. Here are more documents I found to support all this, newspaper stories, police reports, school registration … here's some pictures of Gayle and Bertha in the Teachers club, prom, ball games, wedding …" She passed each document to Mariah and they circulated around the table back to Norela.

"So, when she was sixteen—Gayle had just turned seventeen—she got pregnant and Gayle married her. She was five and a half months pregnant when they were in a bad car accident and she lost her baby. Apparently Gayle didn't want to stay married to her if he wasn't obligated so he filed for divorce, or more probably his parents did, making him sign off on everything. At any rate, here's a transcript of the divorce proceedings. She fought it. With no family, I can understand her not wanting to lose this connection, but I can understand him not wanting to be married at seventeen. Look here…"

Norela flipped through pages of the transcript. "She looses it in court and threatens Gayle. Read this part."

Mariah read the highlighted section of the transcript that Norela indicated.

Judge: Do you understand that your marriage will be dissolved?

Respondent: I don't want it to be dissolved. I love him. He can't just kick me out of his life because our baby is dead. That's not right.

Judge: Legally he can.

Respondent: (crying) But he owes me. He killed my baby and the doctors say I'll never be able to have any kids. He owes me.

Judge: The auto accident was determined to be an accident due to a blow-out. There was no negligence or malice involved. It was an accident and all your bills before the accident and afterward have been paid.

Respondent: (jumping up and pointing at Petitioner, yelled) If I can't have any kids, you can't either. I'll see to that Gayle. You'll pay for this.

Judge: (using gavel) Order in the court. Order. Sit down Ma'am.

Respondent: (yelling) I hate you Gayle. You won't get away with this. You'll pay!

Judge: Ma'am, you're in contempt of court. Deputy, please escort the Respondent out of the courtroom.

Deputy Smith escorts Respondent from the courtroom.

Judge: I hereby declare this divorce degree final.
Bayliff: All rise.

"Wow." Mariah passed the document to Riley. "So what happened to her after that?"

"She got a job at Clinton's Grocery store, working in the deli. She worked there for about a year and a half—until she graduated from high school. Here are some police reports of her stalking Gayle the first couple months after the divorce, but then nothing. The last thing I found was her working at the grocery store. After a year and seven months, she drops off the face of the earth. I think she took off, got some cosmetic surgery, changed her name and came back."

"Show me the pictures of her," Mariah said.

Norela shuffled through the documents that had gone around the table and pulled the picture of Bertha and Gayle out, handing them over. Morgan got up from his chair and looked over Mariah and Riley's shoulders.

"She doesn't look like anyone I've met here." Mariah glanced at Riley. "You guys?"

Riley pursed his lips and shook his head.

"Nope." Morgan stood straight and shook his head.

"Gigi?" Riley glanced at Mariah.

"Maybe."

"Who's Gigi?" Jewel looked from Riley to Mariah.

"Apparently she's the woman behind all this." Morgan, Mariah, and Riley filled Norela and Jewel in on what had transpired so far on the case.

"Where's your computer, Mariah," Norela asked. Mariah got up and went to her bedroom to collect the laptop and bring it back to the table. Jewel and Norela cleared a spot on the table and Mariah set the laptop down. She excused herself and went to the bathroom while Norela fired up the computer.

"How's she doing, Morgan?" Jewel asked.

"She's good. She's had some rough times, but I think she's made it through the worst of it now."

"So that's why you guys are here? To check on her?" Riley inquired.

"Well, yes—and because I wanted to present this information in person."

When Mariah came back to the dining area, Morgan and Riley were discussing Mariah's need to be at the mine when the traffickers showed up. Norela was researching Gigi Daily.

"Norela can probably find maps of the terrain so we can try to figure out a plan. If we leave early enough, we can meet Mariah when she runs into the forest from the drop off point. The three of us can go through the woods together and meet you two there."

"Oh! My! Gawd! Look at this," Norela exclaimed. Mariah walked around behind Norela and looked over her shoulder. Morgan and Riley moved in on either side of her and Jewel was looking over her other shoulder.

"I found Gigi Daily, from Chicago. She was the widow of a Gregory Randolph Daily a copywriter who apparently made millions. Look at this picture of their wedding from fourteen years ago. Looks an awful lot like Bertha to me."

"Sure does," Jewel said.

"Look at this picture of Gigi Daily at her husband's funeral. I was right. She's had extensive cosmetic surgery."

"Save some of those pictures of her to my computer, especially the later ones, and then use my email to email them to each of us. We should take them around to the girls to see if they recognize her." Excitement laced Mariah's voice as she realized they just made the final connection.

"Sure thing."

"Norela," Jewel nudged her shoulder, "can you pull up some maps, topographical and aerial, of the area where the girls were found?"

"Sure, give me just a minute to finish sending out these emails."

"I'm thinking Norela and I can pull up after Hershel takes off and pick you up. I'll rent a pick-up and we won't need to come to a full stop—you can grabbed the tailgate and jump into the bed. If we can find a place closer to the trailhead to pull of and then go the rest of the way by foot, then the cop probably won't be able to stop us."

"Mmm, I don't know about that. I would have to grab his car keys or he'll be on our tail. Besides, the FBI will probably block the road to through traffic."

"Maybe, but won't that tip off the traffickers?"

Mariah shook her head. "I don't know."

"Hey y'all, come look at this," Norela announce. They all gathered around and checked out the map.

"Here's the trailhead," Mariah pointed at the map. "Can you move out from the trailhead so I can view the distance from the drop off?"

Norela manipulated the view on the computer monitor until it moved out, but still there wasn't enough detail. "How's that?"

"No, I still can't tell."

Norela then searched for an aerial map and pulled that up. She tweaked the image a little bit and Mariah pointed to a turn in off the highway. "Here. I think this is where we'll be dropping Hershel off."

Jewel studied the screen.

"So it's about a mile along the highway from the trailhead. Show me where the mine is from the trail head."

Mariah couldn't make out the trails very well on the aerial view. "Could you go back to the topographical map?"

Norela pulled that map back up and displayed it side-by-side with the aerial one.

"Right about there," Riley reached over Norela's shoulder and pointed at the topographical map.

"Yeah, that looks about right," Mariah agreed. "The mine is about equidistant from the middle and the last trail, and west of the main path from the trail head."

"So, that would be about here?" Jewel pointed at the aerial map.

"Yeah. I think that's close. Here's the first trail, and you can barely see the third one down, so the middle one has to be along in this area."

"I think you're right." Morgan reached over and tapped the map. "Look here, the middle trail peaks through the threes right here.

"Yep," came from Riley. "That's gotta be it."

"Look here." Norela traced her finger from the approximate location of the mine to the drop off for Hershel.

"You're going to be even closer to the mine than everyone at the trailhead."

"Yeah. I see that."

"So, Norela and I can go out there," Jewel tapped the map, "early and be waiting for you in the woods here. After Hershel takes off, all you have to do is cross the road and run into the woods and the three of us can make it through to the mine."

"I think that will work. I can tell the Agent that I need to pee or something."

"What time is it now?" Jewel glanced around the room for a wall clock.

Norela checked the time on the computer, "It's six-thirty."

"Norela, you and I should leave about nine and scout out a way to the mine before the Feds are in place and then take our positions to lead Mariah to the mine."

"Why wait. I'd rather have too much time, than not enough. Let's go now."

"Works for me."

"Y'all need to pack some food." Mariah started for the kitchen. "At least take a thermos of coffee."

"Yeah, sure." Norela turned off the laptop and closed the lid.

"And take warm clothes, too."

"Definitely take warm cloths. It gets colder than a witch's tit out there after dark," Morgan added.

"You mean cold enough to freeze the balls off a brass monkey?" Jewel laughed as she poked Morgan in his side.

"Same thing. You know what I mean." Morgan smirked and grabbed Jewel's fingers. They tussled until Jewel conceded defeat.

"A couple sandwiches and a thermos of coffee would be good. Can you do that?" Norela asked no one in particular.

"My camping gear is out in the trunk of my car. I think there's a thermos with it. Let me check." Riley stepped outside to check his gear.

"I packed my Under Armor, wool socks, and hiking boots. Will that be warm enough with what I'm wearing and my all weather jacket?" Norela asked.

"Should be. Riley and I will go with you two." Morgan stood up straight and stretched his back. "We'll go ahead to the mine and wait for Machado's men. I don't trust him to keep his word, so when his men show up and we're already there—won't be much they can do about it without blowing the operation."

"You're right not to trust Machado. If he can keep us from being at the mine, he will." Riley closed the door behind him as he re-entered the room.

"I thought you were going to get vests from Machado." Mariah looked from Riley to Morgan.

"Mariah, I never leave home without mine. Morgan?"

"Yeah, mine's in my trunk."

"Figures." She rolled her eyes and shook her head. "I guess I need to take a page out of your book. I don't even have one anymore."

"Yeah, well you should have one …" Riley delivered a big Stanley thermos to Jewel. "… but the Feds are going to give you one because you're going to show up and ride along with Hershel."

"What am I going to tell them when you guys don't show up?"

"Tell Machado that we went out for target practice and never came back." Morgan shrugged his shoulders. "I don't know—make something up."

"Machado won't care anyway." Riley sat at the table. "He'll be happy we didn't show up. To be honest, they're probably heading out well before ten anyway. He never intended us to participate."

Mariah turned to Jewel. "Did you and Norela bring vests?"

Jewel rolled her eyes. "Mariah! What do you think?"

The guys laughed and Mariah grimaced.

"Silly woman. When have you ever known us not to be prepared?" Norela patted Mariah on the back.

FRIDAY NIGHT

It was dark and cold when they pulled into the drive at ten-forty for Hershel's pick-up. Mariah was dressed in her cold weather gear and was prepared to trek through the woods. The moon was a thin, silver crescent, so there wasn't a lot of light in spite of the cloudless sky.

"Just sit tight for a few minutes. You don't want to show up too early," Special Agent Stack told Hershel.

"We'll wait another ten minutes and then you can get in your truck and go."

"While we're waiting, I'm going to pee real quick." Mariah opened the car door.

"Really? Now?" Stack reached for her arm as she stepped out of the car.

Mariah pulled her arm free. "Yeah. I'll be right back."

"Hurry up and be quiet."

She quietly closed the door and stumbled around in the dark pretending to look for a place to squat. She got behind Hershel's truck which was behind the agent's unit and darted across the road. She could hear the car door open and Stack call out in a loud whisper, "Jeffries, get back here. Jeffries?!"

Once inside the tree line, Mariah found a pink ribbon marking the trail. She grabbed it so Stack or anyone else would have some difficulty following her in the dark. Another ten feet into the woods and she heard Jewel whisper her name. She stopped in her tracks, "Jewel? Where are you?"

"Right here," she heard whispered in her left ear just before a hand rested on her shoulder. Mariah jumped.

"Come on, Norela is up ahead, guarding our path. The Feds are already in place, so be quiet."

Jewel took Mariah's hand and started guiding her through the woods. There was little light, but Jewel was as silent as a whisper and as sure footed as a goat.

Mariah was trained by her Uncle John on stealth ever since she was a little girl, and she was as stealthy as Jewel, if not more so, but the near pitch blackness of the night did present a few problems that Jewel was able to warn her about. When they reached Norela, Mariah realized that her two friends were wearing night vision goggles. That explained a lot.

Mariah considered asking if Morgan and Riley made it to the mine, but decided not to disturb the silence and give away their position.

With Jewel holding Mariah's right hand, and Norela's hand on her back, they crept along, weaving in and out of bushes and trees. They could hear the normal sounds of nature until they were about twenty minutes in and all natural sound stopped. Jewel squeezed Mariah's hand and stopped, Norela stopping behind her. Mariah could barely make out the silhouette of a man standing five feet in front of Jewel. How they got that close without him hearing them was a mystery to her.

Norela took Mariah's left hand, put her finger to her mouth in warning for them to be very quiet, and took the lead. She side-stepped a large stump to her right and went behind a large, full bush.

There was a hillock that they dipped down behind and came up on the other side before ascending up the side of the mountain. After what seemed like an hour, Norela stopped and squatted down, pulling Mariah down beside her. Jewel moved around and squatted down on the other side of Mariah.

"We're directly above the opening to the mine," Norela whispered. "There are Agents watching the front of the mine from the front and each side, but not from here. If we go about twenty paces north and drop down another fifteen paces, we'll be in a perfect position to watch the front and go in behind the traffickers and the Feds. We'll be there for the take down."

"You guys are awesome. Riley and Morgan are inside already?"

"Yes. Machado along with four Agents showed up thirty minutes ago and are set up inside also."

"Let's go then." Jewel scooted back from the ledge. Norela took the lead and Jewel followed Mariah, guarding their back.

When they stopped, Mariah saw the silhouette of another Agent standing about ten feet in front of them. They squatted again. In the quiet of the night the Agent raised his hand to his face and in a hushed voice said, "Gary, Seamus check in. Anything yet?"

There was a brief pause. "Everything's quiet here so far. They should be showing up soon, so be alert. We watch for stragglers and then follow the ..." Jewel had shifted her weight and snapped a twig and he stopped speaking. The women held their breath, but he hadn't noticed the snap and didn't turn to investigate. Instead, he was listening to another Agent talking on the headset. He picked up the conversation.

"Watch for stragglers, and let us know. Get ready boys." It sounded to Mariah, Jewel, and Norela like the trap was about to catch it's prey.

After waiting and watching, the three women finally heard Hershel talking.

"So I'll help you move the girls to the van and I'll be on my way, right?"

"Yeah. That's right," a deeper voice answered in a condescending tone. Mariah figured Hershel's number was up once he turned the girls over to the traffickers. They were going to kill him because they couldn't afford to have any witnesses or leave a trail back to themselves.

A few minutes later, four men appeared, each with a flashlight, following Hershel to the opening of the cave. "This way. Just follow me." Hershel entered the small dark cave. As the last of the traffickers entered the cave behind Hershel, three Agents following them headed for the opening. The women started to follow the agents but stopped short of going into the clearing when another agent came running down the trail and entered the cave behind the two who were guarding the front.

Before they could reach the mouth of the cave, gunfire rang out from inside. Two of the traffickers, running from the cave, ran into Jewel, Norela, and Mariah as the women were trying to enter. The first of the traffickers grabbed Norela, who was in the lead, by the left arm and swung her around, smacking her head against a large rock. She fell to the ground, unconscious. Mariah pulled her Five-seveN and was about to pull the trigger when the second man told her he would kill Jewel if she didn't drop her gun. He had Jewel in an arm lock around her throat and had a gun pointed at her head.

"Drop it!" he snarled.

Mariah held the gun on him as the first man approached her to take her gun. Suddenly a silhouette of a man appeared behind the man holding Jewel, reached up and cut his throat, and threw a knife at the man approaching Mariah. That man went down with the handle of a large knife sticking out of his back. Jewel spun as the man holding her went down. The man who saved her caught her leg mid-roundhouse kick. Mariah ran over to help Jewel and saw that it was Erick who came to their rescue.

"Erick! What are you doing here?" Mariah was astonished.

"I saw you guys taking the girls out earlier, so I decided to sit on the place—keep an eye out." He went to Norela and knelt beside her. "When I saw everyone taking up places for surveillance, I knew something was about to go down so I sat on the place from a distance and watched."

"Is she okay?" Jewel knelt beside Erick as he checked Norela's pulse. Mariah knelt on his other side.

"She's alive, but I .don't know about her head. She took quite a whack to it when she hit that rock." Erick felt around her head. "It doesn't feel like she has a cracked skull so it just depends on how rattled her brain got."

"I saw you three sneaking around the Agents so I figured to hang back in case you needed any help. Are you two alright?"

"We're fine. Just worried about Norela." Jewel took Norela's hand.

"Thanks for saving my life, Riley," they heard Machado say from inside the cave.

Mariah stood and headed for the cave opening and met Morgan, Riley and Machado as they came out of the cave.

"What are you doing here," Machado snapped, looking around and taking in Norela and Jewel.

"I told you I was going to be here for the take down." Two more agents came out with the two remaining traffickers in handcuffs.

Morgan saw Jewel sitting next to an unconscious Norela and rushed over to them.

"What happened? Are y'all okay?"

Mariah turned and noticed that Erick had slipped away into the dark woods. Jewel, who was looking at her, shrugged and raised her right eyebrow to indicate she didn't know where he went. They both kept quiet about his presence.

"I'm fine, but Norela took a bad hit on the head," Jewel told Morgan.

Norela started moaning as she came to and started trying to sit up. Morgan put his hand on her shoulder to stop her and told her to take it easy.

"My head," Norela groaned rolling over on her side.

"Who are you two?" Machado walked over to Jewel and Norela. Mariah followed him and reported, "They're contract employees of our agency. This is Jewel Diamond—Norela Morales is on the ground. She needs to be seen by a medic."

"Who stabbed this man in the back?"

Jewel and Mariah raised their shoulders in unison.

"We're not sure." Mariah knelt back down next to Norela.

"Jesus! What do you mean, you're not sure?"

"Well, the guy over there missing his throat..." Mariah pointed to the man Riley was kneeling beside, "was holding a gun to Jewel's head, and this guy was coming at me when someone cut that guys throat, and threw a knife at this guy. He had a damned good aim too, I might add. I thought he was one of your guys."

"Not one of my guys. Where the hell did he go?" Machado visually searched the area.

"I don't know!" Mariah snarled, frustration rising in her like bile. "There were other things going on."

"Did you see where he went?" Machado gave Jewel his evil eye. Jewel shook her head no but didn't say a word. Riley stepped over the first body and examined the knife sticking out of second man's back but said nothing.

Machado turned to one of his agents, "Seamus, radio Jessie and let him know we need another ambulance and the coroner. We have two dead and two wounded. We need the cars at the trail head to transport two prisoners."

Seamus pushed his prisoner at the agent next to him who was holding the other prisoner.

"Hang onto this one for me, Ryan." Ryan took hold of the cuffed prisoner and Seamus stepped away and started talking into his mouthpiece.

"Where's Hershel?" Mariah asked, looking all around.

"This piece of shit shot him in the back," Ryan said of his prisoner. "He's alive, but no telling for how long."

Mariah pushed herself off the ground and rushed into the mine to check on Hershel. She found him lying in a pool of blood and taking short shallow breaths. Captain Spencer was kneeling next to him, and talking to him with gentle, soothing tones. As Mariah approached, Hershel looked up, "Mariah, did we get them all?"

"Yes Hershel. You did good." She knelt beside him and took his hand.

"Take care of my wife. Tell her I love her."

"I won't need to. You're going to be fine, Hershel."

"Don't think so."

"Hang on. An ambulance is on the way."

Hershel coughed. "It hurts, Mariah."

"I know it does."

"Where's the shock?" he asked her quietly. "I thought you went into shock when you were shot and didn't feel anything." He coughed again and started panting.

"Come on Hershel," Captain Spencer admonished. "You want to see your wife, don't you?"

Hershel nodded his head, closed his eyes, and groaned.

For the second time in less than twenty-four hours, Mariah sat in that old abandoned gold mine waiting for an ambulance. It didn't take as long the last time. Machado anticipated gun play and was prepared. He had two ambulances sitting off the highway not far from the trail head. Mariah followed the paramedic and agents carrying Hershel's stretcher, Captain Spencer beside her.

"Captain." Machado walked up to them as they exited the cave mouth.

Captain Spencer stopped to talk to Machado. "We get them all?"

"Seems so. Seems we have a vigilante out here somewhere. Two of the traffickers are dead by an unknown assailant."

"That's just wonderful! This case has been a nightmare. The last thing we need is a vigilante. Did we catch him?"

"No. Mariah and her friends saw him briefly, but can't identify him."

When the last of them got to the trail head, they found the traffickers box-van in the parking lot, another dead trafficker on the ground next to the back bumper, his neck snapped.

Machado knelt beside the man and scrutinized the scene.

"Bailey!"

Agent Bailey stepped up to his side.

"What happened?"

"I was down the trail, waiting for Hershel and his guys to pass. I waited and when no one else showed up, I followed them. I didn't know anyone stayed behind."

"Well, someone killed him. If it wasn't you, then who?"

"I don't know, sir. I wouldn't kill him unless it was in self defense."

"Seamus, is a coroner enroute," Machado shouted.

"Yes sir."

"Call and let him know there are three dead. Drew, put these other two guys in the car and take them to the police department. Bailey, start taping off the crime scene."

Captain Spencer stepped up to Machado.

"I've got patrol units standing by. We can transport each prisoner in a separate unit to keep them apart. That will free your men up here for the mop up."

Machado just nodded his head and stood. "Seamus, tell the wrecker to hold off. I don't want the van moved until we've finished taking pictures and dusting for prints."

Riley stepped up to Machado.

"We'll get out of your way and meet you at the station later on. We're going to the hospital to follow up on Norela and Hershel." Hershel and Norela had already been loaded into waiting ambulances.

"Fine, fine," he waived his hand to dismiss them. As Riley walked past, Machado started helping Agent Bailey tape off the scene with bright yellow police crime scene tape.

Riley walked over to Morgan, Jewel, and Mariah. "Let's go." He herded them to the road and up the highway toward Hershel's drop off point.

"Where's the car?" Mariah inquired.

"Further down that drive that you were sitting in before coming into the woods," Jewel replied.

Riley grabbed Morgan's arm and slowed down, letting the women get ahead of him.

"Did you get a look at the knife sticking out of that guys back?"

"I saw it, but not close up."

"I saw it before … on Erick. I think he's been looking after Mariah. It seems every time she's in trouble, he shows up to help out."

"You won't hear me complaining."

Mariah turned and waited for the guys to catch up.

"What are you two conspiring about?"

"Your avenging angel!"

SATURDAY

"It's just a little concussion! I'm fine." Norela exclaimed to the group hovering around her bed early the next morning. She was sitting up in the hospital bed wearing one of those funky gowns that opened in the back. The gown hung off one shoulder, her long, silky black hair, a sexy mess. She had a soft white blanket draped over her feet and legs. "Get me the hell out of here, will ya?"

Morgan laughed. "Don't get your panties in a ruffle, woman. You start stressing and raising your blood pressure and they won't let you go."

Norela blew her breath out through loose lips making a motor boat sound, *putt putt putt putt*, before laying her head back on the bed and closing her eyes.

"I'm not wearing any panties and I hate hospitals." She heaved a heavy sigh.

"It won't be much longer," Jewel cooed. "We just need to make sure you're alright."

"How's Hershel?" Norela kept her eyes closed.

"He's was still in surgery last I checked." Mariah brushed loose strands of hair from Norela's face. "I also checked on Gayle Webb and he's come out of his coma."

Norela's eyes popped open. "That's great news."

"Yeah. They're not sure about brain damage, but he seems to be doing alright and he's going to live."

"Does he know the girls have been rescued?"

Mariah already relayed all this information to the rest of the team, but Norela missed it.

"He does now. I talked to Tawnie. The jets are fueling up, getting ready to bring the girls and their families home. Tawnie is anxious to get back to him. She said he woke up yesterday and recognized her voice over the phone. The FBI found Gigi in a townhouse in White City. They have her locked up. She's awaiting arraignment."

Norela, eyes closed, smiled. "I hope they send her to the gallows, or at the least, away for life."

"Me too. Gayle asked about the girls, too. When she told him the girls were rescued he smiled and went to sleep."

"Asleep? Not back in a coma, right?"

"Right. He's resting comfortably. The doctors are monitoring him and they're optimistic for a full recovery."

"That's fantastic," Norela mumbled. "What about that little girl that was in such bad shock. What's her name?"

"Tina." Morgan grinned, proud of how well the girl he nurtured was doing. "She's Gayle's daughter and was the first girl taken. She's doing better. I got to talk to her a few minutes ago and she thanked me for taking care of her when we found her." Morgan shook his head. "I'm surprised she even remembered, but she did. She's excited to sit with her father while he recovers."

"Fantastic. Now all we have to do is get me the HELL OUT of here." Norela slapped her hand down on the mattress and opened her eyes.

The door to the room pushed open on silent hinges and a handsome, fair skinned man with soft brown eyes and a curly, dark brown mop of hair sitting atop his head, entered. The doctor walked up to the side of Norela's bed, Morgan and Mariah stepping out of his way.

He extended his hand. "I'm doctor Faltzgraf. How are you feeling?"

Norela took his hand. "I'm feeling much better. Can I go home now?"

He turned to Jewel, Morgan, Riley and Mariah. "If you'll give me a few minutes to examine her, I'll see if we can let her go."

"Thank you, Doctor." Jewel ushered everyone out of the room and closed the door.

They waited in the hall while the doctor examined her.

"I asked Tawnie about Gayle's first marriage and she confirmed that Bertha was her husband's wife before her. But, she never met the woman, and Bertha never appeared in their lives or communicated with them in any way." Mariah continued. "That's why they didn't' tell me about his first marriage. They didn't even give her a thought. I guess Gayle thought of her and wanted to tell me, but …"

Morgan shook his head. "I guess after this many years, they figured she had moved on with her life. Little did they know she was plotting to destroy theirs."

Doctor Faltzgraf came out and told the waiting group, "You can go back in now. I'll have a nurse prepare her discharge papers. Someone will need to stay with her for twenty-four hours. The nurse will give you instructions."

"Thank you, Doctor. We'll take good care of her," Riley responded, shaking the doctor's hand as they all filed back into the room.

Riley called the police department while Jewel started the car after they all piled in—Riley riding shotgun—Norela, Morgan and Mariah in the back seat.

"Special Agent Machado, please," Riley said when someone answered the call.

"This is Damion Riley. I was helping on the kidnapping case." After a brief wait, Riley continued, "Hi. We're leaving the hospital now. Do you need us to come by the department for debriefing? … No? … Okay. We're headed to our suite, then. Captain Spencer knows where we're staying. … We'll talk later."

"He doesn't want us at the police department?" Mariah asked after Riley disconnected the call.

"No. They're just finishing up interrogating the prisoners. He said he'll come by the suite and take our statements later today."

Jewel eased out of the hospital parking lot to the road while everyone fastened their seatbelts.

"You think he'll tell us what they find out about Gayle and Robert's shootings?"

"I doubt it but we can ask," Riley answered.

"I guess it doesn't matter. As far as the case is concerned, our job is done." Morgan shrugged with a smug look on his face. "I don't like leaving it unfinished, but we got the girls back. The Feds should be able to wrap up the loose ends."

They drove the rest of the way to the suite in silence. When they got there, Paisley was waiting at the door, excited to see all her tired people. They decided to get some sleep before doing anything else. It had been a very long 24 hours for everyone.

"Why don't you and Norela take my bed." Mariah told Jewel. "I'll camp out in the living room."

"Sure. If you don't mind giving up your bed. I can sleep on the floor and you and Norela can take the bed if you prefer."

"No. Get some rest." Mariah walked down the hall with the two women. "I'll come wake you in a couple hours, Norela, and make sure you're not dead." Mariah aimed a mischievous smile at her friend.

"And what will you do if I *am* dead?"

"I'll slap you around until you come back to life." Mariah and Jewel laughed. Norela shook her head, but she was smiling.

"Some friend you are." Norela followed Jewel into the back bedroom.

"Thanks," Jewel mouthed as she closed the door.

Morgan went to his room, muttering something about calling Molly and the kids, and closed the door without saying another word. Riley grabbed his sleeping bag and laid down on the floor. "Take the couch, Mariah. I sleep as well on the floor as anywhere else."

"Thanks Riley, but I have to take Paisley out. We'll take a short walk and be back in a few minutes."

"Sounds good. See you when you get back."

"Get some sleep. I'll be quiet."

Mariah harnessed Paisley and out they went for a quick walk around the complex. The happy little pup did her business and they came back inside.

Mariah was so tired, she could barely stay upright. She set an alarm for two hours and then laid on the couch, Paisley curled up beside her.

"Was it Erick that knocked the guy out and threw the knife at the other man?" Riley asked quietly just before Mariah closed her eyes. He rolled over on his side to face her.

She was startled, thinking he was already asleep. "Yes. He appeared out of nowhere and when it was over, he disappeared with just as much stealth."

Riley closed his eyes. "I thought so." He starting snoring.

Mariah didn't even remember closing her eyes when she was awakened by the alarm on her cell phone. She got up and went to the bedroom to check on Norela. She and Jewel were sound asleep. Mariah shook Norela's shoulder with care, and the woman woke with a start.

"Oh. It's you."

Mariah giggled. "You don't have to sound so happy to see me."

"I'm sorry but you startled me."

"Ah. I had to wake you. Go back to sleep. I was just making sure you could wake up."

"I'm fine, Mariah. Go get some sleep. I'll see you in a couple hours."

"Sweet dreams." Mariah went back to the couch. Paisley had curled up next to Riley and once Mariah was settled, Paisley jumped back up on the couch and stretched out beside her before they both drifted off to sleep again.

It was dawn when knocking on the door woke Mariah and Riley. Paisley jumped down from the couch and barked. Riley got up and answered the door.

Machado was poised to knock again.

"Come on in."

"Good evening." Machado made a cursory search of the room.

Morgan came out of the bathroom, his hair wet from a resent shower. "Hey there, Agent Machado. Here to take our statements?"

"Yeah. Where's Jewel and Norela staying? I'll need to talk to them, too."

"I'll go get them." Mariah stood from the couch.

After Machado took each of their statements, sans any mention of Erick, Riley requested information about Gigi.

Machado sat quietly and looked at each one of them before answering.

"My research guys confirmed all the information you gave us. Gayle Webb had been married to her when they were teenagers. The girl was pregnant and when she was about five months along, they were in a car wreck. She lost the baby and was told she could never conceive again. Long story short, she disappeared and changed her name. Before doing so, she swore that Gayle would never have children of his own if she couldn't. We tracked her down and arrested her. She's the one who was behind the kidnappings."

"Wow! Really?!" Norela's tone dripped with sarcasm. "Did she explain why she took the other girls and she didn't take the Webb's son?"

"When we found her, she was renting a townhouse in White City. She refused to answer any questions, and was booked on a two-million dollar bond. If she posts bail, which I doubt she'll be able to, I'll have an agent keep a tail on her.

"What about the three you have in custody. Did they mention any other cohorts?"

"No. They swear there were just the five of them."

"I'm curious," Mariah threw into the conversation, "did anyone mention how the shooting of Gayle and Robert was connected to the kidnappings?"

"No. As I said, Gigi refuses to answer any questions, but we are certain she was behind it … probably to keep Gayle from talking about her. We just don't know how she knew to ambush him outside that restaurant."

"Yeah. I wonder. What about Hershel. How is he doing?"

"He came through surgery fine. The doc thinks he'll be okay."

****

"If we were to investigate him, I think the trail would end just outside of Medford," Morgan asserted from the backseat of the car.

After a good night's sleep, and the rest of the day relaxing, they were all hungry. Mariah offered to take everyone to her favorite Mexican restaurant for an early dinner. Jewel was driving and Mariah was riding shotgun. Morgan, Norela and Riley were in the back seat.

Mariah glanced back at Morgan. "What do you mean?"

"I think Erick was here looking for the girls. I don't know if someone else hired him or if he is just a vigilante, but I doubt anyone knew him from before the kidnappings or will hear from him now that the case is solved."

"You could be right. I've heard of such a guy who avenges crimes against children." Riley looked around Norela at Morgan. "No one knows who he is or what he looks like. He's known only as The Ghost Soldier."

"And the FBI don't have a clue about him?" Jewel peered in the rearview mirror at Riley before she pulled into a parking space at the restaurant.

"They know about him. He's closed many of their cases. They just can't get a bead on who he is."

"Interesting." Norela pursed her lips and shook her head.

They walked into the restaurant side of the establishment as a loud clap of thunder sounded. Rain drops hit Mariah on the head as she entered behind everyone else.

"You guys did it. I knew you were the right team for the job." Martin shook hands with everyone in the group. When he got to Mariah, he took her hand in his and held it. "Thanks for inviting me to your celebration dinner. I can't thank you guys enough. It's fantastic."

"You're welcome."

"And who are these two lovely ladies?" Martin grinned first at Jewel, then Norela who were waiting beside Mariah.

"They're contract employees of ours …," Mariah smiled, "and very good friends. Jewel, Norela, this is Martin Silkeney. He's the man who hired us."

"Well. Thank you, ladies, for your help. I'm so glad to have this come to an end. Now, all we need to do is get the girls well and over this terrible event."

"It will be a lot easier for them, now that the police have the perpetrators."

"So, who was taking them? Did you catch the guy?"

Morgan cleared his throat, "Um, we believe we got the whole crew that was involved."

"Good. Good." Martin bobbed his head up and down.

A waitress came up to them and Mariah pushed through to the front of the group to claim their reservations under her name. The waitress showed them to their table.

"I'll be right back," Mariah announced as everyone was taking a seat. She walked from the restaurant to the bar and sure enough, there was Jeffrey, holding down his favorite stool.

"Hi, Jeffrey."

"Mariah! Congratulations. It's all over the news. Know what I mean? How are the little girls doing?"

"They're recovering nicely. How are you doing?" She sat on the stool next to him.

"Better, now that you're here, Mariah. Want something to drink?"

"Yeah, my partners and a couple good friends are at a table in the restaurant. I was wondering if you would like to join us?"

Jeffrey looked over at Kate as she set down a cardboard coaster in front of Mariah.

"Kate, honey. I think I'll go join Mariah and her friends in the restaurant. I'll come back here when we're done."

"That's fine, Daddy. I'll send over a pitcher of beer."

"Send three, and put them on my tab."

Jeffrey followed Mariah back to the table and she introduced him to everyone. After making everyone's acquaintance, they chatted for a few minutes until the waitress came back to take drink orders.

"Kate has beer coming to the table, know what I mean? So unless they would rather have something else, I've got the drinks covered. Okay? Know what I mean?"

"Si, Senor Jeffrey. Does anyone want something else to drink?"

Everyone indicated that beer was fine with them, the waitress left and they continued their discussions while they perused the menu. A couple of minutes later, the waitress came back and took their orders.

"How did you and Jeffrey meet, Mariah?" Morgan stuffed a salsa laden chip in his mouth and waited for her response.

"I came into the bar for dinner my second night here. Jeffrey was sitting on a stool and we started chatting. I enjoyed the company and the food so much, I kept coming back."

"I welcomed the company. Know what I mean? She sat there at the bar with me and listened to my stories like they were interesting, or something. Know what I mean?" Jeffrey laughed. "She's a great gal and I like to think she's a friend now. Even Kate, my daughter, likes her."

Morgan cut his eyes at Mariah and raised a questioning eyebrow. Mariah grinned and shook her head.

"Now, I'm guessing you all worked together on the missing girls case, right?" Jeffrey spread his hands out to include the whole table.

"Yes. Morgan and Riley are my business partners and close friends. Jewel and Norela are business associates and also close friends—and Martin hired us."

That led to a lively and fun conversation while they snacked on ships and salsa.

"How do such beautiful women get in the private eye game? Know what I mean?"

Jewel laughed. "We're mean and ornery."

"Yeah, and we're the rebellious type," Mariah threw in.

Norela pounded the table. "And we don't take crap from anyone!"

Morgan rolled his eyes. "And they're frightfully independent."

Riley grinned wide and slow before adding, "They're all three, big pains in the ass, and I wouldn't have them any other way."

"I love it!" Jeffery beamed. "I'm gonna have some new stories to tell. Know what I mean, Mariah?"

"Awe Jeffrey, don't tell me your stories were made up?"

"No. No. Not at all. But they're getting a little old and tired. Know what I mean? I'm thinking a story about the beautiful, young pee-eye who sought my counsel would be a good addition. What do you think?"

"As long as I stay beautiful and young … and ornery as hell."

Everyone laughed.

Martin, Riley, and Jewel's enchilada plates arrived first, followed by Morgan's chimichanga, and Jeffrey's humongous nachos grande. Norela and Mariah's taco salads were last to be delivered. Once everyone was served, they settled down to eat and discuss sites and attractions in the area.

"Mariah, if you bring me a statement, I'll put a final check in the mail to your office." Martin swallowed the last of his bear while they waited for the bill.

"I'll do that first thing in the morning, Martin."

"Are you guys leaving tomorrow?"

Morgan answered first.

"Yeah. I'm ready to get back to my family, but I want to bring them down here for spring break and take in some of the sites. Maybe I can look you up and get some suggestions when it's closer to time."

"Sure. There are so many places to go and things to see around here. I'd be happy to put together a packet of information for your family. How about you, Riley?"

"Headed home. I miss my wife and we have to get back to our business."

The waitress came with the bill and Mariah started to hand her debit card over, but Martin pushed Mariah's hand away.

"My treat. Put that away, Mariah." He pulled out his wallet and gave the waitress a shiny gold credit card.

"Thank you, Martin."

Mariah looked at Riley and Morgan. "I'm going to hang out here for a few days. I want to say goodbye to Velia, the girls, and their families. I especially need to visit with Mrs. Dunn."

"That's fine. Morgan and I can take care of the cases until you get back."

The waitress came back with Martin's card and the receipt. He signed the ticket, adding a tip, and returned the card to his wallet along with his receipt.

"I better go. My family is on their way home tomorrow and I want to make sure everything is cleaned up and perfect at the house."

"That's wonderful, Martin. Thanks again for dinner. I'll come by to see you at the office before I leave town."

"I would like that vey much, Mariah. Stay at the sweet on my dime. They'll bill me once you check out. It was nice meeting everyone. Thanks again for all you've done for this little town."

"Thank you, Martin," Mariah replied as everyone said their goodbyes. He turned and headed for the door.

The rest of the group stayed at the table, chatting. Mariah picked at the remains of her taco salad. Jeffrey regaled them with another of his Viet Nam stories and Kate joined them when she had a break. Mariah introduced her to everyone and Jeffrey finished his tale.

Kate laughed and rolled her eyes. "That was one of his better stories.

Riley ordered a couple more pitchers of beer and Morgan, Riley and Jeffrey took turns competing to see who had the most outlandish war story. Neither Riley, nor Morgan, mentioned their brushes with death—or with angels. Those are things not talked about in public. As the night drew on, the stories grew more wild and everyone was laughing and having a good time.

The band started up for their Saturday night set and Jeffrey asked Mariah to dance.

"You promised you would cut a rug with me. Know what I mean?"

Mariah laughed. "I'll dance one dance with you, but you have to dance with Jewel and Norela too.

Jeffrey winked, took Mariah's hand and led her into the bar and to the dance floor. Riley took Norela's hand and followed Jeffrey. Morgan and Jewel stayed at the table and talked.

The waitress started clearing the table, but when she reached for Mariah's half eaten salad, Morgan asked her to leave it.

"She's a picker and will graze off it until we leave."

The waitress nodded her head and left with the rest of the empty plates.

Jeffrey was very adept at West Coast Swing—Mariah, not so much. Riley and Norela bounced around on the dance floor trying to keep the beat. When the dance was over, a flushed Mariah was led to the table, Riley and Norela following. Jeffrey pointed to Jewel and crooked his finger.

"Your turn. Know what I mean?" His grin grew and he winked.

"Man, that old guy can dance." Riley wiped his brow with a paper napkin.

"He sure can. I was getting dizzy out there."

"Thanks for the dance, Riley." Norela was beaming. "I haven't been dancing in years."

The group switched off partners throughout the first set. Morgan claimed he had two left feet and refused to dance until Mariah and Jewel dragged him out to the dance floor.

When the band took a break, Jeffrey got another pitcher of beer and returned to the table. He refilled everyone's glass.

"We've got to go after this drink." Riley raised his glass. "It's getting late and most of us have an early start home."

"I understand. Know what I mean? I understand, but it's been a pleasure meeting all of you. Thanks for letting me be a part of the celebration. Know what I mean?"

Jeffrey raised his glass of beer. "To new friends and successful outcomes. Know what I mean?"

Everyone chimed in, "We know what you mean!"

Made in the USA
Lexington, KY
17 May 2017